The Crumbling Republics

Heirs of the Mediterranean, Book I

Julius Janeliūnas

Copyright © 2025 Julius Janeliūnas

All rights reserved. No part of this book may be reproduced in any form without permission in writing from the owner, except in the case of quotations in reviews and other non-commercial uses permitted by copyright law.

Cover design by Rem Yumemi – x.com/KowloonsCurse
Assets used for the cover – Pantheon, Rome, Italy by Brian Trepanier and Roman Pilum by Tomsearle16 on sketchfab.com, CC BY 4.0 license

First paperback edition 2025
ISBN: 9798307448052

To the alternate history community, for keeping the genre alive and inspiring me to begin a new series

Contents

Prologue 7
Map of the World 21
Chapter I 25
Chapter II 38
Chapter III 46
Chapter IV 54
Chapter V 66
Chapter VI 78
Chapter VII 88
Chapter VIII 93
Chapter IX 104
Chapter X 114
Chapter XI 127
Chapter XII 136
Chapter XIII 148
Chapter XIV 162
Chapter XV 172
Chapter XVI 176
Chapter XVII 184
Chapter XVIII 196
Chapter XIX 208
Chapter XX 214
Chapter XXI 224
Chapter XXII 231
Chapter XXIII 238
Chapter XXIV 245
Chapter XXV 257
Chapter XXVI 263
Chapter XXVII 283
Chapter XXVIII 289

Chapter XXIX 308
Chapter XXX...312
Chapter XXXI 316
Epilogue...327
End Notes 337
Diagrams and Maps...340
About the Author...349

Prologue

Rome was burning. The city that was founded by the now nearly mythical brothers Romulus and Remus over five hundred years ago, that had been the center of a kingdom and later an even more powerful republic, was now but a ruin. The city had survived a lot – wars with the various tribes of Italy, the Etruscan city states, the Greek coalition led by Pyrrhus, and other numerous enemies. It was sacked once by the Gauls, but the capital and the republic managed to survive and rebuild to become even stronger. The Roman Republic seemed unstoppable at one point, but this streak of victories had now finally been put to an end.

Rome had met its equal – or, rather, its superior. That was, of course, the Republic of Carthage. Founded just before Rome, and starting out as a similarly humble town, it grew for centuries until it became one of the Mediterranean's most prominent states. And while the Romans had managed to defeat it once, receiving all of Sicily for their victory, the gods did not favor the Romans the second time these two giants clashed. The Romans gambled everything, and they lost everything.

The Second Punic War, known as the Second Roman War to the Carthaginians, had started eight years ago when the Romans declared war, but they soon began to regret it. The Carthaginians were now much more powerful, had a larger army and navy, were wealthier – in part due to their newly acquired territories in Iberia and all the gold mines there – and were ready to defend what they had and take revenge on Rome. Not all Carthaginians were so eager to spill blood fighting the hardened Romans, of course, but that was not necessary, as countless mercenaries and allied soldiers were, if the pay was good or if they had their own scores to settle with Rome. And sure enough, the pay was indeed good, and all the possible scores had now been finally settled.

The man who led the Carthaginians to such a momentous victory was none other than Hannibal Barca. A general from the highly influential Barcid family, he was the son of Hamilcar Barca, a leading general during the previous war with Rome. Hannibal followed in his father's footsteps with great success, as now, with the capital of his greatest enemy being destroyed right before his eyes and Roman soldiers surrendering or fleeing in terror, the man felt great joy in having finished Hamilcar's work.

It was not an easy road, of course. The war had lasted years and claimed hundreds of thousands of lives, and the Carthaginians had some setbacks too. Hannibal took an unconventional route by going through Iberia and then the Alps to reach Italy, taking his soldiers, mercenaries, and elephants with him, and losing many on the way. Some claimed this was foolish, and that a naval invasion should be conducted instead. Yet, the plan worked, as the Romans were caught by surprise by the Carthaginians descending on them from the north, and Hannibal was once again vindicated, as were his allies. And he certainly was not lacking them. Rome had made many enemies in Italy over the course of its conquests and many of them did not hesitate to join Hannibal once they realized that this may be the best chance in their lifetime to break free from the Roman grasp. Most notable among these were the Oscan city of Capua, as well as the former Greek colony of Tarentum, though gradually most of southern Italy defected to the Carthaginian side, as their victory became more and more evident. The Etruscans in the north joined Carthage near the end too, as they also had their fair share of grudges against Rome and wanted a seat at the table for when the new order emerged in Italy. Carthage had allies even across the Ionian Sea, that being the Kingdom of Macedon, one of the three major surviving Diadochi states.

Rome was powerful, but even it could not beat such odds, and the people soon realized that the republic had overplayed its hand. Hannibal inflicted a series of crushing defeats on Rome, at Trebia, Lake Trasimene, Cannae, and now the city of Rome itself.

Italy was completely ravaged by war and hundreds of thousands of men fighting on the Roman side were now dead. The Romans had managed to replenish their losses at first by total conscription, later even resorting to drafting criminals, slaves, and other men normally unfit to join the army, but even that was not enough. As the Carthaginians approached Rome, a desperate last line of defense was put up, consisting of the remaining soldiers, who stood loyal to the very end. While it was an intense battle, Hannibal achieved victory once more. Before long, the walls were breached, and the city was taken and sacked.

The Iberian front – where the whole war had initially started – did not look like it would offer much solace to the Romans either. The Carthaginian forces there were led by the generals Hasdrubal Barca and Mago Barca, both brothers of Hannibal, as well as Hasdrubal Gisco. They managed to defend the peninsula against Roman advances and inflict a massive blow to their enemy, which also included killing Publius Cornelius Scipio and Gnaeus Cornelius Scipio, the brothers leading the Roman soldiers on this front. The son of Publius, bearing the same name, had arrived in Iberia to reinforce the rapidly diminishing Roman numbers, but could not do much before he was urgently recalled to help defend the capital. He sailed back from Iberia, leaving it fully in the hands of Carthage and its allies, yet most of his forces did not reach Italy either, as the fleet was ambushed by Carthaginian and Macedonian ships near Corsica. Most of this fleet was sunk and Publius went missing, along with many of his subordinates, and so Rome was dealt yet another devastating blow.

The outcome was clear by this point – Iberia was now fully in the hands of the trio of Carthaginian generals, who had also begun landing troops in Corsica and Sardinia, southern Italy was committed to Hannibal, Etruria was in full revolt, a newly formed Carthaginian army was invading Sicily – which had few troops guarding it, as the Romans lost many men taking Syracuse after it had allied with Carthage – the Gauls, sensing chaos and instability in Italy, joined as well and began sacking towns in the north, and Latium was now overrun with Carthaginians and their mercenaries. There was nowhere left for the Romans to retreat, no more cities to reorganize in, and no more men to conscript. Rome had fallen, and Carthage had won. The question now was, how harshly would the Carthaginians punish the Romans and their allies?

The first matter was the city of Rome itself, and it was being decided right on the battlefield. Hannibal was standing on the Capitoline Hill, near the Temple of Jupiter, overlooking the carnage below. The walls of the city had been torn down, and tens of thousands of restless and angry soldiers stormed the capital from all sides, unleashing their anger at the enemy they had been fighting in some form for over half a century. Hannibal sent some of his most trusted officers and soldiers down to collect important artifacts, documents, literary works, sculptures, and other items of value and send them to Carthage, both to provide proof to the ruling nobles that Rome had in fact been taken by Hannibal and to preserve such things – either in governmental buildings or the personal estates of the Barcids – before they were lost in the ensuing destruction. Hannibal had instructed his soldiers to not ransack or destroy the temples, as while the people of the two republics worshipped different gods, it was still considered dishonorable to desecrate such places, and to try to not harm the women and children still in the city. The Carthaginians followed these orders, but the mercenaries and the Italian allies were less inclined to care about such norms and oftentimes killed everyone in their way, raped the women they came across, burned down the houses, stole what valuables remained, and destroyed several temples, where many civilians had been hiding. Hannibal did not engage in disciplinary measures for such actions, and left these matters for the allied and mercenary commanders to sort out, as he did not have much pity left for the Romans, considering how many chances to surrender they had wasted beforehand, and now wanted to show them the true extent of their defeat. The few Romans who remained in the city saw it very well – the Forum Romanum, the center of the capital, was now almost completely destroyed, Campus Martius, a training ground for Roman soldiers, was now a temporary Carthaginian military camp, and the Circus Maximus, the central chariot racing stadium, had elephants brought in as an additional show of mockery for the Roman capital.

A few weeks later, the city was nothing but a barren ruin. The civilians, those who had not been killed, fled east, away from Carthaginian military presence, while the soldiers returned back to their camps with whatever they could get their hands on during the sacking and prepared to get back to marching once again. Hannibal was expecting the Romans to sue for peace already, but, having fought for this long, he acknowledged the possibility that the Romans might very well fight until the very last man, and so continued making plans regarding the march towards and battles near what few Roman towns still remained. However, that proved to not be necessary, as one morning Hannibal received a message stating that the Romans were finally suing for peace, or at least a truce to stop the fighting before the peace terms were agreed upon.

"The Romans are here, general. Are you ready to see them?" a Carthaginian soldier asked Hannibal, having run up the stairs to the top of the Capitoline Hill where his superior was standing.

"Is the consul among them?" Hannibal asked, looking over the ruins of the capital.

"I believe so, sir."

"Bring him up. Who else is with him?"

"Some guards and other officials."

"Leave them where they are standing. I only need the consul."

"He may not agree to that, general…"

"He is not in a position to make any demands. Either he comes up here, alone, or no one does, and then we march out east. These are the only options."

"Understood, sir. Will notify him right away."

The soldier descended back down the stairs, leaving Hannibal with his guards. A few minutes later, they were joined by some more Carthaginian soldiers who were escorting the Roman representative. The weary looking man was Marcus Valerius Laevinus, the one surviving consul who had been recalled from the Macedonian front after Rome had been sacked. His co-consul Marcus Claudius Marcellus had been killed near Rome, leaving Laevinus the highest ranking Roman and the one chosen to represent them in the negotiations for the ceasefire.

"Marcus Valerius Laevinus, consul of the Roman Republic," a soldier introduced him as he approached Hannibal.

"Greetings. General Hannibal Barca of the Republic of Carthage," Hannibal said in Latin, as he knew both Latin and Punic, while the consul only spoke the former.

"I know who you are. Would be difficult to find anyone west of Greece who still doesn't," the consul replied scornfully.

"Bringing down Rome will have such an effect."

"Yet you still speak Latin."

"I would rather not waste any more time by using a translator. But believe me, the whole of Italy will soon speak Punic fluently, while Latin will be forgotten and remain only in ancient scrolls."

"If that is what awaits us after the peace treaty negotiations, then there is no point to them. Why surrender now if you intend to exterminate all of us and replace us with your settlers?"

"Who said anything about extermination? I was only talking about Carthage being the wealthiest and most powerful trade partner. That's why it would be beneficial for you all to learn Punic. Not because we intend to slaughter you all. But I suppose that could be hard to comprehend for you Romans, when all you do is wage war and destroy entire cultures."

"Don't pretend you are any different. Just look at what you have done to our city here!"

"You have failed to learn your lesson for years, so something more drastic had to be done. Looks like burning down Rome was what it took to get you to come to the negotiating table."

"I may still walk out."

"You may. And then I will follow you with my army and raze even more towns to the ground. So if you care for your people at all, you should choose your words more carefully."

"A consul does not have to bend to a general."

"But who really has power here? Which of us is actually in control of the situation?"

"Aren't you supposed to serve your leaders? Your suffetes and your nobles in their councils at home?"

"The internal politics of Carthage are of no concern to you. All you need to know is that I will be leading the negotiations on our side."

"Very well. Though it is strange how you separate the political and military offices."

"Maybe you should have done the same, considering who won this war."

"Time will tell."

"So are you interested in a ceasefire, or have you only come to waste my time?"

"I am. Unfortunately, I see no other option for my people."

"Wise choice. Here are the terms – you will disband what remains of your armies, you will relinquish all your warships to us, and you will immediately break off whatever agreements you have with outside powers. Those are the conditions for even coming to the negotiations. Otherwise – the war will continue, and more people will die. Mostly yours."

"If that is what you require... It will be done," the consul sighed.

"Good. I will then order my armies to stop the fighting, and will relay that to everyone else commanding forces on our side. I expect to see your representatives in sixty days – exactly two months. Then the peace treaty negotiations can begin."

"Where will they take place?"

"Capua. It is a large enough city and far away from any fighting. It will suit us well."

"Capua it is. We will be there."

"You better be. If you are not – again, the war will continue. And you will have no more chances to surrender."

"I understand. Is that all?"

"It is."

"I should get back to our senate to inform them of this. We will meet again in Capua, general."

"We better. For your sake."

The consul turned around and was escorted back down the stairs by the soldiers.

As was agreed, the two parties met again in two months, this time in the city of Capua. Hannibal's return was marked by grand celebrations, as the locals were overjoyed after hearing about Rome's defeat. The city was the first and most important ally of Carthage in Italy during the war and so was just as invested in its outcome. And now, after the city of Rome had been utterly destroyed, Capua was the most populous city in the peninsula which gave it even more prominence. It was expected that the peace treaty would include provisions not only for its independence from the husk of Rome, but also significant concessions which could make it the strongest power in Italy. Thus, the city was deemed the best choice for the official signing of the peace, with the added benefit for the victors of even further humiliating the Romans.

The Romans were not eager to travel south and seal their fate in such a way, with many of the surviving senators and other officials still clamoring for further battles, but the reality of the situation did eventually set in. Rome had no more men, no more allies, no funds to hire mercenaries, and was surrounded from all sides by hostile powers who were more than eager to wipe it away from the map. The peace was primarily pushed by the senate in Carthage, which felt that Rome was sufficiently crippled and would be of more use as a puppet state paying tribute rather than a desolate wasteland, and Hannibal Barca himself, while having achieved a monumental victory, had still mostly exhausted his army and believed that the Carthaginians should capitalize on this moment and not overplay their hand. Yet it was made clear to the Romans that if they did not stand down and comply with the terms, Carthage would continue the offensive, whatever it took, and so there remained no other option than to come to the negotiating table if the Roman state was to survive in any form.

The meeting was to take place on a mountain just outside the city, in the temple of Diana – the chief goddess of the city. The Carthaginian party consisted of Hannibal himself, his brothers Hasdrubal and Mago, who had arrived from Iberia, and Mago Arvad, one of the two suffetes of Carthage – the highest elected official in the country, mostly equivalent to the Roman consul, but without any military responsibilities, as those belonged to separately selected generals. Also present were Staius Lucius, the recently elected leader of Capua, as well as Polyphemous of Tarentum, the leader of the Italian Greeks who fought alongside Hannibal, Tarxi Hanusa, a representative of the newly proclaimed Etruscan Federation, and Philip V, the king of Macedon. These eight men had spent the previous months discussing the treaty among themselves and eventually managed to come to an agreement which would suit all of them, and they were now ready to present it to the Romans.

The Romans did arrive eventually, despite some speculating that they would go back on their word. Marcus Valerius Laevinus and Quintus Fabius Maximus Verrucosus – a reelected consul who had taken the post of the dictator twice in the early years of the war – led the party, with some lower ranking officials following behind. The men tried to appear strong, but such a veneer did not fool anyone, as they held their heads low in shame, knowing that they were about to sign the most humiliating treaty in the republic's history.

The representatives were allowed inside the temple after being thoroughly searched, but their guards had to stay outside. It was a small contingent of raggedy men who had seen better days, but the Carthaginians took precautions nonetheless. The Roman soldiers stood guard, while surrounded by much better equipped and spirited Carthaginian and mercenary infantrymen, who were ready to attack at the first sign of trouble. The two consuls and their entourage, meanwhile, proceeded inside, slowly making their way through the temple until they reached the opposing leaders. Several translators were also present, as there was no unifying language spoken by everyone, with so many leaders attending.

"Here we are, as promised. Let's not waste any more time – just give us the terms. We are ready to hear your offer," Quintus began exhaustedly.

"It is not an offer. It is a set of conditions that will allow your republic to survive another day instead of being completely trampled by our men and elephants. Let's be clear on this," Hannibal replied harshly in Latin.

"Of course. You defeated us, so we cannot expect anything more. Go ahead then. What are the terms?"

"They are as such," Mago Arvad proclaimed and handed the consuls a set of stone tablets on which the peace terms where listed, written in Punic, Greek, and Latin. "First, Rome shall relinquish all its holdings and claims in Iberia and leave the peninsula to Carthage. Second, the islands of Sicily, Sardinia, and

Corsica are to be returned to Carthage, along with the isles surrounding them. Third, southern Italy shall be granted independence from Rome, including all the territories south of the Volturno river. This new state is to be jointly ruled by Capua and Tarentum. Fourth, the Etruscan Federation is also to be granted full independence from Rome, including the lands between the rivers Arno and Tevere. Fifth, the Roman state shall not expand north of the Metaurus river – all colonies north of it are to be abandoned at once. Sixth, the Roman colonies in northern Illyria are also to be abandoned, or they will be subject to destruction. Seventh, the territories in southern Illyria seized by Rome in the Roman-Illyrian War, including the island of Korkyra, are to be relinquished and handed over to the Kingdom of Macedon. Eighth, after the treaty is concluded, Rome shall not make any agreements with any party except Carthage. Ninth, Rome shall pay tribute for the next twenty years to all of our states, including Carthage, Etruria, Capua, and Macedon, for all the damage caused by this and previous wars and occupations. Tenth, Rome shall not have a larger army than that of ten thousand men. Eleventh, Rome shall have no naval vessels of military nature. And Twelfth, the port of Ostia is to be open to Carthaginian vessels and an accompanying temporary Carthaginian garrison. Is that clear?"

The Roman consuls were stunned as they listened to the terms, and grew more pale by the moment, especially after they read the exact figures of the required tribute specified in the tablets.

"You… You cannot be serious! This is a mockery!" Marcus retorted weakly.

"You may think of them whatever you wish, but these are our terms. And they will not change," Hannibal replied.

"This will destroy us! You cannot expect us to agree to such outrageous demands!" Quintus continued protesting.

"No, you have that wrong. This will save you. But you better believe we will absolutely destroy you if you refuse this treaty," Mago Barca replied almost gleefully.

"You were defeated, and this is the price you have to pay," Hasdrubal added. "You would have imposed similar terms on us if our fates were reversed. You will still retain central Italy, all of Latium and Picenum, as well as parts of Samnium and Umbria. The terms could have been a lot worse."

"This is a decapitation of our great republic, we will be left a rump state with no ability to defend ourselves!" Quintus tried again.

"Your republic was built on the bloody conquest of cities far older and greater than your own," Polyphemous snapped back. "It is time for you Romans to return what you have stolen from Greeks and other Italians and return back to where you belong, before you vermin corrupt and destroy more cultures-"

"That's enough," Hannibal stopped him. "You will be left with more than enough to sustain yourselves and pay your dues, we made sure of that. Of course, that will not leave much, if any, funding for your army, but that may be for the better, considering how much havoc it has caused in the past century. As for defense – do not worry, as we will make sure your lands are defended from any outside threats. Our fleets and armies will make sure of that."

"So, Rome will become a puppet state of Carthage? Like all the Greek cities under the thumb of Macedon?" Marcus asked, already knowing the answer.

"These Greek cities seem to be doing quite well," Philip interjected. "Before you tried to rile them up to rise against us, at least."

"Call it whatever you wish, but, like we said, the terms are final," Mago Arvad repeated.

The Romans, feeling utterly defeated, turned to each other and deliberated for a decision, while the opposing leaders waited patiently for an answer. Before long, however, the Roman consuls returned back and addressed their opponents.

"So it shall be. We agree to the terms," Marcus said with sorrow.

"May Jupiter and Mars forgive us…" Quintus said quietly.

"A wise choice," Hannibal replied as he got the tablets back with the signatures of the consuls. "A very wise choice indeed."

Map of the World
Western Mediterranean

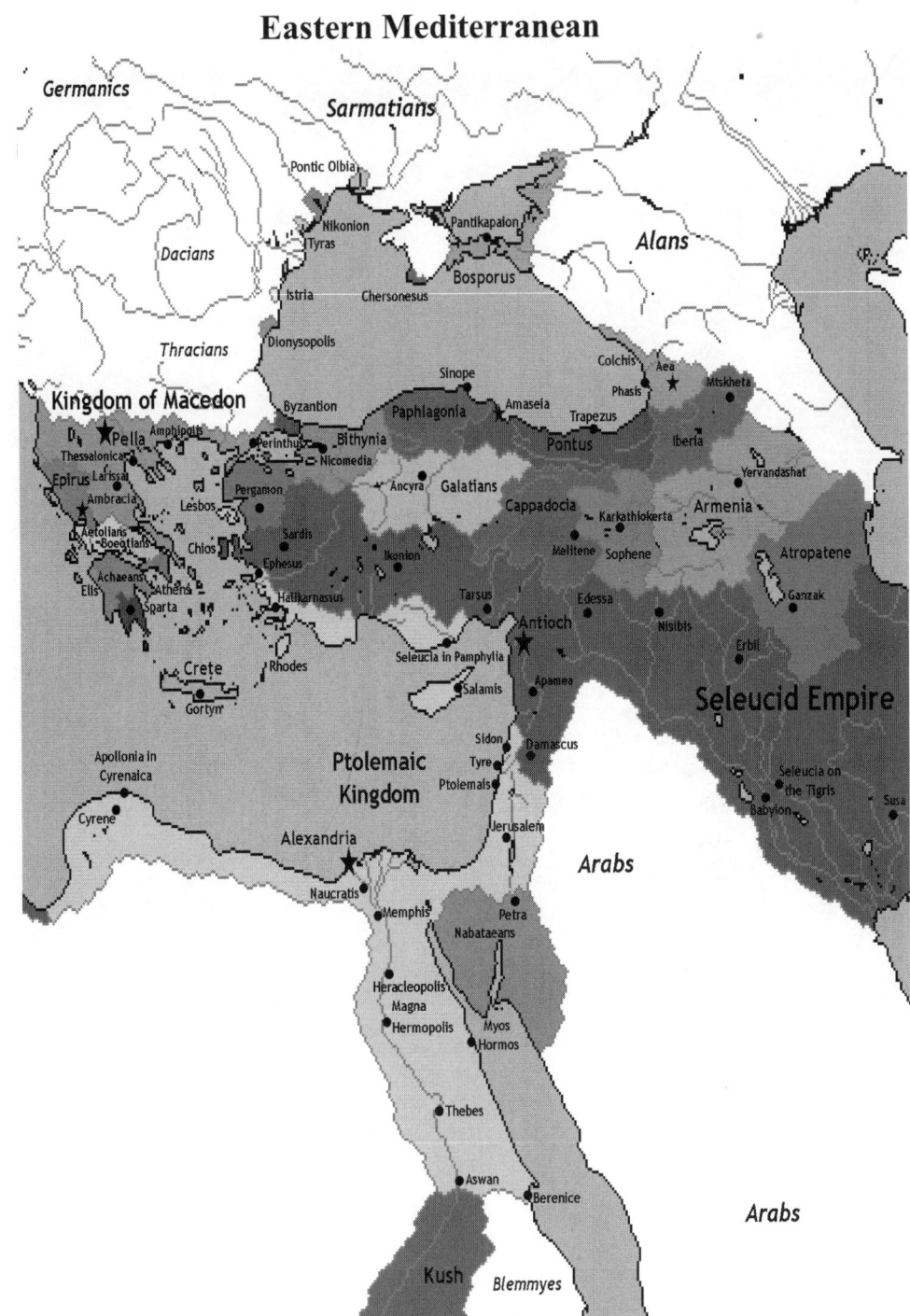

Far East

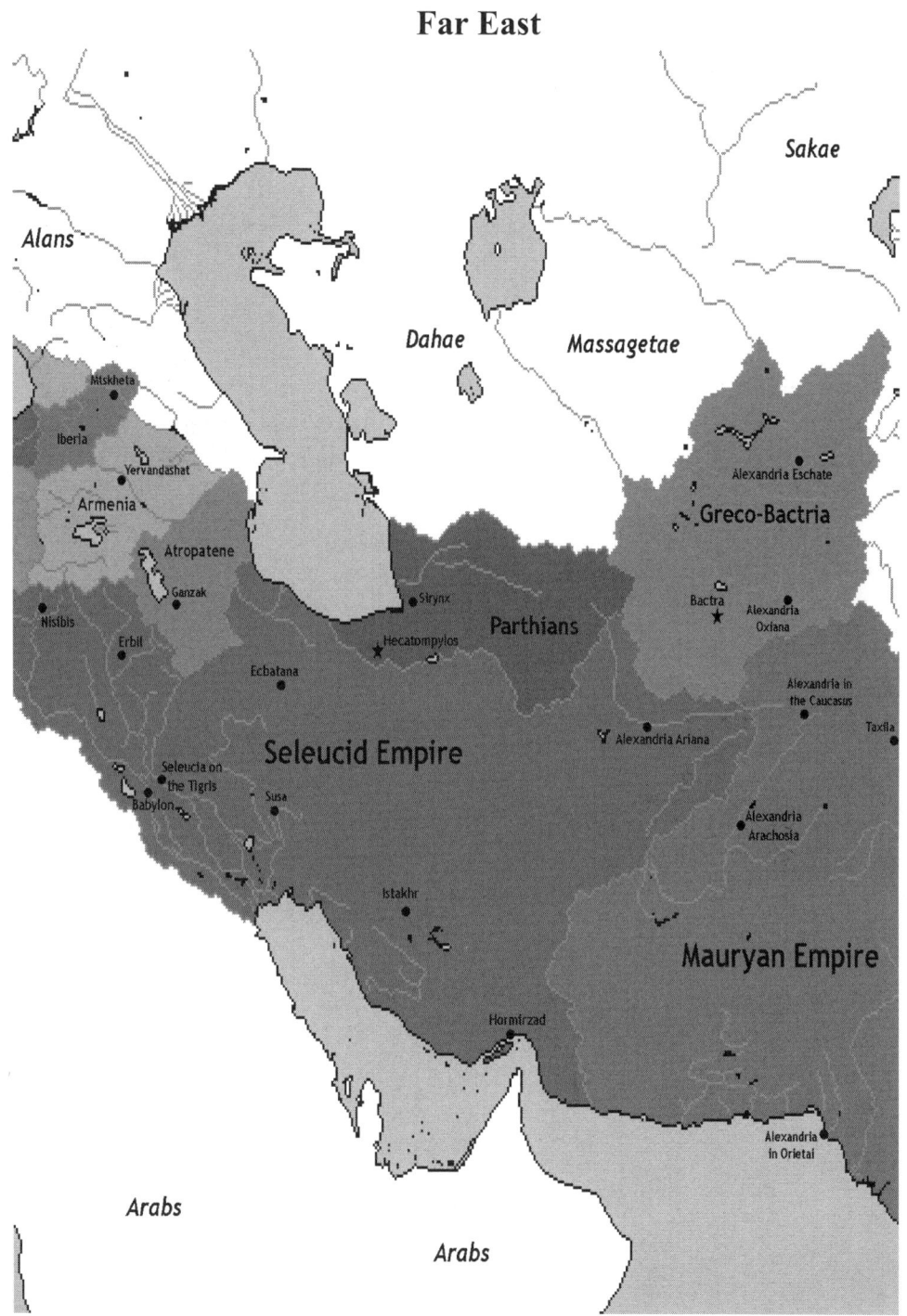

Chapter I

"Citizens of Carthage! Thank you all for gathering here today. It is a momentous occasion – after nearly a decade of continuous fighting, our boys are finally coming back home from the war, after crushing the pathetic Romans and showing them who the true power in the Mediterranean is!" Hyrum Baltsar, one of the two suffetes of Carthage, proclaimed.

He was standing on an elevated platform in the central public square of the capital – also known as the Great Marketplace – addressing thousands of locals who had gathered there. This place was one of the most common areas for large public gatherings, including discussions over new laws and other political matters, as well as important stately announcements, such as this one. The citizens talked loudly, shouted, cheered, and celebrated, many hoping to see the return of their fathers, husbands, brothers, and sons who had gone off to war, while others were just glad that the war now truly was over, and that Carthage was secure once more.

Next to Hyrum stood Mago Arvad, the second suffete who returned back to Carthage and matters of state as soon as the peace treaty with Rome had been signed. Unlike the generals, the politicians had no other reason to stay in foreign lands and so departed just as quickly as they had arrived, while the soldiers and their commanders spent the following weeks packing up and organizing an orderly return home.

Behind the suffetes stood the Great Harbor of Carthage, where hundreds of ships docked or passed through daily, while merchants were setting up markets all around it. The harbor contained a large circular docking area, meant primarily for military vessels, right next to the public square. Inside the circle there was a small island, connected by a bridge, for additional docking space, as well as a base for admirals to oversee their fleets. The circle had a small opening which led to a more open rectangular area, meant for lower priority vessels, mostly merchant ships, or ones which did not intend to stay in the city for long. The harbor was fully surrounded by the city from one side, and the towering seawall from the other to protect against naval attacks. Finally, the harbor opened into the sea by a narrow passageway, guarded by garrisoned towers from both sides and a gate that could be lowered down to fully enclose the harbor and make sure all the ships inside were safe. While many Phoenician and Carthaginian cities had a somewhat similar design, the harbor of the capital was by far the largest and most impressive one, and was a crown jewel of the city.

"However, while all our soldiers, local and foreign alike, fought valiantly and were crucial in delivering us this victory, we must not forget the brilliance of the commanders who led them!" Hyrum continued, with the crowd's excitement increasing by the moment. "Ones such as generals Hasdrubal and Mago Barca, who held the line bravely in Iberia. General Zerom Carthalo, who led our reconquest of Sicily in the last years of the war. General Hasdrubal Gisco, who destroyed the Romans in the field and drove them out of Iberia for good. Admiral Ahirom Arvad, scoring multiple naval victories against the Romans, crippling their supply lines, and demonstrating the supremacy of the Carthaginian navy. And, of course, general Hannibal Barca, who marched his troops across the Alps and crushed the unaware Romans from the north, inflicting one genius blow to them after another, until there was no one left to fight on their side, and Rome itself was but a ruin. Please, welcome our heroes back home!"

As the suffete was speaking, warships were docking at the harbor behind him and soldiers were disembarking, eager to return to their families – or get paid handsomely in the case of the many hired mercenaries. But at the forefront were the commanders, including the various generals and admirals who participated in the war. Chief among them was Hannibal himself, leading the party, with his two brothers behind him. As he came into view, the crowd erupted in cheers and applause. The soldiers had to push some people back to clear the way for the general, but he did not mind the commotion and even shook hands with many of the commoners, who thanked him for his service.

"Hannibal Barca, ladies and gentlemen, the conqueror of Italy and the bane of all Romans. Welcome home, general," Hyrum continued, as Hannibal approached the platform. "But please, give him some space and let him through. I am sure he is quite tired after such a campaign and would prefer some peace and quiet for the time being…"

"Oh no, it's not a problem for me at all," Hannibal replied cheerfully. "I am more than happy to remain here. I'd like to say a few words too," he said as he climbed onto the platform, to the great surprise of the suffetes, who shared worried looks.

"Of course, general… I am sure the people would be glad to hear from you," Hyrum stepped back to give the center stage to Hannibal, feeling rather defeated and mildly annoyed that the general was stealing his show.

"It is good to be back here in Carthage," Hannibal began, as the cheers continued. "I spent over a decade in foreign lands, in Iberia and then in Italy, fighting barbarians and brutes of all sorts. But it was worth it! Why? Because those lands are no longer foreign, they now belong to us!"

The crowd erupted again, now with even more people joining in as they heard the news that Hannibal was home and was addressing the people.

"We won the war!" The general continued. "We got our revenge for the one we lost three decades ago, and a lot more! We destroyed the Romans, and we made damn sure they will never interfere with us again! Iberia is now fully ours. The islands we had lost are now back in our possession. And Italy now bows to Carthage! We proved that we are masters of coin, masters of the sea, but also masters of the land!"

The cheers and applause only intensified, but eventually calmed down, as Hannibal waited for the people to quiet down before he continued.

"It was not without costs, of course," Hannibal now said more solemnly. "Thousands of good men died fighting for our victory. The Romans were brutal enemies, and they did not go down easily. And you people had to suffer too. Increased taxes, constant threats of invasion, enemy vessels trying to cut off our trade routes. I imagine it was not so easy here either. But it was all worth it. Because while we were rich before, we will now become even richer. Unimaginably wealthy. So much to make even the Egyptians pale in comparison! We have the gold mines in Iberia, we have the grain of Sicily, we have access to all of Italy's markets, and we will have great tribute from the defeated Romans! And this wealth will belong to all of us! Mark my words, it will be to the benefit of every last citizen, as everyone has a right to enjoy the spoils of this war, not only the elites in their palaces!"

The people began loudly celebrating once again, though the two suffetes looked quite uncomfortable and glanced at each other with worry, understanding that this was a not too indirect threat against them and their cliques. They were ready to intervene, but Hannibal saw them and realized that it was time for him to go, and so concluded his speech.

"Thank you all for your part in helping us win this war. I would love to stay here for longer, but there are still many matters that need attending to, thus I will have to leave you for now. Please, enjoy the celebrations, and Baal bless you all!" Hannibal waved to the crowd as he was beginning to leave.

"General, would you mind answering a few questions before you go?" one citizen next to the platform shouted.

"I'm afraid the general really has to leave now, please save your questions for-" Mago Arvad tried to shoot down the question, before being cut off.

"Certainly, a few questions won't hurt. What is it you wish to know?" Hannibal turned back to the crowd, despite the silent protests of the suffetes.

Hearing this, dozens of people tried to make their way to the front and ask their questions, with the guards barely able to contain them all.

"Have the Romans truly been defeated for good? Can we be certain that they will never attack us again?" one man asked.

"They have, otherwise I wouldn't be here," Hannibal replied proudly. "Believe me, they are a relic of the past. You can sail to Ostia right now and see what a sorry state they are in. They will never pose a threat to anyone again."

"Are there any other planned military campaigns or will our husbands finally get some rest after their victories abroad?" a woman asked next.

"There is no need for more campaigns. All our soldiers are returning home – what few places need to retain a military presence will be more than adequately served by our mercenaries and the men who signed up to stay there. If your husband survived the war – and I pray he has – he will be home in no time, he will get as much rest as he needs, and will be compensated for his valiant efforts more than appropriately. As will all the other veterans of the war, of course."

"General, it is a great honor to see you here. Thank you for your service. What are you planning to do now that the war is over?" a man asked after pushing through the crowd to get closer to Hannibal.

"Great question. I was thinking about that myself for the last few months. Not much use for generals during peacetime. But there is a need for politicians. So I may get into politics, to set things right here in the capital as well. Elections are coming soon, after all."

"You definitely have my vote, general!"

"And mine!" another man shouted.

"Mine too!" more men joined.

"Hannibal Barca for suffete! Now that's a great and honest candidate for once!" an older man further out proclaimed, with many around him nodding in agreement.

"That's enough time for question, the general is really busy and should get back to his duties," Mago Arvad intervened nervously. "Thank you all again for coming here, great pleasure seeing so many active citizens on this fortuitous day. Please, go and enjoy the celebrations, greet your returning relatives, and take in this victory of ours," he said, as the soldiers started shuffling away the spectators to once again make way the generals who were leaving, including Hannibal, who was more than content with his reception, even as the people were still clamoring to reach him and talk to him more.

A few days after his arrival back home in Carthage, Hannibal was summoned by the government officials on Byrsa hill so that he could be officially congratulated for his accomplishments. While tensions had already been brewing between Hannibal and his supporters and the government of Carthage, which had disagreed with him on numerous occasions, and which had its orders ignored by the general, such a massive victory still could not go ignored. Thus, the senate invited Hannibal to acknowledge his success in the war, but to also learn what he had in mind for the future, as the suffetes began worrying about his next steps after they heard the unexpected speech in the Great Marketplace.

And so, Hannibal appeared as requested, climbing up onto the walled and highly fortified hill in the middle of the city, which stood as both the official government center, as well the last line of defense in case the main city walls were breached and Carthage was under direct attack. It contained some housing, mostly used by government officials, wealthy merchants, military commanders, and other persons of importance. And at the top of the hill, surrounded by yet another wall, stood the government complex, which included the offices of the suffetes, other magistrates, various commissions – such as ones responsible for tax collection, temple preservation, and citizen census – and, most importantly, the senate chambers.

The senate was the main legislative body in Carthage, and included around three hundred members at any given time. The senators, unlike the suffetes, generals, or other high office holders, were not elected and instead were chosen by the suffetes, their fellow senators, and commissions – often through various of backroom deals – which meant that while in theory every male citizen of age was eligible for the senate, only the wealthiest and most important members of society could secure a seat there.

The complex also included the Temple of Eshmun, the Phoenician god of healing, who was also the tutelary god of Sidon in the Levant. It was not the primary god of the city of Carthage – that title belonged to Tanit, who was a goddess of war, beauty, and love, among other things, only worshipped in western Mediterranean, with the Phoenicians in the Levant continuing to instead worship Astarte, their equivalent which had been their deity for millennia. Tanit's cult emerged much later in Carthage, while Sidonians were among the first to arrive in the city, right after it was founded by Tyrians, and so they had managed to build a temple to their god in the most central position when it was still empty. It was right in the middle of the complex and Hannibal walked through its courtyard before finally arriving in the senate room.

"Welcome back, general," Hannibal was greeted by a standing ovation from the assembly as he entered, facing a semi-circular seating area for the hundreds of senators.

The two suffetes were also there, standing on the platform reserved for speakers, and while they were also applauding Hannibal, they were noticeably more wary of him.

"Thank you, senators. It is a great honor," Hannibal said as he came up next to the suffetes.

"Congratulations are in order for such a great victory that you have delivered to us," one of the older leading senators said after the applause had finished.

"I was only doing what I could to serve my great republic."

"And enrich yourself in the process," another senator sneered from the back.

"I enriched every citizen of Carthage, senator. And I made sure Rome would never threaten us again. What have you been doing in the meantime for all these years? I certainly don't remember seeing you on any battlefield."

"We do, of course, appreciate all you have done for us, general," the first senator interjected. "But now that the war is over, we need to focus on rebuilding our strength and refilling our treasury."

"Naturally. But that shouldn't be an issue. There are no more battles to be fought, so the army will recover naturally. And the treasury – well, the Iberian gold is already flowing into it, as are the profits from all the reopened trade routes. And before long, we will begin receiving tribute from Rome. While I am no treasurer, I believe we should have more than enough gold to pay back all our debts, rebuild what is needed, and compensate our troops."

"That is correct. Our financial situation is looking good," another senator replied. "Good years are ahead for us. And do not worry, all the Carthaginian soldiers and mercenaries will be paid more than appropriately, as will the generals with their respective bonuses. The highest one going to you, naturally."

"Good. It is all settled then. But I have a feeling that I am here today for a different reason…"

"Well, there is the issue of our border security," Mago Arvad began slowly. "With all these new changes, there are bound to be some issues. Various local troubles, as I am sure you understand. And to protect all our newfound wealth, we need someone to secure our frontiers and make sure no barbarians or other threats infringe upon our lands... Someone with a lot of military experience, preferably."

"What threats? I made sure there were no credible threats to us when I sailed back to Carthage."

"There is northern Italy, now overrun by Gauls," Hyrum Baltsar continued his colleague's point. "They may threaten our new friends in Etruria, or even our tributary Romans. But more importantly, Iberia. A large portion of it is still untamed. While your family's conquest of the peninsula was swift, there are still tribes hostile to us, and parts of Iberia are still out of reach, in the north and west specifically. We do need a general to finish the job and make sure the peninsula is fully ours."

"And you want me to do that?" Hannibal was perplexed, but soon realized that it was indeed what the senators and suffetes were hinting at. "This is ridiculous! I have literally destroyed our greatest rival and one of the most powerful countries in the Mediterranean, and now you want me to go back to Iberia to fight with some primitive tribes. Absolutely not."

"We do need someone to do this job."

"Then get Hasdrubal Gisco on it. He was in Iberia for a while as well. Or any other general, even a junior would be fine. Iberia is broken, completely. Even a ragtag mercenary band with a hundred men could finish the job of conquering it. Not like there is any need for that anyways, considering how much we are getting from the portion that we own already."

"The senate decides what campaigns are to be conducted, general, not you, and you would be wise to remember that," another leading senator at the front stood up. "We give the orders, and you execute them. You may be a leader on the battlefield, but not here. This is not Rome, as you well know."

"Oh, I do, senator, I do. So that's what this is? You are trying to get rid of me? I have become too successful to be allowed to stay in Carthage, so you are sending me back to Iberia?"

"How much time have you spent in Carthage? Not more than nine years of your childhood, I believe. While you spent about the same in Italy, and twice that in Iberia. What do you know of Carthage, son of Barca? Don't you think Iberia is better suited for your talents? After all, that's where your wife and son are too," a senator in the back laughed.

"You would be wise to consider your words more carefully, senator," Hannibal replied angrily. "Say whatever you want about it, but keep my family out of this."

"Is that a threat?"

"It is a warning."

"Enough!" Mago shouted. "Hannibal, please, let's keep this civil. You have done great work, but there are more enemies that need to be fought. And you are a general. This is your job. And we are not asking you to leave today, or tomorrow, or even this month. But it would be beneficial to everyone to keep our spheres separated in this way. You Barcids can be in charge of Iberia and all the other frontiers, while we will continue to run things here in Carthage and the core of the republic. It has been working well so far, hasn't it?"

"I believe you weren't too happy with us securing Iberia by ourselves at first either. So now, decades later, you are finally willing to concede it to us. How gracious," Hannibal sneered.

"Do you really want to get into a fight over this? It could get ugly," Hyrum warned.

"Oh, it definitely will. But not in the way you think."

"I am pretty sure I know how treason trials for generals disobeying their orders end."

"Is that so? Well, what are you waiting for then? Let's go, we can ask the judges what they think about this situation."

Hannibal began leaving the room, with the two suffetes looking confused but following after him.

"Well, the session is thus concluded," the first leading senator announced after the three men had left, with the senators still not sure of what had actually happened.

Hannibal and the suffetes left the senate chamber and crossed the temple courtyard to head into the main meeting room of the Court of 104. This was a completely independent Carthaginian judicial assembly, which deliberated and delivered verdicts on important legal cases, often relating to the conduct of generals in wars, as a means of preventing the overreach of the military officer class and their potential attempts at overthrowing the civilian government and usurping the control of the state. Historically it had been successful in its work, as there had been no tyrants in Carthage for centuries, and the few attempted coups failed, while the generals retained a very limited influence in the country outside the battlefield, in great contrast to almost every other civilization. The Court was made of 104 high judges, who were all chosen by their peers once someone died, as the court members held their posts for the remainder of their life. This meant that the average member was older and more experienced than a senator, and also wealthier and more highly regarded due to the lower number of seats and a more difficult process of getting in. Overall, however, it was, at least supposed to be, a neutral institution, one which mediated between the internal parties of Carthage – the civilians, the senate, other government institutions and commissions, and the military.

"Good day, honorable members of the court," Hannibal greeted the chamber as he entered it, with the suffetes still behind him.

"Ah, Hannibal. It's good that you are here. We have finished reviewing your appeals and you have arrived just in time to hear our decisions," one of the judges said.

"Wonderful. That is indeed why I am here."

"And I see you have the suffetes joining you as well."

"It concerns them to some degree too, so I thought it would be good for them to hear everything directly from you. To make sure there are no misunderstandings."

"Of course."

"Appeals? What appeals have you made, general?" Hyrum panicked.

"Well, that is one thing I wanted to mention to you before. I am no longer a general. That means you cannot legally command me to go anywhere and fight. I am now just a civilian, same as you two."

"What? That cannot be right," Mago replied.

"Hannibal speaks the truth," another judge said. "He had appealed to be relieved of his command as soon as he returned home. We approved this request, and so Hannibal Barca is now a private citizen, not subject to military laws."

"He can't do that! He can't just leave his post like that!"

"In wartime, yes. But, as the peace treaty with the Romans is now in effect, we are not in any war. Thus, the generals and other military commanders can request to be relieved of their duties at any point, by appealing directly to the Court of 104. Which Hannibal has done, in all the proper ways."

"Why haven't we been informed of this before?" Hyrum asked furiously.

"We are not obliged to tell you everything that we have decided on, considering how many cases we have to review every day. But we are not hiding anything, you could have inquired about it."

"Why didn't you tell us this then?" Hyrum turned to Hannibal.

"Why should I have? So that you could have conjured another reason to send me away?" Hannibal replied. "Besides, I wanted to see how I would be greeted, and I saw it well enough. All you vultures circling around me and just waiting for an opportunity to take me down. Well, I can play this game too, and I have plans of my own."

"You said appeals? What else have you requested of the court?" Mago remembered and asked the judges, bracing for the worst.

"I'm glad you asked. What of my second appeal, honorable judges?"

"It has been likewise approved. You are eligible to run for the office of the suffete, in the elections taking place later this year," a judge answered.

"What? Suffete? How? This man cannot be a suffete!" Hyrum protested.

"He can. He is a Carthaginian citizen, a male of age for the office, and he has more than enough wealth to qualify for it. He has also not committed any actions which would prevent him from running for high office. Thus, Hannibal can indeed run for and be elected as a suffete."

"You treacherous snake..." Mago turned to Hannibal.

"I don't see how exercising my civil rights as a citizen of this republic is any indication of treason, but we may have different definitions in this regard," Hannibal smiled and shrugged.

"Will that be all?" the first judge asked, annoyed at the bickering happening before him.

"Yes, your honor, absolutely. We will disturb you no longer. Thank you for your time."

The three men left the court, with the judges returning to their regular matters, while the suffetes were sharing hopeless looks and wondering what they should do next.

"Well, gentlemen, I must leave you now if there is nothing else," Hannibal stated once they were outside. "The elections are not too far off now, so I must begin preparing."

Chapter II

Just as Hannibal returned home with a great victory after the Treaty of Capua had been signed, so did Philip V, the current head of the Antigonid dynasty and the king of Macedon. While his achievements in the war against Rome were much more modest, with the Macedonians entering the conflict after Hannibal had already been fighting in Italy for three years, and Philip not engaging in many significant battles, it was still another successful campaign that further elevated the young king and granted him more honor and fame in the Hellenic world. Despite still being in his twenties, for the king this was far from the first major victory. He had succeeded his great uncle Antigonus III at just seventeen years and was immediately plunged into a war against a coalition of Greek states which still resisted the Macedonian hegemony over the region. This included Elis, Sparta – both having been previously defeated by his father – and also the Aetolian League, the capital of which Philip had sacked and so ended the war right as Hannibal was marching into Italy and starting to cause terror for the Romans.

While Greeks and Carthaginians had rarely been allies historically, with the two groups constantly competing for trade influence, colonies, and naval domination, Hannibal and Philip found common ground in their hatred of Romans and wishing to destroy Rome once and for all, and entered into an alliance in the middle of the war. The Romans had already began encroaching into Greece in the decades prior, after defeating and crippling Epirus, and were also supporting the upstart Greek states trying to break Macedon's hegemony. Naturally, Philip could not let this continue, and so he took his chance and declared war on Rome, despite some warning against such a risky action.

Nonetheless, Philip's gamble paid off and he was now hailed as the savior of the Greek world from the Roman menace. Of course, not all Greeks viewed him as a hero and savior, as for some states he had now completely dashed all hopes of independence, with Rome no longer able to support them and Macedon remaining the only major power in the European part of Greece.

One such detractor was the Aetolian League, a coalition of the settlements in southwestern Greece, between Epirus and Achaea. It was a harsh and desolate land, with even Greeks considering the region to be a backwater and its inhabitants barbarians, and the Aetolians had a hard time refuting such a claim, especially when many men in the country would often turn to piracy and brigandry to supplement their meager possessions. The Aetolians had entered the war on the Roman side in the last year of the conflict, hoping to get revenge on their enemy who had burned their capital and looted their land just a few years prior, but this proved to be a fatal mistake. Very soon the Aetolians realized that they had made a grave miscalculation, as news of Rome's sacking spread and the remaining Roman soldiers were recalled back to Italy, yet it was too late to back out of the war by that point. Aetolia was excluded from the Treaty of Capua, as the Carthaginians deemed it a matter unworthy of discussion and left Macedon to do with it as they pleased, and Philip was more than satisfied with this arrangement.

Philip landed in Aetolia after returning from Italy and laid waste to the region with no mercy. He assembled Macedonian, recently allied Epirote, and Boeotian soldiers – as the Boeotian League was one of the Macedonian puppet states – and sent them into Aetolia, completely overwhelming the local population and decimating it, until there was no resistance left.

"My king, the capital has been taken," a commander informed Philip on the battlefield, referring to the town of Thermum. "What shall be done with it?"

"Burn it. Raze it to the ground. Leave nothing standing. You may take whatever you find as loot, but I don't want any trace of the city remaining afterwards in this place," Philip ordered coldly.

"With pleasure, my king. And what of the inhabitants?"

"They are beyond saving. These people sealed their fate a long time ago. Don't you agree, commander? Isn't it time we finished the job here properly?"

"Oh, absolutely, my king. It will be done," the commander acknowledged happily.

"You cannot do this! We are entitled to a fair peace treaty!" Pyrrhias, the captured Aetolian general, protested.

"As you can see, I clearly can. And there is nothing you can do to stop me," Philip turned to the captive and smiled wryly. "Might I remind you that your people did indeed receive a fair treaty just a few years ago, when the Romans and Carthaginians were already waging war in the west? But you violated the terms, you attacked us again, and now you have to face the consequences."

"You sacked our capital! You desecrated this holy place! We could not sit idly and let you live with that."

"Well, clearly you savages couldn't. I did sack your capital back then, yes, but I let you live and return here. Clearly, I was too naive back then, too childishly hopeful. But I will not repeat this mistake again. There will be no third chance. Because there will be no Aetolia left after I'm done this time."

"You call us savages? And how exactly are you any better?" the general motioned to the capital which was now once again burning and being ransacked by Macedonian soldiers.

"We conquered the known world. We built great wonders. We unlocked the mysteries of the universe. And what have you been doing all this time? Other than stealing what greater men had created? You are worthless pests, and if I have to destroy you completely to guarantee the security of my realm, so be it."

"The gods will never forgive you!"

"Ares will. And likely Athena too. Probably even Zeus. I can live with that."

Feeling done with the conversation, Philip nodded to the soldiers behind the captives, giving them the go ahead to proceed with the executions. In just a moment, they thrusted their spears through the chests of the kneeling Aetolian leaders, killing all of them, including Pyrrhias. And as they were bleeding out, so were the people being slaughtered in what remained of Thermum, as the Macedonians finalized the destruction of the town.

"It seems that the Aetolians will trouble us no longer," one of the assembled commanders said shortly after.

"Indeed, they will not. Hopefully this will send a stronger message to the other Greeks who still think of challenging our rule on this side of the Aegean," Philip replied.

"It was a great show of force. A very wise move, I would say."

"I prefer a kinder approach most of the time, but the Aetolians are a people who only understand strength, so they had to be taught this way."

"And what are your plans for the region? Certainly not continued independence, I assume?"

"Of course not. I will leave Acarnania for Epirus, as a token of friendship. But the rest, east of the Achelous, I will add to my kingdom. This will give us the port of Naupactus and access to the Gulf of Corinth, allowing for even greater influence over the Peloponnese."

"I see. And what of your personal plans? Are you staying here?"

"No, certainly not. I have had enough of this foul place. The Aetolians have been crushed, for good, just like the Romans. Our job here is done. It is time for us to get back to Pella and enjoy our well-earned victories."

After returning to his capital Pella, Philip was greeted by the local citizens celebrating his victory. It was not a large city, but it had grown in the previous decades due to Macedon's influence, and so large crowds had gathered to see and honor their king. He addressed his people, informing them of the end of the war, the defeat of Rome, and the complete destruction of the Aetolian League, which was met with a lot of praise. Soon, however, the ceremony was over, and the king retired to his palace to get some rest and see his concubine Polycratia and firstborn infant son Perseus.

"I'm home, Poly! Had to burn down a few cities along the way, but I made it back just fine," Philip announced as he returned to his palace.

"Philip!" Polycratia rushed to and kissed him. "I've missed you."

"I haven't been gone for too long, have I? I'd like to think we took care of the Romans in a timely manner."

"Yes, that is true. Still, it can get a bit lonely here without you."

"I know. But I'll make it up to you. And look, I've brought you something," Philip summoned a couple of house slaves, who quickly entered the room carrying a large decorated chest.

"What is it?"

"Open it and see for yourself."

Polycratia opened the chest, revealing a hoard of various necklaces, bracelets, rings, gemstones, perfume bottles, and other jewelry and luxury items.

"It's from Rome. Did not want to return empty handed, and it would have been a shame to let all of this burn along with the city or be taken by scavengers later, so I brought some things back with me," Philip explained.

"Thank you. It looks really nice," Polycratia replied.

"I'll have it put in your room so you could try everything on when you have the time," Philip motioned to the slaves, who acknowledged the order and hurried up the stairs to deliver the chest. "And how about the situation here? Was everything well? Did anyone cause you any trouble?"

"Oh, it was perfectly fine. Everything was in order, and I kept everyone in line. Not like there were many men left here, considering most were fighting in one place or another."

"Good. And where is Perseus? I want to see him."

"He's just over here," Polycratia led Philip over to the other side of the central lounge, entering the room of the king's son, where Perseus was currently sleeping. "Do you want me to wake him up?"

"No, no need. Just wanted to have a look at him. Last time I saw young Perseus was just after he was born... Two years ago, I think?"

"That's right."

"He has certainly grown. He will make a strong soldier and a great king after me, I know it," Philip said proudly as he left the room and began walking across the palace grounds.

"I hope so. But will he be accepted as king?"

"Why wouldn't he be?"

"Well, we aren't married. Some might consider him to be illegitimate."

"Fuck them. They can think whatever they want, but I will make sure that Perseus succeeds me, no matter what. I will strengthen our realm, and he will inherit a great empire."

"I'm glad. I was worried that you might find someone else during your wars and... have them to give you new successors."

"Who do you think I am? I'm not some uncivilized barbarian or a common whore who fucks everyone in their vicinity," Philip laughed, though he looked quite offended. "I only love you, no one else. In fact, now that I have returned, I think we should get properly married. Let everyone know that this is serious," he said, lying down on a dining couch and ordering the slaves to bring them some wine.

"I would love that, but... I don't know. It might be risky," Polycratia sat down on the couch opposite Philip. "It may cause problems in our realm."

"Why? Who would have a problem with our marriage? Who would even dare question it?"

"The Achaeans for one, obviously. I did leave the son of their strategos for you. And now that Aratus is dead, they may suspect that you have killed him and taken me for yourself..."

"I have covered our tracks though, so they have no reason to suspect foul play. Especially since it happened during the war. Many men die during wars, you know," Philip shrugged and started sipping his wine.

"But all three at the same time? My former husband, son, and father-in-law? Might be a hard thing to believe..."

"Maybe. But we hired the best assassins and got the best poisons, remember? Left no trace. Wiped out the whole bloodline just like that, with no one being the wiser. A shame almost, considering how the eldest of them was a good ally. But he stood between us, so he had to be gone too. That's how much I love you. I would poison every other Greek for you if I had to."

"Only every Greek, huh," Polycratia laughed as she sipped some wine as well.

"Who else do you want? Could throw the Romans in too, but I would happily send them all into the underworld even without any reward. The Egyptians maybe? We do need someone to grow our food though, so may not be the best option."

The two laughed again.

"But seriously," Philip continued. "If I want to marry you, and you want to marry me, who is there to stop us? Certainly not the gods – I know that they would approve of us. Anyone else who wants to challenge us is free to make their stand, before I wipe them and their pathetic supporters off the map with my troops."

"You've certainly grown more confident since last time. Feeling ready to conquer the world and follow in the footsteps of Alexander?"

"Why not? Who else is left there to challenge me? Rome is in ruins, the Aetolians are dust, Elis and Sparta received a good beating not too long ago and learned their place, the Boeotians and Athenians remain obedient little dogs, the Achaeans are now leaderless, and Epirus owes me for what I've given them. Otherwise, it's just irrelevant city states and islands."

"And what of the bigger powers? Ptolemies, Seleucids, Carthaginians?"

"I'm on good terms with Hannibal and Antiochus. And the Ptolemies – well, the only threat those incestuous morons pose is to their own realm."

"Can't argue with that."

"See? We are safe, and we are powerful. But my reign is just starting, and I am ready to make Macedon an even greater force. One that is as respected and feared as back in Alexander's days. So maybe I am following in his footsteps. Will you join me on this journey?"

"How could I resist such an offer? Of course I will join you, my king."

"Perfect. Just what I wanted to hear," Philip said as he climbed onto the couch where Polycratia was lying, "my queen."

Chapter III

On the eastern shore of the Mediterranean, and stretching far to the east, stood another realm which was invested in the fate of Rome. It was a large empire, built on the corpse of the Achaemenid Persian Empire and the Empire of Alexander III – also known as Alexander the Great – succeeding it, yet it was a land of contradictions and paradoxes. The empire reached as far west as the Aegean Sea on the Anatolian side and as far east as the harsh lands of Bactria in the east, yet it could barely hold itself together and was plagued by constant rebellions and secessions. It housed tens of millions of inhabitants, yet was ruled by a tiny minority of Greeks – most of them settlers from prior decades – who also made up the majority of the army. It could challenge even the most powerful realms of the land, yet could rarely even keep the peace outside its capital. And while it called itself an empire, and was called as such by others, it was in reality little more than a single dynasty, with no connection to the land, trying to preserve as much of their wealth and power as possible.

Such was the curious case of the Seleucid realm, named as such due to being founded by Seleucus I Nicator, one of Alexander's generals. The Seleucid Empire had been the largest of the Diadochi states by far since nearly the very start, initially holding almost all of Alexander's conquests in Asia. Yet, this behemoth could not sustain itself for long, and began fracturing almost immediately, with foreign powers chipping away at the empire from all its edges. The Indus River Valley was taken by the Maurya Empire in India, the northeastern lands were lost to various barbarians, Parthians, and Greeks who established an independent Bactrian kingdom, while the Anatolian and Caucasian holdings were now divided between a myriad of small kingdoms, varying between puppet states of the Seleucid Empire, independent but allied realms, and hostile entities. And in the years prior, more troubles had begun brewing, as rebellions intensified and threatened to end the Seleucid hold over Persia, Media, and the whole of Anatolia, while the Ptolemies in Egypt were also eyeing the Levant.

However, this was avoided by Antiochus III, the current ruler of the Seleucid realm. He had ascended to the throne at eighteen years of age, receiving titles such as King of Syria, King of Babylon, and King of Asia. Antiochus inherited a fractured realm, but over a decade of his rule he managed to bring it mostly back under control. He put down the revolts led by the satraps – governors – of Persia and Media to its north, secured western Anatolia and access to the Aegean, and brought Armenia back into tributary status, as it had previously stopped paying tribute to the Seleucids. Still, the work was far from finished. Antiochus had plans for continuing his restoration of the realm, including the reclamation of Parthia and Bactria, the pushback of the Mauryas, and the creation of a stronger foothold in Anatolia. There was also the issue of the Ptolemies in Egypt, with whom the Seleucids had been at war many times over the prior decades. The latest one, the so called Fourth Syrian War, ended just six years ago, with Antiochus attacking Ptolemy IV in an effort to take southern Levant and the Anatolian holdings from him, but failed after a major defeat. This did slow down the Seleucid leader's plans, but he vowed to finish this fight later and get his revenge on the Ptolemies.

Antiochus was married to Laodice III, the daughter of the king of Pontus in northern Anatolia, and had six children with her already – three sons named Antiochus, Seleucus, and Mithridates as well as three daughters, named Ardys, Stratonice, and Laodice. The king was also surrounded by advisors, most prominent of them being the general Zeuxis, who rose in rank after the king's right-hand man Hermelas was assassinated, as Antiochus suspected him being engaged in a conspiracy to take over the realm. Antiochus had friends abroad too, such as Philip in

Macedon and Mithridates II, the king of Pontus. And while he had no official alliances or other such agreements with the Carthaginians, Antiochus was cordial towards their leaders and wished for them to succeed against the Romans. Just like Philip, Antiochus feared the rise of the Roman Republic and what it could mean for the Hellenic world, though he did not join the war as he was fighting battles at home at the time. Still, he took great joy at the news that the Romans were defeated and sent a congratulatory letter to Carthage and Hannibal personally, expressing his support for their cause. While Rome was no longer an issue for the Seleucids, the Ptolemies in Egypt still were, and they had the largest fleet in the eastern Mediterranean, which could only be matched by the Carthaginian one – and so, Antiochus was interested in building a relationship with the victorious republic in the west.

Luckily for Antiochus, the Carthaginians, specifically the Barcids, were interested in a partnership with him as well. As Hannibal began his campaign for the post of suffete, he realized that he needed allies to counter the established elites in the senate, and powerful ones at that. Hannibal had Philip, but the Macedonian king could provide little else than his infantrymen, which, while important on the literal battlefield, was of no value in the political arena. The Seleucids, meanwhile, were very wealthy and had funds to spare – from the taxes of their rich holdings in Mesopotamia and the Syrian coast – which Hannibal needed to compete against the senate. He was busy making speeches and talking to the people in Carthage, trying to build up his base, and so he had no time to travel so far, especially with the elections rapidly approaching, but he had people he trusted who could do that job for him.

For this task, he chose his younger brother Hasdrubal. Having been a general in the war and the commander of Carthaginian forces in Iberia while Hannibal was campaigning in Italy, Hasdrubal had acquired important strategic and diplomatic skills as he was dealing with the Romans and the local tribes, and so he was chosen as both loyal and proficient enough to negotiate a deal with Antiochus. Mago, the youngest of the three Barcid brothers, was another option, but he had less interest in such matters and had always been only the right hand of Hasdrubal, and so instead was chosen to stay in Carthage and help Hannibal with his campaign. This was an acceptable solution, and before long, Hasdrubal sailed out of the Great Harbor of Carthage with a delegation heading for the Seleucid realm.

Antiochus was waiting in his palace in Antioch, the capital of the Seleucid Empire. Founded by Seleucus I, it had grown immensely and attracted many settlers due to its favorable position in the Hellenic world. The king had continued to build it up and was proud of his realm's royal seat. The initial city had been situated on the eastern side of the Orontes river, but Antiochus expanded it to include a nearby island in the middle of the river, with this island becoming the most fortified place in the capital, as well as the site of the palace, treasury, residences of important officials, several temples to the Greek gods, and a royal harbor. Antiochus was overlooking this harbor as the Carthaginian delegation approached it and docked there, with several men disembarking shortly afterwards. He was expecting this visit, as he had received a letter regarding it in the prior days. Before long, a palace servant informed the king of Hasdrubal's arrival to the palace.

"Your highness, a Carthaginian delegation has arrived to the city, headed by one Hasdrubal Barca. They wish to have an audience with you. Shall I let them in?" the palace servant asked.

"Yes, I've been expecting them. Send them up here," Antiochus replied.

"Right away," the servant bowed and left.

A few moments later, Hasdrubal Barca entered the room, with members of his entourage carrying in chests full of gifts for the king.

"Good day, your highness," Hasdrubal bowed and spoke in Greek. "Thank you for agreeing to see me. I am general Hasdrubal Barca, representing the Republic of Carthage."

"Welcome to Antioch, general. And congratulations once again on your people's victory against Rome," Antiochus replied.

"Thank you. I come bearing gifts for you, courtesy of my family. We included some pieces from Rome which we thought you might like."

"Oh, wonderful. It should suit my collection well. I'll have my servants take it to my vault," Antiochus summoned his palace servants who took the chests and carried them off, while Hasdrubal sent his own companions back out as well. "Would you like some wine? We have a great selection here at the palace."

"I certainly won't refuse such an offer. Though I know little about wine, so I'll take whatever you are having."

"Good choice."

Another servant came in and handed Hasdrubal a glass of wine, also placing the whole bottle on the table, before leaving the room to only the king and the general.

"It's good that you put that wretched state out of its misery before it got too powerful for everyone's good," Antiochus said. "I must admit, even we were getting a bit worried about Rome's rapid growth and were preparing for a war with it, but fortunately the balance of power now seems to be restored in the Mediterranean once again."

"Indeed. It was not an easy war, the Romans really did fight to their last, but we beat them anyways. Raw ferocity can't win against superior tactics."

"Absolutely. What your brother Hannibal did, crossing the Alps with his entire army, elephants and all, truly was a genius move, one which will be remembered for the ages. Were you accompanying your brother on this journey?"

"Unfortunately not. I stayed in Iberia and defended against the Romans there while Hannibal was campaigning in Italy."

"Fair enough, that's just as important a task. So where is your brother now? On some new campaign in Europe?"

"Actually, he is running for the office of suffete right now. The elections are approaching, and he is rallying the people to his cause."

"Ah, interesting. Well, considering his accomplishments, I imagine many citizens will vote for him over whatever bureaucrat was sitting in your capital during the war."

"Well, it's not so simple. While many do indeed adore Hannibal, particularly the soldiers and the urban poor, his opposition is still quite powerful. He is basically fighting the entire senate, who do not wish for an outsider like Hannibal to enter such high office, while also fearing the reforms that he is proposing."

"I see. So you need more help to succeed, is that right?"

"That is why I have come here, yes."

"I am glad you came here instead of Alexandria, as while the Ptolemies are rich, my realm is doing just as well, if not better. What do you need?"

"Gold, mostly. We need to spread our message far and wide in our republic, build up our base, hire experts who can help us navigate the political landscape, hire private security in case the senate starts threatening us – those sorts of matters. Also, your political support for Hannibal would be greatly appreciated, as having such a powerful ally would deter any internal and external enemies even better."

"Carthage is certainly a good ally to have, I don't doubt that. I would not be opposed to an alliance with you. But, with your state being a republic, why should it matter to me who is in charge of it, especially as the leaders are changing every year? By allying specifically with Hannibal and the Barcid family, I would be alienating the senate faction, which could renege on our agreements if they came to power again. Why shouldn't I just ally with your senate and avoid your internal politics, leaving you to sort out your elections by yourselves?"

"Well, for one, you know Hannibal. You know he is not just a typical Carthaginian politician. He is a man of action. He is a warrior, a conqueror, a great strategist. You two could get along very well, I imagine, and help each other, which I don't think I could say about other choices for suffete. As for the term limit – while it might be an obstacle, I don't believe it would hinder the alliance as much as you may think. Like I said, Hannibal has a lot of interesting ideas in mind, many changes that he wishes to enact. He seeks to reduce the power and influence of the senate, the high court, and all other institutions of old fueled by ancient wealth. He wants to transfer this power, or at least some of it, to the people, both political and economic, and so he is loved by the populace at large. If he wins, our faction may become the frontrunner in the political struggle for a long time to come, and the senate will have little to offer to get its preferred candidates reelected."

"You do make a compelling point. While I do not care for your internal policies, that is none of my business after all, a strong man like Hannibal would indeed be preferable as a leader with whom I could make dealings. I imagine a lot of the unnecessary bureaucracy could be avoided to make the process smoother. And having your family stay in power for longer would also help, as I wouldn't need to reestablish a relationship with Carthage once again every year. I like this…" Antiochus paused for a few moments while sipping the wine. "Say I support Hannibal, give him what is needed. Would he answer the call when I request his aid in turn?"

"This would constitute an alliance between the two realms – in the event Hannibal wins, of course – so he most definitely would. Hannibal is a man of his word, and he never lets his allies down. He is honorable, I don't think even his critics in Carthage would argue against that."

"He would be willing to assist me in a war then? His military knowledge, as well as the whole Carthaginian fleet at his disposal would greatly aid me and be most valuable in a campaign that I am planning."

"Yes, unless it conflicted with one of his other alliances. It would become a more difficult situation to manage in that case."

"Do not fret, for I am not planning on invading Macedon. Not yet, at least," Antiochus laughed, and Hasdrubal followed. "No, I don't believe there would be any conflict of interest. I am talking about our mutual neighbor, the blight on the rich Nile valley, otherwise known as the Ptolemaic dynasty. I failed to defeat them once a few years ago, but I have grown more experienced since then. And if I had allies such as Carthage – well, our victory would be all but guaranteed. I don't believe it would even be a long campaign at all, considering how flat and easily navigable Egypt is. And, of course, Carthage would be well compensated with the spoils of war."

"While I cannot speak for my brother, this does sound like a reasonable request, one that Hannibal would be more than likely to accept. Of course, we would need time to rebuild our forces, since the war with the Romans certainly took its toll. But rest assured, we don't care much for the Ptolemies either."

"I thought so. This could become a very fruitful alliance."

"Indeed. I will write to my brother of this potential arrangement and will let you know as soon as I get an answer."

"I will await it. In the meantime, enjoy Antioch, general."

"Thank you, your highness. I believe we will meet once again quite soon."

Chapter IV

"And what would you do about the rising inequality in Carthage, if you were elected to be a suffete? We won the war, and are now supposed to be the richest and most prosperous country in the world! Yet there are thousands of people languishing in the streets of our capital and many other cities, the elders are dying in front of temples because no one will take care of them, mothers are forced to become prostitutes to feed their children because their husbands died fighting the Romans, and even if those veterans survived the war – they return home, possibly sick or crippled, and are immediately relieved of their post and benefits, with no support from the government, and have nothing to look forward to! How can such a state of affairs exist if Carthage is so famously wealthy?" a concerned citizen asked in the Great Marketplace of Carthage, with hundreds of others around him nodding and agreeing with the sentiment.

The question was addressed to the candidates for the post of suffete – Hannibal Barca and Hyrum Baltsar, one of the current suffetes. There were more candidates in total, the others being Mago Arvad, also running for reelection, Hanno Baalmun, a young senator presenting his candidacy for the post for the first time, Aradus Reshgal, an ally of Hannibal from a lesser-known family, and Bomilcar Hadad, an independent with no affiliation to the others, but a wealthy one as he had profited greatly from his mercantile activities. However, at this time only Hannibal and Hyrum were present in the marketplace for a debate and to answer questions given by the voters, while the others were campaigning in different areas. For the senatorial faction, which included Mago, Hyrum, and Hanno, the concern was also covering the entire city and countering Hannibal's campaign as much as possible, and so while Hyrum was sent to debate Hannibal when the former general was seen interacting with the voters in the marketplace, the other allied candidates continued their campaigns in districts further out, hoping to get as many voters on board as possible. However, in the marketplace, Hannibal was so far dominating the conversation and was the crowd's favorite by a large margin.

"That is an excellent question, sir. What is your name?" Hannibal asked.

"Esh, same as my father's, who died in the First Roman War," the citizen replied.

"Esh, believe me, I understand your concerns. I personally think it is shameful that we have built such a great country, yet allow many of our people to suffer, especially veterans who brought us to this greatness. The gods surely cannot be satisfied with such a situation. Tell me, Esh, did your family get compensated for losing your father in the war?"

"Not at all, we were completely abandoned by the government, and had to survive without our main breadwinner at the time."

"What a disgrace. And I imagine such a story has repeated itself thousands of times, has it not? It is time we addressed this issue. If I am elected, I swear on Tanit, I will do everything in my gods given power to resolve this matter. As you well know, I fought many battles, met many soldiers, and I know their plight well. I will make sure all our soldiers get paid what they deserve, no matter how low their rank was in the war, and if they had to give their lives to defend us – their families will be taken care of and compensated for their losses. I will make sure that every citizen of our republic is provided at least the most basic of necessities and can live in dignity instead of total poverty and misery."

"But how would you achieve that?" another citizen asked.

"I have many plans in mind, but one of the first things would be a grain dole, provided for a reduced price for the people who cannot afford it at market rates, and for free for the poorest citizens. We have grain, we have more than enough of it for everyone – all that we grow around Carthage in Africa, and now in Sicily too. It is only a matter of distribution. Another task would be constructing a lot of new housing, as well as various public facilities. Our city has grown immensely in the previous decades, yet there has not been much expansion recently. People are forced to live in overcrowded areas and sometimes are even thrown out on the street. We need to build more and provide everyone with a decent place to live, as well as work and engage in activities in their free time."

"Very noble goals, absolutely. But please, Hannibal, tell us how you would pay for these programs? You would need to buy the grain so you could distribute it, you would need to buy land to build on it, as well as buy materials, hire workers. This all costs money, and it wouldn't come cheap. Where do you intend to get this much gold from?" Hyrum snidely asked.

"Great question, Hyrum, I was just about to talk about it. You probably think that my answer will be increased taxation, right? Taking the hard-earned gold of the merchants and landowners to support the urban poor? Well, it actually is not. Do not worry, taxes will not be increased either, even on the highest earners, so you can rest easy in one of your dozen mansions," some in the crowd laughed and Hannibal continued. "We have the money as well, there is no need to be concerned about it. Our trade activities, our tariffs, our docking fees, our gold mines in Iberia, our spoils from the war, our income from Roman tribute – it all adds up and fills our treasury to the brim. The question now is, where does all that gold go? And that is the question that I intend to answer. I will conduct a thorough investigation and make sure all the embezzled money is recovered, and corrupt practices are put to an end. It is time the wealth is shared properly between all the people who serve our country and does not only go into the pockets of senators and high judges in the Court of 104, who live lavishly and ignore the suffering of the masses."

"This is an outrageous accusation! We are not stealing any money that is not rightfully ours! You are making claims with no evidence in reality!"

"Oh, but I do have evidence. And I will have even more once I am in the high office and can access the treasury records in full. And thank you for letting me know that you are also in on the whole operation, as I did not mention you among the embezzlers, but I will make sure to add your name to the list," Hannibal said to the great amusement of the crowd, who laughed and clapped for him after the retort.

"And what about your plan, Hyrum? How would you solve these issues?" a citizen asked once the crowd quieted down.

"Well, it is indeed a complicated matter, and we can't just throw money at it blindly and hope to solve it that way," Hyrum began. "We need gold to maintain our army, navy, border fortifications. We can't waste it all away just because we have it right now, we need to prepare for the future. And while soldiers should be compensated for their efforts – and they would be under my rule, of course – not everyone can be supported by the government. Carthage is a land of freedom and opportunity, and I believe it is every citizen's individual responsibility to provide for themselves, without relying on handouts from us. This will make us a stronger country, even if sometimes one has to suffer to a degree…"

"If this is the land of freedom, why am I paying such high taxes to you then?" another citizen asked.

"How are we supposed to provide for ourselves if we are crippled in a war you started?" another added.

"Your personal guards, yachts, and palaces don't count as armies, navies, and fortifications!" a disgruntled man from the back shouted.

"Very true," Hannibal agreed with the crowd's sentiments. "You see? You can, of course, vote for Hyrum here or anyone else in his clique, and then things will stay the same. Or you can vote for me, and actually see some positive change in the country for once, where our victory starts benefiting everyone instead of just the ones at the very top."

"You often talk about elites at the top of our society. If you were elected, would you do anything about them, to curtail their power and give it to the common people?" a man at the front asked Hannibal.

"Another great question. And while I cannot guarantee any results, I would certainly try. It has always bothered me that the people can vote on the suffetes, yet cannot do so for the assemblies overseeing them, which often makes the suffetes just tools of the established elites. So yes, I would definitely have to do something about this situation, because without the senate's or the court's approval, none of my plans would come to fruition. Now, for the senate – while the situation is not ideal, I believe it can be improved without massive changes. It does contain hundreds of members and so organizing elections for every seat would take a very long time and be highly inefficient. And with such a high number of senators, there are many factions within the assembly, with different beliefs and interest groups, so anyone can potentially take their place if they want that enough and have some political skills. Yet it is a different story with the Court of 104. It is a smaller assembly, while at the same time the members are much more entrenched there, usually serving for life and being chosen by their predecessors. This makes the court rather unrepresentative of the population at large and impossible to get into for anyone except members of the most powerful and ancient families. But I believe this can and should be changed. The world is changing, and the court should too, which is why I believe it should become open to elections. The citizens should have the power to elect all the judges, thus making sure they are trusted by the community and serve its interests, instead of only serving the noble families."

"Does this mean that every citizen could stand for election to the court?"

"Yes, I believe that should be the case. If a person proves himself and gets elected, why not? But the term should be just one year, same as it is for suffetes, or a few years at most, so that the judges could not sit on their accomplishments for decades, and would instead have to continuously prove their worth, or be replaced by better candidates. This would prevent such stagnation and dominance of old families that we see now and open the way to actually skilled candidates, no matter their status."

"And does this include citizens from other cities in our republic?"

"As long as they can make it here and find a place to live. While every city has its own suffete and local assembly equivalent to our senate, the Court of 104 is one of a kind, only present here in the capital. I believe it would be more than fair to allow at least some members to come from other great cities in our realm, be that Hippo Regius, Iol, Gades, New Carthage, Panormus, or any other Punic city in our republic. They pay taxes not only to their local treasuries, but also to the one in the capital, so they should have at least some representation here as well."

"This is a sacrilege!" Hyrum interjected angrily. "You are talking about upending a tradition which has lasted centuries. You want to replace the wise judges with commoners who know nothing of our law! This man cares nothing for our legacy, for our culture, he is willing to destroy everything that we have built if it means getting more votes!" Hyrum turned to the crowd and addressed it passionately, hoping to win it back.

"What the fuck did you say about us?" a citizen shouted back at him.

"Hyrum does not care about us, he is just a tool of the elites!" another added.

"Wait, wait, no, I did not mean it like that! Obviously, I just wanted to say-" Hyrum panicked.

"Even more proof to confirm what everyone already knew," Hannibal interrupted his opponent gleefully. "Hyrum certainly does not care about any of you – you just heard what he thinks of the common people, the regular citizens. He cannot stop treating you with disdain even when he is supposed to be campaigning! What a pathetic performance! Hyrum, you should run back to your friends in the senate, as it does not seem that you will find any here!"

"Please, everyone, it's just a misunderstanding, of course I care about all the citizens-"

"I believe we have all heard enough from you today. I will not waste my breath arguing with you further. As for the rest of you – I would gladly address any other concerns that you have and discuss issues and my plans for solving them. Meet me at the chariot race in the evening. If you do not have tickets yet – I would be more than happy to buy them for you!"

Hannibal left the marketplace, with the absolute majority of the citizens there cheering him on and some following him further.

"The situation is quite dire at this point," Mago Arvad said, as he was eating and drinking wine at dinner, in his villa on the outskirts of Carthage, where he was joined by Hyrum Baltsar and Hanno Baalmun to discuss political strategy.

"No one can argue that. Hannibal is clearly the men's favorite, pulling them to his side with all sorts of idiotic promises and populist nonsense," Hyrum agreed, finishing his wine and asking one of the house slaves for more.

"His military history certainly helps him, I suppose," Hanno suggested.

"Maybe, but I imagine for an average citizen the promises of free food and him distributing tickets to the chariot races are even better incentives. He is literally bribing the people to vote for him!"

"To be fair, aren't we doing the same thing?"

"You could say that, except we are trying to bribe the nobles and other elites. Which is turning out to be quite expensive," Mago replied.

"Well, fuck me, I guess we picked the wrong people then. We could get a hundred commoners to vote for us for the price that wouldn't even make a well-off merchant budge," Hyrum exclaimed.

"True, but then we would have to actually proceed with whatever populist propaganda is fed to them, or otherwise we would never be elected to any post again."

"And what about his Iberian connection? Is that something that we can use against him?" Hanno asked.

"I don't believe that strategy is very effective, not among the commoners at least."

"Of course not, it doesn't matter to them that Hannibal and all his brothers spent most of their lives in Iberia and barely set foot in Carthage before the elections. Or that he has a barbarian wife, and a mongrel son tucked away in that forsaken peninsula. But when half the city is now composed of Greeks, Numidians, Jews, and other foreigners, I suppose that fact can be easily ignored…"

"At least those foreigners can't vote."

"Yet."

"Yet… Right."

"Who knows, maybe Hannibal will grant them citizenship too and allow them to vote, so he could increase the number of his supporters for the next election."

"I don't think even he would dare attempt it… Nonetheless, that is a grim possibility."

"What a damn mess. You know, maybe we should have remained a kingdom. Could have become the Achaemenids of the west, if not the entire Mediterranean. What have any republics accomplished? The Greek cities have been continuously fucked for centuries, first by the Persians, and now the Macedonians. And the Romans – well, nothing further needs to be said about them."

"If Carthage remained a monarchy, you wouldn't be in charge of it now, would you?" Hanno asked.

"Maybe not. But I don't feel very much in charge right now either. What king just allows his general to campaign in the streets, gather supporters, and take the throne with no resistance? And if we tried to do anything about it, we would be sanctioned into the underworld by the court, if not exiled or outright executed. Fucking ridiculous…"

"The very same court that Hannibal is interested in completely dismantling and replacing with commoners…" Mago added bitterly.

"Exactly! That fucker is setting himself to be a king anyways, and the morons in the streets are cheering him on. All so some common whores on the street could get free grain and leech off the state even more."

"Right… Yet, we have to face the reality of the situation – however much we do not like it, Hannibal will win. There is overwhelming support for him. Even among the rich, considering the Barcids are far from nobodies and have connections even at the very top. Not to mention all the soldiers and generals rallying behind him. No matter how much electoral interference we can create, everyone could still see that Hannibal is the clear winner. Thus, we are no longer competing for the first place – we have to adjust our goals and hope to at least win the second place, so that the second suffete could hinder Hannibal's disastrous plans."

"That means consolidating our voters. Even without Hannibal, any of us alone would struggle against Aradus or Bomilcar, and we can't allow them to win either, as they would just support Hannibal and agree to whatever he proposed."

"Even Bomilcar, you think?" Hanno asked.

"Absolutely, he is nothing but a spineless coward. He just cares about appearing to have power, but does not give a shit about actually ruling the country. It would be the same as having one suffete only."

"So we have to work together, make sure everyone who supports our common cause is voting for one of us, so as not to split the vote and to at least get more votes than Bomilcar and Aradus," Mago pondered.

"That's what I said. We can't have our already small pool of voters split into three camps. Then we would all certainly lose."

"Which means somebody would have to drop out…"

Mago and Hyrum turned to Hanno.

"Who, me? Why would I do that?" Hanno protested.

"Well, you are the least well known of us and would fare the worst, I would say…" Mago cautiously suggested.

"I've grown in popularity immensely in the last few months! I'm very popular with young voters, in fact. If anyone should drop out, it should be Hyrum! He's doing nothing but embarrassing himself in public when debating against Hannibal!"

"That is quite true…"

"What, are you attacking me now?" Hyrum was taken aback.

"We would need two people to drop out, so that does include you…"

"Oh, so it was decided that you would be the one remaining?"

"Well, yes."

"Fuck you, I'm not going anywhere. I'm the most experienced, and the most capable of tackling Hannibal in the political arena. You two would get completely sidelined and become irrelevant within the first week of your term!"

"You barely won last time, you idiot! You only became the second suffete because, other than me, there were no other decent candidates the previous year!" Mago now started shouting as well.

"You're getting old, you can't handle this job as well as before."

"I think I am perfectly capable of doing that. And look, it's not like you would lose everything if you drop out. I could grant both of you some good magistrate positions, or place you in charge of commissions…"

"Oh, thank you for your generosity, great Mago!" Hyrum mocked him. "Of course I will drop any chance of becoming the suffete again for a promise to be given the honor of leading the fucking sewage oversight commission!"

"This is getting ridiculous, it's getting us nowhere. You two clearly aren't fit for this position in my eyes…" Hanno interjected.

"Oh, shut up, boy. You are not even part of this conversation."

"Yeah? Well, fuck both of you, this is a waste of my time and I'm leaving," Hanno got up from his chair. "I was willing to meet with you and see what arrangements could be made, but clearly, I misjudged the situation and now see that you don't need me. Fine, if you don't want to treat me with respect, I won't stay here any longer. I must get back on the campaign trail anyways."

"Hanno, please, what are you doing? We can figure something out…" Mago begged.

"No, I'm done with this."

"You have no chance of winning on your own!"

"That's fine. It will be valuable experience in any event, and I have many future elections to look forward to and continue my rise, unlike you two. But dropping out now for you would do no favors to my career. So goodbye, and may the gods have mercy on you."

"Baal fucking Hammon, this is a disaster…"

"What an astute observation. I think I'll be taking my leave as well," Hyrum stood up, drunkenly staggering towards the front door.

"You can't leave! We need to work something out! I can't win alone without your support!"

"I bet, good luck though. And by the way, your wine is trash. Can't even get the good stuff out for your supposedly honored guests, huh?"

"Stop acting like a fucking child. Are you seriously going to risk the stability and prosperity of our republic for your own damn pride?"

"Maybe I will. I don't see you trying to be the bigger man and stepping down voluntarily. So maybe I will try my chances as well, I still have many supporters."

"Fine, if you believe such political suicide is your most dignified option, then by all means! Just don't come back begging to me after I become the suffete, you son of a whore!"

Chapter V

While Carthage was a very wealthy and agriculturally secure state with a massive fleet to defend itself, there still remained one other country which could rival it in all these categories. This was the domain of the Ptolemaic dynasty, one of the three surviving major Diadochi dynasties that, along with the Antigonids and Seleucids, managed to endure the first few decades of chaos and constant warfare in the wake of Alexander III's death and establish a reliable foothold in one of his conquered territories. The Ptolemies held Egypt, as well as some territories around it, which they had managed to acquire over the previous century. These included Cyrenaica, southern Levant, Cyprus, as well as some portions of southern Anatolia. In a way, the Ptolemaic realm was the most stable and secure of the surviving Diadochi states, helped by natural defenses that had protected Egypt for millennia – vast and untamed deserts to the west and east, the Mediterranean Sea to the north, and the weak Kingdom of Kush to the south. The only real threat was the Seleucid dynasty on the narrow Levantine border, with which many wars had been fought over the region's control, but the latest one had been won by the Ptolemies.

The situation was also helped by the demographics of the country – the Greeks were still relatively few and so they stuck together in order to retain control over the capital Alexandria and the realm at large, while the vast majority of the population was made up of native Egyptians, who were content to let the Greeks rule them as long as the local ways and gods were properly respected. Navigation in the country was also easy – all the holdings were connected either to the Nile or the Mediterranean, and so every part of the kingdom could be reached relatively quickly, similar to Carthage, and unlike the vast mountainous and desert ridden swathes of the Seleucid Empire.

The Ptolemaic Kingdom had a large army, made up of both Greeks and Egyptians, and a massive fleet, while the historically fertile Nile river valley helped produce more than enough food for the local population while also making Egypt the primary grain exporter, serving regions such as Greece and Italy for many centuries. This naturally made the realm much wealthier than any of its competitors, though Carthage was quickly catching up. And Carthage was becoming a problem for the Ptolemies.

During the Second Roman War, the Carthaginians greatly reduced the food producing capacity in Italy due to their campaigns in the region, but the Romans found a way to sustain themselves by way of imports from Egypt, though that did not prove to be enough to stop Hannibal's purple tide descending on them. Still, the Carthaginians did take note of the Ptolemaic involvement and began to see them as potential rivals, despite the Ptolemies officially remaining neutral during the war. And now, the rulers of Egypt really did begin to feel cornered, with Carthage having allied with Macedon and even more recently with the Seleucids – both Diadochi dynasties being less than friendly with the Ptolemies – while they had no allies of their own left anymore, with Rome having been burnt to the ground, the Aetolians – whom the Ptolemies were trying to protect – crushed by the Macedonians, and all the rebelling factions in the Seleucid realm stomped out. The situation was starting to look dire, especially as rumors and fears of Antiochus III rearming and preparing to invade Egypt were beginning to spread.

"Oh, I love this wine! Really makes me feel like a god, you know? Of course, I am a god, so it is only natural," Ptolemy IV, the pharaoh of Egypt, exclaimed as he was lying in his bed and caressing the body of his mistress Agathoclea.

"Isn't the pharaoh only a son of one of their gods, not a god himself?" Agathoclea asked, lying naked next to him.

"Maybe, I don't remember. Their traditions are difficult to understand. But I am a pharaoh, so I can make whatever rules I want, and if I say that I am a god, then who is going to contest this claim? It only makes sense."

"It does, I suppose."

"And they are not only their gods, they are our gods now too! We own this place after all. So the Egyptian gods now bless us just as much as anyone here. Especially Horus. As I am the pharaoh, he should be speaking to me, and no one else."

"Has he spoken to you yet?"

"Why, yes, of course! How else would I be the pharaoh then? And Ra too, and Osiris… And others, also. Yes, the gods here, they like me. We have an understanding."

"Oh? And what are they saying to you."

"Well… I can't reveal that, otherwise they might feel insulted that I shared their secrets."

"I understand."

"Yes…" the pharaoh finished his drink and threw the empty glass away. "I think I'm ready for another round of action."

"Already, huh? Well, let me just-"

The two were interrupted by a knock on the door.

"Who is it?" Ptolemy shouted angrily. "Have you come to refill our wine? We are running quite low on it."

"Uh, no, your highness. I'm afraid not. I have come to you with an urgent report. But I can call the servants to bring you more wine, if you wish," Sosibius, the vizier of the kingdom, answered from behind the door.

"Oh, Sosibius, it's you," Ptolemy sounded quite disappointed. "Can't you hear that I am busy? And I told you to not disturb me until at least noon!"

"I understand, however, I am afraid that it is already more than four hours past noon."

"Huh, is that so? Well, fine, I'll see what you have."

"Shall I come in?"

"No! I mean, unless... You want to join us? No, bad idea, I'll come out instead," Ptolemy quickly got up and put on some robes. "Don't go anywhere, I'll return for more fun in just a moment," Ptolemy said to Agathoclea and left the room.

"Good day, my pharaoh. Is everything alright?" Sosibius asked.

Sosibius was the chief government official and right-hand man of Ptolemy. He had been active politically before the pharaoh's ascension to the throne eleven years ago, and had quickly become his most trusted advisor, despite having mysterious origins and not being part of any major noble house.

"Yes, it's fine, other than your interruption," Ptolemy replied, still annoyed.

"I apologize, but I have received this missive today and I believe you should read it..."

"Read it? Who do you take me as? Just tell me what it says!"

"Of course. Well, it appears that, according to our latest reports, Hannibal Barca is about to win the election for the position of suffete in Carthage. The highest office there, that is."

"Hannibal... Is that the, uh, the man who... Who is he again?"

"The general who conquered Iberia for the Carthaginians, and then invaded Italy and burned down Rome. He has become quite popular and powerful back home."

"Right. Rome, the country we supplied all that grain too. That's not good for us, is it?"

"No, I'm afraid not."

"Because we won't be able to charge the Romans for the grain again?"

"Well, that too, yes, but there is the bigger problem in Carthage."

"What could be a bigger problem than losing such a lucrative source of income?"

"The fact that Hannibal, the main enemy of what could have been considered our ally, is about to become the leader of Carthage. Which would make Carthage our enemy as well, as Hannibal does not think fondly of us."

"What do I care what some nobody thinks of me? Especially one elected by the filthy commoners. I thought we buried this idiotic notion of letting people choose their leaders a century ago. The Egyptians clearly had the right idea from the start."

"That may be true, however, the issue still remains. Carthage is a powerful country, even more so now, with all their allies and puppet states in Italy, and they have a large fleet which could threaten us."

Ptolemy pondered on this information for a moment.

"And why would they threaten us? Aren't they a merchant country anyways?" the pharaoh asked.

"They may be, but they still defeated Rome, a very martial country. So we must be careful," Sosibius explained. "And our spies report spotting one of Hannibal's brothers in Antioch, supposedly conspiring together with Antiochus. That means that Hannibal is in league with both the Seleucids and the Antigonids. His victory might prove to be disastrous for us, as we can barely fight one opponent at a time – fighting three would seal our doom."

"The way you put it, it does indeed sound dire."

"Because it is."

"But haven't we come to an agreement before? I let you decide what the best course of action is and steer our country in that direction, while I get to enjoy the good life here in the palace, as the great gods intended. Can't you deal with this alone? Or are you incapable of such a task?"

"Not at all. I will deal with it. I just thought to inform you of these developments and ask if you wished to take any… extraordinary actions."

"Such as?"

"Well, it may not be possible to influence the election from our side. But there are other ways to remove Hannibal from the equation."

"Assassination?"

"That is a possibility. Do you want it done?"

"I… I don't fucking know. Listen, you deal with it. I don't care how, just do it. Just keep me and my realm safe, however you can manage it. I really don't care. Let me enjoy my life, while you go make sure my kingdom doesn't get fucked both ways like a common whore in Corinth."

"Yes, my pharaoh. I will do what I can."

"Good. You can go now. Oh, but before you do, get the slaves to bring me some more wine. And oil. And some food too would be nice," Ptolemy said as he went back into his room.

"It will be done… your highness," Sosibius sighed and said through gritted teeth.

Some time later, as Sosibius was leaving the palace, he was met by Agathocles, another of Ptolemy's officials and the chief priest of the cult of Alexander the Great, as well as brother of Agathoclea. He had known Sosibius for a few years, as both of them had met and bonded during the war against the Seleucids, leading the kingdom against Antiochus.

"Good day, Sosibius," Agathocles greeted his colleague. "Hard day at work today, serving our beloved pharaoh?"

"When has it ever been easy?" Sosibius replied.

"Indeed, it never has been. We get all the duties and responsibilities, but none of the rewards, and all the blame and punishments if something goes wrong. Anything new today?"

"Not really, except the fact that our kingdom may very soon be invaded from all sides and be burned down to the ground, while the pharaoh is content to remain in his chambers and drink and fuck until he passes out."

"It is what it is. The Ptolemies sure have been on the decline since the second one."

"The inbreeding which only continues to intensify does not help the situation."

"Of course not. While his father marrying a cousin was not unheard of, marrying your sister is pushing the limits, in my humble opinion," Agathocles noted, referring to Arsinoe III, the sister and wife of Ptolemy IV, with whom the pharaoh recently had his son Ptolemy V.

"Though today I believe he was fucking your sister instead."

"Well, that's great."

"Really? I wouldn't be so overjoyed if I was in your place, but if that's your thing, don't let me ruin your fun-"

"Don't get me wrong, I'm far from thrilled by the idea, but I understand the reality of the situation. Having someone so close to him does indeed have benefits."

"That is true, I imagine neither of us could get to him in such a close and vulnerable state as your sister. Unless he likes sleeping with men too, but I don't believe that to be the case."

"In any event, I'm not volunteering to test this hypothesis."

The two men laughed as they continued outside the palace.

"So did you want anything else from me? Otherwise, I believe I should be getting home, it is getting quite late," Sosibius said.

"Well, actually I wanted to invite you over to dinner, if you are not terribly busy," Agathocles explained. "Courtesy of my mother."

"That is very gracious of her. And who else would be there?"

"Just us four. Me, my mother, my sister – if that fat defective son of Horus is done with her by then – and you, if you choose to join us."

"I see. Is there any particular reason you are inviting me?"

"Well, we just believe that some matters need to be discussed, considering the news that arrived today. And, since the pharaoh clearly cares for none of it, why bother him? So that leaves just us."

"And what would we be discussing exactly?"

"Well, the state of our kingdom, what should be done about, the leadership, and the like. Would rather not say too much here, but we could talk about everything in much more detail in private, I'm sure you understand why."

"Yes, of course."

"So will you be joining us?"

"Gladly. Just let me quickly get home and change into more proper attire."

"We can meet in an hour, if that suits you?"

"It does. I will be there, I know the way."

"I am pleased to hear that. See you at dinner."

"Ah, I see our guest has joined us. Good evening, Sosibius, glad you could make it," Oenanthe, the mother of Agathocles, greeted the guest.

She was lying on the dining couch at the head of the dinner table, filled with various dishes and drinks. Her children Agathocles and Agathoclea were to the right and left of her, on their respective couches, and now Sosibius took his place on the final couch in between them, sitting down opposite of Oenanthe and taking a glass of wine offered by one of the house slaves.

"I am glad to be here. Thank you for inviting me," Sosibius replied. "This is a really nice house, you know."

"I suppose it is, though there are always even grander ones that could be taken as a residence," Oenanthe chuckled.

"Such as the pharaoh's palace," Agathocles suggested.

"Oh, please, our guest has just arrived. This is no time for discussions of treason. That will come after the first meal."

"Sorry, mother."

"It's alright, I don't mind getting right to business," Sosibius said. "I imagine none of us here are the biggest supporters of Ptolemy, and would like to see some change, is that correct?"

"Yes, you are indeed correct," Oenanthe replied. "The fourth Ptolemy of his name is far from the most suitable person for running this kingdom that our ancestors have granted us."

"That would be an understatement," Agathoclea scoffed and drank some more wine. "Ptolemy is a disgusting dirty inbred animal, who cares for nothing but sex, alcohol, and other forms of mindless entertainment and pleasure. The sooner we get rid of him, the better."

"Now, Clea, there will come a time for that. But we all need to make our sacrifices in the meantime for our plan to succeed."

"Easy for you to say that, when you don't need sleep with him almost every day."

"That must not be easy," Sosibius agreed. "Not to say that my time spent with him is any more taxing necessarily, but I have had to deal with a lot of his antics lately as well, and it has been highly frustrating. I basically have to run the country on my own, while still having to adhere to his random whims and deal with the consequences of his anger if something does not go according to his plan."

"That's precisely why we are all here today," Oenanthe replied. "We need to decide on the future of this country, as clearly the way things are going right now are far from ideal."

"I understand. But why now? He has been on the throne for over a decade. We waited this long, can't we wait for a little longer? He certainly doesn't seem that healthy anymore, he may just drop dead one day and solve the problem for us."

"I'm afraid time is of the essence here. Forces are amassing against us already," Agathocles explained. "The Seleucids seem to be preparing for another campaign in Syria, the Antigonids are looking for a new target to attack, and Hannibal may become the new suffete of Carthage, and would most likely become even more aggressive towards us. War may be coming, of a scale not seen in decades, and we cannot afford to have infighting during it. We need to take charge before then and prepare the kingdom the best we can."

"That's right. Ptolemy does not seem interested in preserving his realm whatsoever, and he would be a poor war time leader," Oenanthe added. "Granted, seeing his downfall during an invasion would surely bring us all at least some pleasure and relief, but it would not bode well for us either in the end. Our enemies may very well want to burn Alexandria down and execute all of us for being so high up in the hierarchy. To increase, or at least preserve, our power, we need to make sure our realm survives. And I see only one way to do that."

"A coup," Sosibius thought about it for a moment. "I see. It does make sense."

"And Ptolemy now has a son," Agathoclea interjected. "Not by me, thank Serapis, but by his sister. A little ugly inbred creature, that is supposed to be Ptolemy's successor. What a cruel joke by the gods. But this is a great moment of opportunity for us. The pharaoh is more distant from his wife than ever, now that she has fulfilled her duty to him, and is even closer to me and so more vulnerable. His son's birth also reduces the risk of a succession crisis considerably, since we could just place the fifth Ptolemy on the throne, while having all the actual power ourselves, without anyone commanding over us."

"All good points. But what would happen later? When the successor comes of age and decides that he actually does want to rule the country?"

"Well, we will have a couple decades to figure that out. Or you will, at least," Oenanthe laughed. "I don't know if Hera will grant me so many more years in the realm of the living."

"Yes, there will be plenty of time for dealing with this issue," Agathocles nodded. "But one of us could definitely end up on the throne as the official pharaoh before too long."

"That does indeed sound exciting," Sosibius said as he ate some cheese and figs and drank more wine. "Say we do go ahead with this plan. How would it work? What would the immediate future look for us?"

"I could deal with Arsinoe and Ptolemy, and then take the kid into the care of myself and mother..." Agathoclea began.

"Meanwhile I would rally our supporters and secure the city," Agathocles continued. "If the capital submits to us, the rest of the country would follow, as most Egyptians do not care which Greek sits on the throne. And then you, as the highest ranking official, could proclaim the new pharaoh and, since he is just an infant, the regents who would actually be running the kingdom."

"Regents?" Sosibius asked.

"Well, you and me, of course. We need your high status, as well as my family's resources."

"Two regents, huh? Just like the two consuls of Rome or two suffetes of Carthage... It could work though. We definitely need each other if we are to succeed, that is certain. Speaking of Carthage though – the problem of Hannibal remains, and it would remain still even if Ptolemy was removed. It needs to be dealt with just as quickly."

"Have you thought of anything already?" Oenanthe asked.

"Well, at first I was about to just sit back and let Ptolemy reap what he has sown, but now... Now the future does look a lot more promising, so maybe I should act to preserve it. I have my network of spies, some of them already in Carthage, so I could definitely arrange something to make this problem disappear."

"That would be fantastic," Agathocles smiled. "Doesn't really matter whether his opponents get elected, or the country turns to chaos, as long as Hannibal is not at its head, since then his alliances with Philip and Antiochus would become void."

"Indeed. I will get to it then. Time is of the essence, as you said."

"You are fully on board with our plan then? If we begin, there will be no turning back."

"Yes, I am. Whatever comes, I am ready for it."

"Wonderful!" Oenanthe raised her glass. "I am so glad we are all on the same page here. There is a lot of work to be done, but I believe the gods are on our side and will guide us to success. Now, please, eat, as there is more than enough food for everyone, and we should celebrate this occasion."

Chapter VI

As the suffete election day in Carthage was rapidly approaching, Hannibal continued campaigning in the city and rallying the people to his cause. He was walking through the narrow streets of the inner city, together with his brothers Hasdrubal – who had returned from the east after securing a deal with Antiochus – and Mago, some guards, as well as Aradus Reshgal, who was also running for the office, hoping to get elected as the second suffete after Hannibal. As Hannibal already had plenty of support, he was now helping his ally convince the remaining undecided voters to choose Aradus, rather than one of the other candidates, so that the second suffete's seat would also not fall into the senatorial faction's hands.

"I don't know, I'm still hesitant about this, to be honest," a merchant said as he was selling various foreign wares at his stall next to his house. "I respect Hannibal, and I appreciate what he has done for our country. Saved us from those bloodthirsty Romans and their barbarian ways. I thank the gods for that. And I do not disagree with his ideas, they all sound nice. Could really help us honest folk. But he is a military man. All he has known is war. Shouldn't the post go to someone… less involved in such matters? At least with the current suffetes, you know that nothing would change too much. I could live with that. But Hannibal? What if he uses his military mindset and skills to take over the country? Become a tyrant? That scares me somewhat."

"I understand your concerns perfectly," Aradus replied. "They are not unfounded. Not that I think that Hannibal would become a tyrant, but it is always good to be skeptical of politicians who appear to be larger than life. After all, that is how we can preserve our democracy and make sure it is not exploited unfairly. But that's where I come in. You see, I share most of Hannibal's policies. Giving back to the people, investigating the mismanagement of the funds, reducing the power of the elites. But what's even better, I'm not a general, never have been. In fact, I have never participated in a war, not directly at least, so my hands are clean from bloodshed. I am just a Carthaginian citizen, who has lived here my entire life, and who wants the best for the people."

"Aradus, right? I remember hearing about you. You were on some commission, if I remember correctly?"

"Yes, indeed. I was on the public works commission during the war, and before that. Helped build the new marketplace in the north, as well as restore the public baths nearby. Also expanded the library out west, as it was in dire need of some new material. Along with many other similar projects."

"That's good. Especially the baths, I do very much enjoy visiting them. But still, I fear the instability that could take place after the elections… Would prove to be detrimental to my business."

"Well, then I'm still your best bet. Hannibal is the clear frontrunner now, there is no doubt about that, but if someone else got elected as the second suffete, they would only be focused on fighting Hannibal, which would definitely create instability. Meanwhile, if I got elected alongside him, I could smooth things over and moderate the situation much better. All the good policies would still get passed, but I would make sure he does not get out of line and start tearing down our republic."

"When you put it that way, it does indeed sound like the best of both worlds."

"I'm very glad to hear that. So don't forget, vote for Aradus Reshgal in just a week. And tell your friends about me, if they still have doubts."

"Oh, I will. They might very well be interested. Good luck with the election!"

"Thank you! Tanit bless you and your family!"

Aradus left the stall, continuing down the street until he met up with Hannibal and his brothers once again.

"How is it going?" Hannibal asked.

"The people are receptive to my message. Some are still hardened supporters of Hyrum, or Hanno, or even Bomilcar. But my numbers are rising, I am pretty sure of that," Aradus proudly replied.

"See? The people want change. So much so that there can be more than enough votes for the both of us."

"Indeed. And what about you? Any interesting encounters today?"

"Not really. I'm just enjoying the stroll while my brothers are out speaking for you," Hannibal chuckled. "Would be rather strange if I was promoting another candidate, so I have them do the talking. Not like they have anything better to do."

"This better be worth it, because I really would rather be in Iberia fighting the Celts, rather than do more of this political campaigning business…" Hasdrubal sighed.

"Oh, cheer up, this is fun!" Mago replied. "We are in the heart of the city, really getting to see and feel how the common people live. Quite a fascinating experience."

"Not in a good way though."

"Speak for yourself. I was in a whorehouse just now, and managed to convince the owner to vote for our Aradus."

"Seriously?"

"He has a lot of contacts and could really spread the message far."

"I don't think those are the contacts we actually need. They seem to only be spreading diseases instead of anything worthwhile to society."

"Hey, he has many prominent clients visiting his place. It's quite a high-end establishment, don't be so quick to discount it like that."

"High-end, huh?"

"Yes, the prices are quite steep, but the service is great. You should check it out some time, it's on the Second Baal street, just next to the-"

"Oh, so that's where our Seleucid funding is going."

"Well, come on, I needed to make sure it was legit. You don't want our reputation to be tarnished by associating with low-quality brothels, do you? Besides, it would have been bad manners to just leave without paying for any service."

"In any event, thank you, I appreciate the support," Aradus said, as the group continued down the street, turning to a short alleyway.

"And I appreciate yours," Hannibal replied. "I have many enemies in the city, so it is good to have an honest friend and ally here. We both need each other, if our plans for Carthage are to succeed."

"We will do great things here, I am sure."

"I believe we could now go to Dido street, there should be some more potential voters there, especially now that-"

"Looks like someone is blocking our way," Hasdrubal pointed to the three men who were standing at the other side of the alleyway.

"I see. Juba, could you tell these gentlemen to clear the way, so that we could pass?" Hannibal asked one of his guards.

"Right away, boss," Juba, the large Numidian bodyguard, nodded and went up to the men in front of them. "Hey, you three!" Juba addressed them. "Can you step out for a moment? We have people coming through and you are blocking the street."

Without saying a word, the three men turned around, all wearing masks that covered their faces, and pulled out their daggers. One immediately lunged at Juba, and before the Numidian could react, slit his throat.

"Oh fuck! We need to get out of here!" Mago exclaimed as he saw Juba's body drop to the ground and the masked attackers approaching the remaining group.

"Turn back! Better to fight them on more open ground than squeezed in here," Hannibal reacted quickly and began running back from where he came, with the others following behind him.

However, they quickly stopped again, as three more attackers, dressed the same as the others, now appeared on the opposite side of the alleyway, trapping the three Barcids, Aradus, and the four remaining guards between them, as another one had also already been killed by the second group of assassins.

"Help! We're being attacked!" Aradus shouted, hoping that the locals would notice the skirmish and help in some way.

A struggle ensued between the assassins and their targets, and while the latter group did draw their daggers and swords, and were all trained in hand-to-hand combat, they were not as experienced or agile as the unexpected attackers. In a few moments, two more guards were cut down, giving their lives while trying to protect Hannibal. One of the assassins was injured, but continued to fight alongside his allies, hoping to quickly finish the engagement before bleeding out.

The situation was looking desperate for Hannibal and his friends, but this changed as a local merchant, having heard the cries for help, went up to the alleyway to investigate and saw the scene for himself.

"Hey! Someone is attacking Hannibal and Aradus! We have to help them!" the merchant shouted, alerting more of the locals to the ongoing fight.

Before the assassins realized what was happening, about a dozen local men sprinted into the alleyway, armed with knives, cleavers, clubs, and other makeshift weapons that were on hand, and descended on the perplexed masked attackers.

"Get away from them!" a butcher shouted as he struck one assassin in the chest with his cleaver.

The assassins were now seriously overwhelmed, fighting nearly three times their number, and being completely surrounded and barely able to maneuver. The three nearest ones were disarmed and dragged into the crowd, which proceeded to stab and beat them to death. The two remaining guards meanwhile used this opportunity to knock back another assassin and kill him. This left only two assassins, who now realized how low their chances of success were, and decided to flee, before the other side of the alleyway was blocked too.

"Should we chase after them, sir?" one of the remaining guards asked Hannibal.

"No," Hannibal replied, still catching his breath. "I can't imagine they will attack us again, after what happened. And the soldiers should catch them before they get far."

"Understood. Are you hurt?"

"No, just a few scratches. Is everyone else alright?"

"I'm fine," Hasdrubal replied.

"Don't worry about me either," Aradus confirmed.

"Well, for me… I might be in a more of a predicament," Mago said, as he was holding his bleeding side. "Those fuckers cut me pretty deep. Probably should not have skipped so many of father's sword fighting lessons, heh…" he let out a weak laugh.

"You need to be taken to a doctor, right now! Zel, Syph, take him to be treated before it's too late!" Hannibal ordered his two guards, who swiftly picked up the injured Mago.

"I know of a good doctor nearby," one of the men said as he pushed through the crowd. "He's very close, I can take you there."

"Thank you, please do that. Just show them the way," Hannibal replied, taking out some coins and preparing to give them to the man.

"No need for money, it's really no trouble. You can pay the doctor once he is done. He should be able to at least stabilize your brother, before he is taken to a more proper place."

"Thank you, I really appreciate it."

"Come on, it's just around the corner," the man said as he led the two men out of the alleyway and into the street.

"What about you though?" Zel turned and asked Hannibal.

"I'll be fine, I have more guards not too far away," Hannibal reassured him. "You just make sure Mago is safe and taken care of."

"You got it!"

"This was quite unexpected. Did you know who these ruffians were?" one of the men asked, as all the remaining people moved back out into the street.

"I have no idea. But clearly someone fears my election so much that they are willing to send assassins to kill me beforehand," Hannibal replied.

"Must be the work of the likes of Hyrum," another man pondered.

"Or Mago Arvad. One of these senatorial backed snakes who cannot play fair and are resorting to disgraceful methods," the merchant who had originally alerted the people added.

"The elites really are getting scared of our victory, and doing everything they can to prevent it," Aradus said. "But that will not deter you, good people, from making the right choice, will it?"

"Absolutely not! These sons of bitches must learn that the people still have the power in this city!" a man shouted.

"We will not let them intimidate us like this!" another added.

"Fuck the senate! For Hannibal!" yet another shouted, as more and more people gathered around the scene after hearing about the commotion.

"And for Aradus!" a merchant shouted back.

"Thank you! Thank you for your support, everyone!" Hannibal said. "People like you keep the city alive! But I believe I can't stay here for much longer, I must report this incident to the authorities."

"I'll come with you," Aradus joined him. "This might have been an attack on me just as much, so I should be there as well."

"I'll go see Mago then," Hasdrubal replied. "And later have him taken back home once he is well enough."

"Look after him," Hannibal said to his brother. "I'll try to figure out who sent these assassins after us in the meantime."

Later in the day, after Hannibal and Aradus had arrived at the office of the commander of the city guard and informed him of the situation, he sent out his men to collect the bodies of the killed combatants and search for the two surviving assassins. In a few hours, they were found, trying to escape the city through the harbor. They were intercepted before they could board any vessel and were shot and killed by archers after they refused to surrender. Their bodies were brought in alongside the others, and now Mago Arvad and Hyrum Baltsar were summoned to the office, after Hannibal had accused them of conspiring to kill him.

"What is the meaning of this? Why are we being called here at this hour?" Hyrum annoyedly inquired as he entered the commander's headquarters, where Hannibal and Aradus were already waiting.

"Oh, I'm pretty sure you know exactly why," Hannibal stepped in front of him. "You tried to get me killed, but, as you can see, your pathetic plan failed."

"What on Baal's green earth are you talking about? Kill you?" Hyrum replied in shock. "Politically, maybe, but I don't think you can accuse me of manslaughter just because of my speech in the marketplace today, about how your policies will raise the taxes for the common people."

"Seriously, what is going on?" Mago asked. "These are some very serious accusations, and I have no idea where they are coming from."

"They are indeed. But, as you may have heard, today Hannibal and his brother, along with Aradus here, were attacked by a group of masked assassins in an alleyway while they were talking to their voters in the inner city," Adherbal Hadash, the commander of the city guard, explained. "Luckily, with the help of his guards and the local men, their attack was foiled, and my soldiers picked up the remaining ones before they managed to escape the city. Do you happen to know any of these men?"

The commander showed the two suffetes outside, where six corpses had been laid on the ground, now with their masks removed. Two looked like Carthaginians, two were darker colored Numidians, one was a West African, and the final one appeared to be an Iberian.

"I have never seen them in my life," Hyrum defended himself.

"Me neither. I don't know any of them," Mago likewise added.

"Lies! You hired them to attack us!" Hannibal approached them again.

"Listen, I may not like you, but I would not resort to such measures. I still respect the democratic process, and I will make sure it goes through according to our law. I never had any intention of killing you."

"I can't believe it needs to be said, but I didn't hire them either, I swear on Melqart!" Hyrum said.

"My brother is now injured, and while he managed to recover – thank the gods – he could easily have died because of this attack. Your empty words mean nothing to me, I know how your kind operates!" Hannibal grew even more furious.

"Listen, Hannibal, while I absolutely understand your want for revenge, you have to understand… You have many enemies in the city, let alone the whole republic," Adherbal tried to calm him down. "It could have been any one of them. These assassins could have been hired by some Roman sympathizers for all we know."

"Oh, come on, as if the Romans would care about when our election is taking place or know where I would be campaigning in the city! The other candidates in the election are the prime suspects, that's a fact. You can't just ignore that!"

"I am not ignoring it. I will dedicate as many resources to this case as I can. But I cannot make any charges against either

Mago or Hyrum. They are just as innocent as anyone else at the moment. We searched the bodies of the assassins, and they do not have anything that could link them to the suffetes. I'm sorry, but we just do not have enough evidence to make any certain claim, and I will not wrongfully arrest these men just because you believe they were behind this terrible crime."

"So you will just let them go? And allow them to continue their campaigns unhindered?"

"I must. Rest assured, I will look into every avenue and follow every lead, but for now, there is no definite conclusion. There could be hundreds, maybe even thousands of potential suspects, and that's not even counting participants outside the country, since these assassins could easily have come from abroad. The elections will proceed as normal."

"Fine... I understand that, commander."

"You could try bringing the case in front of the high court, but I doubt they would come to any different conclusion."

"No, that won't be necessary. I would not be surprised if some of the judges were involved in the conspiracy against me as well."

"Well, whoever it was, it wasn't me, or Mago," Hyrum interjected. "I assume we're done here, then? You can question and investigate me and my servants all you want, you won't find anything."

"Maybe. But you can be sure of one thing – I will not hide, and I will continue my campaign just as before. And I will let everyone know what happened. Whether the voters actually believe your story is for them to decide, but I doubt you will find many supporters among them..." Hannibal snidely remarked as he left the commander's office.

Chapter VII

About a week after the assassination attempt on Hannibal and Aradus, the election finally commenced. Despite the elected officials being granted the authority to rule the entire country of now over four million inhabitants, only the capital city of Carthage could participate, with the other Carthaginian and Phoenician founded cities having their own elections for local suffetes on their own schedules. And further, of the nearly three hundred thousand inhabitants of the capital, only about a tenth had officially been granted voting rights, as women, males below the voting age, slaves, freedmen, foreigners, criminals, and some others could not participate in any elections, as was the case in most other republics in the Mediterranean. However, this still left tens of thousands of eligible voters, as well as some men who arrived from other cities – one did not have to continuously reside in Carthage to vote, the only requirement was to have official citizenship, which usually required one to be born into a citizen family. This was an important provision for Carthage, as it was a merchant republic after all, and so many people spent most of their time outside the capital, engaged in trade, naval exploration, colonization, and other matters. Thus, it was important for them to be able to return and vote for their leaders, though many did not make the trip, instead being content with voting only for their local suffetes in the city of their stay.

The others, however, were interested in deciding the fate of their country, and so, after disembarking from their ships, joined the thousands of others in one of the marketplaces to cast their vote. Initially, after voting was first established in Carthage, everyone voted in the Great Marketplace near the harbor, but since the city had grown so much since then, it was now divided into districts, each with its own designated voting zone and officials to oversee the process. The zones had been divided by the census commission according to the latest demographic data, and the overseers were chosen by the election commission, with the Court of 104 giving the final approval.

And as the day dawned, the voting process officially began. It went as such – first, a citizen made his way towards the voting area for his district, usually a local field, arena, marketplace, or any other relatively open area where many people could fit. The election overseers would check if the person was indeed a citizen and if he was in the right district – to prevent anyone from voting more than once by going to multiple districts. If someone was in the wrong place, they were directed towards where they should go, and if a non-citizen attempted to enter, he was asked to leave, with local guards being stationed in the area to make sure such orders were obeyed. But if everything was in order, the citizen was then asked to make his choice from the available candidates. He publicly stated the name of his chosen option, and the overseer marked it down on a tablet, along with other votes. The citizen then left to return to his business, while the next one in line stepped forward and the procedure was repeated again.

Later in the day, some voting districts began closing down, as all the expected citizens had voted, and the overseers brought their results to the central voting district, located in the Great Marketplace. It was the last one to close, as it had by far the most voters there – with all the foreign arrivals also voting in this location – but in the evening it was closed as well, and the final results were brought in to be counted. It took some more time for all the tablets to be sorted and all the tallied votes to be combined, with the election commission and some judges presiding over the process to make sure there was no fraud involved.

All the while, thousands of people, both citizens and non-citizens, continued anxiously awaiting the announcement of the results in the marketplace. All the candidates were present there as well, talking, eating, and drinking with their supporters and guessing what the outcome might be. Some were willing to put some money on their predictions and went to place a bet in a prominent local gambling den that did not miss an opportunity to make additional income on this day. There were many available options, from gambling on who would become a suffete, to who would place last, and to how many votes a particular candidate would approximately receive. So even those who did not care much for the political situation still were heavily invested in the outcome, as they hoped for a big life changing payout and feared a loss that would bankrupt their family.

Eventually, however, a few members of the election commission arrived and stepped onto the elevated platform in the center of the marketplace, holding the tablets with the final combined results. They were met by cheers and applause from the crowd, but it soon quieted down as everyone was eager to hear the results clearly.

"Glad to see so many of you here today!" the lead commissioner announced. "It is indeed an important day for our republic. A day when we partake in one of our most sacred traditions. One that should continue to be highly revered, as few people in the whole world ever get such an opportunity to choose their leaders. Fortunately, you seem to agree, since today we had a great turnout of over twenty-eight thousand citizens from the maximum of about thirty-two thousand. But it has been a long day, so I will not tire you further and will get right to the results. Starting with the sixth place…"

The crowd now stood almost completely silent, awaiting the name with bated breath.

"…And 782 votes," the commissioner continued, "we have Hanno Baalmun."

"What did I say, should have stayed with me, kid," Mago Arvad snidely remarked from his camp while sipping wine, with his supporters laughing at the losing candidate.

"In fifth place, with 1921 votes... We have Bomilcar Hadad."

"We did good, people, even if we came short of some votes," Bomilcar announced. "And we will do even better next year! Vote for Bomilcar Hadad in the next suffete election!"

"Now, before we proceed with the second to fourth places, I believe the candidate who placed first should be mentioned now, as it will probably come as a surprise to no one. The man who gained 10617 votes and will become a suffete is, of course... Hannibal Barca."

The crowd erupted in cheers and started swarming Hannibal to congratulate him on the victory.

"Thank you! Thank you, everyone, for putting your trust in me!" Hannibal said as he was shaking the hands of his voters. "Together we will fix Carthage!"

"And now let's return to the fourth place," the commissioner continued after the people calmed down somewhat. "4017 votes go to... Hyrum Baltsar."

"Oh, fuck this," Hyrum said as he chugged some more wine and then threw the glass onto the ground.

"You too should have stuck with me," Mago chuckled. "We had a good thing going and could have continued together, but you threw it away on a pathetic attempt like this... What a shame."

"Fuck off..."

"At last, we come to the third and second places," the commissioner began again. "These men received 5360 and 6043 votes, respectively. Quite close, but only one of them will become a suffete along with Hannibal, and the other one will not. Thus, the name of our second suffete for the upcoming year is... Aradus Reshgal."

The crowd erupted once again, even more than before, with some celebrating this victory and shouting victory slogans for Hannibal and Aradus, while the others cried out in despair or became enraged and shouted back at their opponents, claiming that the votes were counted wrong. The situation quickly started spiraling, and the guards moved in to separate the crowd and avoid any further hostilities between the two factions. At the same time, Hannibal and Aradus came up on the platform and, after being congratulated by the commissioners, addressed the crowd.

"Thank you for your amazing support! Today you showed that the people of Carthage want change, real change, something that will benefit the lives of the people and make the sacrifices of the war worth something," Aradus began. "And we intend to make these changes, whatever it takes! It will not be easy, and the obstacles are plentiful, but, by the will of the gods, we will persevere! I know many of you doubt us or our methods, and think that we will ruin the country, but trust me, our changes will improve the lives of everyone in Carthage!"

"Indeed! The will of the people has been expressed clearly today, and we intend to carry it out," Hannibal continued. "We defeated the senate backed candidates today, but our fight is just starting. Like my friend said, we will do whatever it takes, no matter how many more politicians we are up against. All for the good of our great republic. Thank you again for taking this step today, may Baal Hammon, Tanit, Eshmun, Melqart, and Astarte bless you all. And may they bless our magnificent Carthage!"

Chapter VIII

As the election season was coming to a close in Carthage, on the other side of the Mediterranean the Seleucid king Antiochus III was leading his troops into Parthia. He had previously reestablished control over the rebelling governors to the west, but in the eastern reaches of the vast empire the influence of the Seleucids was waning, and Antiochus set out to remedy that. He wanted to secure his eastern border and restore Seleucid control at least to what it had been when the dynasty was founded by Seleucus I, now about a century prior. The first target in this campaign was Parthia, ruled by a local Iranian chieftain Arsaces II.

Arsaces was the successor of his father of the same name, who had established this kingdom three decades ago. The first Arsaces had managed to unite the Parni tribes – which at that point had been living on the borders of the Seleucid realm and were part of the loosely organized Dahae tribal confederation – and become a renowned local warlord. He used the instability of the Seleucid realm to conquer the regions of Parthia and Hyrcania, which at that point had just been seized by the Greek governor Andragoras. Andragoras, however, failed to defend his newfound kingdom and was killed in battle with Arsaces, who then proceeded to secure the city of Hecatompylos, make it his capital, and proclaim himself the king of Parthia. He too had some trouble maintaining his throne, as he was soon engaged in a two-front war with both the neighboring Greco-Bactrian kingdom – another polity established by a rebelling Greek governor – and the Seleucids, who were seeking to restore control over Parthia. Still, Arsaces did manage to maintain his realm until his death, when the throne passed to his son – around the time when Hannibal was crossing into Italy.

Yet the second Arsaces proved to be a much less competent and feared warlord, and everyone around him could see that, especially Antiochus, who deemed it a perfect opportunity to retake the region. He raised an army of about seventy thousand men and, after meeting up with his trusted commanders in Ecbatana, marched east through the mountainous and desert ridden Media into Parthia.

The capital Hecatompylos, being right on the border, was naturally the first target, and Antiochus set his sights on it immediately. Arsaces then realized that he did not have enough time to assemble a proper army to counter Antiochus, and so sent some soldiers to disrupt the Seleucid supply lines and destroy the underground wells providing water in order to weaken and delay the advancing menace. This did not go to plan, as Antiochus sent his own forward force, a cavalry detachment led by the commander Nicomedes, which quickly overran the unprepared Parthians and sent them scattering north. Thus, the Greek march continued unimpeded, and the capital was soon within view. Seeing that there was no chance of victory at this time, Arsaces ordered a retreat from the capital, so that he could gather more troops and face Antiochus at a more opportune time and place.

Antiochus proceeded to enter Hecatompylos with no fighting, and established it as his temporary base of operations. Some locals welcomed him, treating him as a savior from barbarians, though others mourned the loss of their relative independence. The Seleucid king did not stay in the city for long though, as he wanted to catch the Parthians before they came back to full strength. He resupplied his army, and proceeded to march further northeast, into the coastal region of Hyrcania, which bordered the southern part of the Caspian Sea.

However, this required crossing some narrow mountain passes, which presented an opportunity for Arsaces. He hoped to nullify the Seleucid numerical superiority by trapping the large force inside the passes and destroying it over time by attacking it from all sides. The Parthians set up barricades, traps, and various ambushes, seeking to turn the heavy equipment and rigid structure of the Greek phalanx against itself, but this too did not go all according to plan. Antiochus had prepared for such a possibility by sending out a detachment of light infantry skirmishers under his commander Diogenes to seek out Parthian bands and clear the way for the main army.

Diogenes led his skirmishers up the mountains and killed the Parthians or forced then to retreat, catching them unprepared and ambushing them before they could commence their own ambush. All the while, Arsaces continued retreating with his core force, every day growing more worried as his already small force was diminishing without hindering the Seleucids in any meaningful way. Antiochus was not too far now, as his army was making swift progress and disposing of anyone who stood in its way. And now, a week after they had entered the pass, the Greeks were almost through and ready to descend on the plains north of the mountains. Arsaces realized that there was no way of avoiding a pitched battle now, and that if he faced Antiochus in the flatlands to the north, he would surely lose. Thus, he recalled all his remaining soldiers and prepared to meet his enemies while they were still in the mountain pass, where the Parthians had a relative combat advantage due to their lighter gear and experience of the local terrain.

"We are nearing the end, I believe," Nicolaus, one of the generals of Antiochus, said to the king as the army was marching. "If the gods do not throw any obstacles our way, we might be out by sunset."

Nicolaus was an Aetolian born general who had first served in the Ptolemaic army during the recent war between the Ptolemies and the Seleucids, but after the war defected to Antiochus, seeing more potential in serving him rather than Ptolemy.

"I hope so. I spent enough time in this miserable place for a lifetime. And there are other traitors that need dealing with, so I would rather not waste any more time on quelling these barbarians," Antiochus replied.

They continued through the pass, until shortly afterwards, they received a message from the front of the phalanx, which was led by Polyxenidas, a young but experienced Rhodian general who had been exiled from his home island and later joined Seleucid ranks. He was now leading the vanguard of the army, which also included mercenaries from Crete, and was the first of the Greek commanders to notice trouble ahead, of which he sent word to the king.

"The Parthians? They want to fight us here?" Antiochus asked, as the soldier who had delivered the news to him nodded. "I see. Well, there is no way out now, except forward. Through the Parthians. Send word to the general to close ranks and advance. We have the numbers, we have the weapons, we have the morale. We can push through."

The soldier acknowledged the order and rushed back to the front of the phalanx.

"So they finally stopped running, huh," Nicolaus said.

"That's good. It means they exhausted all their other options," Antiochus replied confidently. "If we are lucky, we will destroy their entire force here and crush this little rebellion completely."

"What are your orders?"

"Go back to the rear, make sure it is secure and that we are not attacked from both sides. Send Nicomedes to scout the surrounding passes and keep them clear. We need to have our exits guarded, as while I do not intend to lose today, I need to be prepared for all possibilities."

"Understood."

"And also tell him to find Diogenes. Don't care how, just get it done."

"May I ask why, exactly? I think we already have more than enough troops right here, and I don't believe more could fit anyway."

"On this side? No, of course not. But behind the Parthians? I bet there is plenty of room there. Diogenes is already way ahead of us, it should not be difficult for him to sneak behind the Parthians with his troops and help us surround them."

"That is a good strategy. I'll make sure it is done."

Nicolaus turned around and proceeded to head back to inform Nicomedes of these developments and the new orders, while Antiochus remained in the center, surrounded by his hoplites.

"Listen up, men!" Antiochus proclaimed to his troops. "We are approaching an army of Parthians. Get ready to fight them with all you have! This is not perfect terrain, but we are Greeks, and we've faced much worse odds before. We can fight and win anywhere! These Iranian bandits think they own the place, and they seem to have forgotten some important lessons from the prior century. Let's teach it to them again! Just like Alexander crushed the Persians before, we will crush the Parthians and return this land to us Greeks! Let's make Ares proud!"

Before long, the battle commenced. The Parthian soldiers smashed into the Greek lines, but they were unsuccessful in breaking through, as the phalanx line held without letting any Parthians through. However, the Greeks could not advance much further either, as their enemies were determined on holding the pass. Thus, both forces remained frozen in place for a while, with the killed or injured soldiers being replaced by new ones from behind them, but even as the casualties climbed into the thousands over the hours, there was little progress being made.

The Parthian force was weakening, if rather slowly, but so was the Greek one. In an attempt to disrupt the enemy lines, the general Polyxenidas pulled his soldiers back, hoping that the

Parthians would rush to secure new ground and so break their own lines, but this maneuver helped little, as the hoplites were unable to significantly capitalize on this and so the battle returned to the stalemate that it had settled on before.

More hours passed with more casualties being suffered, and Arsaces was starting to feel rather confident, believing that the Greeks might soon give up and abandon the pass, ceding it to the Parthian king and granting him the victory. However, such hopes were dashed once frantic reports about an additional Greek force arrived from the rear of his army. The Greek commander Diogenes had finally assembled all his skirmishers and went behind the Parthian lines without being noticed. And now he struck the completely unprepared and exhausted Parthian soldiers in the back, decimating their ranks.

Arsaces realized that he was surrounded, and began to panic. He sent some of the elite troops from the front to the rear of the army, and while that did temporarily stop the onslaught caused by Diogenes, this also weakened the front and gave an opening to Polyxenidas. The general finally broke through the line and his newly energized men overran the desperate Parthians, causing great havoc in their ranks. The Parthians were now unable to inflict any considerable damage on the enemy and soon could not even defend themselves, as attacks came from all sides.

Thousands more Parthians died in the slaughter, and Arsaces now knew that there was nothing he could do except flee if he wanted to survive, which he did. He escaped the battle by one of the narrow nearby passes, which could only allow a few men though at a time, along with some of his personal guards and local guides who knew the way. The rest of the army was left to fend for itself. Some managed to find similar passes and escape through them, but the majority died where they stood, with the Greek forces eventually reuniting and crushing what little resistance remained. Antiochus won the battle, but he did not want to stick around for much longer, and so quickly led his army through the remainder of the pass until the flatlands of Hyrcania were reached. The Greeks finally set up camp for the night, ready to rest after an exhausting day of fighting.

"Today Ares has granted us a great victory!" Antiochus proclaimed to his gathered officers later, as he raised a toast. "But it would not have been possible without the contributions of all of you and your men. And especially my good friends Polyxenidas, Nicomedes, Nicolaus, and, of course, Diogenes, who masterfully sneaked behind enemy lines and helped us crush the Parthians! We destroyed their army, and sent whoever remained scurrying away like scared rats! But the war is not yet over. Their king has managed to escape, and so we must find him and bring him to heel. And if we need to conquer the rest of his kingdom for that, so we will!"

The rest of the campaign proved to be little trouble to Antiochus. The rest of Hyrcania folded quickly, as there was no resistance left and the locals were not too fond of their current rulers, so they allowed the Greeks to continue onwards. Some fortresses stood in the way of the Seleucid army, but they were secured expediently as well. Before long, the Greeks arrived at the walled city of Sirynx near the Caspian Sea, which had become Arsaces' new capital after the fall of Hecatompylos, and where the Parthian king was currently staying with what remained of his supporters. Such men were few, as the nearby Dahae tribes refused the call to help Arsaces, having heard of his disastrous performance in the previous engagements, and now even some of his own soldiers and officers left him, fleeing to the relative safety in the north and hoping that the Seleucids would not pursue them into the desert.

Antiochus ordered a siege of Sirynx, and the city was soon surrounded and its supplies were cut off. Arsaces was now completely trapped, while the Greeks spread out around the area to clear any remaining threats. The siege lasted a couple months, over which time Antiochus received news of Hannibal's victory in the Carthaginian suffete election, and began planning his next moves.

Eventually, as the defenders of Sirynx grew exhausted and demoralized, the city walls were breached. The Greeks stormed the city and killed all who resisted, but left the civilians mostly alone, as Antiochus wanted reliable locals to be left in charge of the city, instead of having them despise him and possibly allow the Parthians back in. The king did not want it destroyed either, as there were few cities in the region, and so it needed to stay up to maintain consistent supply lines and hinder potential barbarian advances from the north. And so he left Sirynx intact, only removing any indication of it belonging to an independent kingdom instead of being just another town in the Seleucid empire.

The elite Greek soldiers finally made their way to the small palace, where they disposed of the remaining Parthian guards and forced their way into the central chamber, facing the terrified Arsaces, now left without any allies of his own.

"Please, let's not make any hasty decisions here," Arsaces pleaded in Greek, as he was backing away from the approaching soldiers, pointing their spears at him. "You have won, that is quite clear. And I probably should have realized this sooner, but I am willing to admit it now. There is no need for us to fight any longer."

"You are right on that point, there really is no point for anyone to continue fighting," Antiochus said as he entered the throne room. "In fact, there was no point for anyone to start fighting in this region in the first place. You people had plenty of space to yourselves to the north, yet you decided to invade my family's realm."

"Well, that was under my father. I just succeeded him – I never wished you any harm, really."

"The soldiers who died on their way here would beg to disagree. Sure, we killed many more of your troops, but I lost some good men as well, dying here in this harsh wasteland, far away from their homes."

"I understand how you feel, but... But I can still be useful to you!"

"How so?"

"I... I could... I could submit to you... And lead a tributary kingdom here, while recognizing your supremacy. I could send tribute, resources, soldiers... Provide safe passage for your troops. All while keeping your realm safe from barbarians!"

"Could you though? I don't think can I trust you to keep it safe, considering your rather unimpressive military record..."

"Please, I can-"

"And I don't think anyone places great trust in your skills either. Even your own people don't seem to be too fond of you, and I think if I left you here, they would quickly replace you with someone else, which would start all this trouble once again. And, by the Twelve Olympians, am I tired of putting down such insurrections in my empire. I think I will deal with this issue for good right now, and give a clear message to everyone about what happens to rebels and invaders."

"What was I supposed to do? I had to defend the realm that I inherited, is that worthy of death now?"

"We all pay for the mistakes of our fathers," Antiochus said as he drew his sword and approached. "A decade on the throne, and I am still picking up the pieces of the empire that my father failed to protect."

"You can't kill me! I have powerful allies and they will avenge me!"

"No, they won't. They did not even show up to protect you."

Antiochus took another step forward and plunged his sword into the chest of Arsaces. He pulled it out and let the Parthian king's body drop to the floor and bleed out.

"Any remaining relatives of his here?" Antiochus turned around and asked.

"It does not appear so," Diogenes replied. "At least not in this city. They might have fled even further north, possibly out of the kingdom, but we did not find any evidence of where they might be. Or if there even is anyone important left alive."

"That's right. Just a bunch of whores in his bedchamber, but nothing else of note," Nicomedes confirmed. "It appears the Arsacid line is truly finished."

"Not that it was ever anything more than an upstart barbarian tribe," Antiochus sat down on the makeshift throne.

"Indeed."

"What are your next moves? Parthia is secured, but I imagine the campaign is far from finished," Nicolaus asked. "Are we proceeding to Bactria?"

"Well, that's a good question. I first did indeed think of going to Bactria and putting those rebels to the sword in the same manner," Antiochus replied as he was cleaning the blood off his sword with a cloth. "But, as you may have heard, our good friend Hannibal has just won the elections in Carthage. And he has promised me help in my fight against the Ptolemies. Now, the Carthaginian rulers are not kings, they only rule for a year, so time is of the essence here. I decided that I want to make the most out of this opportunity, and so I will head west and prepare for war with Egypt, one which will hopefully commence before Hannibal is replaced."

"That does make sense. Egypt is a far greater price than anything that could be found here, short of maybe the Indus river valley itself," Polyxenidas agreed.

"Yes, but securing our eastern border is also important. That's why I killed Arsaces, instead of allowing him to become a puppet king. I couldn't trust him to keep the peace, and I wouldn't be here to watch over him. But Bactria still stands defiant. I cannot allow that to continue. I have decided that I will leave some of my forces here to crush the Bactrians, while taking the rest back to Antioch."

"I see. And who will be left in charge of the Bactrian campaign then?"

"Well, I need you to come with me. You are a Rhodian, you have the Cretans following you, and you have experience as an admiral as well. A war with the Ptolemies would surely be a naval war just as much as a land based one, so I will need your experience in this conflict. It would surely be more useful in the Mediterranean, rather than in this desert. But I need Nicolaus too, since he served under Ptolemy and so could be helpful in countering his tactics, maybe even getting some Greeks from Egypt to defect to my side. So that leaves you two," Antiochus looked at Diogenes and Nicomedes. "Diogenes, for your great contribution in this campaign against Parthia, I am promoting you to a general. You will lead the remaining men, about a half of the initial army, and bring Bactria back into the empire. And you, Nicomedes, will be the second in command. In case anything happens to Diogenes, you will replace him and continue the fight. Is everything clear?"

"Yes, my king," Diogenes bowed. "I am honored to receive such a duty. It will be carried out to the utmost of my ability."

"And mine too," Nicomedes also bowed. "We will take your rightful lands back, and there is nothing these pathetic rebels can do to stop us."

"Good, I trust that you will do your job here well," Antiochus got up from the throne. "But we should get some rest now. Some of us have a long trek back to the capital."

Chapter IX

In Egypt, the Ptolemaic royal family was sailing on the Nile on Ptolemy's newly built luxury yacht. This was the Tessarakonteres, a massive catamaran galley which the pharaoh had commissioned a few years ago in order to have the largest ship ever built. It was a drain on the treasury, but the pharaoh's will was not questioned by his subordinates, and so the vessel was constructed – mostly using slave labor in a drydock in Alexandria – and launched into the sea. It had two large hulls connected by an open central area, with each hull having two thousand rowers, a thousand for each side. This was further divided into fifty sections, each with twenty men. The sections were similar to those found in regular triremes, except requiring more men due to the immense size of the ship – the bottom file had five rowers per oar, the middle one had seven, and the uppermost one had eight. The catamaran also had an additional crew of about four hundred, including officers, deckhands, cooks, Ptolemy's personal slaves, and others. Finally, the vessel could also transport about three thousand marines, as well as catapults and other siege engines, though for this voyage there were only about a thousand marines present – mostly to oversee the rowers – and the central section was left to Ptolemy. He ordered it to be filled with large couches for himself and his companions, massive tables with lavish feasts, and statues of himself and his predecessors, so that they could be seen by the people as the ship was passing through their cities.

The Tessarakonteres was built under the pretense of it being a military vessel, but everyone quickly realized that it would be of no use in naval warfare. Ptolemy's advisors and admirals warned him that the ship would be too large and too slow and so would quickly be destroyed by ramming or fire in an event of a battle, but the pharaoh dismissed these criticisms and continued with the project, despite its huge cost. Ptolemy wanted his extravagant pleasure yacht, and nothing was going to stop him – certainly not budgetary concerns, even if such a price could otherwise have given the Ptolemies an additional sixty battle ready triremes.

Eventually the Tessarakonteres was finished and, after a short cruise on the Mediterranean coast, sailed into the Nile. Ptolemy wanted to have a tour of his realm and decided to show off his new luxury project to the people along the way. The pharaoh had received news of Hannibal's victory shortly before this trip, and while he blamed Sosibius for the failure to prevent this outcome, he quickly dropped the matter and returned to planning his tour, unconcerned with political matters. The ship had now passed Alexandria, Naucratis, another prominent city founded by the Greeks, Memphis, the old Egyptian capital during the reigns of various dynasties in the Bronze Age, Heracleopolis Magna, and Hermopolis, and was now well on its way to Thebes, the largest and most prominent city in Upper Egypt and another historical capital, where the Valley of the Kings – a royal necropolis used a millennium prior – was located.

Ptolemy was joined on this cruise by his concubine Agathoclea, as well as his wife Arsinoe, though the latter he only took on this journey out of obligation and so he could keep an eye on her. The young Ptolemy V was also here, looked after by the slaves and trusted servants of the pharaoh. Sosibius, meanwhile, was left back at the capital, charged with running the state while his superior was enjoying himself on his travels – as had often been the case in previous years.

"What a marvelous land this is," Ptolemy IV said as he was eating and drinking while overlooking the Nile and the fields around it. "I truly must be favored by the gods for being granted command over such a place."

"Of course, my love. Egypt is most prosperous indeed, and there really couldn't be anyone better suited to ruling it than you," Agathoclea, lying next to him on the couch, replied.

"Yes, you are right, as always. Only I can make sure this land remains as prosperous as it is and does not fall into chaos. Those brute bastards can have their decrepit mountainous holdouts for all they want, nothing that they have will ever compare to my possessions."

"Absolutely."

"I can't imagine living in a place like Macedon. What a shithole that place is. I imagine even the poorest Egyptian peasant is still better off than an average noble there."

"But what about Alexander?"

"What about him?"

"He came from Macedon."

"He did, but why do you think he left? Macedon was such a gods' forgotten corner of the world that he decided to try conquering the Persian Empire instead of spending any more time there!" Ptolemy laughed, gulped another glass of wine, then threw it overboard. "But now his body is here, in Egypt, joining the dozens of other great rulers of the land under my protection. I will make sure no barbarians desecrate these graves and tarnish them with their unholy and unclean bodies."

"But what if they invade our kingdom?"

"I will beat them back. I defeated Antiochus once already, after all. I have my loyal soldiers who would gladly die for this kingdom and their gods. Our gods, I mean, of course. Since Osiris and Horus and others have chosen me to carry out their will in the world of the living."

"But what about Hannibal? What if we get attacked from the west as well?"

"It doesn't matter. I will beat them back just the same. I trust in the gods to help me win. You don't need to worry about such trivial matters," Ptolemy took a handful of dates from a bowl and crunched them all at once.

"What should I worry about instead?"

"Well, what about whether you can handle me again today?" Ptolemy pushed Agathoclea down and crawled on top of her, pressing down with his overweight body.

"Right now? But we're right in the open! Everyone would see and hear us!"

"That wouldn't be too bad, would it? What can they do about it, except appreciate the gesture? Truly, maybe my loyal servants here do deserve to get a glimpse at their pharaoh's god like virility and his chosen maiden's beauty…"

"But-"

"Don't worry, I do not plan on having new successors just yet. I will finish in the Nile, as the good pharaohs of old would do. That's what a priest told me at least, I think. So I want to honor such traditions."

"But your wife is still here. Do you think she would approve of such a display?"

"It doesn't matter what she thinks, does it?"

"Well, no… But I would feel much more comfortable if she wasn't watching over us… And I would like to have you all to myself, instead of her taking you away from me…"

"Hmm… I agree. I wouldn't want her to see us either," Ptolemy got up and pondered for a moment. "She has been a nuisance to our relationship for a while now, hasn't she?"

"Yes, you are right. I wish you weren't married to her, so that I could become your wife, and we could enjoy our time together, undisturbed by anyone…"

"I know, I know… You should be the queen, instead of her. But I can't have two wives, the priests would now allow it, even for me! And divorce would turn her allies against me, despite everything that I have given them, those ungrateful leeches…"

"You can always take matters into your own hands… You are the pharaoh, after all. You are blessed by the gods and are here to carry out their will, are you not? No one can stop you, if you are determined in your decision."

"Indeed, indeed... I am blessed. I am one of the gods, truly. I shouldn't be worrying about such petty problems like a lowly nomarch. You are right. Like Horus, I should take matters into my own hands. I have waited long enough."

"What are you planning-"

"Just wait here, don't go anywhere. I will return in just a bit. I will go to my wife and make sure she does not bother us. Ever."

"Thank you, my love."

"Anything for you."

Ptolemy hastily made his way from the front of the ship to the back, where his wife Arsinoe was standing. She was guarded by a few soldiers from each side, though Ptolemy quickly waved them away after he reached her.

"Dismissed. Give us some privacy," Ptolemy said to the guards.

They moved further out, giving some space to the two siblings.

"Do you know what privacy means? Go back to your quarters!" Ptolemy shouted at them, and the soldiers quickly scurried away. "I will summon you when needed."

With the two now left alone, Ptolemy approached Arsinoe on the edge of the ship.

"Were you sleeping with that bitch again?" Arsinoe asked disappointedly.

"You will not call her that. And what does it matter who I sleep with? It is none of your business," Ptolemy retorted.

"It is, actually. I am your wife. And now that we have a son, you should be more careful. We do not want any other potential successors from different women to contest the throne from our child."

"I think I know how to manage my own family line."

"Oh, do you? Then you should know that we should be trying for more children, to increase the chances of our dynasty's survival."

"Maybe. But I'll be the judge of that. It's a problem for the future."

"You should take all this more seriously. What are you leaving for your son, really? You are making enemies all around you, you are wasting away the gold on such idiotic projects as this ship, and you do not care for your realm at all, except how much you can drink and eat and how many whores you can fuck!"

"And that is my Horus given right, damn it! I can do whatever the fuck I want here. I am the pharaoh, and I make the rules."

"If you continue to act this way, you will not be one for much longer. Even people in the kingdom do not respect you anymore. You need to stop acting like a child and become a responsible ruler, before you lose everything."

"So what do you want me to do, huh, sister? Want me to fuck you instead of Agathoclea, would that soothe your nerves?"

"It would be a nice change, instead of you sleeping with that bitch all the time."

"I told you not to call her that. But if you want me so much – turn around then."

"Wait, what-"

"You asked for it."

"What, here?"

"And why not? If you are so eager. I dismissed all the guards from here, so no one will see us anyways."

"You are ridiculous," Arsinoe said as she turned around and bent over.

"Look, there are some crocodiles swimming below us. Great omens from the gods. You like crocodiles, don't you?"

"I told you, I don't. I'm scared of them, they look like terrible beasts who could devour a person in a moment."

"What a coincidence! I just thought the same thing. Let's test this hypothesis, shall we?"

Ptolemy then suddenly pushed Arsinoe out of the ship, and his wife fell into the Nile. Before she could swim up or scream for help, the crocodiles lunged for and killed her, with the water turning red around them.

"Thank you, Sobek, for helping me out of this predicament," Ptolemy said calmly as he looked over the carnage and his wife's body that was being devoured by the crocodiles. "I shall build another temple to honor you for your service."

"So he just threw her overboard like that?" Sosibius said in disbelief.

The vizier of Ptolemy was now once again at dinner in Oenanthe's villa, joined by his usual companions Agathocles and Agathoclea, who had just returned from the Nile tour with the pharaoh.

"It seems that way," Agathoclea shrugged as she sipped her wine. "I did not see the action up close, but Arsinoe was not seen anywhere afterwards, and some rowers reported seeing crocodiles and blood in the water. Of course, they would not question the pharaoh, nor would anyone else."

"Devoured by crocodiles. What a way to go," Agathocles said.

"Indeed. He did not seem too bothered about it and just mentioned that Arsinoe would trouble us no longer. I did not press the issue further, since I did not want to end up with the same fate."

"Can't blame you for that, sis."

"While this is a rather unconventional method of getting rid of someone... This still serves our needs just as well," Oenanthe pondered. "With his wife out of the picture, we can make sure no one is closer to Ptolemy than us."

"Both Ptolemies, in fact," Sosibius added. "There is no one else left in the pharaoh's family to protect them. We can now take the kid and dispose of the older Ptolemy with little trouble. Now, not even Arsinoe's friends would come to his aid, considering how they rightfully suspect that she was killed by the pharaoh during his little Nile trip."

"But who would deal the final blow to Ptolemy?" Agathoclea asked. "I may have managed to convince him to kill his mother and then his sister-wife, but I doubt I could talk him into a suicide. He cares for himself most of all, so he would sadly not fall for my charms this time, I'm afraid."

"Well, it can't be me, because I'm busy gathering armed support," Agathocles replied. "I need to be near the generals and officers, make sure they hear everything directly from me before making any conclusions by themselves. Besides, I think Ptolemy is starting to be wary of me, so it might be for the better to avoid him."

"I could do it, but it would be very risky," Sosibius said. "It would be quite suspicious for the pharaoh and his second in command to meet, only for me to leave his body behind and then proclaim myself the new ruler of the country. Maybe the people hate him enough that they wouldn't care, but maybe that is not the case. It would still be better to give at least some credibility to the story that we are not responsible for his death."

"I could get my contacts to do the job for us."

"And do you trust any of them enough to execute the plan as instructed and not fuck it up? Or not betray us to Ptolemy in hopes of gaining a promotion or a big payout?"

"No, I suppose not."

"I will do it," Oenanthe said simply.

"I appreciate the confidence, but I'm not sure how-" Sosibius began, but was cut off.

"What, you don't think I could? I'm not just some old hag who comes to sit with you all at the table and listen to the gossip without contributing to anything. I can and will do my part to secure your future. I did my fair share of nobleman killing back in the day, so I can do it again just the same."

"Of course, I apologize. I did not mean to insult you. I was just... simply wondering how you would get an audience with him?"

"Oh, that's simple. Now that Ptolemy has no wife anymore, he is planning a wedding with my Agathoclea... Am I wrong?"

"No, that is correct. He wants a wedding to be held soon, maybe even in the next month or so," Agathoclea confirmed.

"As I am her only surviving parent, it only makes sense that I meet with the pharaoh to discuss the event in detail. Under the pretense of talking about the wedding financing, guests, venues, and so forth. I am sure he would not object. And after I'm done, you take over."

"Wouldn't it be wiser to wait for the wedding?" Agathocles asked. "Then Agathoclea would be his official consort and would have a better claim. Maybe even a child who could be placed on-"

"Absolutely not," Agathoclea responded furiously. "I am not putting the spawn of that demon inside me!"

"That, and also we do not have any time for such matters," Sosibius added. "It would take at least a year, and we can no longer afford to wait. Antiochus is moving to the Levant, Philip is also certainly planning something, and Hannibal is in the office only for a year, so he will try something before his term expires. We have months to prepare, and not that many of them. We need to move now, otherwise it might be too late. Having a wedding and then immediately killing Ptolemy would also look way too suspicious. I would argue for a different approach."

"Well, his son is the only one who would really matter in terms of legitimacy afterwards," Oenanthe said. "It is only important that we have him in our custody, everything else is just details."

"Precisely. No point in bothering with a wedding or a new successor. We will get one when we have control of the country anyways."

"I am glad to hear that," Agathoclea said with relief.

"It is set then. I will arrange for Ptolemy to leave our mortal realm, while you better make sure everything else is taken care of," Oenanthe said. "I have never been much of a public figure, and will not become one, so I doubt there would be much fallout to deal with for you afterwards. I will happily recede into the shadows once again, and only advise you from there, if needed. The rest will be up to you three."

"I will take the young Ptolemy and make sure he is in my care for the enthronement that is to come," Agathoclea added.

"And I will deal with the nobles and military commanders, make sure they remain calm and support the transition. I will also procure some mercenaries to secure the city so that no one disturbs our plan," Agathocles replied.

"And I... Well, I guess I will wait around the corner and do my best to act surprised when I see Ptolemy's corpse," Sosibius said. "And then I will announce his death, proclaim the new pharaoh, and introduce us as the regents. Let's hope the people will accept this."

"I think they will. Everyone is tired of Ptolemy's ruinous reign and is ready for someone more competent and less deranged to take over."

"To the end of Ptolemy's tyranny!" Oenanthe raised her wine glass and the others followed. "And to the start of a new era!"

Chapter X

As the year ended in Carthage and the two former suffetes left their posts, Hannibal and Aradus took their place and did not waste any time in getting to work. First, Hannibal reorganized the still recently conquered lands in Iberia and granted governorship over it to his brothers – southern Iberia to Mago Barca, who had now mostly recovered, though he had developed a limp due to the injuries, and northern and eastern Iberia to Hasdrubal Barca. Meanwhile Aradus assigned new governors to the reconquered islands of Sicily, Sardinia, and Corsica. Hannibal also oversaw the collection of the first round of tribute payments from Rome and established a new commission for Italian affairs, one responsible for maintaining relations with the newly established states in the peninsula – the Etruscan Federation and the Greco-Italian Confederation – as well as watching over the rump Roman state and making sure it did not become too powerful.

The two suffetes also worked to recover funds from inside the country, namely dealing with cases of embezzlement by the senators and judges of Carthage. In some cases, the persons being investigated cooperated and gave away what was deemed to have been stolen from the treasury, but some resisted and did not expect Hannibal to push the issue further. However, Hannibal proved to be quite dedicated to this task, and did not let the issue go. Already from his first weeks in office, he started publicly shaming various senators and judges who did not cooperate, turning the public's opinion against them. Many locals were angry at the accused and would sometimes even assault them or try to break into their homes to get back what was supposedly theirs. While Hannibal did not publicly endorse such actions, he did little to stop them or protect such targets of the mob, forcing many to resign or even go into exile. Hanno Baalmun, a candidate for the suffete post in the latest election, was one such target who fled to Egypt after a mob vandalized his house.

This all naturally turned the senate and the Court of 104 even more against Hannibal, but there was little they could do for the time being. They were still divided and could not agree on how to solve various issues or deal with the suffete overreach, and everyone was for the most part concerned with protecting their own assets rather than participating in some greater effort. Thus, Hannibal and Aradus were left with a lot of freedom, relative to prior suffetes. Carthaginian law did not help the senators much in this case either. While suffetes did have to get approval from the senate for many of their actions, if the senate refused and the suffetes were determined enough, they could then present their case to the popular assembly. This was an assembly made up of randomly selected eligible citizens, which was convened on request to provide final input on new laws or other cases of importance. While the previous suffetes did not often take this route, as they could not predict who would be selected for the assembly and how they would react, while also not wanting to drag the process any longer and tarnish their reputation among the upper classes, Hannibal and Aradus had no such qualms. They were already known as men of the people and disliked, if not hated, by the elites, and their policies were time and again received much more positively by the populace at large rather than the senate.

Still, the political battle had just begun, and the senatorial faction was not about to give up yet. While Hannibal was popular in the capital and Iberia, the rest of the republic did not view him as favorably. The inland Carthaginian territories – the largest breadbasket of the Mediterranean after Egypt – was controlled by the old wealthy families who supported the senate as much as they could, fearing the loss of their estates. Many coastal cities were also wary of the new suffetes, as they feared that this overreach might mean a reduction in their autonomy, and the senate used this to their advantage to gain new allies. Thus, the fight between the aristocracy backed senate and the populist suffetes continued, and would only intensify in the following months.

"Greetings, my good senators!" Hannibal announced cheerfully as he decisively strode into the senate hall on Byrsa hill, as he had done many times prior, with Aradus following behind him.

"Good morning, Hannibal, Aradus," Ahirom Gamon, a prominent older senator who had been selected as the speaker of the senate, greeted the two. "I assume you have a new proposal for us to consider, am I correct?"

"Certainly won't be a good morning for us if that is the case..." a senator murmured from behind.

"Why, you are indeed correct, honorable Ahirom," Hannibal confirmed as he took his spot in front of the senators.

"By all means then, go ahead," Ahirom sighed.

"Thank you. It's not a difficult concept to explain or understand, so I will be brief. The grain dole," the senators already began sighing and protesting upon hearing those words. "It's time we implemented it. Our people deserve it, and we do have the money for it."

"Money that you stole from us, you mean," one senator scoffed.

"I do not remember stealing anything. I do remember returning the stolen money to our treasury though, to be used for the collective good of our republic instead of your new country villa."

"Where it goes is none of your damn concern."

"Oh, but it is. Remind me, what was your name again? Maybe I should take a closer look at your assets as well, now that you mention it. I may find some interesting things there..."

"Gentlemen, please, let's not descend into mindless bickering again," Ahirom stopped them. "Hannibal, please get back to your proposal. What would this grain dole entail?"

"It is simple – we buy grain, a lot of it, and then distribute it to the people on a monthly basis," he began, as he and Aradus distributed some copies of the proposed law to the senators. "Those who could not afford it at market prices could buy it from us at reduced rates, while the absolute poorest could get it for free. Thus, we make sure no one starves in our great capital. And, if it works as intended, other cities later as well."

"It's an enormous expense," a senator argued.

"I know, but it is achievable. And it may not be as expensive as you may think."

"I don't think you quite realize how much the estates would be charging for so much grain," another senator retorted.

"I do, but we can negotiate the prices."

"Believe me, they will not lower them, especially not to you."

"Then they won't be able to sell the grain at all. Carthage controls all the ports through which it could be exported, after all. They will bend the knee soon enough, and in the meantime, we can use the Sicilian grain to support ourselves."

The chamber erupted in uproar after this suggestion.

"This is preposterous! You would drive our farmers destitute just to fulfill your twisted desires?" a senator shouted from the back.

"Please, the farmers will be fine," Hannibal replied. "But I assume the people you are actually worried about are your landholding cronies. Well, maybe now they will have to find legitimate ways of making money instead of just charging ridiculous amounts for the produce they sell."

"This is going to destroy our country!" another senator shouted.

"The gods will not forgive you for this!" one from the opposite side of the hall added.

"The gods would welcome it, actually," Hannibal replied calmly. "I don't know of a god who would prefer you hoard all this wealth instead of sharing some to feed our citizens."

"And what, pray tell, would be the benefits of such an action?" Hyrum Baltsar, now a senator, asked once the room had calmed down. "We already have plenty of vagrants living in the streets, scurrying around like rats and polluting our great capital with their filth. At least now they can die off pretty quickly if they continue to not contribute anything to our society. But with this grain dole, we would be tasked with ensuring free food supply to all these bottom feeders, certainly worsening this infestation."

"Hyrum, glad to see you made it to the hill today. Certainly an achievement, considering your busy schedule of whoring around and gambling away your sorrows. It is funny you throw such insults at the people while not contributing all that much to our city yourself. You should consider this proposal more seriously, it may save your life once you fall low enough and your debts catch up to you," Hannibal countered, eliciting some laughs from the senators.

"And do you have any actual answers, or is mocking me all you can do these days? I think you still haven't realized this is an actual sacred place, used only for discussing matters of importance, not your army camp where you drunkenly joke around with your officers in between bouts of local pillage and murder."

"Gentlemen, again, please," Ahirom pleaded. "You can fight and throw insults at each other all you want outside, but not here, not during these meetings! We have important topics to discuss... Hannibal, do you have a proper answer?"

"I do," Hannibal became serious again. "It is for the good of our society. We are a rich country, and there is no excuse for us to let our citizens starve. But I understand that you will not accept such an answer, so how about this – I think we can all agree that fed men are better workers, farmers, merchants, soldiers, and overall more productive members of society. Fed women give birth to healthier children, and fed children grow into healthier adults. Of course, these people seem useless to you now, but what else can they do if they spend their days just begging for food and trying to survive? If we gave them this bare minimum, they would be able to move on to tasks which could benefit more people."

"Right. Such noble goals," Hyrum said dryly. "And what about you Aradus? Are you, the ever-loyal hound at Hannibal's side, also in favor of this proposal?"

"Of course I am," Aradus replied. "We worked on it together, and I contributed my fair share to it. Like Hannibal said, it will be a huge benefit to our society in the years to come and will help grow a more productive population."

"Interesting, considering I clearly remember you campaigning on being totally different from Hannibal and curbing his excesses. Was that all just a lie to get more votes?"

"I am still committed to this idea. And you must be misremembering something, because I was always talking about Hannibal's military career and future plans related to it. Curbing excesses related to those matters. This is a purely civilian matter, and we are both in favor of it, so I have no idea where your accusations are coming from."

"Well, maybe you should consult with your electorate about it. Do you think all those merchants would be happy to know that their taxes are going to supporting all the local vagrants and petty thieves stealing their wares?"

"You know, maybe we should consult with them," Hannibal interjected. "The two of us agree on the proposal, but the senate does not seem to share our sentiment. That's fine, it just means we will have to take this question to the popular assembly. I am sure the people will be thrilled to hear that a plan to offer them cheaper or free grain has been rejected because of some senators who want to protect their landowning friends... The assembly would approve the plan on the first day, I know as much."

"You don't know that. You are overplaying your hand."

"Am I? Let's go test it out then. Sure, maybe the assembly will decide that they do not want free grain, and you win. Or maybe, and I think more likely, they will decide that it is a good idea, and will also remember the names of the senators who blocked this proposal, making sure to never support them in any campaign, at the very least. You can choose – do you want to settle this matter here, in a proper and civilized way, or shall we ask what the people think?"

"You have made your point, Hannibal," Ahirom said. "The senate shall now vote on your proposal. If you choose to contest the senate's decision, the proposal will go to the popular assembly."

"And just to make it clear, I will most definitely contest it if the vote fails."

"As will I," Aradus added. "And then the decision will be in the hands of the people."

"Let the voting begin then," Ahirom stated. "We have 279 members present, a quorum has indeed been reached. We now need to decide on the proposal presented by the suffetes, which will pass if it gets at least 140 votes here. Those of you in favor of it, please move to the right. Those opposed – to the left."

The senators began moving to their intended camps, until there was a clear divide in the middle between the two. Many who moved to the right did so with great reluctance or even shame, but they did not want to risk the proposal going to the public and even further tarnishing their reputation, and so they decided to agree to the grain dole.

"161 in favor, and 118 against," Ahirom confirmed after counting. "The vote has passed."

"Thank you, senators," Hannibal said, as he was leaving the hall. "I greatly appreciate your cooperation."

A while later, as Hannibal was in his office drafting proposals for new laws that he could present to the senate, he was informed by his servants that a guest wished to see him, one arriving from the Seleucid Empire. Upon hearing who it was, Hannibal promptly told the servants to allow the guest in before dismissing them.

"General Hannibal Barca, I am honored to finally meet a legend such as yourself in person. Allow me to express my congratulations to you once again, for your recent victories in both the military and political fields," Polyxenidas began in Greek as he entered the suffete's office.

"Thank you, but I am a general no longer. Just a suffete trying to help his country in peace, as I did in war," Hannibal replied. "Please, sit. I've heard a lot of good things about you as well, admiral Polyxenidas. Or is it general now?"

"I carry both titles and assist my king both on land and at sea, wherever there is an enemy to be found."

"Most impressive. Few men have such skills to command both domains competently. Would you care for some wine?"

"I would greatly appreciate it. And I hope I am not interrupting your work, as I have heard that you are quite busy."

"It is absolutely fine," Hannibal dismissed the concern and called his servants to bring some wine to the room. "While it is true that I have many matters to oversee, I would still much rather spend my time discussing them with an honorable and accomplished figure such as yourself, rather than the crooks sitting in the senate."

"I can imagine. They must be quite a burden to deal with."

"They are, but it is manageable."

"That is good to hear. And what about your second suffete? Is he causing any trouble?"

"No, absolutely not. He is a good ally of mine and helps my work proceed more smoothly. Would you like me to invite him as well, so that both of us could hear what you have to say?"

"That will not be necessary," Polyxenidas said as he took the glass of wine offered to him by a servant and sipped from it. "We prefer speaking directly to the man in charge, and no one else. And that would be you in this case."

"Well, both suffetes are equal, at least according to our law."

"Yes, but… Well, we all know who is really in charge of Carthage now, don't we? No need to mince words."

"You are not wrong."

"And you were the one who contacted Antiochus, so it only makes sense that I speak to you. Though I must admit, this system of government that you have is still very foreign to me and not as easily understood as the ones in the east."

"It's not as uncommon as you might think. Rome has two consuls, and Sparta has two kings. And you Greeks are the inventors of democracy, aren't you?"

"And yet, Rome is in ruins now. And Sparta is a mere shell of its former self. And while we were the first to embrace democracy, that is true, I don't believe it helped us all that much. We struggled against the Persian hegemon for centuries, unable to even resolve our inner petty conflicts, until Alexander united and brought glory to us. Now we control half the known world."

"If you can't beat your enemy, join them, right?" Hannibal laughed.

"You could say that. Great empires aren't built by the public consensus. They are built by great men, acting only on their own wisdom and the blessings granted by the gods."

"You sure do have plenty of such great men on your side of the Mediterranean."

"But only one true king. Only one true heir to Alexander. That's Antiochus, and he is ready to restore the empire to its prior greatness, and much more. It does require removing some pretenders though. Such as the inbred mongrel playing pharaoh in Egypt."

"So you are already planning on attacking it. Isn't Antiochus still on campaign in the east though?"

"He defeated the Parthians and left some capable commanders to deal with the Bactrian insurgents. It will be handled in no time. Meanwhile he returned west and is preparing to gather forces in Antioch for a march down the Levant, and eventually into Alexandria itself."

"I see. And who else will be joining you in this war?"

"Macedon, namely. Though we would rather they did not get involved too heavily, lest Philip starts believing that he is an equal to Antiochus and becomes too greedy with his claims…"

"That should be more than enough men to defeat the forces of Ptolemy on land. Yet he does possess a numerous fleet. One which could be countered only by one other country, by my estimations…"

"Yes – your republic. We need your help in this matter. The Carthaginian navy would be invaluable, and with it, we could crush the Ptolemies in no time."

"I can imagine. But there is little reason for Carthage to go to war with Egypt."

"You would get your fair share from the spoils of this campaign. And even some lands, if you wish, such as Cyrenaica."

"While I appreciate the suggestion, Carthage is already rich as it stands, and we do not need plunder to sustain ourselves. As for lands – our republic is already overstretched, and we need to consolidate our Mediterranean and Iberian possessions before we can even think about expanding further. Cyrenaica is full of Greeks, and would probably be more useful in the hands of a Greek king in any event…"

"Those are all valid claims. But what about honor and trust?"

"What about it?"

"You did promise Antiochus that you would fight beside him against the Ptolemies when the time came."

"I do not believe I have ever made such an explicit promise. I certainly wouldn't be fighting beside him, since I'm no longer in charge of any army."

"However you want to call it, Antiochus did fund your campaign with you joining him in the war as the goal in mind. Was he mistaken in the assumption that you would not renege on this?"

"Don't get me wrong, Antiochus is a great friend and ally of mine. And I am a man of my word. I do not intend to abandon him, but I just did not expect that he would begin his campaign so soon."

"You have already become a suffete though."

"I have, but I have barely begun my work."

"We do not have much time. The term is only one year, isn't it? Who knows who the suffetes will be next year? It's a much safer option to begin now, while you are in charge and can be relied upon."

"Well, I am pretty sure that next year I will still be the suffete."

"Are you running for reelection?"

"Why not? I have many plans in mind, and it will take far more than one year to execute. So you do not need to rush, as there will be plenty of opportunities."

"I would like to believe that, but time is of the essence to my king. He has many enemies all around him, and he cannot just wait for another year."

"Well, I am sorry, but he will have to. Carthage has just finished its war with Rome, and still needs to recover. We cannot charge into another conflict, one which might be just as, if not more, destructive than the last one."

"You use mercenaries for most of your roles anyways. You don't need to wait for your army to recover, you can just buy a new one! And besides, like I said, we won't even need your soldiers. Just your ships and their crews to defeat the Ptolemaic navy and secure sea access."

"Still, war is expensive. The treasury has just begun to be refilled, and I do not want to waste all our wealth just yet."

"Your senators and judges hoard plenty of wealth. Can't you take it from them? You are in charge, after all."

"I am in the process of doing just that. But it's not so simple. There are rules, laws in place. I have to adhere to them. And I can't just force the whole senate to bow to me, it would cause a civil war here!"

"Yet leaving the elites to fester would only cripple Carthage further. Few men could deal with such a growing problem, but you could."

"Those institutions are here for a reason. The senate, the Court of 104, the commissions, the two suffetes, and the others. It is what makes Carthage great, what makes it stable. What prevents tyrants from arising here. I do not intend to destroy these institutions, merely reform them to serve the needs of the people better."

"Those institutions seem to be only hindering your potential and stealing valuable resources at the moment. Don't you think the people would be better off without them entirely?"

"No. It is a flawed system, absolutely, but it's still far better than unchecked power granted to one man. I want my people to have a choice."

"But they did have it. They chose you. They knew exactly what electing you would mean."

"Listen, while I do appreciate your input, I would rather not discuss my political choices any longer. You want us to join you in the war, I understand that. And we will, eventually. But not yet. I need more time. I need to stabilize the budget, repair the fleets, get the senate in line. I need at least a year. I can get it done, but you have to trust me and wait."

"So I should tell Antiochus to wait for the next election and hope you will be chosen once again?"

"Yes. Is that too much to ask? If he trusted that I would win once, is it such a stretch to believe that I could do it again?"

"Well, that is for the king to decide. At least he won't need to get the approval of hundreds of senators to make his decision."

"Good for him."

"Maybe you should consider becoming one too…"

"What, a king?"

"A king, maybe even an emperor. You certainly have the skills, the wealth, and the lands needed for the title."

"It did not go well for the last monarch who tried to seize control of the state and reestablish absolute authority. It led to the end of his line and the abolition of the monarchy. And above all else, such an act would be high treason. I am many things, but I am no traitor."

"Just offering some ideas. You only have a year in the office guaranteed for now, who knows what will happen later. It would be wise to spend this time efficiently," Polyxenidas finished his wine and stood up to leave. "I apologize if I caused any offense to you, but I am just relaying what my king thinks. I will let him know your answer. Should you change your mind, be sure to contact us. And thank you for the wine, it was really good. But I'm afraid I will have to take my leave now, as I cannot afford to linger here for long. Preparations are underway, and I am needed to see them through."

"Of course. Give Antiochus my regards, and please just ask him to postpone the war. There is no need to blindly rush to it right now."

Chapter XI

In Macedon, king Philip had now officially married Polycratia, who had previously only been his concubine, though most already knew that they were much closer than that. Few opposed this decision, and so the ceremony went ahead and took place in Pella, with a lavish feast for hundreds of guests to accompany it. The Achaeans were the ones most displeased with this action, as some of them rightfully suspected Philip of secretly eliminating their ruling family and taking Polycratia for himself. Yet they could do little about it for the time being, since the league was already fragile and each city had its own goals, with many refusing to condemn Philip and treating it as an internal family matter in which the Achaean League should not be involved in any official capacity.

Still, tensions were brewing in the European part of the Greek world. While Philip had styled himself as the defender of the Hellenistic world against Roman expansion, Rome had now been dealt with, and no other unifying threat had emerged which could help the Macedonian king keep the cohesion across his domain and those adjacent to it. Some Greek cities were now once again clamoring for independence or at least autonomy, and Philip's popularity was declining, with him being called a tyrant more and more often. This was especially notable in the Peloponnese and Crete, which were difficult to oversee due to their distance from the capital and the relatively small Macedonian fleet being overstretched. Philip knew that to maintain or even expand his realm and secure a future for his dynasty, he needed to do something special that would earn him the approval of the people once more. Fortunately for the king, such an opportunity soon appeared.

It was a busy morning in Delphi, as the locals had gathered in its central marketplace, near the Temple of Apollo, to witness what was about to happen. The arrival of the Macedonian king was announced, and surely enough, Philip confidently rode right into the marketplace on his horse, followed by a few of his commanders, elite guards, and a small detachment of regular infantrymen trying to keep up on foot. To some locals it was an exciting sight, witnessing their king in person, but to others it inspired only fear or anger. Delphi had spent the better part of the century as part of the Aetolian League and its destruction and annexation to Macedon was dire news for some natives of the city, but Delphi remained untouched despite having been an enemy combatant. The city was still considered a most sacred place to Greeks, and so Philip did not exact any retribution, allowing the citizens to continue living as they had, only now paying taxes to Macedon instead of Aetolia.

And Philip was not visiting the city to punish it any further, instead, he came there to deal with a very specific local issue. A few weeks ago, a certain Echecrates arrived in Delphi, seeking guidance from the oracle – the high priestess of the Temple of Apollo, also known as Pythia. He was originally from Thesally, just north of Aetolia, and so had some connection to the area, which allowed him easier access to the oracle, skipping past hundreds of others from all over the Mediterranean waiting for their turn. However, he was also a general of Ptolemy, serving under him for over a decade. He fought in the war against the Seleucids, and now that it was peace time, he departed on a more spiritual journey in an effort to ask the gods what his next steps should be.

All went well, until Echecrates entered the room with the oracle in it. The general's priorities quickly shifted once he saw the young woman who was supposed to speak the prophecies, and instead of proceeding as was expected in this ritual, he grabbed the woman, dragged her out of the temple, and raped her. The locals soon heard of this and while some wanted to punish the general for his crimes, the others feared that the city would face serious retribution, as Echecrates was still a prominent general of Ptolemy and would likely be avenged. Thus, he was begrudgingly let go, and allowed to continue on his way as if nothing had happened. Philip, however, had different ideas. As soon as he received news about this event, he immediately signaled for the general's detainment, and dispatched messengers to carry out the decision to other cities.

Echecrates was not a difficult man to find, as he did not take any safety precautions, and continued through Greece unbothered and not even realizing that he was a wanted man. The general and his accompanying soldiers ventured through many towns on their way to Athens, which he also wanted to visit, drinking until they passed out in many taverns and sleeping with many women, both with those willing and not. Yet his luck soon ran out, as he awoke one morning only to see a dozen men surrounding him and pointing their swords at his throat. The general and his companions were arrested and brought back to Delphi for judgement. Naturally the man protested this action and tried to scare his captors with threats of Ptolemaic fury, but this did not work in his favor. Eventually the party reached Delphi, and the Ptolemaic party was thrown in a dark underground cell, where they were to be kept until Philip's arrival.

"Welcome to Delphi, your highness," Antidoros, the leader of the city, greeted the king and bowed before him.

"I assume you know why I am here?" Philip asked as he dismounted his horse.

"Oh, yes. What a terrible tragedy…"

"Indeed. And while I unfortunately can do little to ease the pain of your oracle, I can at least bring to justice the man who has committed such a heinous crime."

"Shall we bring him to you? He is currently kept locked with the other prisoners."

"Yes, bring him right here."

Antidoros acknowledged the command and sent his men to retrieve the captive. A few moments later, they returned, dragging the grimy and exhausted looking Ptolemaic general towards the Macedonian king. The people now got to see the perpetrator up close, and began shouting slurs at him and pelting him with rocks that they could find. The soldiers did not interfere, and just dropped the disgraced man on his knees, in front of Philip towering over him.

"This is the man who committed the crime? General Echecrates of Thessaly, now serving the Ptolemies?" Philip asked.

"That is correct, your highness," Antidoros confirmed.

"So, general Echecrates, do you have anything to say for yourself?"

"You have no right to treat me like this! Like some common criminal! I am a distinguished general of Ptolemy, and he would have your head if he heard of what you did to me!" Echecrates growled.

"Do you mean to say that you did not commit the crime of which you are accused? That you did not rape this most honored priestess? Are you willing to state that right in front of the gods, not to mention all the witnesses gathered here who saw you do it?"

"No, I admit I did it... And I would do it again! That whore was just asking for it, the way she looked and how she was dressed... I did what I had to do, and I do not regret it!"

The people in the crowd gasped and started shouting at the general even more furiously, until Philip stopped them.

"You admit it," Philip continued. "You are guilty of everything that you are accused of, and you have nothing to defend yourself with, except the fact that you are a filthy disgusting animal who cannot control his primal emotions. Pathetic. The

Ptolemies really must be scraping the bottom of the barrel if the likes of you are in charge of their armies."

"And you can't do anything about it, can you?" Echecrates laughed. "Mock me all you want, but I will go back to Egypt and continue to live as I have, and do whatever the fuck I want."

"That would be true, if this land was ruled by a weak-willed king. But this is not Aetolia any longer. This is Macedonian land. Under my protection. And I will protect my land and all the people here from whoever attempts to do harm, including degenerates like you."

"You can't be serious! You can't kill me! Ptolemy would not ignore such a transgression! It would cause a war, one that you would certainly lose!" Echecrates now panicked, as a couple guards restrained him and put his head on a stone slab.

"We shall see about that. But I would rather die fighting, than live out the rest of my days as a coward," Philip unsheathed his sword and held it over the captive's head.

With one swift motion, the king landed the blade on the general's neck and decapitated him, with the head falling down on the ground, followed by the rest of the body.

"This is how we deal with criminals in Macedon!" Philip held up his sword and proclaimed to the gathered people, who cheered him on for his decision. "The time spent in the Aetolian League has not served your city well, considering all the lawlessness it brought here. But under Macedon, Delphi will rise to its former glory once more, I can guarantee that. I will make sure it is never desecrated again and remains a safe and holy place for all Greeks. Though maybe you should take a closer look at your local leaders and reassess their capabilities, considering they allowed this to happen..." Philip looked at Antidoros. "They had almost allowed the rapist to escape with no consequences, while also pinning the blame on Pythia herself at first. Are these the people you want in charge of this sacred precinct? Well, I will let you decide... Just know that you can always count on Macedon to protect you, as from now on my soldiers will be stationed here at all times to make sure no such heinous crimes are committed ever again."

The public continued cheering on Philip, but also now turned to Antidoros and began expressing their disapproval of him.

"Well, it was not that simple... at first... He was a general, after all, so we could not... do much to... stop him," Antidoros began sweating as he felt the whole city now turning against him.

"Be that as it may," Philip said. "What about the other captives? Were they involved in the act as well?"

"The soldiers? No, they were not here. They were only escorting their general to and from the city. What shall be done with them?"

"Release them, and send them back to Egypt. Together with the remains of their general. Ptolemy will be wondering what happened to Echecrates, so I will let him know in these rather simple terms. Maybe that will get the message across and make him reconsider disrespecting my realm like this."

"It will be done, your highness."

"Good. Then, I suppose my business here is done."

"But before you go... Allow us to offer you a gift in gratitude for your help in this matter. Would you like to meet the oracle and hear her prophecies for you? Usually, it takes months to see her, but you have done more than enough to be the first in line right now. And, from what I have heard, she does indeed have something to relay to you from the gods..."

"Huh, that is interesting. I have never been to the temple, so I suppose now is as good a time to visit as any. Yes, I will see her, and hear what she has to say."

"Wonderful. My servants will show you to your accommodations nearby and I will inform you as soon as she is ready to receive you."

The oracle preparation ritual soon began. It included purification – Pythia bathing in the sacred spring nearby and drinking from the waters flowing into the temple – and a sacrifice. For this purpose, the servants brought a goat in the temple courtyard and killed it, before checking its organs. The omens were deemed favorable, and so Pythia descended into the adyton, a closed area at the back of the temple where she would give her prophecies, and sat down on a tall seat. She was, however, a different woman from the one assaulted by the now executed general, as the oracle was supposed to be a virgin, and so the previous one was let go from her position and compensated from the city's treasury. Yet it did not take long to find a new one, as there were hundreds of candidates in the region, with many young women hoping to be selected as the high priestess. Thus, by the time Philip arrived at the city, the new Pythia was already in place.

Philip was then informed that the oracle was ready for him, and that he could now go to the temple to receive guidance from the high priestess. He left his temporary suite and proceeded to the Temple of Apollo, led by a few local priests. They explained the process to the king, including how he should act in front of the oracle, and vetted his questions, to make sure they were appropriate. Upon entering the temple, the king made a generous gold donation to it, as was customary, and proceeded further. Upon reaching the adyton, the priests left him, and the king ventured into the room alone.

He saw the oracle in front of him, a young woman sitting on a golden tripod and wearing a white dress. The room was filled with vapors and fumes coming from an opening in the ground – the spirit of Apollo according to the priests. It took a few moments for Philip to acquaint himself with the unfamiliar atmosphere, and he felt somewhat dizzy at first, but soon found his footing and approached the high priestess closer, preparing to ask his questions.

"Speak, Philip of Macedon, son of Antigonus. What answers do you seek from Apollo?" Pythia asked slowly.

"Thank you, high priestess. I am honored by this opportunity to speak with Apollo himself," Philip replied. "I want to ask him this – what is the biggest threat to my kingdom right now?"

The oracle began swaying in her seat and uttering unintelligible sounds, which made the king quite uncomfortable, but he continued to stand there and await his answer.

"The threats are many, but one stands above the rest, one which could quickly cause great ruin on your realm, if you are not prepared," Pythia now once again spoke normally. "An ancient state that has been defeated, but continues to exist. One that will one day rise again and cause great havoc in the world, if it is not stopped…"

"I see… Yes, thank you," Philip replied, not quite sure what to make of it, but did not press the question further.

"What other answers do you seek from Apollo?"

"I wish… I wish to know how I can prepare myself and my kingdom for these challenges?"

The oracle once again began her ritual of communing with Apollo, before turning back to the king.

"There are those who conspire against you," Pythia began. "Those who wish to see your downfall. They are closer to you than you can imagine. They cannot be trusted as they will only bring troubles to you. If your realm is to survive, you need to remove such evildoers. And you, Philip, need to strengthen and unite your home to prepare it for facing all its adversaries…"

"I understand. Yes, this makes sense. Thank you," Philip nodded.

"What other answers do you seek from Apollo?"

"Well, since I have so many enemies around me… Who can I truly trust?"

"There are many, but few who have the knowledge and experience you seek," the oracle replied after her communing ritual. "In the end, you can only trust yourself, the wise philosophers of old, and the gods. All others may wish you harm for their own gain..."

"Thank you. I will be sure to heed this advice."

"What other answers do you seek from Apollo?"

"How long will my dynasty survive and rule this land?"

"Countless generations, if you act as a wise ruler and guide it to prosperity," Pythia responded after the ritual. "But if you act recklessly, you will be its last ruler, and your realm will be buried in the ashes of thousands..."

"Yes... I understand... Thank you for this."

"What other answers do you seek from Apollo?"

"Only one more thing. Can I ever reach the same greatness that Alexander the Third had achieved?"

The oracle now began shaking and uttering unintelligible sounds very quickly and violently, shocking Philip who decided to take a few steps back. The high priestess now began screaming and a few priests rushed in to check on her. They saw that it was only part of the ritual and that no physical harm had come to her, and so left her with Philip once more. The king continued witnessing the hysterical reaction of the oracle, but could not do much, and so just hoped that she would stop soon. Some moments later, she did, and turned back to Philip.

"Apollo does not wish to answer this question, Philip," Pythia said once she had calmed down.

"But-" Philip protested, but was immediately cut off.

"Or any more questions. He is tired now, and does not wish to be disturbed."

"I... I understand, and respect his decision. I apologize if I offended Apollo in any way, that was not my intention. I suppose I shall take my leave in that case," Philip said as he headed out of the room. "But thank you again for the answers you have given me, I will think about them carefully and make sure to act in a way that would please the gods."

Chapter XII

"Sosibius! Get over here right now!" Ptolemy shouted from one of the balconies in his palace in Alexandria.

"How may I be of service, my pharaoh?" Sosibius asked tiredly as he quickly made his way to Ptolemy.

"Have you seen this?" the pharaoh threw a papyrus scroll at the official.

"I believe I have, my pharaoh," Sosibius replied as he picked it up from the ground and unrolled it to read the contents.

"You have? Then why have I not been informed before? And, more importantly, why has nothing been done about it yet?"

"I believed we had other, more pressing matters to deal with first-"

"More pressing matters? What could that be? What could be more important at this time than my general being killed in a foreign country? Echecrates was one of my best commanders, and now his rotting corpse and cut off head showed up at my palace with this note from that shithole Macedon!"

"Well, it does say that he had assaulted and raped the high priestess of Delphi. That's a serious accusation…"

"I don't care what he did there! Those brutes had no right to kill him, he's an honored general! He could have raped all the women in Greece for all I care."

"He was in a foreign country, and on a personal visit at that, not an official one. He should have followed the laws. I don't think we can do anything about this situation now."

"What do you mean we can't?!" Ptolemy got up and roared. "I will have Philip's head for this! We need to prepare for war!"

"War? With Macedon?"

"Yes, we have to teach them that the Ptolemies do not take such insults lightly."

"My pharaoh, with all due respect, I don't think that would be wise. We are already preparing for a potential invasion from the Seleucids, as well as one from Carthage. We cannot afford to enter into yet another conflict right now. Especially one with such a powerful kingdom as Macedon."

"We must! My honor, my family's legacy, my empire depends on it! Do you think Ptolemy the First would have allowed such an insult to go unpunished?"

"I think he would not have blindly rushed into action and would have considered all the options…"

"I considered the options. And the only option is war! That's the only language those Macedonian scum understand."

"Surely you must-"

"I've made up my mind. We must strike now, while that fool Philip does not expect anything. We will sack Pella, and I will parade their beaten king through the streets of Alexandria, before feeding him to the crocodiles. And Delphi will be sacked too, that city has long outlived its use, as the gods now reside here in Egypt."

"It will be done," Sosibius sighed, having given up on the discussion.

"You better make sure it is! You have already failed me by not killing Hannibal and now allowing this travesty to unfold, but I am giving you one more chance to redeem yourself."

"I understand."

"Good, then go! Get out of my sight and get to work! My wedding is coming up, and I do not wish for you to disturb me any longer with your foul presence. But you better make sure that as soon as the ceremony is finished, you have the fleet ready to sail out and transport our soldiers to Macedon. Otherwise, Philip will be the least of your concerns…"

"Of course, my pharaoh. I will make sure our army and navy is prepared for… whatever awaits them," Sosibius said as he bowed and left the balcony.

Shortly after Sosibius left, Ptolemy received another guest. This time it was Oenanthe, the mother of Agathoclea, who the pharaoh intended to marry very soon.

"Oenanthe! Thank you for coming here. We have not met in a long time, I believe," Ptolemy greeted her, sitting in the same spot in the balcony as before.

"I am honored to have an opportunity to meet you and discuss such matters directly, your highness," Oenanthe said as she sat down next to the pharaoh.

"Please, you are always welcome here. I would always prefer speaking to someone like you instead of the myriad of court clowns that I have to deal with everyday…"

"I can see that. It must be very difficult being responsible for this entire kingdom."

"It is. Luckily, Horus and Osiris have granted me infinite wisdom and strength to cope with such a task."

"Well, I can't imagine a person who is more worthy of such gifts from the gods."

"Indeed. Us Ptolemies are meant for ruling this realm. But there will need to be more Ptolemies after me. There is one already, but it would be most beneficial to have more, in case something happens. And now that my previous wife is dead, the sweet Agathoclea seems to be the best lady to take up this role."

"Of course. And I am very sorry for your loss, I am sure losing your wife and sister must have been difficult."

"Not at all. She was an annoying wench. I am glad she has left this realm. Now I can spend more time with your Agathoclea and make her my royal wife officially."

"I am glad to hear that. I suppose we should start discussing the wedding arrangements then?"

"Yes. But before we begin, would you like some wine?"

"I was actually about to ask you the same question. I have brought you wine from one of my estates as a gift. Would you like to try it?"

"Oh, absolutely. I am getting rather tired of the same old palace wine, so I will gladly see how yours tastes."

"Wonderful. My servant here has a sample, and will bring more if you enjoy it," Oenanthe summoned her servant, who promptly showed up with an intricate wine jug, decorated with Egyptian and Greek symbols.

"Interesting. Let's see how it tastes," Ptolemy said as the servant filled his and Oenanthe's glasses with the wine from the jug and then placed it on the table before leaving.

"Shall we?" Oenanthe sipped from her glass.

"Oh, it's... it's very strong," Ptolemy said as he gulped down the wine. "Got this rich flavor and nice texture and... Yes, it is good. Why can't my servants bring me such good wine," he chuckled as he finished his glass. "I'd definitely take more."

"Please, allow me," Oenanthe picked up the jug and refilled the pharaoh's glass.

"Oh, this is good. This is what being a god feels like," Ptolemy leaned back in his chair and continued drinking. "But we should get back to the wedding. It is starting soon, and we need to organize it quickly."

"Of course, you are right. Do you have any ideas already?"

"I have plenty. I think it should last at least five days, maybe more. Let the people know that this is real and important. It could take place in the palace, but we should also make our way to the Temple of Serapis, to get blessings from the priests. And maybe some other temples too, can never have too many blessings. And then a massive feast! No celebration can be held without an extraordinary feast. I will invite our realm's most prominent members to attend it, Greeks mostly, but maybe some local Egyptians too, so that they could witness this monumental occasion as well. And I should use my Tessarakonteres somewhere, the wedding would be a great occasion to bring it out of the harbor again…"

"Very ambitious plans. Though I imagine quite costly too…"

"Yes, but it's just gold from the treasury, so what does it matter really?" Ptolemy chuckled as he was finishing the second glass now. "We can always get more. Just raid the Blemmyes and take over their gold mines. Surely even my incompetent Sosibius would be capable of performing such a task…"

"I see. Well, we should probably start inviting our guests already, considering how soon the wedding will take place, so that they could arrive in time and properly prepare."

"You are right, they should be informed as quickly as possible. Would be a shame for them to miss out on such an important event."

"And what about the entertainment? Surely we should hire some talented musicians, dancers, and other performers for the event."

"Absolutely. I will spare no expense in this regard either. Especially the…" Ptolemy tried putting his empty glass on the table, but dropped it on the ground and shattered it. "The… uh… Oh, this wine really is strong… I would not mind some more, but… Oh, gods, what is happening? Have you come to take me already?" Ptolemy started convulsing in his chair, while Oenanthe remained unmoved opposite him.

"What was that? I am sorry, I am getting quite old and can't hear as well as before," Oenanthe calmly continued sipping her wine. "Did you say you want more wine? Why, of course, I will help you with that. Anything for my pharaoh."

She stood up and poured the wine from the jug directly into his mouth, with the pharaoh now barely able to move or properly speak.

"Horus… help… me…" Ptolemy slurred his last words, before fully collapsing in his chair.

"Could you summon Sosibius for me?" Oenanthe called her servant, who had been outside the balcony. "It appears the pharaoh had a bit too much to drink and needs someone to help him up."

"It appears he is, in fact, dead," Sosibius confirmed after examining the body.

The vizier, along with Agathocles and Agathoclea, had been secretly waiting just outside for the signal from Oenanthe, and as soon as they received it from her servant, they made their way to her. Sosibius and Agathocles dragged the deceased pharaoh's back inside and placed it on his bed, so it would look like a more natural death, while Agathoclea cleaned up the scene on the balcony to not leave any evidence behind.

"Good fucking riddance," Agathoclea said as she joined the group inside.

"How did you do it, by the way?" Sosibius asked Oenanthe. "Looks pretty clean, I'm impressed."

"Oh, please, this was child's play," Oenanthe replied. "I just gave him some poisoned wine, that's all."

"But you drank it as well, right? Did you have an antidote?"

"There was no need for that. I simply brought my assassin's jug that I acquired from an eastern merchant once. A part of it is filled with regular wine, and another with poisoned wine, which you can pour by holding it in a certain position. I just poured him the poisonous version and myself the clean one, and he did not suspect a thing until it was too late."

"Marvelous."

"Indeed. But I believe my part is now done, so I will leave this to sort out amongst yourselves. I will retire to my villa and watch how this unfolds."

"Very well. If anyone asks, just tell them that the pharaoh is sleeping now and does not wish to be disturbed. And thank you, your help has been invaluable."

"Anything for my children," Oenanthe said as she left the room.

"It's up to us three now. Agathoclea, you make sure the young Ptolemy is secured. He is a greatly valuable asset, and we cannot afford to lose him to anyone else. He might also become a necessary bargaining chip if our plans go south."

"I can take him. Last I checked he only had the palace servants looking after him, and they trust me enough by now, so it should not be a problem," Agathoclea replied.

"Good, we will need him in the ceremony. And you, Agathocles, inform your friends so they would secure the city for us. Meanwhile I will begin the necessary preparations here and make sure everything is under control."

"That's the plan," Agathocles replied. "I don't believe there is anyone who could significantly interfere with it anymore."

"Yes, that's what I'm hoping too. So let's reconvene in, what, four hours, maybe? And then make the announcement before it gets dark. Time is of the essence."

"But do we really have to rush so much? Can't we wait a little longer before the public hears of this?"

"And why would we do that? The more time passes, the higher the chances of someone finding out about our plan."

"I don't think we need to worry about that, we control all the information flows after all. And I believe if we announced it too early, there might be some serious suspicion."

"How so?"

"Well, look – Ptolemy had a meeting with you, got angry, sent you away, then you return, and just a few hours later proclaim to the world that the pharaoh is dead. Don't you see how some could have doubts about your story?"

"Fuck, you may be right. I did not expect to be summoned by him just before he met your mother, so this does indeed complicate things. But what other choice do we have now?"

"We could just wait. Say, maybe a week," Agathoclea suggested. "Let everyone believe he is still alive, and by the time we announce that he is dead, everyone will have forgotten who he had met with before and what he had discussed."

"Yes, that's what I was thinking as well," Agathocles added. "Just leave him here, tell the guards and servants that he does not wish to receive anyone else in his chambers until stated otherwise, and let him rot. A few days later we send a servant to check in on him, because we are now supposedly very concerned for his wellbeing, and the unlucky servant discovers, well, this…" Agathocles pointed at the corpse. "We are the first to get the news, act shocked, and proceed as planned."

"I can see a whole lot that can go wrong with this approach… There are many people in the palace, and we can't account for all of them to not accidentally sabotage our efforts…" Sosibius replied.

"Well, do you have a better plan?"

"Wait… What about the priests?"

"Which priests?"

"Your priests. The ones serving the cult of Alexander. And since you are the chief priest of the cult, they must be loyal to you above anyone, save for the spirit of the conqueror himself. Am I wrong?"

"I suppose not. Though I have never asked them to do anything of importance before…"

"A good time to change that and put them to work. You could bring them in, so that the priests would immediately proceed with the mummification and then quietly transport the body from the palace to their temple. All the while, they would make sure no one else enters the room or hears of this, except you."

"And prevent any doctor from determining the actual cause of death," Agathoclea added.

"Indeed. So what do you think, Agathocles?"

"It is a solid plan. The priests have no allegiance to anyone, and they couldn't be bribed, so all they can do is listen to me and do what I think benefits our cult the most, with total devotion to the task. Otherwise, they would never meet Alexander after they enter the underworld," Agathocles chuckled.

"Which makes them the perfect allies for the occasion, much more preferable to the random soldier, mercenary, or servant who could betray us at any point."

"I know where I'm heading then. But since you are here – maybe you should forge a will in his name, to help our case?"

"I don't think Ptolemy is one who would bother leaving a will, since he cared for no one but himself and thought himself to be invincible," Agathoclea scoffed.

"I agree, it would not be in character for him," Sosibius confirmed. "But I could forge some other documents, make it look like he signed them after today's meetings."

"That's a good idea," Agathocles replied. "I will leave you to it."

"I suppose we declare him dead in a week?"

"Yes, seems good enough."

"Very well, let's make sure everything is truly in order before that point. I hope it will not be too late…"

Over the next week, the group executed their plan as they had discussed. Agathocles informed his allies of the new developments and received confirmations of support from them, most notably from Scopas. This was a mercenary turned general who had fled from Aetolia and recently arrived in Egypt. He had no prior loyalties to the Ptolemies and only cared for whoever could pay him the most – which in this case was Agathocles, who now had full access to the royal treasury. Scopas thus mobilized his troops and secured the capital, making sure it was under full control of the new leadership. The other commanders soon followed suit and obeyed the orders given by Agathocles, who was in some cases supported by fake signatures of Ptolemy, forged by Sosibius.

Agathoclea meanwhile took hold of the infant successor Ptolemy V and replaced some of the palace staff with loyal servants to reduce the risk of a counter coup from the inside. And Sosibius secured the support of the remaining officials for his new government while dismissing the ones he deemed untrustworthy or inefficient at their job, by way of forged orders with the pharaoh's seal on them. All the while, the priests of the cult of Alexander were secretly and diligently working to mummify the late pharaoh's body, with no one apart the coup instigators being the wiser.

Yet the group did not want to wait for too long, as some rumors were already beginning to spread outside the palace, and so they wanted to get ahead of them. Once he got the approval from his co-conspirators, Sosibius informed the palace of the passing of the pharaoh, stating that he died of natural causes. Ptolemy V was the next pharaoh in line and was quickly blessed by the priests who made the appropriate rites, while Sosibius was confirmed as the highest ranking official, with all being forced to defer to his authority now. He was the vizier and there were no direct surviving relatives of Ptolemy IV who were of age, so few questioned this choice, and none publicly. Sosibius announced the coronation event and Agathocles gathered all the important officials, commanders, and nobles in the city to the courtyard in front of the palace, with Scopas and his forces making sure that no one acted out of line or caused any trouble. This event had been long planned and was executed very swiftly and efficiently, so that in the same noon, just hours after the death was first reported, the ceremony began.

"Good people of our realm, blessings be upon you!" Sosibius proclaimed once everyone had gathered. "I have asked you all to come here to inform you of a terrible tragedy – our beloved pharaoh Ptolemy, the fourth of his name, beloved of Isis, has sadly passed away this morning, due to natural causes."

Some in the crowd seemed pleased or relieved at the announcement, while others were shocked, anxious, or disgruntled at these news, though some had already suspected it and so did not display much emotion, instead being much more interested in what the consequences of this change would be.

"Ptolemy has ruled our realm with grace, wisdom, and honor for twelve years," Sosibius continued, receiving some chuckles from the audience at the pharaoh's description, but that quickly ceased. "He was taken from us at only thirty-five years of age, which is a terrible loss. But he will be in a better place soon, sharing the Field of Reeds with his predecessors and gods such as Horus and Serapis. Ptolemy will be mourned, and a funeral will be held for him in ten days."

Sosibius paused for a few moments, gauging the crowd's reaction, before continuing.

"But we must think about the future. Our enemies will not let our realm rest and may exploit this loss with no decency, so we must prepare with no delay. Ptolemy is survived by Agathoclea, who had been his great royal wife in all but name for years, and his namesake son. Thus, allow me to present you the new ruler of this kingdom, Ptolemy!"

Agathoclea stepped forward, holding the young Ptolemy in her hands, and raised him up for everyone to see.

"And until Ptolemy is of age to rule, he will be in the good hands of Agathoclea, who will continue to take care of him and make sure he is safe," Sosibius continued. "As for matters of the state – until the pharaoh can rule in his own right, two regents will lead the kingdom in his stead. That will be me, Sosibius, the vizier of our late pharaoh and his trusted advisor, as well as Agathocles, the chief priest of the cult of Alexander and the late pharaoh's most loyal servant."

The crowd started murmuring, with some being less than content with this new power sharing arrangement, but they quickly quieted down again once they saw that Sosibius wished to continue his proclamation.

"Our situation may seem uncertain now, but we have the backing of the gods, and with the power of Serapis, Isis, and Horus, we will persevere!" Sosibius picked up the pschent crown – symbolizing rulership over lower and upper Egypt – from the nearby high priest, and slowly placed it on the head of the new pharaoh. "All hail Ptolemy, the fifth of his name, the heir of the two gods who love their father, chosen by Ptah, the strong one of the ka of Ra, the living image of Amun, and pharaoh of Upper Egypt and Lower Egypt!"

Chapter XIII

Hasdrubal Barca, who had recently been appointed as governor of northern Iberia by his brother Hannibal, was not a man who took his duties lightly. The region had been in disarray since the war with Rome, as it was a war zone between the Carthaginians, Romans, and the locals who wanted to use the war as an opportunity to reclaim the peninsula for themselves. And while the Roman threat had now been dealt with, the locals still continued to cause a lot of trouble. Tribes from further inland were assembling raiding parties and attacking Carthaginian colonies, mines, and supply caravans. Hasdrubal could not let that continue and sought to resolve the situation. Immediately upon arriving, he ordered the border fortresses to be rebuilt and security patrols to be increased, as well as any suspected hostile combatants to be killed on sight before they could bring more of their tribesmen. He also assembled together a sizable new army of over thirty thousand men, though only about a tenth were Carthaginians, with most of them being officers or specialist soldiers – the rest were Numidian, Balearic, Greek, and Iberian mercenaries.

Iberians themselves did not mind joining with the Carthaginians, as they had established a working relationship together, which was also helped by Hannibal marrying Imilce, a daughter of a prominent Iberian chieftain. The Carthaginians had not infringed much on their way of life and mostly left them to their own devices, while the Iberians realized that it was much more lucrative to join the Carthaginian army as a mercenary for a fixed payment rather than try to plunder the lands together with the rampaging tribes. However, not all locals were satisfied with such an arrangement, most notably the brothers Indibilis and Mandonius.

They were the co-chieftains of the Ilergetes tribe, situated in the northeast between the Carthaginian holdings and the Pyrenees mountains. While the brothers had been allies of Hasdrubal during the war with Rome, over time the relationship deteriorated, especially when Hasdrubal Gisco was sent in to take command over the Iberian front. The general had demanded tribute from the brothers, as well as their wives and children to be sent to New Carthage, as a guarantee of the chieftains staying loyal to Carthage. They deemed such a demand outrageous and broke the alliance with Carthage, which resulted in the general accusing them of having defected to the Romans and so the tensions were raised on the peninsula even more. The war ended soon after, and Gisco was relieved of his command, but the damage had been done. The Ilergetes brothers no longer trusted Carthage and assembled a coalition of independent northern tribes to push the Carthaginians south of the Ebro river and possibly even further, with some chieftains going as far as hoping to kick Carthage out of Iberia entirely. This was a diverse coalition which included Iberian, Aquitanian, and Celtiberian tribes, and was partially funded by the nearby coastal Greek colonies, which feared Carthaginian expansion and wanted to stop it just as much as the natives did.

And while Hasdrubal Barca tried to negotiate with the Iberians, there was no breakthrough, and the locals only intensified their attacks. Thus, the general donned his armor and set out on campaign once again against the Iberians, as his brother Hannibal, and his brother-in-law Hasdrubal, and his father Hamilcar had all once done. Meanwhile Mago Barca, who had been named as governor of southern Iberia, stayed behind in New Carthage, the political and economic center of the peninsula, and pledged to support his brother with men, supplies, ships, food, gold, and whatever else was needed for the campaign to be successful, while making sure that what lands were already in Carthaginian hands remained this way and did not descend into chaos.

Hasdrubal began in Tarraco, a native town with a significant Greek presence that had been taken over by Rome just as the war had begun, but was later occupied by Carthage once the Romans had retreated in an attempt to relieve their forces in Italy. It was now right on the Carthaginian border and, after receiving the final mercenaries, Hasdrubal departed north from it, heading towards the last known position of Indibilis and Mandonius.

The general encountered resistance from the local tribes almost immediately, but they were outnumbered and at a severe technological disadvantage compared to Hasdrubal's army, and so were beaten with few casualties on the Carthaginian side. Hasdrubal soon approached the small settlement which had been the capital of the Ilergetes, but found it all but abandoned. He put what remained of the town to the torch, and continued westwards, in pursuit of the renegade brothers. His forces marched through the lands of the Iacetani and the Vascones, the largest Aquitanian tribes, and survived several ambushes, in return pillaging some local settlements and executing what hostile soldiers could be found.

Still, the wanted chieftains were nowhere to be found, though some locals were bribed into talking. This led Hasdrubal south of the Ebro river again, where yet more resistance was encountered. The Iberians fought ferociously, but Hasdrubal came out on top nonetheless, and secured himself some more victories along the way. Not all the Iberians were hostile either, and some tribes joined his side as mercenaries, hoping to profit from the conflict that was unfolding. Eventually, scouts spotted the Iberian coalition's forces moving towards the city of Edeta from the east, with an army rivaling that of Hasdrubal in the number of men. Edeta was an important logistics hub, as well as the factual capital of Hasdrubal's holdings, and the general understood that if it was taken or destroyed by Indibilis and Mandonius, his control over the region might shatter. He realized that he had been outflanked, but was still hoping to catch the attackers before it was too late, and so ordered a forced march towards the city, while also sending some couriers to inform Mago of these developments.

Hasdrubal soon arrived near the city and found it under siege by the Iberians he had been searching for. He set up camp further away, so that his forces would not be easily noticed, and prepared for a battle to relieve Edeta. However, Hasdrubal was not fully satisfied with the situation, letting his commanders know that he felt something was not right, and so sent out scouts to make sure the surrounding area really was secure. This took a few more days, and some of Hasdubal's men protested this waiting, instead insisting on attacking the Iberians before they took the city or received reinforcements, but they were promptly silenced.

Hasdrubal's intuition, however, proved to be correct, as his scouts eventually returned with news of another Iberian army hiding and waiting just to the west of their position. The Carthaginian scouts also managed to capture an Iberian soldier who had wandered too far out and interrogated him in Hasdrubal's camp. The captured man divulged his superiors' plans, which involved Indibilis besieging Edeta and baiting Hasdrubal into attacking him, while Mandonius waited in the nearby hills with half the army, ready to attack the Carthaginians from behind when they were close enough and encircle them with the help of his brother's force. Hasdrubal thus adjusted his plans and ordered an assault on the army under the command of Mandonius.

On one morning, just as the day was dawning, Mandonius awoke to his soldiers alarming the camp of an impending attack, but it was too late. The army which intended to ambush Hasdrubal was now the one being ambushed, as thousands of Numidian horsemen charged into the camp, overwhelming its few defenses and slaughtering the unprepared Iberians. This was followed by a volley of arrows from Carthaginian mercenaries, which further reduced the Iberian numbers. Mandonius tried to rally his men to fight back, but it was now futile, with many of his men, especially the Celtiberians who held little allegiance to him, choosing to flee while they still could. The Carthaginians meanwhile continued surrounding their opponents, forcing them into an ever-shrinking area. Mandonius eventually did manage to break out, but with only a portion of his soldiers, and they could not advance far, as they could only travel on foot and were at a constant disadvantage in speed compared to the cavalry on the Carthaginian side.

Indibilis was soon informed of what had occurred and immediately shifted his forces so they would link up with those of his brother, hoping that the unified force could still win him the day. Yet it proved to be too late. Mandonius, having fulfilled his role of baiting Indibilis into lifting the siege, was deemed of no more use to Hasdrubal and was swiftly captured and killed. This enraged his brother, who tried charging through the Carthaginian lines with his most loyal men to get to Hasdrubal. He killed many mercenaries and Carthaginians in his way, but Hasdrubal simply pulled further away, leading Indibilis into a pocket of the most elite Carthaginian warriors, who swiftly killed the worse equipped and less trained Iberians with no mercy.

Before long, the gates of Edeta opened and soldiers from the city joined the battle as well, now completely surrounding the desperate Iberians and preventing anyone from escaping. Many soldiers dropped their weapons and surrendered, begging to be spared, and while their chieftain commanded them to continue fighting, his calls to action were mostly ignored. Still, Indibilis continued fighting, attempting to at least get to Hasdrubal and avenge his brother. Yet even that goal failed to be accomplished, as he was overwhelmed by the Carthaginian soldiers, disarmed, beaten, and brought to the general as ordered. The remaining Iberians, now leaderless, soon surrendered, realizing that all was lost now. The battle was over, and the Carthaginians were once again utterly triumphant.

"Any last words, chieftain?" Hasdrubal asked the bleeding captive who had been brought to his knees.

"Fuck you, you son of a motherless whore," Indibilis replied in Punic, which he had learned during the war with the Romans while fighting alongside Hasdrubal.

"It is a shame it has come to this. You have served me well before, and you were a competent and honorable commander. You could have accomplished much more by remaining on our side instead of going on this pointless rampage."

"I have never served anyone but my gods and my tribesmen. And I would rather die in this mud, having fought for our freedom, than become a slave to the likes of you and your wretched family."

"That is exactly what you will receive. I know some would prefer you to be shipped in chains to Carthage and paraded in the streets, but I will spare you from such humiliation. Since we fought the Romans together, I will execute you right here as a sign of respect, instead of dragging you like a helpless animal to the senate."

"Then get on with it and let me join my brother without further delay. May the gods curse your whole dynasty and may your greedy republic crumble into dust, you son of a bitch."

Hasdrubal raised his sword and swiftly decapitated Indibilis, before turning to his commanders awaiting further orders.

"Execute all the remaining members of his tribe if there are still any. We do not want anyone trying to avenge their failed chieftains," Hasdrubal instructed. "As for the others – take them as slaves. We will need some more hands to rebuilt what was destroyed here in recent times."

Hasdrubal's campaign was not finished yet, however. While the Iberians had been defeated, the Carthaginian general was not about to go home and rest yet, as he wanted to go after the source of funding for the insurrection – the Greek colony of Emporion. This was a coastal town on the very northeastern corner of Iberia, which had allied with Rome for a time, but had up to this point been left independent and suffered no punishment, as it was not involved too much in the war against Carthage and was too far to be effectively occupied at first. It had been let off with a warning, and the Carthaginians had hoped that it would cooperate with them and not cause any further trouble, but Emporion nonetheless continued acting against the interests of Carthage.

Captured Iberians confirmed that Emporion was indeed the main source of their foreign support, including gold to pay some less willing tribes to join the coalition of the now defeated chieftains. Hasdrubal decided that it was now time for the city's independence to end and for it to become part of Carthaginian Iberia. Thus, after resupplying in Edeta, the general marched north again, leaving some soldiers to watch for more potential incursions into the region, while taking the rest all the way back to the Pyrenees. Along the way a few more Iberian tribes were subjugated, but most accepted the Carthaginian occupation with no resistance, having heard what happened to Indibilis and Mandonius and all their allies. Finally, after the rest of Iberia north of the Ebro was secured, Hasdrubal approached the city of Emporion, surrounding the city with his men who were prepared to conduct a siege if it was ordered.

"Citizens of Emporion!" Hasdrubal announced in Greek as he rode up to the city gates on his horse, surrounded by his elite guards. "I am Hasdrubal Barca, a general serving the Republic of Carthage. Your city has time and again worked to undermine my country and violated the neutrality agreements by supporting our enemies, including the Romans and the Iberians. I ask you to stand down and allow my army to enter your city. I assure you, Baal Hamon as my witness, that no harm will come to you if you allow us in. However, if you choose to decline our gracious offer, your city will be placed under siege by my soldiers and the fleet that will arrive within days, and in that case, I can no longer guarantee anyone's safety or even survival."

A few moments later, the gates opened, and a man surrounded by his guards and advisors stepped outside the city and approached Hasdrubal.

"I assume you are the leader of Emporion?" Hasdrubal asked.

"You could say that, yes," the man replied. "I am Meleagros, the former overseer of the city's temples and public works, but I am now in charge of the whole city as of four days ago."

"How come? Where are the previous rulers?"

"They are no longer here, that's all I know. They left me in charge before they departed, as I remained the highest-ranking official in Emporion."

"I see. And do you by chance know where they have fled?"

"Unfortunately not, general. But it is safe to say that they no longer speak for the city."

"But you do? You have enough authority to ask the citizens to stand down?"

"I believe I do. As well as enough authority to ask them to fight for the freedom of their city."

"Naturally. But I don't think that would be in anyone's interest. I have more men with me here than the entire population of Emporion, and enough ships to enforce a total and uninterrupted naval blockade. Do you really want a fight?"

"I suppose it wouldn't be very wise."

"Not very wise indeed. Only one other option remains. Will you let us in?"

"Permanently, I imagine?"

"Well, your city's independence caused us some serious trouble in the past, so yes, it will have the honor of joining the Carthaginian Republic for good."

"I see. And do you truly mean that no one in the city will be harmed if I agree to your demands?"

"I do. I am interested in finding the leaders who have fled and making them answer for what they had organized, but the regular citizens did not have anything to do with it, and so they will continue to live as they had before."

"That is a relief to hear. And what about me? Is there a way for me to keep my head?"

"Only if you order the city to surrender. As I see it, you have just been left as a scapegoat to deal with the disaster that the previous leaders have left, but you are not guilty of anything except being in the wrong place and at the wrong time. So if you just stand down and tell everyone else to follow suit, you will be as safe as anyone else. I may even allow you to remain in charge of the city, if you are truly innocent and prove to be loyal to me. Because, as you may know, I am the new governor of northern Iberia. And I do not wish for any needless conflict, I just want to restore order to this lawless place at once."

"Not much of a choice then, is it? Well... Allow me to welcome you to Emporion, governor. I hope you enjoy your stay."

Hasdrubal's army entered the city, and while the local population was less than pleased with this change and their new overlord, there was no resistance. Emporion was secured within hours and became yet another addition to Hasdrubal's rapidly expanding holdings.

To commemorate Hasdrubal's victory over the Iberians and their allies, a celebration was held in Emporion by the Carthaginians. This included a large feast to which Carthaginian and local elites were invited, so that Hasdrubal could meet with them and learn more about regional matters. Chariot races were also organized to appease the citizens and distract them from recent events. The general's family soon arrived at the city as well to congratulate him, which included his wife Elissa, brother Mago, sister-in-law Imilce – Hannibal's wife who had remained in Iberia – and her twelve-year-old son Haspar, all of whom had sailed together from New Carthage. To the surprise of some, Hannibal himself also made his way to Emporion. He informed the senate that he wanted to see what the situation in Iberia was for himself, reassess the material situation together with his governor brothers, and reassure the local people that Carthage had not forgotten about and would take good care of them. He left his co-suffete Aradus in the capital, which the senators did not mind at all, instead being glad to receive some temporary reprieve from Hannibal's schemes and new law proposals.

Upon arriving, the Barcid family joined Hasdrubal in his new residence – a townhouse which had been claimed by the general and redecorated according to his will. It had previously belonged to the strategos – general – of Emporion, who had fled the city together with his family as news of Hasdrubal's approach reached him. Thus, Hasdrubal saw it only fitting to take it for himself, and now had the slaves prepare a grand feast for his guests.

"I must say, you really have outdone yourself, brother," Hannibal commended Hasdrubal. "Restoring order to Iberia, defeating those treacherous barbarians, and even claiming this great city for our republic. Excellent work."

"Thank you. I can't say it was nothing, because the Iberian brothers were indeed quite difficult to find and ambush, but I do enjoy a good challenge. Along with the well-earned rewards," Hasdrubal replied as he bit into a piece of roasted wild boar, hunted and brought to the house by his soldiers, and drank it down with wine.

"Naturally. And what about you, Mago, did you participate in this campaign as well?"

"I did. Well, maybe not directly, but I helped materially. Someone needed to stay behind and manage this mess of a peninsula," Mago replied.

"He really did help, believe it or not," Hasdrubal confirmed. "He kept my troops supplied and provided the necessary resources for recruiting more mercenaries. Without his help the campaign would not have gone nearly as smoothly."

"That is good to know. I am glad you are putting your post to good use, Mago," Hannibal said.

"And what about you? Any important news from Carthage?" Hasdrubal asked.

"Nothing's changed much. Still fighting the senators, judges, and landlords however I can, though it is proving difficult to break their stranglehold on the country."

"I imagine. Military tactics only get you so far, right?"

"Indeed. I wish it was so simple as routing a band of Iberians on the battlefield or sacking a Roman town…"

"Well, I for one believe in your skills, brother. Keep fighting the good fight in the capital."

"I will. And what about you, what are your plans for the future?"

"We shall see. I will stay here for some time, but will probably go back to Edeta soon, as it is in a better position to oversee the region. And, hopefully, my child's birth…" Hasdrubal turned to Elissa.

"Huh, is that so?" Hannibal said in surprise.

"Yes. The priests read the omens and said that it will be a boy," Elissa replied.

"Congratulations! It is always a great pleasure to welcome a new member into our family. You should take note Mago, as there are still no successors from your side."

"Oh, uh, don't worry about me, brother… There will be plenty of successors…" Mago chuckled and gulped some more wine.

"Let's hope you're not talking about all the bastards you've left after touring the whorehouses of New Carthage," Hannibal, Hasdrubal, and Haspar laughed.

"Oh, please, why must you be so mean to your brother?" Imilce looked angrily at Hannibal.

"It is fine, I pay no mind to Hannibal's poor attempts at humor," Mago said. "I am used to it, it's just good old brotherly banter."

"So Imilce, are you staying in Iberia for long, or will you be going back to Carthage with Hannibal?" Hasdrubal asked.

"I think I will remain here for as long as I can," Imilce replied. "This is my home after all, and I'm not very fond of sea travel. Besides, I never much liked Carthage. I stayed there for a few years during the war, but I found it rather filthy and full of the most disgusting and depraved people. I would prefer to stay in Iberia."

"I can understand that. Never liked Carthage myself either. It's all just schemers and people trying to take advantage of you. Here everything is much clearer, and matters are easier to settle."

"That's certainly true," Hannibal added. "Don't get me wrong, Carthage is a great city, built by skilled architects, craftsmen, and merchants, but it is a difficult maze to navigate, and there are unseen enemies on every corner. If you are not careful, you can easily be devoured by greater forces at play before you even realize it…"

"You seem to be managing fine so far. Dare I say, even enjoying your new position there," Mago said.

"The capital definitely has a lot to offer, that is certain. But it takes a specific kind of person to succeed there. And I'd rather Haspar grew up as an honorable warrior here in Iberia, rather than a scheming senator back in Carthage. It is probably for the best for Imilce and Haspar to stay here for a while longer."

"Yes, I can't argue with that," Imilce said.

"But I liked Carthage. I think it is a pretty great city," Haspar interjected.

"Well, don't worry, you will have plenty of opportunities to explore it in the future," Hannibal assured him.

"So what will I do in Iberia before that? Will I get to fight the barbarians here?"

"Not a bad idea, now that you say this. It may indeed be time for you to mount your horse and see what a real battle looks like."

"Hannibal, he's far too young for that!" Imilce protested. "He's just a kid, you can't send him into battle with real enemy soldiers just yet!"

"Nonsense, he is old enough. Better to start preparing early anyways, because who knows what could happen in the future. I was already campaigning here in Iberia with my father when I was even younger than Haspar is now. Isn't that right, Hasdrubal?"

"Oh, yes. Our father led us into all sorts of battles from an early age," Hasdrubal reminisced as he sipped his wine.

"And it forged us into who we are today. I think Haspar should follow in our footsteps. What do you say?" Hannibal turned to his son.

"I'm ready, father! I have been waiting for this for a long time," Haspar gleefully replied.

"Fine, just please be careful and do not take unnecessary risks," Imilce relented. "I do not want to lose you for nothing."

"I entrust Haspar's training and safety to Hasdrubal," Hannibal decided. "Unfortunately, the only battles I will be fighting in the near future are political ones, so I can't provide much actual military training. And I can't imagine Mago will be going on many campaigns either…"

"Not if I can help it," Mago replied.

"Right. But staying in New Carthage and learning only theory with no real practice can only go so far. I believe joining Hasdrubal on one of his adventures would be the most beneficial course for Haspar. Would you be willing to take on this task, brother?"

"Of course, I would be glad to. I will take good care of you, Haspar, and make sure you see plenty of action on the battlefield," Hasdrubal proudly stated.

"Are you planning on marching to battle again soon?" Haspar asked.

"Absolutely. We have achieved temporary peace, but there are still many tribes in the peninsula who are hostile to us and need to be dealt with. There will be plenty of campaigning and plenty of opportunities for you to learn."

"I am most glad to hear that, brother. Let us raise a toast to your past and future success," Hannibal raised his glass, and the others followed suit. "And to a prosperous and unified Barcid Iberia!"

Chapter XIV

Past the eastern edge of the Seleucid empire, war raged between the forces left there by Antiochus and the Kingdom of Bactria. Seleucid general Diogenes, along with commander Nicomedes, had been left in charge of the campaign as Antiochus departed west, and while they expected it to be a simple and straightforward endeavor, it was anything but that. The recently promoted general had confidently marched into Bactria from the eastern Seleucid fort of Alexandria Ariana with about thirty thousand men, including about five thousand cavalrymen led by Nicomedes, but these numbers began dwindling almost immediately.

While the initial advance proceeded relatively smoothly, issues already started arising in the first weeks of the campaign. The advancing Greek soldiers were not used to the scorching and barren terrain, and had trouble navigating through the deserts and mountain ranges, while the locals had decades of experience and so could easily outmaneuver their attackers and cause serious casualties. The cities – or any settlements for that matter – were also few and far between, while the closest Seleucid outposts were already far behind them. Resupply for the army of Diogenes was a difficult matter, unlike the Bactrians who were fighting on their own land and could count on their country to provide what was needed.

Finally, there was the issue of the Bactrian military. While the Seleucid commanders expected the Bactrians to only have a meager untrained infantry force and barely fortified cities, in reality the Bactrians were much more prepared. The current king of Bactria Euthydemus – the third ruler of the country, who assumed power fifteen years prior after usurping the throne from Diodotus II – had begun preparing for war immediately upon his ascension, ordering the construction of formidable fortifications for all the major cities in his realm. He had also expanded Bactria and unified the Greek inhabited regions of the east, as his predecessors initially controlled only a much smaller area. Euthydemus had come to power with the Oxus river still being the northern border, but soon he expanded his holdings even north of the Jaxartes river and claimed the distant Greek city of Alexandria Eschate in the Ferghana Valley. Having expanded his realm and increased its population, the king reformed the army, expanding its size, training its army in advanced tactics, hiring mercenaries to supplement the local forces, and inviting experienced officers to serve under him. Thus, over the years Bactria had grown into a force to be reckoned with, and neither its king nor the people living there had any intention of allowing Antiochus to subjugate it or turn it into a puppet state.

    The first major target of the Seleucid forces was Bactra, the capital itself. The commanders hoped that by seizing it, the kingdom would fall to chaos and be easily swept up, and so they focused all their efforts on taking it, whatever the cost. Yet that cost proved to be quite high, and growing by the day. The soldiers hoped to approach a simple undefended town, but were instead met with a massive fortress and thousands of defenders willing to die for it. Undeterred, Diogenes and Nicomedes set up a siege and began waiting for the city to fall.

    Yet Bactra continued to hold. Days turned into weeks, and weeks into months, and there was little noticeable progress. The capital was well supplied, as the king had prepared for such an eventuality. Furthermore, the Bactrians had thousands of cavalrymen, with both the men and their horses being armored, continuously breaking through enemy lines and resupplying the city, while also escaping before the Seleucids could catch them. The rudimentary siege engines that the attackers had brought with them also helped little, and were often burned by the marauding cavalry before significant damage was inflicted upon the city.

Seeing that the initial approach was clearly not working, Diogenes decided on a different strategy. He sent Nicomedes out with his cavalry to scout out the surrounding area, which soon yielded the general the location of a Bactrian cavalry camp, from which the attack and resupply efforts seemed to be coordinated. Diogenes ordered a swift attack on the camp, so that the Bactrian forces there could be eliminated, and the capital would be left isolated and easier to take.

Under the cover of the night, Seleucid forces left their original camp near the capital and set up another one, closer to their new target. And as a new day dawned, Diogenes charged into the enemy camp, with Nicomedes at his side commanding the cavalry, and the infantrymen following behind. The Bactrians were taken by surprise by such a maneuver, as the Seleucids breached their defenses and started wreaking havoc on them, though they quickly assembled their own forces and got into formation, not willing to give up just yet.

The battle raged for a few hours, and while the Seleucids took some casualties, they were still inflicting more on their enemies, with the Bactrians slowly being pushed back and failing to successfully strike back at their ambushers. Diogenes was satisfied with this course of events, as was Nicomedes, and the two expected the fighting to end quickly as they had planned.

However, a new variable was soon introduced into the battlefield. Having noticed the besiegers leaving the capital, king Euthydemus sent scouts to follow them and, in the meantime, assembled an additional force of infantry and cavalry from the city to march in pursuit of the Seleucid army. Once he got word of where Diogenes was spotted, Euthydemus led his army to meet the general, while leaving his fourteen-year-old son Demetrius temporarily in charge of the capital. Before long, the Bactrian king arrived at the site where the battle was raging, and charged towards the rear of the Seleucid infantry, alerting Diogenes to the presence of a new foe.

"Nicomedes! You have to pull your troops back and stall the new arrivals!" Diogenes shouted to his second in command as the new force was rapidly approaching.

"What? My men are tied up fighting the first batch, I can't afford to pull them out now, especially since we're so close to crushing it!" Nicomedes replied as he rode towards Diogenes.

"I'll take care of whoever remains here. But you need to get your cavalry to the rear right now, since your men are faster. Otherwise the infantry will be crippled, and we will be squeezed between their two units! You need to hold off the enemies behind us before they reach my men."

"I can't do that alone! There are too many of them!"

"There aren't, these are probably only the soldiers from the capital following us. And you only need to hold them off for a little while, before I can rejoin you with the rest of the army."

"Zeus almighty…"

"What is it?"

"It appears we have a much larger problem now…"

Diogenes turned north to see what Nicomedes was looking at, though he could already tell from the terrifying sounds approaching from that direction. A third Bactrian force was now joining the battle, and this was not a regular infantry or cavalry regiment – this was a unit of over a hundred war elephants, with the beasts trumpeting and trampling everything in their way.

"I think that's the end of the line for us, brother," Diogenes said as he was turning his horse around. "We need to retreat to save who we can and fight another day."

"Wait, we don't need to give up just yet," Nicomedes stopped him. "That's exactly what the Bactrians want us to do – get scared of their beasts and flee, probably right into their grasp again. No, we must fight them!"

"How? We don't have any elephants of our own!"

"We don't need them. My horsemen can do the job just fine. I can charge into the elephants with my soldiers and scare them away! They are probably just here for show, they can't be trained very well. Once we face them and start throwing spears into their faces, they will break formation and start trampling the Bactrians themselves! We can use this to our advantage to win the battle!"

"You can't rely on that! You don't know how well they are trained, these beasts might very well be our own doom!"

"I can feel it. Ares is on my side, and I trust in his wisdom that this is the right move. There is no time to waste. Cavalry, form up on me!" Nicomedes shouted to his troops as he rode away.

"No! You can't do this! Get the fuck back here, I am still your superior!"

Nicomedes did not listen, and instead assembled his cavalry forces and charged into the Bactrian elephants. They started throwing their spears at the elephants and managed to scare and even kill a few, but the results were not nearly as significant as expected. The elephants continued onwards, trampling many cavalrymen on their way and rapidly approaching the main force of Diogenes. Nicomedes tried to continue his attack, but it had failed, and many of his men were now scattering in an attempt to avoid the elephants. His formation was now completely broken and could do little to stop the enemy's advance, which, in just a few more moments, smashed into the frightened Seleucid infantry.

Chaos ensued in the Seleucid ranks. Diogenes desperately tried to reorganize his forces, but to no avail, as few could hear his orders, and fewer still listened. Seeing as the remnant of his army was now being slaughtered from three sides and that there now truly was no hope, the general ordered a full retreat south, via the only pass that was still clear of enemy forces. Some of his men managed to join the general, but many simply fled in any direction they could find, while more still perished on the battlefield, crushed by the war elephants or skewered by enemy spears. Nicomedes survived the ordeal and withdrew the remainder of his cavalry as well, before linking back up with Diogenes. Both commanders escaped the battle, but they had suffered a catastrophic defeat, and neither had much hope in their continued survival, let alone any victory at this point.

In the following weeks, the Seleucid commanders led their remaining men south, back towards Alexandria Ariana for resupply. Yet Euthydemus had predicted such a move and so blocked their path back to the Seleucid realm. Realizing that they could not breach the Bactrian blockade, the Seleucids turned east, while continuously being pursued by the Bactrians. The army was now trapped – it was too weak to fight its enemy in any way, and all the paths back to the relative safety of the Seleucid Empire were now blocked. Diogenes could only continue to flee, but his options were growing short by the day.

He now commanded fewer than fifteen thousand men, including a couple thousand cavalrymen, and most were exhausted and ready to give up, with morale being at an all-time low. Many had already deserted or even defected to the Bactrians, seeing Euthydemus as just another Greek king to pledge allegiance to, no different from Antiochus. The Bactrians meanwhile were celebrating, but were still intent on pursuing the Seleucid force and making sure it was fully destroyed if Diogenes was not willing to surrender. Euthydemus had over twenty thousand men, with the number growing as news of his victory spread, and acquired even more elephants, having seen their effectiveness at the recent Battle of Bactra.

"It's fucking over…" Nicomedes lamented, as he was eating together with Diogenes in their temporary camp, south of Alexandria Oxiana. "We can't beat them. We couldn't at first, and we certainly can't now. No amount of strategizing could give us a battlefield victory now…"

"Yes, and I think everyone here knows that," Diogenes replied somberly. "I failed. I failed my men, and I failed my king."

"Well, we both did. I am as much to blame, if not more… Those fucking elephants…"

"Maybe. It doesn't matter now, does it? They're coming for us both."

"So what are you thinking? What are our next steps?"

"I don't think there are any. We can't attack, but we can't leave either, we're cornered here."

"What about reinforcements?"

"Even if there were any, we would be dead long before they arrived. Besides, we already got as many soldiers as Antiochus could spare. He needs everyone else for his campaign against the Ptolemies, which is probably underway already."

"So... We surrender then."

"What? You can't be serious."

"Well, what else is there? Would you rather just be killed right here, knowing full well that your sacrifice means nothing because the battle has long been lost?"

"I would rather go out with dignity, than be executed for entertainment, or left to rot away in a cell."

"These aren't barbarians, the Bactrians are our fellow Greeks! They are civilized people, they clearly would understand us and probably treat us relatively well. Euthydemus must know that otherwise Antiochus would eventually arrive himself and unleash his full fury, so it would be beneficial for him to keep some well cared for hostages as a bargaining chip. We could very well come out of this alive."

"Is that what you are willing to stoop down to? Become a mere bargaining chip?"

"There are far worse fates than that. Besides, I imagine most men would prefer that instead of having to fight an unwinnable battle which would surely end in their death."

"No. I will not go down this route," Diogenes did not relent. "We all knew what we had signed up for, we can't abandon our duties just because we are no longer on the winning side. It would be dishonorable. I am loyal to Antiochus, and while he is battling the Egyptians, I am charged with keeping his eastern enemies at bay, which is what I will continue to do until my last breath. Even if we kill a few more Bactrians, it will be a better outcome than surrendering and allowing their forces to march into the realm of our king uncontested."

"That is unfortunate. But if you insist…" Nicomedes sighed.

"You are free to leave. But I will continue the fight, along with all the men here."

"No, I'm not leaving, not yet at least. But I have an alternative, if you would be willing to hear it out."

"What do you have in mind?"

"While it is true that we are cornered at the moment, that does not have to be the case if we expand our horizons and include more than just our two realms in the equation."

"And what other realms could help us?"

"There is one just south of here."

"The Mauryan Empire? How in the name of the Twelve Olympians could the Indians possibly help us out of our predicament?"

"Oh, the Indians don't have to do anything. It's simple – we head south and reorganize there. Regain our strength, hire some mercenaries, prepare battle plans, and strike back at Bactria."

"And the Mauryas are just going to let us in, instead of treating it like an invasion and killing us on the spot?"

"Their empire is crumbling. Rebellions, secessions, all sorts of troubles are plaguing the once mighty realm. It is already reduced to half the size it was just a couple decades ago. And the regions in the west, where we would be going, are now controlled by local tribes, warlords, and whoever else decided to claim them, with the Mauryas only having nominal control, which is being further reduced every year. It's no man's land, so we don't have to worry about any army stopping us. Not one larger than the Bactrian army, anyways."

"Let's say we manage this. But what then? Wouldn't the Bactrians just pursue us into these Indian lands as well? What would stop them?"

"Nothing. They could very well pursue us. But after a certain point they will have to turn back. Because, you see, we have nothing to lose. We are dead men, essentially, so we could go all the way to the eastern edge of the world if we wanted to. But the Bactrians, well, they just won a major victory and defended their home. They have a lot to lose, and they still have many enemies – more potential Seleucid forces from the west, barbarians to the east and north, and maybe even some Indian warlords to the south. They can't have their army mill around for months searching for us – they need to get those men back soon so they could go back to farming, training, manning the forts, fighting other enemies, and what have you."

"You believe we can successfully escape them for long enough to rebuild our army and attempt our attack again?"

"Yes, I would say so."

"I can't say I am willing to put much trust into your plans, considering how well your last one went... But it appears there are few options in the matter. Surrender would mean the end of our campaign, and so would continuing to fight here, as we would be slaughtered. So maybe crossing the border is our best chance at success, no matter how small."

"It is risky, no doubt about that... But it is the only way that gives us a fighting chance."

"That's true. And I suppose with us on the run, Euthydemus would be kept busy and unable to attack our country directly, fearing that we could emerge from behind at any point and take their undefended cities."

"Indeed. So what do you say? Shall we go ahead? There is a pass which I know of that we could use to safely get away before it's too late."

"Fine. Let's move out. Maybe we can still make Antiochus proud. Though I certainly hope our king's campaign is proceeding better than our own…"

Chapter XV

"Borvonicus, another chieftain that we have captured, your highness," a Seleucid officer had his men drag a beaten Galatian chief in front of the tent where Antiochus and his general Polyxenidas were sitting.

"My brothers will hunt you down, you disgusting worm!" Borvonicus growled in broken Greek. "They will avenge me! They will burn your precious cities down, and they will rape your wife and children to death, and only then will they allow you to die!"

"Oh, this one speaks Greek," Antiochus remarked boredly, while sipping his wine. "Sadly, he doesn't use it to say anything intelligent."

"What shall be done with him, your highness?" the officer asked.

"What do you think? He clearly isn't willing to cooperate – you heard what he said, didn't you?"

"Yes, of course."

The officer raised his sword and struck the prisoner in the neck. However, the move was not enough to behead the chieftain, as he had a rather thick neck and so his head still clung onto the body.

"I, uh, apologize, your highness," the officer tried a few more times, hacking away at the now fallen body, until the head was finally separated. "There, it is done."

"Yes, I can see that," Antiochus sighed. "Maybe try sharpening your blade. And take the body further away next time, I don't want any blood getting in my drink."

"Absolutely, your highness, I will... see to it. Shall I now bring forth the next chieftain in line?"

"By all means..."

While Antiochus had initially planned to use his forces to attack the Ptolemaic kingdom, he could not secure timely support from his Carthaginian ally Hannibal, and so he had to postpone the campaign. However, the tens of thousands of soldiers gathered near Antioch were becoming restless, and it was a drain on the treasury to keep them all fed and equipped, so the army needed to be put to some use. General Nicolaus suggested turning to the nearby Cappadocia, which Antiochus had wanted to subjugate for a long time, but it was a well-fortified and mountainous region and so the king did not want to risk losing many soldiers on such a campaign. General Polyxenidas instead suggested attacking the Galatians, who were further to the west, but were not as organized and had fewer defenses, so Antiochus agreed, deciding that it would be better to keep his soldiers active while waiting for the Ptolemaic campaign, while also dealing with the Galatian threat for good.

The Galatians originated in Gaul, between Iberia and Italy, and raided their way through Europe until they were stopped by the Macedonians. Some turned back north, but others continued the fight, moving to Thrace, and eventually crossing the Bosporus Strait into Anatolia, where they settled about seventy years prior. Over the years the Galatians fought with and against the local kingdoms, including Pontus, Bithynia, and Pergamon, both for their own gain and as mercenaries, though they had suffered a major defeat in recent times during a battle with Pergamon, which reduced Galatian influence in Anatolia. Still, the land remained in the hands of the Gauls, who continued their raids all around them. The Seleucid realm was no exception, as the Galatian chieftains did not fear Antiochus and often attacked border towns in his kingdom as well. Now, the Seleucid ruler had had enough of this and invaded Galatia with his full force, to the surprise of the locals who were not prepared for such a response. They scrambled their warriors for a battle, but it was not enough – it was a massacre, with the Seleucids suffering few casualties while killing thousands of their Celtic enemies, as well as taking even more as captives.

"This is pathetic," Antiochus grumbled. "By now we were supposed to be marching down to Egypt, preparing for a battle that would be remembered for ages… And yet, instead I am now stuck with quashing these pests. These barbarians who do not even deserve to witness my elite army. Gods know why they even arrived here in the first place…"

"We can always turn somewhere else. But you agreed yourself that the army cannot be kept idle, they need some enemy to be turned towards," Polyxenidas cautioned.

"That is true. As long as we do not lose too many men, this is probably the best place for them to be right now. And I suppose I can take some solace in knowing that these brutes are finally reaping what they have sown."

"Indeed. It will be good to eradicate this blight upon the land."

"But I don't even know what I will do with all the slaves. They are still quite aggressive and not intent on following orders, not to mention that no one else speaks their tongue here, or even anything close to it, so they would be mostly useless to our slaveowners."

"We could send them to Carthage. They have plenty of Gauls, both as slaves and as mercenaries, so they would know what to do with them."

"I'm not sending a single coin to Hannibal until he fulfills his end of the deal. I already showered him with gifts, yet he is still stalling and delaying my campaign. He sends his brother to continue the conquest of Iberia, yet refuses to help me with the Ptolemies. Or whoever is in charge of Egypt right now. This regime change is an opportune moment for an attack, but it will not last forever."

"Do we still consider Hannibal as our ally?"

"Well, he is not an enemy. Which is more than I can say for most rulers. Carthage can still prove to be very useful, but its democratic system often works against our interests…"

"Good day, my king," general Nicolaus arrived at the tent as the two were speaking.

"General, good to see you here. Do you happen to be bearing any news of significance?"

"Yes, I would say so."

"Would they happen to be related to Hannibal? Maybe he finally decided to help us in our campaign?"

"Unfortunately, that does not appear to be the case yet. However, I believe I have something that may be of interest to you, as it still relates to Egypt."

"Go ahead."

"As you may know, the transfer of power in the Ptolemaic realm did not go without issues. The sudden death of Ptolemy IV has left the country in a rather unstable position, and some have used it to great effect to achieve their goals at the expense of the new rulers. I still continue to receive news from Egypt through the contacts I made during my service to Ptolemy. And I recently learned of a rebellious warlord who could be of great use to our cause."

"Another ally against the court in Alexandria?"

"Not yet, but he may soon be. In one way or another."

"Who is he?"

"He calls himself Horwennefer, and he claims to be the rightful pharaoh of Egypt."

"And does he have anything to back up that claim?"

"An ever-growing army of native Egyptians, marching north along the Nile, my king."

Chapter XVI

To the terror of the Greeks residing in the region, Horwennefer – literally translating to Horus-Osiris – continued his relentless march north. He had previously been a local noble advocating for the native Egyptians to rise up against their new Greek overlords, before crossing into Kush to the south to build up his forces out of the reach of the Ptolemies. He had been preparing for years, and when news reached him that Ptolemy IV was dead, Horwennefer knew that his time had come. He assembled the Egyptians who had flocked to him, as well as the thousands of Kushite mercenaries that he had hired, and crossed the First Cataract of the Nile which formed the border between Egypt and Kush.

This was an unofficial declaration of war, with Horwennefer also quickly proclaiming himself the rightful pharaoh of all of Egypt, but the Ptolemies were slow to react to the threat from the south. Most of their forces were tied down in the Nile Delta or the southern Levant, focused on maintaining order during the transfer of power and defending against a potential Seleucid attack, so Upper Egypt in the south was only lightly manned. Upper Egypt was also mostly inhabited by native Egyptians and Kushites, with very few Greek settlers residing there, so support for Horwennefer was high, especially since he had made many allies in the region in prior years.

The claimant pharaoh's first target was the border city of Aswan, which the Egyptians called Swenett. The town was unprepared for the coming ambush and fell quickly, with the locals happily greeting their new ruler. The Greek garrison at the nearby fortress of Elephantine, or Iebu – which had been circumvented by Horwennefer as he led his initial force through the desert – sent out some soldiers to take care of their enemy, but this failed miserably. Horwennefer completely routed the Greeks and then proceeded to capture the undermanned fortress. Having recruited more soldiers for his army and installed loyal administrators for the region, Horwennefer continued north, claiming one city after another.

Along the way he captured the Sobek worshipping town of Kom Ombo, the city of Apollonopolis Magna with its nearby pyramid, the ancient pre-pharaonic seat of power Hierakonpolis, and other settlements, while also renaming them back to their original Egyptian forms – Nubt, Edfu, and Nekhen, respectively. The few Greeks who were found along the way either kept their heads down or fled, while those who resisted the new order were promptly executed. At the same time, the Egyptian ranks swelled, as news of Horwennefer's victories spread and his army was joined by both individual volunteers, as well as retinues pledged to him by the local Egyptian nomarchs – governors – and other native nobles.

But now, Horwennefer came close to his main goal for this phase of the campaign – the grand city of Thebes, or Waset as the Egyptians called it. Situated near the legendary Valley of the Kings, a necropolis containing nearly a hundred tombs for Egyptian pharaohs, their families, pets, and items of significance, the city was among the largest ones in Egypt, only rivaled by the likes of Memphis and Alexandria in the very north. It was the political, cultural, and economic center of Upper Egypt and had been the pharaonic capital for centuries in the prior millennia, which made it a very attractive target for Horwennefer not only for its strategic value, but for the ceremonial and religious significance as well.

"Sir, our enemies have already been spotted outside the city. Their attack now appears imminent," Chalcon, the commander of the garrison of Thebes, grimly informed the nomarch as he entered the palace.

"That is... troubling," Telephos, the nomarch of the region surrounding Thebes, replied as he stood up to join the commander.

"What are your orders?"

"How many men do you have?"

"About five thousand. That's the most I could gather from Thebes and the nearby towns. And unfortunately, many are far from being in their prime. All the best soldiers appear to be in the north."

"I see. And the reinforcements have not yet come, I assume?"

"No. And I do not foresee them arriving soon."

"So we are on our own..."

"It appears we are indeed."

"Have your scouts counted how many we are facing?"

"It is hard to say, sir. Could be twenty thousand. Thirty. Maybe forty. Or even more."

"In any case, not a favorable situation for us to have a pitched battle."

"No. It would be a massacre."

"We must prepare to defend then. The city is well fortified, the supplies are plentiful, and our enemies are not used to siege warfare. We will stay right here and await help from the north, while the rebels exhaust themselves and wither away. In a few weeks, this will all be over."

"I agree. This appears to be our best strategy. I will deploy my men immediately so we would be ready when the enemies arrive at the gates."

"And I should make an announcement to the people. Reassure them that we have the situation under control and that the city is no less safe than before."

"Will you be heading to the town square now?"

"Yes, I suppose I will. There is no time to be wasted, as unrest is already starting to spread."

"Allow me to escort you."

"Thank you, commander."

The nomarch left his palace with haste, with the garrison commander in front of him and the guards forming up all around the men. However, just as the group made their way onto the street, a few of the guards fell, having been struck with arrows.

"There! Shoot them down!" Chalcon shouted, pointing to a few Egyptians with bows on a roof of a nearby building.

The Greek soldiers got their bows out and started shooting back at the Egyptians, but they soon realized that the arrows were coming at them from different directions, and that there were far more than one group of Egyptians attacking them.

"It's an ambush! Get the governor back to safety!" Chalcon turned around, before being struck with an arrow to his leg and falling to the ground. "Go! There are too many of them!" the commander ordered as he was helped up by the nearby guards.

The group now turned back, hoping to get to the safety of the palace in time, but they were too late. A group of ambushers had gathered behind them and blocked the way, and dozens more were now emerging from everywhere, completely outnumbering the Greeks.

"Push through them! We have to get back to the palace!" Chalcon shouted, as he now pulled out his sword and started slashing the Egyptians attacking him.

The Egyptians were much more numerous, but they were mostly civilians with no armor and improvised weapons, such as daggers, short swords, clubs, and whatever else they could get their hands on. Many of them were killed, more still injured, and some fled as they feared the same fate. Yet, the Greeks were still rapidly losing men. Each soldier was fighting multiple opponents at the same time and eventually got overwhelmed. The palace guards were dragged into the skirmish as well, but they did not fare much better, and soon the Egyptians started flooding into the palace, denying the Greeks a safe zone to retreat to.

Before long, Chalcon was hit with a few more arrows, and then a final one to the neck, which felled him to the ground for good. The remaining Greek soldiers were killed as well. Telephos tried to flee in the chaos, but he was captured by a few men who subdued him with their daggers.

"Please, let me go!" Telephos pleaded. "We can still negotiate this! You don't have to kill me!"

"No," Khafnofru, the leader of this attack, said as he walked up to the captured nomarch. "There will be no negotiations. Death to the Greeks! Death to the usurper! And victory for Horwennefer!"

Khafnofru plunged his dagger into the chest of Telephos, and the other Egyptians joined him, stabbing the Greek from all sides, until they dropped his corpse to the ground, in the pool of blood along with the other fallen combatants.

This was just the start of the insurrection. Soon order in the city broke down completely, and the civilians marched out into the streets with the intent of ousting the Greeks. Khafnofru was chief among encouraging and leading them, and his warband massacred their way to every Ptolemaic ally in the city that they could find. Many quarters in the city were enveloped in this violence, before no place in the city remained safe. And as the Egyptians grew more and more organized, the Greek command completely collapsed, with everyone on their side being left to fend for themselves.

The garrison was of little help, as many soldiers were dragged from their posts by the mob and stabbed or beaten to death. Some guards were also Egyptians or of mixed ethnicity, and they joined the Egyptians in attacking the Greeks – if not for their conviction to the cause, then at least to preserve their own life by siding with the victors.

The remaining Greek officers, administrators, and other elites who feared for their lives fled north along with their relatives by whatever means they could find – some left on foot, others on horseback or carriages, and the rest sailing out on their ships. Their abandoned homes were subsequently ransacked by the Egyptians, who claimed them as spoils of victory. The few Greek temples in the city were also destroyed, including that of Serapis, whose statue was torn down and replaced with that of Horus.

In a few days, the fighting was mostly over, with the Egyptians having secured the city. Horwennefer, meanwhile, was patiently waiting outside the walls, having heard about his loyalists fighting inside the city and deciding to not intervene too early. Thus, he won the siege without a single casualty from his army. Khafnofru soon opened the gates to him and Horwennefer's army marched triumphantly into Thebes, with the locals overwhelmingly supporting their new ruler.

"My pharaoh, allow me to welcome you to Waset," Khafnofru bowed before Horwennefer, who had just entered the city. "We have been awaiting your arrival most eagerly and now we have been blessed by your presence. The gods have been good to us lately. Surely they must be pleased with these victories against the enemies plaguing our holy land."

"Do not assume to know the intentions of the gods," Horwennefer replied as he looked around. "Their plans are far greater than mortals can comprehend, and far above such earthly squabbles."

"Of course, forgive me, my pharaoh. I am but a simple man who only wishes to see our glorious Kemet returned to the hands of its rightful rulers."

"You have done well so far. You have not let me down and have taken Waset as I expected. For that, you will be rewarded. As all who fulfill their duties to me are."

"I am most grateful, your highness. But while we did cleanse the blight that was the Greek control of this city, there are still some Greeks who continue to live. What shall be done with them, my pharaoh? Shall I have them executed and sent straight into the jaws of Ammit?"

"No. There is no use for that. The city is already ours. We need to restore order here as soon as possible, and more bloodshed would only hinder these efforts. Am I understood?"

"Absolutely, your highness. In that case, shall we proceed with the coronation? I believe such a momentous victory is the perfect opportunity for it. The priests are already prepared for the ceremony."

"Very well. Let us proceed."

A few hours later, the coronation ceremony began. It took place in the Karnak Temple Complex, which had been a prominent site for nearly two millennia and continued to be expanded and maintained all the way into the reign of Ptolemy III. It was a large walled area, divided into several precincts which included many temples, pylons, monuments, a couple sacred lakes, and the Great Hypostyle Hall in the center, which was decorated with scenes of battle where pharaohs of the previous millennium had led the Egyptian armies to victory against the Hittites and their other foes. It was here that the thousands of observers had gathered to witness the coronation of the first native Egyptian pharaoh in centuries.

Horwennefer emerged from the temple, now dressed in his royal attire and matching jewelry instead of his battle garments. The priests around him conducted their rites, said their prayers, and blessed their new ruler with the water taken from the nearby sacred lake. They then handed him the symbols of pharaonic power – the crook and flail wielded by Osiris. Finally, the priests took the pschent crown – one which had just been made, as the original was still in Alexandria, and was now worn by Ptolemy V. As Horwennefer sat down on his throne, now in full regalia, the high priest of Amun – the chief deity of Waset – turned to the people in front of him, standing below and looking up in respect or awe at the pharaoh, and proclaimed the ascension.

"All hail Horwennefer, the first of his name, the strong bull beloved of Maat, the defender of Kemet against the foreign lands, the great champion who has struck down the Greeks, he who delivers the justice of Ra, the manifestation of Horus and the living image of Osiris, and the rightful pharaoh of all Kemet and Deshret!"

Chapter XVII

"Good morning, Aradus, I am glad you could join me," Hannibal greeted his co-suffete as he was walking through the central courtyard of Byrsa Hill. "What news do you bring?"

"Morning, Hannibal. Fortunate ones, I believe," Aradus replied as he joined Hannibal. "The preparations for the judge elections are well underway. There have been some protests here in the capital, but it should proceed without too much trouble."

"And what of other cities?"

"Well, communicating with all of them in a timely manner is quite a challenge, but it's nothing that can't be dealt with. Most cities are happy to have any representative of theirs in the capital, and only a few are trying to protest this decision. Mostly those still controlled by allies of our senatorial faction…"

"Of course. These vermin will never stop trying to hinder our efforts. No matter, their power is quickly slipping away, and it will not be a threat to our plans for long."

"I hope so. But I am still worried about one thing – what if the current judges refuse to step down? Few of them have agreed to this change yet, so it may be difficult to force a change in leadership."

"They can resist all they want, they cannot do anything to change the outcome. All are old men who spend their days bickering with each other over minute issues, who will realize that their time has come only when it is too late."

"Don't you fear that the senate will support them?"

"I don't think that will happen. The senate has long been at odds with the Court of 104. Partly because the judges sided with me, allowing me to become the suffete right after the war."

"You had it all well planned. Divide and conquer. Just like in Italy."

"Just like in Italy," Hannibal chuckled. "I suppose the political battlefield is not too different."

"You certainly are proving to be great in both arenas. Still, I worry about the ramifications of this new law on the election of the judges. I fear it may cause great instability in our realm. Should we not wait before enacting it in full?"

"I understand your concerns, my friend. But we have no time to lose, we have to act fast. Otherwise, our opponents will figure out ways to counter us, and our plans will be foiled."

"What is your plan if the judges refuse to surrender their posts?"

"I'll create my own court, a shadow court you could say, but one which would be just as, if not more legitimate than the old one. After all, the new judges will have been officially elected by our citizens, all in accordance with our new law. Then this court would disband the old one, and that would be the end of it. Some could protest still, of course, but they would become criminals, and be imprisoned or even executed. And I doubt many would be willing to die for such a matter. The judges must surely prefer retiring to their estates and spending the rest of their days peacefully, rather than losing everything for a position that barely pays anything!"

"That's... Quite an extreme approach. But it could work, I suppose."

"Tanit willing, it will. It will. And what about the other elections? New suffetes are to be chosen soon. Who is our opposition this time?"

"It's... difficult to say at the moment. Many potential senatorial candidates are ready to rise to the challenge, for sure. But they seem disorganized and not too much of a threat right now."

"Careful now. Just because there is no clear frontrunner and no one campaigning in the streets doesn't mean that our opponents have given up just yet. Surely they must have some plan of defeating at least one of us and taking our place. Just maybe not a conventional one. We need to figure out what it is and put a stop to it before it's too late."

"Not the easiest task…"

"Nothing is ever an easy task in this job, Aradus. Do not worry, I will have my people look into this matter ."

"Good. I certainly wouldn't mind another term here, could do a lot of good work."

"A year is definitely not a lot of time, not nearly enough to implement sweeping reforms as the monarchs in the east do. And making sure they are not immediately reversed is even more difficult, so we need as much time as we can get. I, for one, am ready to serve the republic in this role until Resheph himself claims me. And as long as the people accept me as their leader, of course."

"Well, I can't say I am as committed, since I would like to retire one day, but I am with you, at least for the foreseeable future."

"That is good to hear."

"There is one other matter that I wanted to discuss though."

"What is it?"

"I've received a couple letters, and the senders are expecting a reply soon…"

"Ah, I see. You are talking about Egypt, I take it? In that case, I received them as well."

"So you've heard the news by now."

"Definitely. I need to keep a close eye on foreign politics as much as on internal ones."

"What shall we send as a reply then? This is a rather extraordinary situation, with Ptolemy IV having perished in circumstances which are suspect at best, and now there are two claimants to the throne. Ptolemy V in the north, installed by his father's courtiers, and the native Horwennefer in the south. We clearly can't recognize both… can we?"

"No, that would not do us any good, only inflame tensions further."

"We must choose one. But neither option is great, to be honest."

"An infant who is clearly just a ceremonial face for the clique which committed a coup, or a rebellious warlord. Not the best pickings indeed. And choosing to recognize either would have dire consequences for us as well."

"If we recognized Horwennefer, our own southern natives might get emboldened and may rise up," Aradus stopped to ponder. "A Numidian rebellion might be on the table then."

"Correct. But if we recognize the young Ptolemy – wouldn't that embolden, say, our senators to try a coup here?"

"We don't know if it really was a coup though…"

"Yes, but… We do, actually. He just had a son, then his wife died – not due to childbirth or any complications, just on some unrelated trip down the Nile as I'm told – and now the pharaoh himself croaks. And from what – natural causes, really? Give me a break. We can't trust their new leadership. And we shouldn't recognize them."

"There is also the issue of Antiochus, who seems to want the throne for himself…"

"Oh, he wants all that Alexander once had, I'm sure. But now that Egypt is fracturing, I think it's only a short while before his armies cross into Africa."

"Which means that by recognizing either claimant we also risk offending our eastern ally."

"Most likely."

"So what then? Do we just stay silent and wait for the situation to unfold?"

"No, but we don't have to pick a side either. How about we simply send a reply that says we do not recognize either ruler, because there was no clean transfer of power. That would diminish Egypt's position even further, and would hopefully give pause to any rebels or insurrectionists, as they would realize that even if they achieved their goals, the great powers would still not recognize them."

"That's a bold move, but it could certainly help keep the stability in the Mediterranean. But what about the Egyptians? Wouldn't they treat this as an act of war?"

"Even if they did – what could they do? They are in a civil war already, and the Seleucids are breathing down their necks – they cannot afford to fight us, let alone attack us. One of their generals was killed in Macedon, and what did they do? Nothing. Because they already have plenty of enemies and have no resources left to fight even more."

"Fair enough. Though now that I think about it, a war with Egypt might not be to our detriment at all. I think it might be wise to finally accept the Seleucid call to arms against the Ptolemies, don't you think? It's over for Egypt in any event."

"Yes, but only on our own terms. And that means after the election. We don't want the opposition taking our voters away by promising them peace."

"I see, that does make sense… Maybe we should indeed postpone it. Perhaps the war will start and end before the next term is even finished, increasing our standing with the populace even more, since we would be credited with this great victory."

"I'll get my scribes to draft the reply. I will only need a signature from you so it would have the approval of both suffetes."

"Anytime. I suppose the end is near for our last major foreign enemy."

"It may be. But with the enemies we have made inside this very city, who needs foreign ones?"

"Evening, gentlemen," Hyrum Baltsar said as he sat down at a large feasting table near his colleagues. "Hope I'm not late in joining you."

The former suffete, along with many other senators and influential elites, had made their way to the large mansion on the outskirts of the city of Zama, deep into the agriculturally rich Carthaginian inland. They had agreed to gather to discuss strategy once again, as they realized that their power was rapidly slipping, and that Hannibal was ready to introduce yet more laws which would erode it even further. This time, however, the meeting was arranged by the new leader of the clique, who had provided the venue for the occasion from one of his many estates.

"Good evening, Hyrum. I don't believe you are late, we have not begun discussing anything officially yet," Ahirom Gamon, the speaker of the senate, replied.

"That's good, would not want to miss anything," Hyrum said as he immediately began pouring wine for himself.

"Don't worry, the old man is still nowhere to be seen. Probably sleeping. Or maybe already on his way to the underworld, who knows," Hanno Baalmun – who had secretly returned to Carthage after his short stay in Egypt – chuckled as he finished his glass of wine.

"Oh, I'm not sleeping. And I am sure not leaving for the underworld anytime soon, boy," Hanno Nermun slowly made his way to the table and sat down at the head of it. "I don't know why I still invite such an insolent fool as yourself here, even with you being married to my granddaughter."

Hanno was an old general and politician, already past seventy years old, who had been active in Carthage even before the First Roman War. He hailed from a prominent line of nobles stretching back centuries, with his great-great-grandfather – also named Hanno – having defeated the Greeks in Sicily and been the wealthiest figure in Carthage about one and a half centuries prior. However, Hanno did not follow in the footsteps of his ancestor and went the opposite way in terms of strategy. He decried the expansion of the Carthaginian navy, as well as any notion of war with Rome, instead urging the republic to focus on becoming a land power and fully securing northern Africa for itself.

Over the decades he fought numerous battles against the Numidians and made his fortune by acquiring vast swathes of fertile land from them, making Hanno by far the most powerful agricultural magnate in Carthage. He also fought in the First Roman War, where he achieved some victories as a general, but eventually demobilized the navy. The war was ultimately lost, and this vindicated Hanno in the eyes of some, but made him a traitor to others, such as Hamilcar Barca and his family. Hamilcar had wanted to continue the war against Rome, whatever the cost, and blamed Hanno for sabotaging the war effort, while Hanno blamed Hamilcar and the others for starting such a war in the first place and compromising the security of Carthage. This feud continued through the interwar years, with Hanno continuing to expand his domain and influence in Africa and urging the leaders to focus on this continent only, while Hamilcar began his conquest of Iberia and waited for a chance to defeat Rome.

Eventually, the Barcid faction had their way, as another war with Rome did begin about two decades after the first one had ended. Despite Hanno's protests, Carthage was once again fighting its northern adversary, and before long Hannibal's armies descended down the Alps into Italy. Hanno still did not let up on his message at first, but when news of Rome burning down reached him, the man knew that he had already lost the political battle, and so retired to live out the rest of his days in his country estate, away from the capital which was now full of Barcid supporters.

Yet, his work was not finished. As Hannibal grew more and more powerful politically, the senators, judges, landowners, and other elites looked for a powerful conservative figure to rally behind, one who could represent and defend their interests against Hannibal, Aradus, and their new laws. The former suffetes were found to be ill suited for this task, and no new challengers rose to the task. Thus, despite having many disagreements with him, the senatorial faction now turned to Hanno Nermun, who they believed to be the only person powerful enough to stop Hannibal.

"So, is this lousy lot all that we've got for today?" Hanno Nermun asked after a pause.

"I believe so," Mago Arvad confirmed. "Everyone is here. Unless you have also invited someone we are unaware of."

"I wish, but, unfortunately, this is all I have to work with. A bunch of failed politicians who have never worked, let alone fought, a day in their lives. Who are now whimpering because the plebs have elected a populist intent on taking your wealth and power away. Certainly not the best crop…"

"Maybe tone it down, old man, this tough guy talk is not impressing anyone," Hyrum retorted.

"Shut the fuck up, kid. I was a general before your daddy even impregnated the whore you call your mother. So I won't have you talking back to me while wasting my good wine, got it?"

"I think what he was saying was that… We are on the same side, there's no need to be hostile," another senator interjected. "We have a common enemy and we should focus our energy there. We need each other, after all…"

"Please, I don't need any of you morons. I have made a life for myself, and I could spend the rest of my days without any worries, and so could my children and grandchildren. I only agreed to this because I still, for some goddamn reason, care about this republic and do not want it to fall to ruin. The gods have given me a lot, and I feel like I have to repay them in this way. I do not want to stand idly by while this Iberian mongrel Hannibal desecrates our sacred city and ancient traditions by catering to the feeble-minded masses. But you certainly need me much more, as all your power and wealth comes from your positions in the capital, and you fear losing them."

"Wouldn't hurt for you to not be such an ass about it though…" a judge noted.

"Wouldn't hurt for you to stay fucking silent. Now, if any of you don't like the way I talk, feel free to leave, no one is holding you hostage. Run back to your single mothers and cry about how mean I was to you, because clearly none of you had a father in your lives to teach you how to act like a fucking man. So I guess I will have to step in. But if I get interrupted one more time, you are getting fucking whipped. Understood?"

"Yes, yes, we got it. Now can we proceed to the plan?" Mago asked tiredly.

"The plan to defeat one Hannibal Barca, yes. Something that you weaklings could not manage, even with all your combined resources. Though who am I kidding, of course there was no combined effort, all of you were fighting each other and ignoring the real threat. I remember the election well. But maybe you have now learned your lesson. Carthage hasn't fallen yet, so we can still salvage this. Anyone want to guess how?"

"By uniting our forces, I assume," Ahirom answered.

"Correct! You are a sharp one, Ahirom, clearly raised in a more civilized age than these children. Yes, we need to unite. And not only because of any bullshit philosophical reason. We need that for the cold hard numbers. Last time none of you even managed to get a second place, and so essentially gave Hannibal control of both suffete positions. Great fucking job. This time, you will not engage in such nonsense. There will be one candidate, and all the resources will be spent on him. Now is not the time for vanity campaigns."

"Alright, great, so we send only one suffete candidate out. But we still can't beat Hannibal, can we?" Hyrum asked. "Even with all our combined votes we could not overtake him."

"Good thing that we are not trying to overtake him, you idiot. No one can beat Hannibal in an election, the masses love him too much for feeding the whores and vagrants and giving away tickets to the races for free. But luckily for us, there are two suffetes. We can beat Aradus, or whoever else is chosen to be Hannibal's lackey for this election."

"That would still leave Hannibal in his post," a senator replied.

"Of course. But as I recall, one is less than two, which means that it is easier to deal with one opposing suffete than two, don't you agree? Even if that happens to be Hannibal. He is still just a man. And he can be removed from power much more easily if there is no second suffete protecting him."

"Couldn't he still pass his laws, even if he was the only one in support of them?" Hanno Baalmun asked.

"I would be surprised if even a bunch of wimps such as you allowed that to happen. Bad enough that you allow the suffetes to bully you into signing their laws, in fear of the deluded masses, but it will hopefully not be an issue with one of your own as a suffete. For a law to become official, it has to be approved by both suffetes. Hannibal will thus be either forced to compromise, or stonewalled completely. In any case, at least partially neutralized and prevented from ruining our country further."

"Who will this new suffete be? Are you aiming for the position?" Hyrum asked.

"Of course not! I despise anything to do with the elections. Having to walk through the filthy streets, speak to the morons complaining about their taxes, put on a whole show for their entertainment. No, absolutely not. I will continue my work from the shadows. One of you will have to be the public face of our movement, but I am sure that will not be a problem. We have plenty of candidates for such a position here, don't we?"

"In that case, I would be glad to take up the mantle of the suffete once more-"

"Who are you again?"

"Hyrum Baltsar, the former suffete…"

"Don't be a fucking retard, Hyrum, you lost enough times already. We need a serious person and someone who could be relied upon."

"Maybe I could-" Hanno Baalmun began.

"Don't even think about it… Fine, since this approach is not working, let me present an option. How about Zimri Germelqart? A senator in his prime, with enough political experience, no scandals that I know of, and potentially broad voter appeal. Nothing special, but a good enough choice to get everyone from the anti-Hannibal crowd. What do you say, Zimri?"

"I would be honored. If you all agree, I would be more than willing to step into this role," the senator replied.

"Of course you would. Now, does anyone have any objections? Or a candidate in mind, who you believe would be better suited for our goals?"

No one spoke up, and so Hanno continued.

"Good. It is settled. Zimri will be our suffete and will keep Hannibal in line."

"I will do everything to the best of my ability," Zimri replied humbly.

"See that you do. I will fund your campaign, have my men spread word about you, send proper security forces, and do whatever else is needed to ensure your success. But you better make this investment worth my while… As for the rest of you – just keep the senate in check, and make sure Hannibal does not get to replace the court with his commoner judges. The election is soon, and you need to hold out and contest the results for as long as possible, no matter what the suffetes try."

"It should not be a problem," Ahirom replied.

"Good. I will be ready to intervene, if it is necessary. I have many men serving me, along with various useful contacts."

"We appreciate the help," Mago said.

"Just don't forget that I am not doing this for any of you, I couldn't care less about that. I am just serving the gods and our republic, as I always have. Maybe Carthage can still be saved after all…"

Chapter XVIII

"Is everything alright, Philip?" Polycratia asked, as she approached her husband standing on the balcony of his palace in Pella and overlooking the city.

"Oh, don't worry about me. Everything is fine," Philip replied unconvincingly.

"Really? You seem quite troubled in recent weeks. Ever since you came back from Delphi, in fact."

"Well, I had quite a profound experience there. Gave me a lot to think about."

"I can imagine. Few get the privilege of an audience with the oracle."

"I don't know if it's a privilege actually. Maybe it is a curse, and now I have to bear it."

"Are you still concerned about that... prophecy that the oracle told you?"

"Yes..."

"And you are still having dreams about it?"

"How could I not? It has now infested most of my dreams, and I can't escape it even during my sleep. I must do something about it..."

"Maybe you should stop focusing on it so much. I know that's not an easy thing to do, but you can't let it consume you."

"I would like to, but I can't just ignore what the oracle said, can I? Apollo is speaking to her, and his warnings can't be disregarded easily. Otherwise, why would thousands of great men be clamoring to go to Delphi and meet the oracle, for centuries now?"

"In that case, maybe you should do something about the prophecy. Act on it, before the situation gets worse."

"Yet I still do not know who my real enemies are. What the oracle said was... vague, conflicting even."

"About those who seek your downfall?"

"Yes. There was mention of an ancient state, which has fallen in power, but will rise up again to threaten my realm. That has to be Sparta, right? They have been on the decline for over a century, but they are still a potential threat. But that's just one candidate…"

"Who else do you think is plotting against us?"

"Well, there was also something about my supposed allies betraying me, and that I shouldn't trust anyone but myself. This can't be Sparta, since they've always been our enemies."

"Seleucids, maybe? Or Carthage?"

"No, I doubt it. There is no reason for either to attack me. And they're not even my allies – Seleucids are only the lesser of two evils when compared to the Ptolemies, and with Carthage I am only allied with Hannibal, not the myriad of the republic's other politicians. It has to be in Greece."

"That sounds reasonable. We do have a lot of cities paying tribute to us, which may want to break free."

"None powerful enough to achieve independence, let alone challenge my armies. Except, of course… The Achaeans. They are powerful enough to inflict some damage if they chose to. And they may find a reason to attack Macedon. If they find out what happened to your former husband…"

"That would be very troubling."

"It would. You see why I'm so conflicted. If I preemptively strike to cripple the Achaeans, the Spartans might use the opportunity to attack us. But if I focus on Sparta, the Achaeans could break their allegiance and stab me in the back while I am on campaign."

"Might I offer an idea?"

"Of course. What do you suggest?"

"Why not have them fight each other? This way, you would not need to put yourself in danger and send your men to die, while taking both opponents out at the same time."

"Huh... That's an interesting thought. But I don't believe the two sides would be equally matched."

"That doesn't really matter, does it? One would come out on top, but they would still be weakened by the war. Doesn't matter whether that's the Achaeans or the Spartans. You could easily sweep away whoever remains, as they would be too exhausted to fight Macedon afterwards."

"I could. And then Macedon would control all of Greece, with no one to oppose us! That's what the prophecy was about, wasn't it? That has to be it. Thank you," Philip kissed Polycratia and then rushed back inside the palace.

"Don't thank me yet, it's just a suggestion," Polycratia followed after him. "Do you have a plan of how you will get the two to fight each other?"

"Shouldn't be difficult. The Achaeans and the Spartans have never liked each other, so they should not hesitate to start another war in the peninsula if I pushed them to it."

"And what would that be?"

"Well, I have my spies in both realms," Philip said as he went through the various reports he had received on his desk. "They have not delivered much of use to me yet, but I could have them influence the leaders and pit them against each other."

"Oh, I like that. Now that's the Philip that I know and love," Polycratia laughed.

"Say, if I spread rumors about Spartans being the ones responsible for killing Aratus and his family... Because they wanted to destabilize the north and retake Messenia... The Achaeans would be forced to act! While the Spartans could be led to believe that the Achaeans are plotting against them and trying to unify all of the Peloponnese under their rule. The Spartans would take to arms to defend their kingdom, and would be vindicated once they see the Achaeans already advancing upon their lands..."

"That's a great way to engineer a war."

"You think it could work?"

"I think it will. I know how much the Achaeans loved Aratus and his whole dynasty, so they would not miss an opportunity to avenge him. And if they are convinced that Sparta is behind this… Well, Sparta will burn then."

"And Sparta will not give up easily. They will take down as many Achaeans as they can before they fall. Leaving the peninsula desolate of troops and with no defenses against my own army…"

"It's a very ambitious plan. But if there is anyone who can pull it off, it's you."

"It must be kept secret though. No one can know except us, and my spies."

"Don't worry, I will make sure no one learns of this. And if they do… They won't live long enough to act on it."

"I will send out instructions to my agents. But after that – I think we have good cause to celebrate, wouldn't you agree?"

A few weeks later, the Achaeans were already marching to war. They were led by their new strategos Philopoemen of Megalopolis, who had been elected to the position just a year ago. However, he had already managed to gain the trust of most of the Achaean soldiers, and so they were willing to follow him to war against Sparta. He had decades of experience fighting the Spartans in the southern Peloponnese, as well as on Crete, so this was far from his first campaign against the southern neighbors of Achaea. The strategos had a very favorable track record, as he had won many battles and saved the Achaean League on numerous occasions.

Thus, while few in the League doubted the success of their strategos, some were unconvinced by the motive of the new war against Sparta. While Sparta was almost a mortal enemy to the Achaean League, some citizens started voicing concerns almost immediately, criticizing the war as a way for Macedon to expand its influence and tighten its grip on the Peloponnese – the one place in Greece which had still remained for the most part independent. Yet Philopoemen remained unmoved, and quickly assembled a force of nearly ten thousand men to punish Sparta and avenge their former strategos Aratus, as well as his son and grandson of the same name – former husband and son of Polycratia – as that was what the Achaeans had been told by Macedonian spies. Men from Aegium, Sicyon, Corinth, Argos, Orchomenus, Mantinea, Megalopolis, and other cities in the region rallied to form the army of the Achaean League, and soon they crossed the border into Sparta.

"We can still turn back, you know," an officer under Philopoemen suggested to the strategos as they approached the first town in enemy territory on their way to the capital. "There have not been any casualties yet, the campaign can still be called off if we act quick!"

"And why would I do that?" Philopoemen retorted. "Why would I run away from a fight like a coward? Flee before the first battle has even commenced?"

"With all due respect, you don't know what you're walking into. None of us do. This has all happened so fast, and, well, we may just be walking into a trap! I know that I've already told you this many times, but soon it may be too late to change course!"

"I have fought the Spartans many times… And won all the battles against them. They are not as formidable as they may appear at first. And they are a bunch of dumb brutes. They are incapable of laying traps, they only know of charging headfirst into the enemy, until one side is destroyed. We will quickly crush them, and we will go home before any one of us is missed."

"But what about the Macedonians? Doesn't this all sound a bit too coincidental? Don't you think this could just be a ploy to get us away from our homes and weaken our League?"

"I've thought about it plenty. And believe me, I don't trust Macedon any more than you do. But there was no other choice. If I refused, I would be saying that Philip is lying to us, that he is deceiving us for his own gain. It would lead to our relations deteriorating even more, probably even to war with Macedon, and we are not prepared for one. Not with Sparta breathing down our neck and trying to retake Messenia by any means. So we play along for now. I don't like this, but it has to be done."

"I suppose you are right…"

"We just need to strike fast and cripple Sparta before they can put up a solid defense. In the best-case scenario, our army remains intact, and we take control of the entire peninsula, giving us ample leverage against our northern…"

"Allies? Rivals? Masters? Enemies? I don't even know what they are at this point…"

"I don't know either. But I want to be as prepared as possible for the time when they decide to make their move. For that, the Peloponnese must be secure and Sparta must be defeated, no matter what comes next."

"A wise move. However, I believe we have a problem already. Our plan about assaulting the Spartans before they suspect anything… I don't think that will be happening."

A large Spartan force emerged before the Achaean army, fielding about five thousand hoplites from the region, as well as some mercenaries behind them.

"Well, only one way out now…" Philopoemen sighed. "Not an ideal battlefield, but we will make do. I will get the troops ready. Let's hope they are in a mood for a good fight right now…"

The Spartan army now marching towards its opponents was led by Machanidas, a mercenary leader turned regent. It was a peculiar situation – while Sparta normally had two kings, this tradition was abolished during the reign of Lycurgus about seven years ago, as he had dethroned his fellow monarch Agesipolis III. Yet soon after, Lycurgus himself died, leaving only an infant son Pelops as a successor, and in turn a chaotic succession crisis, proving to the Spartans that perhaps the kingdom really did need two monarchs. At the same time, Sparta's army was led by the mercenary general Machanidas, who had arrived from Italy with a host of soldiers from Tarentum, after the war in Italy was concluded. Sensing an opportunity, Machanidas marched to the capital, put it under control of his mercenaries, and proclaimed himself as regent of the kingdom, in charge of it until Pelops came to age – which would be at least fifteen more years. The ephors – a council of five Spartan magistrates, elected to oversee the kings – protested this and argued that it was against the law, but that had little effect, considering they had no soldiers to back them up. Machanidas had the support of the mercenaries, as well as the native soldiers who had come to trust him over his previous campaigns. Anyone who continued to oppose him was quickly put to the sword, quashing all dissent in a quick fashion.

The new ruler of Sparta was eager to prove himself, and he did not hesitate to raise the army once more and march north once he was informed that the Achaeans were plotting against him. He had suspicions as well, but knew that staying idle would only rouse his opponents and give them an opportunity to overthrow him, so Machanidas accepted the challenge and went out to meet his adversaries.

"Citizens of the Peloponnese! Today is a day that will be remembered in history! We have fought the Spartans countless times, and we have claimed many victories, but now the final great battle has come!" Philopoemen proclaimed to his soldiers, as he was about to charge into the enemies. "At long last we will prove that the Spartan army's superiority is nothing but a myth, and we will wipe this sorry state off the face of the earth! We will deliver righteous justice to them for what they-"

"Strategos! There is something you should hear!" an officer rode up to Philopoemen and interrupted the speech.

"Not now, you fool!"

"It is of utmost importance!"

"What can be more important than the battle which is about to begin?"

"Well, maybe that the battle may in fact not begin at all today…"

"Huh… What do you mean?" the strategos turned around and followed his officer, leaving his soldiers confused.

"Our scouts have returned. And, I know it sounds strange, they report that the Spartan leader wants a parley."

"Now?"

"Yes, right now. Before any hostilities have begun."

"That is strange. A Spartan asking for a parley, and one before the first battle has even been fought?"

"I know it is hard to believe, but the offer appears genuine. He is over there," the officer pointed to a hill west of the two armies, where Machanidas was already waiting with a small retinue of soldiers behind him.

"He wants me to go there as well?"

"It appears so."

"I might as well try. I am curious as to what he has to say."

"I shall accompany you-"

"No, you stay here. In case things turn south, I need someone to take care of the army. I can risk myself, but I will not risk my officers at the same time."

"Very well, if that is what you wish."

"Stand by until I return, but be prepared for anything. And if I don't return… Make them regret their decision."

"Absolutely, sir. Good luck."

The strategos accepted the offer and took a small retinue of his own soldiers to accompany him to the hill where the meeting was to take place. The Achaeans slowly approached the spot, wary of anything that could threaten them, until Philopoemen came standing face to face with Machanidas.

"Good day, strategos. I am Machanidas, leader of Sparta. I am pleased to see that you have agreed to discuss matters here," Machanidas began.

"Philopoemen, strategos of the Achaean League," Philopoemen introduced himself. "What does the king wish to discuss with me?"

"Oh, I am no king, though I certainly wish to be one someday. I am just a regent for now."

"Where are your kings then?"

"A complicated story. But they are all either dead or have just been born. Tragic, I know, but no need for your condolences."

"Did you take any part in that?"

"No. Just arrived at an opportune time and stepped in to stabilize the country."

"Right… Well, in any event, it is most peculiar to see a Spartan asking for negotiations before a single drop of blood has been spilled. Has Ares finally abandoned this forsaken place?"

"That's where you are wrong once again, strategos. I am no Spartan. I come from elsewhere. And while native Spartans would most likely be glad to fight your men and spill as much blood as humanly possible, I have some more practical ideas in mind."

"Such as?"

"That maybe, just maybe, we do not fight each other this time, and instead unite to fight our common enemy."

"We do not share any enemies. The only enemies of the Achaeans are standing right in front of us."

"Oh please. Is Sparta really your biggest enemy? Or is that what your northern overlords have told you?"

"They are not our overlords. Merely allies. To help against the likes of you."

"You can call them allies all you want, but everyone can see who is actually in charge. You can't tell me you aren't simply following Philip's commands."

"We are not. The Achaean League has its own goals."

"What goals? Why are you marching on Sparta once again, with no provocation at all?"

"To avenge Aratus of Sicyon, our former strategos, and his descendants that you are responsible for murdering. And I should ask you the same thing – why are you marching your men towards our lands? We have just crossed the border and can already see you moving north."

"Aratus? Really? Is that what they told you? Believe me, we did not kill Aratus. Or anyone in his family. I have been around for a while, and I am rather sure that Sparta was not involved in this matter whatsoever. Spartans are brutal, yes, but they prefer settling a score on the battlefield, rather than with shadowy assassinations."

"So who killed them?"

"I don't know who. But I do have a prime suspect in mind. Philip's wife was married to Aratus before, the son of your strategos, wasn't she? How awfully convenient for him to die just as Philip starts to take a liking to his wife... And for his whole family to die at the same time as well!"

"You are saying that... Macedon is manipulating us into fighting your kingdom... To distract us from finding out the real truth?"

"Yes. And you seem to have taken the bait hook, line, and sinker."

"Yet you still haven't answered my question – why you are marching north with your troops?"

"Well, I may be just as guilty of taking the same bait. You see, I was informed that an attack on my kingdom was imminent. That you were already on the way to Sparta, so I had to mobilize. I doubted the information at first, but here you are, with your entire army behind you. Strange, isn't it? Normally, a Spartan king would take this at face value and charge into his opponents with no second thoughts, but I am a mercenary – I have seen my fair share of dishonorable practices in warfare. And this sure does seem like one. Only two realms could have known about your soldiers advancing and where they would be. The Achaeans obviously wouldn't reveal this to us. So that leaves only one…"

"Macedon. Sending us out to fight you on a basis of a lie…"

"That's right. So you can see now why I called for this parley, instead of engaging in the senseless battle that was arranged for us by the Macedonians."

"Even if that is true, why shouldn't we still fight you? We can defeat Sparta, and then fight Macedon."

"You can't. While you may be able to defeat my forces – and even that is not a given, with all the mercenaries I've brought along – you would have a Pyrrhic victory at best and become easy prey for Philip."

"You may be right, unfortunately… But the same applies to you, I assume? Even if you win, you still get swept up by Macedon later."

"I would say so. Win or lose, it doesn't matter, both of us would be killed and have our realms conquered. Thus, we can either do Philip's bidding and guarantee that all of Peloponnese becomes just another province in his kingdom… Or, as I said, we can unite."

"Fighting alongside a Spartan, huh? Might be a tough sell to many citizens."

"Oh, same for mine, believe me. But isn't that preferable to destruction and indefinite subservience to the northerners?"

"I suppose it is…"

"The cities in this peninsula have been at war with each other for centuries, but that does not have to continue."

"Still, fighting Macedon will be no easy task.

"I understand how challenging it will be. But we had united once before. When the Persians came to subjugate the last of the Greeks, the Peloponnesians came together and fought back with all they had. And, against all odds, they won the war. Against the goddamn Persian empire. If we could beat them, with millions of

Africans and Asians in their service, who says we can't defeat Macedon?"

"Maybe we can beat them. Maybe we can... But what do you want in return? Surely you are not doing this out of kindness. You could just ask us to leave, while you return to Sparta and rule it for years, if not decades, before the Macedonians start troubling your realm."

"You are right. But if we waited for your league to fall, we would not have enough men to oppose Macedon. Better to fight them while there are still allies to be found. Besides, Sparta has fallen on hard times, so expanding and bringing glory to it would serve the kingdom well. Crete would be nice, and some more islands in the Aegean too. Sparta never had any naval capabilities, which hindered it greatly, and I believe that should be changed."

"And what about other lands? Athens, Boeotia..."

"They are right next to you. You can choose what becomes of them. All of this can be discussed later, after we defeat the Macedonians. But since you are already asking about that, I assume that you agree to this alliance?"

"I do," Philopoemen shook hands with Machanidas.

"I am pleased to hear that, strategos. Together, we will be unstoppable."

Chapter XIX

In Egypt, the situation continued to deteriorate. The self-proclaimed pharaoh Horwennefer continued to advance north, seizing town after town, and while his march was finally slowing down, he still remained a major threat to the leadership in Alexandria. The co-regents did not have a clear plan of how to deal with him, as they wanted to maintain the integrity of the kingdom while also retaining the support of the native Egyptians, who still outnumbered the Greeks at a rate of nearly ten to one. Yet the new leaders of the kingdom struggled to bring even the Greeks in line, as many noble families distrusted Sosibius and especially Agathocles, and refused to fully cooperate with them. What made the situation even worse for them was the fact that they had also inherited all the enemies of Ptolemy IV – Antiochus, Philip, and Hannibal – and so a major war seemed unavoidable. Sosibius sent out envoys to try to cool tensions down and at least stall for time, so that Egypt could prepare more, but it had little effect. The future looked dire, and so Sosibius called for a meeting of his inner circle, which included himself, Agathocles, Agathoclea, Oenanthe, and general Scopas.

"Well… It could be worse," Agathocles shrugged after Sosibius finished explaining the situation to the assembled council.

"I fail to see how," Sosibius retorted. "The country is in the most precarious position it has ever been since its creation."

"Maybe, but that doesn't mean that all is lost. We still have the Red Sea ports, for example. Horwennefer has not taken any of them. That means that he is isolated and has little contact with the rest of the world. And he can't be supplied by any of our other enemies. Meanwhile we retain the full naval access to Arabia, India, and everything else to the east of us."

"That gives little comfort, as these ports will not matter if he is marching on Alexandria…"

"That won't happen," Scopas said. "He may have taken a few cities in the south, but he will not be able to break through much further. In the north, the cities are larger, more fortified, we have more soldiers here, as well as more Greeks. His nativist cause will find little support here, and he will have no one to open the city gates for him anymore. Horwennefer's initial progress was remarkable, I must admit that, but it will not go any further. We have good men fighting to push him back, but if you wish, I can go there and deal with the rebel myself…"

"Thank you, general, but that won't be necessary. We'll make do with what assets we already have in the area. Your expertise will be needed more on the crucial fronts against our primary enemies, of which we have many. It seems that everyone is out to destroy us, and we have no allies of our own."

"Oh, don't just give into despair yet, Sosibius. There is still plenty we can do," Oenanthe replied. "When you put it that way, yes, the situation does indeed look grim. But we should look at one issue at a time and see what can be dealt with, instead of just bemoaning our fate and talking about impending doom."

"You're right. Other than Horwennefer, we have Carthage, Macedon, and, of course, the Seleucids that threaten us. We could combat one of them at a time, but certainly not all three."

"So we need to eliminate two," Agathocles pondered. "That can't be too hard. What about Carthage?"

"What about it?"

"Well, you still have your agents there, don't you?"

"Some, yes. The thing about Carthage – Hannibal is the only one there who is really interested in a war with us, so if we get rid of him, we get rid of the Carthaginian problem. My spies are trying to make that happen, but whether they will succeed is another matter…"

"Right, though it didn't go that well last time…"

"It didn't. But new elections are about to take place, and they may be more fortunate for us. This time I'm trying to make inroads with the opposition instead of just attacking the man in question. Hopefully this will result in the election of at least one suffete who is not in line with Hannibal and who could block any attempts to drag Carthage into a war."

"Do you have anyone in mind?"

"I do. I am in contact with them, and they seem to know what they are doing. Who knows, maybe this could even make Carthage into an ally of ours."

"You seem confident about it, so I take it as a good sign. Well, that's one down then."

"Seleucids and Macedon are still left. That's a lot of manpower between the two of them," Scopas pondered.

"And I can't imagine we would be able to get rid of the Seleucid threat just as easily, right?" Agathoclea asked.

"No, I don't think so," Sosibius sighed. "This has been building up for decades, there is no turning back now. Antiochus wants his revenge for the last war, and it seems only a matter of time before he invades."

"He was defeated once already, that can be done again," Agathocles suggested.

"He is older now, and more experienced. His realm is also more united, wealthier, and he has a larger army at his side. It will be a tough fight for sure."

"Could we perhaps make a rush for his capital? Take it in a swift strike, and cripple his empire this way?"

"I doubt it," Scopas answered. "The terrain is rough, and Antioch is well fortified. This would only compromise our positions and give Antiochus an opportunity to trap our forces. I wouldn't risk it. Not in the situation we are in."

"I agree. Even with all the Greek and Egyptian troops that we can get it would still be too risky," Sosibius added.

"We could get some more mercenaries too. Provided your treasury is not empty yet…"

"That is a good idea. I will have to start looking for experienced companies to aid us. The one thing we have plenty of is gold, thank the gods for that."

"Even still, I would suggest going for a defensive strategy. Let the Seleucids exhaust themselves and lose men to attrition. Only once they are weakened enough should we strike north."

"Also, don't forget Bactria," Agathocles interjected.

"Bactria?" Sosibius asked.

"Yes. Antiochus was on a campaign in the east, but ended it prematurely to return to the west. Bactria was still left standing, and it may be a useful ally in opening a second front against Antiochus."

"Isn't Bactria besieged by some of his generals?"

"Not anymore, from what I have heard. Apparently, the Seleucid forces in the east have been defeated. The war hasn't ended though, so the Bactrians may start marching into the eastern reaches of the Seleucid Empire. If they haven't done that already."

"I don't know much about the Bactrians and how much we can trust them… But it's better than nothing. Have you contacted their king already?"

"Oh, don't worry, I am already on it. I am trying to establish contact with him. If it works, Antiochus would be in quite a tricky situation."

"Seems like it. With Scopas leading our troops in the Levant, and the Bactrians coming from the east… We may actually win against Antiochus once again. Maybe for good."

"See, it isn't so bad after all. We can overcome this crisis," Oenanthe said.

"There is still Macedon, and I don't have many ideas of how to deal with that."

"Would they really join the war against us though?" Agathoclea asked. "I thought they would remain neutral, since they are still struggling in Greece."

"That may have been the case before, but not anymore. We can't assume that Macedon will stay out of the conflict. Especially after this recent debacle, with our general raping a priestess there and getting himself killed in the process... Fucking idiot. Now Philip has cause to attack our kingdom, as he thinks that we are responsible for this sacrilege."

"Well, what's done is done. We can only try to remedy the situation," Agathocles said.

"Have any suggestions?"

"Not really."

"I have one," Scopas said. "While the Aetolians are unfortunately out of the picture already, we may have some new allies in Greece. The Achaean League is now in open revolt and is marching against Macedon. And they are not alone – Sparta has reportedly joined them. This makes for a force to be reckoned with, and it could grow even larger. Who knows what other Greek cities could join this coalition?"

"Interesting. Do you think it could defeat Macedon? Or at least keep it away from us?" Sosibius asked.

"It depends. But they could if we decided to help them. If we fund the Greeks, send them ships, provide supplies – that could certainly turn the tide of the war against the Macedonians."

"I don't know about that... It sounds risky. We would guarantee that Philip would turn his full attention on us after he is done with the southern Greeks, and it is unclear of how much use they would be to us."

"No, I agree with the general," Agathocles said. "We have to strike first. We can't just sit around and wait until Philip and Antiochus decide it's the perfect time to strike. We have to be proactive. Send the Achaeans and Spartans whatever they need, and we make sure Philip is occupied for years before he can even venture out of Europe. Besides, if our allies win, we could open yet another front against the Seleucids!"

"If they win. Otherwise, we would be stuck in a losing war which would be difficult to leave."

"Maybe, but what other choice do we have? You said it yourself, Macedon is an enemy of ours, that is clear. So why should we be cautious around them? They killed our general after all, fuck them. We need to show our strength and resolve to the world. We should support enemies of Macedon, maybe even send troops on the ground there to help the war effort. What do we have to lose?"

"Well, I would have preferred to negotiate diplomatically with Philip. Maybe talk him down from all this…"

"Come on, you know that's not possible. The time for diplomacy with hostile kingdoms is over."

"I suppose you are right, however unfortunate that is…"

"I'm confident it will work to our advantage. Don't worry, I will arrange everything. You take care of the west, I'll take care of the north. And Scopas will deal with the east, right?"

"That's right," Scopas nodded.

"Sounds like a plan," Sosibius said. "May Serapis help us see it through successfully."

Chapter XX

The Carthaginian suffete elections were once again upon the republic. A year had already passed since the previous one, and so citizens once again began lining up to cast their votes for their preferred candidates. This time, however, there were fewer choices. The only viable options in this election were Hannibal, Aradus – the two outgoing suffetes – and Zimri Germelqart, an opposition candidate from the senatorial faction. Everyone else had dropped out of the race before the election day, either due to realizing how low their chances were or because of bribes – and in the few cases where that did not work, intimidation as well.

The voting once again continued into the evening, and afterwards thousands gathered in the Great Marketplace, where the results would be announced. There were even more attendees this time than the previous year, and now there were two clear camps – one supporting Hannibal and Aradus, and one supporting Zimri – though it was more of a protest vote against Hannibal's faction, with Zimri only being the face of the coalition. Hannibal's reforms gave him many new supporters, but lost some as well, and many citizens who had previously been neutral on the matter now vehemently opposed him. Many felt that he was needlessly wasting resources on the poor by providing free and subsidized grain and also betraying the traditions of Carthage by allowing the judges to be elected.

The court reforms were indeed highly controversial, and the matter remained far from settled. Some judges were reelected and retained their posts, while others agreed to step down and allow the elected ones to replace them. Some, however, stood their ground and refused to cooperate, paralyzing the court's work. Some judges gave extended speeches, one after another, just to prolong the process and delay their departure. They were also sometimes attacked on the streets by mobs of Hannibal's supporters, and a few were seriously injured, with the violence only intensifying as time passed. In response, private guards and mercenaries hired by the judges and the senatorial faction went after Hannibal's supporters and attacked them, brutally beating and sometimes even killing them, further perpetuating the cycle. The senators also used their connections to delay or cancel the elections of the judges in some areas, so that their newfound allies in the court could retain their posts. The senate and the Court of 104 were never too close and often had major disagreements, but by now both felt threatened enough by Hannibal to temporarily put aside their grievances and work together.

Thus, these reforms became one of the main talking points in the debates between the potential suffetes. Zimri vowed to annul the results of the judge elections and restore the court to its previous form, while Hannibal promised to carry out his reforms to the fullest and crack down on the old holdouts even more. Hannibal also took a more hardline approach to Egypt and finally began openly suggesting that war with the eastern neighbor might be necessary, while Zimri wanted to rebuild the relationship with the Ptolemaic realm, officially recognize the new pharaoh in Alexandria, and avoid any further meddling in the eastern Mediterranean.

With these and many other pressing matters being contested, the thousands of Carthaginians eagerly awaited the official announcement, which came soon enough. The lead election commissioner appeared on a platform in the middle of the Great Marketplace and began his speech, which went the same way as it always had. And, just like the previous year, he skipped the second and third places and began with the candidate who had the most votes, since that was not supposed to be a big surprise to anyone.

"Hannibal Barca, with 11874 votes! Hannibal will once again serve as our suffete, for his second term now," the lead commissioner announced.

"Thank you for your continued support, citizens!" Hannibal stood up and proclaimed. "There is still much work to be done, but it will be completed, trust me. Together, we will save our republic and make it a better place than it has ever been!"

"And now for the second and third places..." the commissioner continued after the crowd quieted down. "7690 votes for Aradus Reshgal... and 10436 for Zimri Germelqart, who will be replacing Aradus as the new suffete."

The crowd erupted into an uproar, with the senatorial faction celebrating and cheering for their new leader, while the one across them was swearing and throwing insults to the opposite side. Further out, on a balcony of one of his buildings, Hanno Nermun was sipping wine and witnessing the event. It was the first time in many years that he had gone out to see the announcement firsthand, and it pleased him greatly. He cracked a rare smile, as his plan to make Zimri into a suffete to counter Hannibal had succeeded just as expected.

"It is a great honor to be chosen as the suffete of our glorious republic," Zimri began. "It has functioned well for centuries, and in the past year we have seen that change is not always good – in fact, most traditions are there for a reason. I will honor them, and I will honor our ancestors and the founders of this city by maintaining them, making sure that they are not trampled on by some Iberian foreigner!" this remark received a lot of cheers and applause from his camp. "Carthage will once again become a safe, proper, and respected city and these populist games will cease at once!"

"I'm sorry to leave you to this, Hannibal," Aradus said to Hannibal as Zimri continued his speech. "I wish I could have led a more successful campaign."

"Don't worry, you did more than enough already, my friend," Hannibal replied. "It will be more difficult, surely, but nothing that can't be managed. This guy is a nobody, he is just there to regurgitate the senate's demands. I've faced far more able opponents and won."

"Good luck to you. If you ever need anything, I'll be there to help."

"Thank you, that is greatly appreciated."

A few weeks later, the official transfer of power took place. Hannibal remained in his post, and Aradus was replaced by Zimri. It did not take long for the conflict between the two to begin. The suffetes rarely interacted and stuck to their own supporters, but when they did meet, it rarely went well. Both had their own proposals and laws that they wanted to pass and could not agree with each other on almost anything. Hannibal turned to the Court of 104, but found little help there – many of the original judges were still part of it and continued to oppose Hannibal and refuse to step down. The former general then created his own so called shadow court, consisting of the newly elected judges, but this assembly was not recognized by anyone else, with all its edicts proclaimed as void by Zimri, now firmly backed by the original court. Thus, Hannibal disbanded his court and went back to trying to reform the old one. A few days later, he drafted a new law that would allow the use of any force to remove officials refusing to do so of their own volition, once they legally lost their post to another member. He did not specifically mention the court, instead including all government offices – such as the senate, the commissions, and even that of the suffetes. Hannibal did not tie it directly to the issue at hand, instead speaking about it as a measure to safeguard the republic's institutions and in doing so hoped to attract more senators to his proposal.

Still, the anti-Hannibal faction in the senate was too large, and contained too many hardliners who would not accept the law in any form. The former general had a plan, however. On the night before the vote was scheduled to take place, he sent out his loyal supporters to create distractions and obstructions for some senators so that they could not arrive to Byrsa Hill the next day on time. A few of the pro-Hannibal senators also participated by agreeing to skip the vote, in order to make the list of absentees not look too suspicious, but the final numbers were still supposed to be on Hannibal's side.

"Maybe we should still wait before we begin... We are missing quite a few senators," Ahirom Gamon suggested, looking over the senate chamber.

"We have waited long enough," Hannibal retorted. "There is much work to be done, and we cannot afford any delays. I call for a vote now!"

"Well, I suppose it is past the time when we were supposed to start... Let's begin then. We have 217 members present here today, just barely enough for a quorum. That means at least 109 votes are needed for the proposal to pass. Those of you in favor of Hannibal's proposal on the use of force to remove government officials, please move to the right. Those opposed – move to the left. Should be plenty of space now."

"This is ridiculous! It's a sham! Hannibal, I know you had something to do with this!" one senator shouted.

"Did you kill all the others? Wouldn't be surprised if you did," another added.

"It's not my fault they are late. Or decided that it's not worth bothering to vote. That's their decision," Hannibal shrugged.

"Don't pull this shit now, it's clear you were responsible!"

"Gentlemen, please," Ahirom turned around to calm them down. "You will have all the time later to voice your concerns, but it is time to vote now. Will you join us?"

"You know, I don't think I will," one senator replied and got up to leave the room. "Fuck this nonsense, I will not participate in this farce of a vote. It has clearly been rigged in Hannibal's favor, and I will not stand for it."

The senator was followed by a few others, who all left the room without voting for the law.

"By all means, go, leave right now if you wish. Clearly you have more important things to do than deciding the future of our republic," Hannibal mocked them as they passed by him on their way out. "But don't worry, we still have enough reasonable people who will do just fine without your whining."

"Well, this changes things now..." Ahirom said. "We have fewer senators now, so we may not have enough for-"

"It doesn't matter, Ahirom, the vote has already commenced. We had enough senators when you announced its start, so it is legally binding now. No matter if someone left or did not vote."

"Well, yes, but you can see how-"

"Shall I cite the voting law to you? I have the scrolls right here, so I can refresh your memory if it is needed. Let me see, right here, it says-"

"I understand, you're right. The vote has indeed commenced now," Ahirom sighed.

The senators were indeed quite confused as to what was going on, but in a few moments continued moving to their respective side to cast their vote. After everyone was in place, Ahirom tallied the votes and returned to the center of the room to announce the outcome.

"Let's see what the results are. 118 for the proposal, and 85 against. The law has passed in the senate," Ahirom proclaimed.

"Good. Now I'll just sign it and be on my way to-" Hannibal began.

"What is the meaning of this?" Zimri marched into the room and addressed Hannibal. "What in the name of all the gods do you think you are doing?"

"Why, saving our republic, of course."

"I saw some senators leaving, and they told me what had happened. This is unacceptable."

"Don't blame me, blame the senators for not showing up. Not my problem that they can't manage their time properly..."

"How convenient is it that the ones missing are all your opponents, huh?"

"Not all, clearly. Some of my supporters are missing too, as you can see. Do you happen to know where they are?"

"I was under the assumption that both suffetes had agreed to this proposal…" Ahirom interjected.

"Well, clearly not," Zimri replied angrily. "I didn't even know that this vote was taking place right now!"

"It has already taken place. And the law has passed. But it does need the approval of both suffetes, which, I now understand, it does not currently have."

"It will," Hannibal stated. "Just sign this, Zimri."

"Absolutely not," Zimri took the scroll and threw it to the ground. "I am not a fool, I can clearly see what you are doing. And I am a rightfully elected independent suffete, not a lapdog like Aradus was. I won't sign anything that I don't agree with."

"Come on, it's over already. The senate has voted. Everyone has agreed that it is for the best. Just sign it and be done with the matter. No reason to drag the matter further when the outcome is already clear."

"Oh, it's far from clear for me. I will not give in to your demands. I was elected for a reason – I was elected because people were getting tired of your desecration of this country and its traditions. And the least I could do is prevent you from desecrating it even further," Zimri retorted as he left the room.

"Zimri, wait, listen!" Hannibal went after him. "It doesn't have to be this way."

"I don't see any other option," the suffete continued walking.

"Alright, I get it, you have your act that you have to perform. You charge in there, attack me in front of your senate friends, claim that you are the only one standing between the republic and its destruction. Fine, we all have to give our voters what they expect of us. But can't we talk about this normally, now that we are in private? Can't we reach some sort of an agreement? You can win from this as well."

"No, I'm not entertaining this charade any longer."

"You can drop the act now, it doesn't do you any favors. I know you're not that kind of man…"

"Yeah? What the fuck do you know about me?" Zimri turned to face Hannibal.

"Not much actually. I don't think anyone knows much, considering you seemingly appeared out of nowhere one day. Which does make me wonder how you managed to get elected…"

"What are you implying?"

"Nothing. Not yet, at least. Listen, I don't mind you being my co-suffete. But if you are going to obstruct my work like this, we are going to have a problem."

"Well, you will just have to learn to deal with it."

"Or maybe I will have to take a closer look at the voting results. See who all these mysterious voters supporting Zimri Germelqart are…"

"Are you blackmailing me now? Is that what you have stooped to?"

"No, but I am saying that it would be most beneficial for you to cooperate with me. Otherwise, you might face unforeseen consequences."

"Do whatever you want, I still won't sign any of your mad decrees. And I was elected fairly, so you will not find whatever you are looking for anyways."

"Maybe not," Hannibal replied as Zimri walked away. "Or maybe I will…"

"So how is it going with your new colleague?" Aradus asked Hannibal, as they, along with some other friends and allies of Hannibal, were feasting in the suffete's house that evening.

"Just as how you would expect, he's an obstructionist little rat," Hannibal replied and chugged some more wine down.

"Oh, I can imagine. Must be annoying to have to work with one such weasel," another man said. "Have you thought about how you could get around him maybe?"

"Yes, actually. I have an idea of how to bring him in line."

"Please, tell us if it's not a secret."

"I'm trying to scare him into submission. I told him that I may be about to uncover some voter fraud that was used to get him into power. I could threaten to release this information if he continues to reject my law proposals."

"That is serious. If it is true. Is it actually true?" Aradus asked.

"To be honest, I have no idea," Hannibal laughed, and so did his guests. "I'm just fucking with him right now. But it could still work."

"How would it work if he knows that there was no voter fraud though?"

"That's the thing, he may not know either. He's a nobody, just a completely random senator who appeared suddenly and won the office of the suffete. I suspect someone far more powerful is behind his campaign. Thus, even Zimri himself may not be aware of the entire operation to get him to the office. He seems to be a puppet for our real enemies in the country."

"Huh, that's interesting. Better to keep him guessing too. Make him distrust his allies maybe. That's smart."

"And hopefully that will force him to yield to me. At least on some issues."

"You have to be careful though," another one of Hannibal's friends cautioned. "It could go very wrong. Besides, you wouldn't be able to use this threat every time, at some point it would lose its effectiveness."

"Oh, I know that. I will be strategic about it. I just need to get Zimri's approval for one major change, so I could proceed more easily afterwards. Still not quite sure what that would be though…"

"Luckily, you actually only need to pass one law, and then you can do whatever you want," another man suggested.

"And what's that?"

"Simple – you just change the law so there would only be one suffete!"

"No, that's impossible... Isn't it, Hannibal?" Aradus asked.

"Huh... It's certainly unprecedented..." Hannibal pondered for a few moments. "But it's doable. The laws are what the lawmakers agree them to be. If both suffetes agreed to it, only the senate would be left. And it would be far from the first time I got them to sign a law they hated... Besides, I could always bring it to the popular assembly as well, it might find more support there."

"But what about the court? Don't you think the judges would protest such a change?"

"Not enough of them to protest it now, with much of the old guard replaced by the newly elected judges."

"Right, that's true. So it could work then..."

"It could. Maybe I really should go ahead with the idea. Put an end to the petty squabbling and start working on solving actual issues."

"That's fucking right! I for one support Hannibal as our sole suffete! Maybe even as king!" one of Hannibal's friends shouted.

"I appreciate the enthusiasm, but maybe let's not go that far," Hannibal chuckled. "A suffete is good enough, I think."

"You should move forward with this plan, I wholeheartedly support it as well," another friend added. "You were an unconventional commander in the battlefield, but it won us the war. Why not try something just as unusual in the political arena too? The second suffete is often a hindrance anyways, and powerful states are forged by a single great man, not two sharing one post."

"Thank you. And those are good points. Look where having two rulers led Rome... Maybe Carthage really does need a single leader who can guide it to prosperity..."

Chapter XXI

The situation was getting dire for the Kingdom of Macedon. Philip's and Polycratia's plan to pit the Achaeans and the Spartans against each other had failed and totally backfired. The two southern armies had united instead of engaging each other in combat, and they were now marching north. The new coalition was also soon joined by Elis, which had its own grudges against Macedon, and so the entire Peloponnesian peninsula was now set against its northern rival. Philip's hopes to stop the advancing armies at the Corinthian isthmus were also dashed, as the city of Megara – which controlled most of the isthmus – stayed loyal to the Achaean League and let its forces pass unimpeded. Thus, by the time the Macedonian troops had reached their opponents, they were already in Attica and could no longer be so easily contained as Philip had initially hoped.

The initial engagements were inconclusive, as neither side had a definite advantage and were at first mostly just testing their opponents. Philip had a large and elite fighting force, but his opponents were well prepared too, and led by Philopoemen and Machanidas – of the Achaean League and Sparta respectively – who were both well versed in military strategy. Realizing that his enemies were not going to be defeated easily with such competent generals among them, the Macedonian king planned to overwhelm them with numbers. This was working so far, as the sheer size of the Macedonian army prevented the Peloponnesians from advancing much further. Still, there was no guarantee that this would remain the case for long. While Athens and the Boeotian League remained loyal to Macedon as its tributaries and provided access to their lands, as well as some troops, there were fears that they might also join the Achaeans in their uprising. This would not only deprive Macedon of some of its soldiers and increase the enemy's numbers, but also trap the main bulk of Philip's army in a now hostile area, with few ways to escape it. Yet the king could not afford to have his forces abandon Boeotia and Attica now either, as that would allow the Peloponnesians to take them with no struggle and entrench themselves in a much better position with more resources available to them. Thus, Philip ordered his commanders to stand their ground and continue to defend against enemy advances.

The Macedonian woes did not end there though. The southern coalition, having been stopped on land for the time being, refocused their efforts on a different front – naval warfare. The Achaeans, using Elis as the staging ground, had managed to sail to and seize the islands of Zakynthos, Kefalonia, and Ithaki, while the Spartans used their island of Kythira to launch an offensive on Crete. The Macedonian navy could not defend against these incursions and was forced to fall back, much to Philip's dismay. He knew about the naval capabilities of cities like Corinth – which was the largest city in the Achaean League – but was confident that his own naval forces could hold against them. Yet the king was soon faced with a terrible revelation – he was not just going against the small Achaean fleets and the almost non-existent Spartan navy, but also against the naval might of Ptolemaic Egypt. Macedonian sailors, returning from lost battles, reported that they had spotted dozens, if not hundreds of Egyptian vessels, which had first only delivered supplies to the southern Greeks, but now were also actively engaged in supporting their military operations. While there was still no official declaration of war, many in Macedon now understood that the primary enemy in this conflict was Egypt. The Kingdom of Macedon was among the three major surviving states that had emerged from the ashes of Alexander's Empire, but it was still leagues behind Egypt in almost every way and could not hope to fight it alone. Luckily for Philip, he knew someone who could help him balance the scales.

Antiochus was getting tired of waiting to begin his attack on the Ptolemies, as were his soldiers, who were becoming more restless by the day. Fighting the Galatians was not enough, and the king knew that he had to act fast, or he would be forced to disband his army due to the costs of keeping it active becoming unsustainable. He did not want to attack the Ptolemies alone, as he still remembered vividly what happened the previous time he had attempted it, and the humiliating defeat he had suffered. The king vowed to not allow that to happen ever again, and so he had been engaged in trying to find serious allies over the previous years. The seemingly spontaneous uprising in southern Egypt was a nice surprise and gave him more time to prepare, but it was not enough.

Enlisting the help of Carthage had been his primary objective, as the Punic republic's riches and massive navy was crucial for Antiochus' plan to succeed, but it now appeared clear that the western state was going to be of little help. Hannibal had stalled during his first term as suffete, never fully agreeing to join Antiochus, and now the country was in a political gridlock, with the two suffetes having completely opposite foreign policy approaches and unable to steer the country in any way. The Seleucid king had thus abandoned the idea and was left with two choices – disbanding his army and going back to his capital, which would anger many in the empire, or going against Egypt alone, with whatever that may entail. But, fortunately for Antiochus, he was relieved of having to make this choice, as a new opportunity soon presented itself.

An envoy from Macedon arrived at the camp of Antiochus, delivering news from the west. The king was informed that Egypt was now actively aiding Macedon's enemies in the war, and that Philip wanted to meet with Antiochus to discuss prospects of an alliance against their now common enemy. Antiochus had never been close with Philip and was somewhat distrustful of him, but he accepted the invitation with little hesitation, as that appeared to be the only viable opportunity to defeat Egypt. The meeting was set to take place in Sardis, the westernmost major Seleucid city, which was still far enough from any current or potential frontline, and so both kings agreed to travel there with haste.

"Good to meet you, Philip," Antiochus greeted the fellow monarch as the two entered a tent set up for their meeting, in a military camp near Sardis.

"Likewise. Wish it was under more favorable circumstances, though," Philip replied.

"Indeed. But they may soon become much more favorable."

"Hopefully. So… The Ptolemies. They are a fucking pain in the ass for both of us, isn't that right?"

"That's a mild way of putting it. Though I question whether it's actually still the Ptolemies at this point. With the fourth Ptolemy croaking – good riddance, might I add – and the fifth one still a child, I believe we are dealing with new faces. Regents who have assumed control of the country."

"That may be so, but it does not matter much. They are continuing the previously set policies, except they seem to be efficient at it. Which makes it even worse for us."

"It does. With no Ptolemy to reign in the voices of reason, Egypt may actually pose a very serious threat now."

"Which is why we must unite. That's the only way to win."

"That's one way, yes."

"You know it is the only choice. Otherwise you wouldn't have come here."

"Currently I'm only assessing my options… I'm not committed to any one of them yet."

"Bullshit. You know that there is no other way, and I know it too. You want Egypt, for whatever reason – not my concern, really. But if you had other options, you would have attacked them already. But you haven't, so this alliance must be your last hope before you have to disband your forces and go home with no spoils. I just want you to acknowledge that this is just as crucial for you as it is for me, and that we would both benefit equally."

"That is true... We both need this alliance. What are you proposing?"

"It's simple – we give a joint declaration of war against Egypt, and all its allies. Sparta, Achaea, Elis, and so on. And whoever else is foolish enough to be swayed to their side. With our combined forces, our enemies don't stand much of a chance."

"There is still the naval issue though..."

"For now, yes. But we can build or hire more ships easily. Carthage would have been most helpful here, but we can do just fine without them."

"We can. But what then? What about the aftermath?"

"What about it?"

"You do realize that the expected outcome is for Egypt to fall under my protection at the end, in one way or another. Will that be an issue?"

"No, you can take Egypt. For me it is a defensive war, so my goals are much more modest."

"Well, but that's the thing – it shouldn't only be a defensive war for you."

"How so? You do realize that my armies are pinned down right now and can't do much until the Peloponnesian issue is resolved."

"For now, yes. But I can't just have you sitting in Greece for the entire war – only gods know how long it will take – while I do most of the actual fighting with the Egyptians. If you want us to be equals in this war, both of us have to contribute equally to defeating the sun and falcon worshippers."

"That would be much more costly for me..."

"War is costly, no doubt about that. But I thought that the idea behind this alliance was both of us helping each other in our campaigns. Otherwise, it would be just me protecting you, like a...

tributary. And I imagine you wouldn't want that sort of relationship?"

"No, of course not."

"Right. You are a king, same as me. Descended from an honorable and prominent dynasty. From a general and trusted companion of Alexander the Great himself. Not just some upstart noble snatching a piece of land for himself. The two of us are the last successors of Alexander. So, act like one."

"I will. But in that case, I'll need something more in return. Something more to show for all this effort, rather than just the fact that I maintained hold over my realm."

"Not a problem. The Ptolemies still have plenty of holdings that can be carved up. I'll take Egypt, as well as the rest of the Levant on the way, naturally. I'll also take their remaining Anatolian territories. And you can have all of Greece – as long as it is over the Aegean, it is not my concern, I'll leave it all up to you. And you can take Cyrenaica too. I promised it first to Carthage, but they are not showing up anytime soon, so I have no issue with you taking hold of the region."

"But I assume Alexandria will still go to you, right?"

"Yes, that is a rather large prize to pass up."

"Not a very equal bargain then, is it?"

"Well, what can I say – Egypt at its core can't really be divided. It's just one river and continuous farmlands surrounding it. You either hold Egypt, or you don't. Splitting it arbitrarily would only lead to inevitable future conflicts. But you can have the entire coastal stretch in the west, all the way to Alexandria. That way both of us could easily access the great city."

"I see. That's good, but I would also take Cyprus."

"Do you really need it?"

"Yes. It would be quite beneficial for me to have the resources from the island which my current realm is lacking in."

"Fine. Anything else?"

"Also, all the Aegean islands would be in my sphere. That includes Lesbos, Chios, and Rhodes. Just so we would have a clear border of where Europe and Asia meet."

"You drive a hard bargain. That's quite a few islands in total…"

"Are you claiming them as well?"

"No, it's fine, you can do with them what you want. But if we are dividing the world into spheres of influence, I assume you would be fine with me claiming all of Anatolia? From Pergamon to Colchis. It is all in Asia, after all."

"I could accept that. But then I would claim the rest of the Euxine Sea coast. Everything to its west, north, and east – as long as it is north of the Caucasus Mountains."

"You can have it. Everything else to the east would be in my sphere."

"And to the west in mine."

"Sounds fair to me."

"So we are in agreement."

"We are. We declare war on our enemies, defeat them with the combined might of both our armies, and then divide the spoils as equals."

"I do like the sound of that. Though I imagine it will be a bit more difficult than how you just put it… It might be a long war indeed. What do you think we should start with?"

"Why not Ephesus? It's right here. A quick and clean strike to start the campaign. My forces would move from the west on land, while yours could land from the east, as you hold Samos, which is right next to the city. Then we could march south to Halicarnassus to seize it before the Ptolemies reinforce it."

"Sounds like a solid plan. Let's begin the preparations then. There is much work to be done."

Chapter XXII

Diogenes and Nicomedes, along with their remaining Greek soldiers, had spent months traversing the harsh terrain they found themselves in, full of mountains and treacherous passes between them. The Bactrians had not pursued them, instead deciding to focus their full attention on reorganizing their forces and preparing for a march west, into the lands of the Seleucid Empire, which was the preferred outcome for the stranded commanders. Yet, even without such foes on their heels, Diogenes and Nicomedes had plenty of other problems. The crippled Seleucid army faced mass desertions, with the soldiers either defecting to Bactria, fleeing back to their homes in the Seleucid realm, or simply forming their own warbands to scavenge and pillage their way across India. Now, only about five thousand remained under Diogenes' command, and even they were losing hope and becoming restless. The Seleucid men had no supplies left and so began taking what they could from the locals, which led to many conflicts and even skirmishes with the Indians. The Greeks were better equipped and trained, but they would still lose a few men in such cases, and so their numbers continued dwindling. The situation was getting more dire every day, but Diogenes insisted that the soldiers needed to push on and that turning back now would mean certain doom.

"We're lost! Admit it, man, we are lost! It has been weeks since we entered this valley, and we have fuck all to show for it!" Nicomedes groaned.

"It's not too far now, I just now it," Diogenes tried to reassure him. "The maps show that we are in the right place…"

"The maps… Of course it's your damn maps! When have they been drawn, a century ago, back when Alexander first arrived here?"

"Maybe, but that doesn't mean they are wrong. Cities don't just suddenly lift up and float to a different place!"

"I wouldn't be surprised if that was a regular occurrence here. Who knows what these Indian monks are up to…"

"Just have patience, we will be there soon enough. And stop whining like a child, it was your own goddamn plan that got us here in the first place!"

"Yes, but I would have taken a different route. We could have stopped in Alexandria along the way, would have avoided all this trouble."

"I told you, we couldn't have. That city was full of Bactrian supporters. They would have imprisoned and turned us over to Euthydemus for a reward."

"And the rulers of this magical city of yours won't?"

"No. It is said that its king is a good friend of Antiochus. He could help us turn the campaign around."

"I don't think even Ares and Athena arriving could help us turn it around by this point…"

The group continued travelling north as they had, led by Diogenes and his collection of maps drawn by Greeks who had been to India. However, as the remnants of the once mighty army stopped to make camp for the night, they found themselves surrounded by a large force of Indian soldiers, armed with spears and bows, as well as a dozen or so war elephants.

"Great, more elephants. Guess that's it for us then," Nicomedes sighed.

"Wait," Diogenes said as the Indian commander approached them. "This doesn't have to end in bloodshed. We can negotiate our way out of this."

"Can we?"

"I think so. If they wanted to kill us, they would have ambushed instead of just surrounding us like this. Let me try to talk to them. If that doesn't work… We will have to make our last stand here."

"Would be quite a sorry end to our campaign... Maybe we should have stayed in Bactria and fought until the bitter end as you wanted, after all..."

"Maybe. But I'm not giving up hope now, not after everything that we have been through to get here."

The Indian commander stopped in front of the Greek general and called for one of his officers in a few moments.

"Good evening, gentlemen. Do any of you speak Greek, by chance? It would make communication between us much easier," Diogenes asked.

"I do," the Indian officer stepped forward and replied. "I am fluent in both Sanskrit and Greek and have been assigned by our general to be the interpreter for this occasion."

"I am glad to hear that. In that case, I would like to know why my men have been surrounded by your soldiers in such a manner. We are only passing through, no harm intended."

"Are you the leader of these troops?"

"I am. General Diogenes, with Nicomedes here being my second-in-command."

"Well, general, your troops are trespassing in the territory that belongs to the Kingdom of Gandhara. There have also been reports of supposedly Greek soldiers pillaging our villages, so we have been instructed to apprehend you and everyone in your command."

"I apologize for any harm we may have caused to your realm. But I doubt you would really want to apprehend us. We serve Antiochus, the ruler of the Seleucid Empire. I am sure he would reward you greatly if he heard that you helped his troops. Or, if he got news of you harming us... the consequences would be most dire..."

The translator consulted with the Indian general, before returning to Diogenes.

"Seleucids, huh? You are far from your home. Is Antiochus marching on India now?" the translator asked.

"No, he is not. He only sent us to put down a rebellion in Bactria. He has no intention of invading India."

"This place is still far from Bactria."

"Yes, well, you see… We suffered some losses and had to retreat. We do not wish to overstay our welcome here, only to regain our strength and then get back to the fight. So if you could only let us go, we would be out of your lands in no time."

"Where did you plan to go? After leaving Bactria, that is?"

"Well, we had a few options… But our current destination is Taxila, if you know of such a city."

"Know? I am from there. Taxila is the capital of Gandhara."

"Oh? That is great! That means we are on the right track."

"Yes, and that's why the king instructed us to find and deal with you. If you want to get to Taxila, you will have to go with us."

"Very well. We will follow you."

"I don't think that's a great idea, could be a trap," Nicomedes cautioned.

"Do you have any better alternatives? Ones that do not involve us getting immediately trampled on by their elephants?"

"Not really…"

"Then we will follow the Indians."

After a few more days of marching, the soldiers finally reached Taxila. Some Greeks expressed their dissatisfaction with the situation, arguing that they were now prisoners being led to their slaughter, but most trusted Diogenes and were relieved to have finally reached the city. The Greeks were allowed to enter it, though at first most of them were restricted to its outermost part, away from the center and the palatial district. Diogenes and Nicomedes were allowed to proceed further, but Diogenes left Nicomedes to oversee the troops and went to see the king by himself.

Taxila was a moderately large city, though it had quite a varied population. Most were Indians, but there were also many Persians, and even some Greeks, as the city had previously been part of the Achaemenid, Macedonian, and Mauryan empires before seceding along with the rest of Gandhara. The city stood on the Grand Trunk Road, which was constructed by the Mauryas and went through northern India to connect the westernmost and easternmost portions of the empire, and it brought many merchants and other travelers to Taxila. The city also hosted a unique center of learning, consisting of several monasteries engaged in the teaching of Buddhism and Vedism, the two main religions in India. However, law, medicine, military science, elephant husbandry, archery, and other subjects were also taught in this institution, and so Taxila had become a popular destination for prospective students from all over northern India in the last few decades.

Diogenes, however, had no time for sightseeing at the moment and went straight to the royal palace to meet the king, as he was told that the ruler was expecting him. The palace had formerly belonged to the Mauryan governor of the region, but had been repurposed to serve as the seat of power for independent Gandharan kings. Currently this title was held by Sophagasenus, a newly enthroned ruler who almost immediately declared the full independence of his realm and began raising a personal army to protect it – though Gandhara had unofficially been independent for a couple decades, with the Mauryan Empire continuously losing influence in its borderlands. Still, Sophagasenus wanted to officially confirm this status and gain more legitimacy this way, and so he proclaimed the secession of his small kingdom, though one that was growing rapidly.

"Your highness, thank you for seeing me," Diogenes bowed as he entered the throne room of the king in the palace. "And thank you for granting safe passage for my troops to this great city, it is most appreciated."

"You are most welcome, general. Diogenes, is it?" Sophagasenus asked in Greek. "I have been taught your language, by the way, so there will be no need to interpreters."

"Yes, indeed. General Diogenes, serving my king Antiochus."

"That's good. A friend of Antiochus is a friend of mine."

"I am very glad to hear that. Have you two met already?"

"No, but I had been contacted by him. Antiochus informed me that he would support my campaigns against the Mauryas."

"I see…"

"Though he is not here, is he?"

"No, unfortunately not. A war broke out in the Mediterranean and he had to leave to fight there."

"So he left you in charge of the eastern front, is that correct?"

"Yes, I was made the general of the army left in Bactria."

"But you were defeated."

"Well… Yes, that is correct. The Bactrians overwhelmed my forces, and we had to retreat. This is why those of us who still remain are here in India. We are trying to escape the Bactrian soldiers and recover our strength so we could strike back and fulfill our king's mission at last."

"A noble goal indeed."

"Would you be willing to help us?"

"I might. What do you need?"

"Supplies, weapons, a place to stay and rest in for a while… And, I know this may sound like too much, the help of your soldiers against the Bactrians, if that is possible."

"Those are hefty requests."

"I know, your highness, and I would understand if you refused. But, if you did help us, I am sure Antiochus would reward you greatly, especially once he gets back here with all his plundered riches from the west."

"I see… Well, in any event, I'm afraid I can't supply you with much right now. My soldiers are fighting enemies all around, from the Mauryas to the various other kingdoms which have emerged near us, as well as the resurgent barbarian tribes, and not much can be spared. But I do see a path forward that could help both of us, especially since we are both friends of Antiochus. You do not have that many soldiers left, from what I have seen, but you do have knowledge of Greek military tactics. Meanwhile my realm is full of men who are ready to fight, but they are untrained and have little to no experience in battle. Do you see where I am going with this?"

"I think I do."

"You could leave right now and search for a better place for your men. Or you could help train my officers and soldiers and aid them in battle, guaranteeing victory against any local foes who stand against me. In return, you would all have free access to Taxila, as well as other cities in my realm, to stay in and enjoy yourselves for as long as you wish. And you would receive as many supplies and weapons as I can give you. I am sure this would only increase over time, as we crush one opponent after another and take their cities. Finally, once your troops are ready, and my realm is secure, we could march together to Bactria and put down their insurrection, as their continued independence threatens my realm just as much as it does yours. What do you say, general?"

"You want us to act as advisors… Well, that doesn't sound too bad. And it's not like we are in any shape to do anything else at this point… Very well, I agree. I will need to consult with my troops about the specifics, but I don't think there will be any issues."

"I am pleased to hear that. I believe this will be a very fruitful partnership indeed. I will send for you once I am in need of your services. In the meantime, have some rest and enjoy my capital. I am sure you will find everything you need to satisfy your desires, both physical and intellectual."

Chapter XXIII

"You are here, at long last. I was beginning to wonder whether you would show up at all. You certainly took your damn time," Hanno Nermun remarked to his guest, while continuing to sip wine and overlook the city of Carthage from his balcony.

"I am a busy man. And that's no way to talk to a suffete, so you should watch your words more carefully," Zimri Germelqart replied, as he joined Hanno in his residence and sat down next to him.

"I will speak however the fuck I wish, you should be the one to watch your tone, boy. Without my help, you would not have got this position. I gave it to you, and I can just as easily take it away. There are hundreds of others clamoring to have it, so I am not short on candidates."

"Have you called me here just to threaten me? I... I could have you arrested for this!"

"Really? I'd love to see you try. I wonder who would be willing to do it for you? Your four personal guards? Everyone else who is armed in the city is now either on Hannibal's side or on my payroll. You don't have many friends here. But I wasn't threatening you, simply reminding you of your place. Making it clear who is actually in charge."

"Fine, fine...I got it. Let's just get down to business."

"Are you ready to listen to me now?"

"Yes, yes, so what is it? What do you want from me?"

"I just want you to do your damn job, that's all."

"Well, I have been doing it. I blocked Hannibal's every move, prevented him from ruining our country even further. I did everything I said I'd do. What the fuck else do you want?"

"For you to be truthful to me, for one. You have failed to report one crucial detail."

"What, am I your personal courier now, supposed to relay every little thing to you every day?"

"If it concerns me or our plan, then yes. That's the whole point of putting you in the damn office. I need eyes and ears on the very inside of this rotting republic."

"I have no idea what you're even talking about. What have I supposedly failed to report?"

"Don't play stupid with me now."

"Is it about Hannibal's new proposals? To permit the use of force in removing non-compliant officers and to retain only one suffete, so that he could have even more power? Well, I've blocked them, so I did what I thought we wanted!"

"Partly, but we will return to that later. No, I was referring to the fact that my spies reported Hannibal's men searching the voting archives, on more than one occasion already. Do you know why that is?"

"Hannibal did accuse me of voter fraud or something of that sort a while back, but I paid it no mind. We are clean, after all… We are, right? Right? Or did you, actually-"

"Does it matter? But no, I didn't manipulate the votes, if that's what you are concerned about. You don't have to worry about it. I have thought about such a solution, certainly, but I discarded the idea. If I had gone ahead with the plan, why would Hannibal be a suffete now?"

"Because he is too popular and no amount of electoral fraud would make his loss believable, so he would have to be allowed to become a suffete anyways?"

"That's true, he is still very popular. But I could have chosen two suffetes instead of just you. Both getting almost the same number of votes, but just a little bit more than the former general."

"So why not take that route?"

"Too risky. Can't have such extreme maneuvers so early in our plan. Besides, Hannibal would still be on the loose, and his support would not evaporate overnight. No, he would still be a threat, which is why he needs to be caught in the act. While he is still a public figure, a suffete committing one blunder after another."

"Fair enough. What's your problem then? Why is it an issue that his thugs are searching the records? They won't find anything to support their case."

"You really believe that, don't you, you goddamn simpleton? You think Hannibal will just accept such an answer and let the matter go? After all he tried already? Didn't you think, for just a moment, that he is going to get what he wants from there, no matter what the truth actually is? That he is just going to fabricate the evidence to indict you?"

"This is ridiculous. It wouldn't work, he would be accused of the same crime himself for tampering with the results!"

"A few years ago? Yes. But now, with the court stacked in his favor? Who knows. He might very well win the case. And then it's over for us."

"But you don't even know if he is attempting that."

"You're right, I don't. But are you willing to risk it all on this assumption? Are you willing to trust Hannibal, of all people, to play fair?"

"That is a good point… What's the plan? How do we get out of this mess?"

"It's simple – Hannibal has already laid down all the cards he had, and now we can turn them against him."

"How, exactly?"

"Let me worry about the specifics, I don't want to overwhelm you with all the details right now…"

"I still need to know what you want me to do though."

"All you need to do is go back to Hannibal and sign his proposed laws."

"What?" Zimri said with complete shock in his voice. "Am I hearing this right? What laws exactly?"

"The two important ones you mentioned – so that there would be one suffete, and the military could remove any undesirables from Byrsa Hill," Hanno continued calmly.

"Are- Are you out of your damn mind?! Have you gone senile? What the fuck-"

"Calm the fuck down, boy, no need to make a scene."

"What do you mean? If I sign these laws, I'm a dead man!"

"You would be if you don't sign them. Then Hannibal would implicate you in a voter fraud conspiracy and remove you from office. And then I would make sure that you are removed from the mortal realm for your incompetence."

"Why do you even care? If that is true, the result is the same. Hannibal removes me one way or another. I should at least go out fighting, rather than surrendering my office with no protest."

"I can't tell you, because I can't afford this information getting leaked to anyone else. But it is of utmost importance. If you agree to step down, Hannibal will remain as the sole suffete. If you don't, you will be removed and replaced with Aradus. We would have two hostile suffetes to deal with. That cannot be allowed to happen again, as even I could do little at that point."

"So I give up and leave willingly? Is that the plan?"

"Yes, precisely. You tell him that you can't handle the pressure anymore, and you give the keys to the republic to Hannibal, so he could do what he wants."

"This is ridiculous."

"Maybe. But life often is. This is the only way forward, though we will have to move fast."

"You do realize what will happen, right? Hannibal will basically have absolute control of the state afterwards. I'm one of the last people preventing him from having that, at least legally."

"Let me worry about that part. You just do as you are told, and it will all be fine. You trust me on this, right?"

"Absolutely not."

"But at least you fear me, which will suffice. I believe I have explained the consequences of your potential failure. But your job entails only signing a couple documents, that's all. A child could easily do it."

"I suppose I have no choice in the matter then. Will I at least be protected from the masses in the aftermath if I agree?"

"Oh, absolutely. One could say you will be set up for life. You got the easiest role in this whole play, you know."

"There are worse fates, I suppose. I'll do as you ask. I'll sign the laws. And I pray that you know what you are doing."

"I know that very well. I may be old, but I am as sharp as ever. Now, go. There is no time to waste."

"Now? Right now?"

"Yes! I told you, time is of the essence. And from now on, until this immediate situation is resolved, report everything to me. I don't want any more surprises like before."

"I can't imagine there will be much left to report…"

"Maybe not. But my instructions still stand."

"Hannibal! You're still here, I see. That's good," Zimri said as he entered his co-suffete's office on Byrsa Hill.

"Why, yes, I am," Hannibal replied. "Still have some matters to deal with after my recent meeting with the senate. Though I am surprised to see you here at this hour. What do you want?"

"I was thinking about it for a long while… But I have made my decision. I am looking forward to finally putting an end to this useless and tiring conflict between us."

"Is that so? Well, I'm listening."

"I'll admit it, you won. I can no longer fight you, and I don't want to end up like the Romans, so that's it – I surrender. I'll sign your laws so we can be done with it for good."

"I am very glad to hear it. But why the sudden change in your stance?"

"I just can't handle it anymore. Your supporters keep attacking me, both verbally and physically, I can't do any useful work because I am constantly preoccupied with shutting down your proposals, and with you now looking into the voting records... Not to say that there was any foul play, but being implicated in such a scandal would be terrible for my reputation, no matter the outcome. Besides, like you said – I am just a puppet of the senators, who are using me to fight your laws, and I am tired of serving their needs. They can reap what they have sown themselves."

"It is most fortunate that you have finally seen reason and acknowledged the need for these reforms, if Carthage is to have a better future."

"Oh, please. Don't think for a second that I am on your side now somehow. I am just tired of this and wish to leave the capital... To return to the peace and quiet in my country estate and spend the rest of my time there. You can burn Carthage down for all I care."

"In any event, I appreciate the gesture."

"Just... Call off your men. There is no reason for them to harass me or my family even more."

"Rest assured, you will no longer be troubled by any of my followers. Granted, they should not have resorted to such measures in the first place, but there is only so much I can do to control them. From now on, I will make sure to bring anyone who causes you harm to full justice, as you are a citizen of Carthage like any other, and deserve to have the appropriate treatment."

"Thank you, that's all I need."

"I could even arrange for you to be guarded by some of my most trusted soldiers. The senators may feel betrayed by your actions and may want to retaliate. I am willing to help you whether this storm in any way I can."

"That will not be necessary. I have my own guards, and I trust them enough."

"Very well. But the offer will continue to stand, if you ever change your mind. You are a very important part of this process to transform Carthage, and I always make sure to treat my allies well – even if you still don't consider yourself as one."

"Yes, I got it. Let's just get this over with. I have already made up my mind, you don't need to convince me of anything. Just give me the documents."

"Of course. Believe me, I don't want to prolong this process either," Hannibal placed two papyri documents on the table, in front of Zimri, and gave him a pen and a bottle of ink. "I just need your signature here... And here."

"Tanit forgive me..." Zimri sighed as he put his signature down slowly on both documents. "It's done."

"Thank you."

"Is this it? Am I out of my job now?"

"Well, not quite yet. The single suffete law still needs senate approval. That could take up to a week, with its busy schedule and all the drama happening here. But it will be approved, I am sure of it. I managed to bend the senate to my will more than once, and this proposal is already endorsed by both of us, so I imagine there will be little opposition left."

"I'll start packing up then. Leave everything nice and tidy for when you are in total and undisputed control of the country."

"You think I'm trying to become a dictator, don't you?"

"Trying? You have always been one. In Iberia, in Italy, and now here in Carthage. That's your nature. Who you have always been."

"All I am trying to do is preserve and increase the prosperity of our republic, as well as that of its citizens. And if that requires going against some ancient laws, so be it. You can't move forward without breaking some things in the way."

"Maybe you are right. You did win us the war. Let's now hope you can win the peace too."

Chapter XXIV

With the combined might of the Seleucid and Macedonian armies, it did not take long for the city of Ephesus to fall. Other Ionian cities to the south followed, but the troop advance was stopped in Halicarnassus, which proved to be a more difficult obstacle to capture than initially expected. The island of Rhodes, a long-time ally of the Ptolemies, had joined the war against Philip and Antiochus, fearing their total domination of the region, and sent ships and soldiers to reinforce the now besieged city. The two kings had no time to spare, and so agreed to deal with this issue later, with Antiochus continuing his march east, and Philip sailing back to Macedon to fight the Peloponnesians, leaving a token force under general Alcetas to prevent the Ptolemaic and Rhodian forces from breaking out.

Antiochus also made one more stop in Anatolia before leaving for the Levant. This time it was the city of Seleucia in Pamphylia, a regional Ptolemaic stronghold. The irony of the Seleucids now having to fight to take this city was not lost on Antiochus, and so for him it was not only a strategic target, but also one for propaganda purposes and raising morale. The town was founded by Seleucus I but later taken by the Ptolemies, and so Antiochus insisted on righting this wrong and returning Seleucia back to its original masters. For this purpose, he left general Polyxenidas in charge of the siege, who was also later supposed to launch a naval attack on Cyprus and from there rejoin his king in the Levant – or even Egypt, if the king had made it that far by then. With Anatolia now secure, Antiochus marched forward with the rest of his army into the Levant, ready to meet the bulk of the Egyptian army on the battlefield.

Upon reaching Apamea, Antiochus joined forces with his general and right-hand man Zeuxis, who had been looking over the region and fending off Ptolemaic probing attacks while the king was away. Antiochus now had an army of about fifty thousand soldiers at his disposal, consisting of everything from phalangites and skirmishers to elite cavalry and even some war elephants, though all the men were Greeks. It did not take long for them to find their opponents – shortly after crossing into Ptolemaic held lands, just north of the city of Sidon, the Seleucids encountered the main enemy force. Led by general Scopas, this was a slightly larger army, and one that was more ethnically diverse, as it included not only Greeks, but also native Egyptians, Nabataean and Arab mercenaries, Aetolians, and other peoples from around the Eastern Mediterranean. Egypt had far fewer Greeks than Macedon or the Seleucid Empire, and manpower was hard to come by – especially now, as the Ptolemies were fighting in southern Egypt, Anatolia, and the Levant at the same time – and so enlisting the aid of the natives, as well as mercenary companies, had become standard practice decades ago. Antiochus refused to engage in such practices, deeming the natives and the mercenaries as untrained and unreliable, while the Egyptians were happy to continue with this method. Ptolemy IV had employed this strategy to win the previous war against Antiochus, and the new leadership in Alexandria hoped that the same would apply in this conflict as well.

The battle began as Antiochus ordered his cataphracts – the elite heavy armed and armored cavalry, which originated in Persia and was adopted by Antiochus, after his campaigns in the east – in the center to charge into and weaken the enemy phalanx, headed by the Egyptian commander Aeropus. Zeuxis, commanding the right wing of the Seleucid forces, and Nicolaus, in charge of the left wing, stayed on the defense along with their light infantry and light cavalry forces, awaiting further orders. Scopas, meanwhile, deployed his own cavalry to counter the Seleucid charge and protect his infantry, but it went rather poorly for the Aetolian general. The Egyptian cavalrymen were far less armored and trained than the Seleucid cataphracts, and soon crumbled under the pressure, suffering heavy casualties while inflicting few. It was now up to the Egyptian phalanx to defend against the cavalry charge. To the relief of Scopas, the phalanx held the line and was not defeated as easily. This resulted in a stalemate for a while, but Antiochus was undeterred. He now sent Zeuxis to engage the enemy, and the general's men soon began clashing with the native Egyptians and the Aetolians on the coastal side of the battlefield.

"Everything is going according to plan," Scopas smiled as he was overlooking the battlefield.

"How so? I know it's not my place to question your tactical skills, but I believe we are losing men at a more rapid rate than our enemies," Aeropus replied. "And they have not even sent out the elephants yet…"

"You are right that it's not your place to question my orders. You clearly don't know anything about elephant warfare, huh?"

"Well, I think I know a thing or two…"

"Clearly not the important bits though. Why do you think I brought all these Arabs with their camels here? There are cheaper mercenaries closer to home."

"For their camels then, I presume?"

"Yes. We can scare the elephants with our camels and have them turn around to crush the Seleucid soldiers, giving us an easy victory."

"How would that work, exactly?"

"The soldiers tied some straws around the camels and are going to set them on fire once I give the order. The camels will then rush forward and completely disrupt the elephant attack, turning it against our enemies."

"But… why? Why would the elephants be scared of camels, which are much smaller than them?"

"I don't fucking know, I'm a general, not a goddamn animal handler. Ask the Indians or one of their elephant gods."

"Well, I just hope it works as you expect."

"It will, don't you worry. Antiochus doesn't know what's coming for him."

Not too long after, Antiochus finally gave the word to unleash the elephants, which were sent to the center of the battle to deal with the Ptolemaic phalanx, weakened by the repeated cataphract charges. The Seleucid troops stepped back and made way for the beasts, who were now about to trample the scared and exhausted phalangites, and the even more terrified native Egyptians around them. However, Aeropus commanded them to stand their ground, as he had been told by his superior.

Upon seeing the elephants begin their charge, Scopas wasted no time and put his camel counterattack plan to action. The straws were set alight, and the camels were set loose from the general's right side in the direction of the elephants. They reached the intended targets soon enough, though the effect was not what Scopas had envisioned, to his slowly building dismay. The elephants were indeed terrified of the flaming and screaming camels, but they were already upon the Ptolemaic troops, and so their trampling only intensified. The elephants also did not turn around and rush back to the Seleucids, as Scopas had hoped, but instead turned and dashed to their right. Some Egyptians were crushed along the way, but the main obstacle for the elephants now was the Aetolian unit, completely unaware of what was coming for them. The Seleucid forces managed to pull back just in time, with relatively few casualties, but the Aetolians were not so lucky, as their formation was now completely destroyed by the dozens of elephants trying to escape the battle and crushing anyone in their way.

"What in the name of Zeus is happening there?" Antiochus asked in disbelief as he was witnessing the unfolding carnage.

"Our elephants seem to have… strayed away from their intended path," Nicolaus replied, similarly confused. "I think the camels scared them and forced them to go right."

"Not what I had hoped for…"

"They are making good work of the Aetolians though, by the looks of it," Nicolaus shrugged. "Maybe they can still serve our needs."

"You may be right. And I believe Zeuxis made it out of there in one piece, I can see his men pulling back in order. We need to regroup and strike back while the Egyptians are still disorganized."

"At the center, perhaps? The elephants still cut through there and inflicted some casualties. And the camels are now running wild and disrupting the formations. It's still a complete mess there by the looks of it. If we attacked now, we could destroy them completely."

"That's good thinking, general. It's time to finish this."

Once Zeuxis returned with his men to Antiochus, the army was quickly reorganized and, after the king gave the order, descended on the still reeling Ptolemaic center. The Egyptians had managed to kill all the remaining camels which were still causing them trouble, and the elephants were now far away enough to not be a concern – at the expense of almost the entire Aetolian regiment – but the soldiers were still not at all prepared for what was to come. They were struck by Nicolaus and his infantry and cavalry flanking from the left, with this unit still being at full strength, then by the forces under Zeuxis from the right in the same manner, and finally pummeled by the Seleucid own phalanx directly under Antiochus in the very center. The Nabataeans and Arabs were sent to relieve the Ptolemaic phalangites, but this had little effect, as these mercenaries were now nowhere as effective as they had been before, having lost most of their camels.

The battle soon turned into a massacre. A portion of the Ptolemaic army was completely encircled and could not break out, with Antiochus and his generals proceeding to eliminate what remained of it. The native Egyptians further out, seeing how desperate the situation had become, started fleeing in all directions to the south, fearing what other horrors could be unleashed on them if they continued fighting. The Aetolians were similarly unwilling to get back into the fight and retreated south, despite Scopas shouting and trying to get them to stay.

"Get the fuck back into the fight, you cowards!" Scopas screamed as hundreds were rushing past him. "I will have you all burned alive if you retreat without my permission! You hear that? All of you, and your families too! Fuck!"

"General-" Aeropus rode up to him.

"What? What are you doing here? You should be out there fighting!"

"It's... It's over... The battle's lost, general."

"No... No, it can't be. Not like that. We, we still have the Arabs, right? What the fuck are they doing?"

"Revolting, by the looks of it. Or deserting. They, uh... I don't think they are going to be helping us anymore."

"What? Why?"

"They didn't really like what you did with their camels. And how this whole battle turned out afterwards... Some are surrendering, I think. Others are just fleeing. The east is mostly open, so no one is stopping them. And the Nabataeans are following behind them..."

"And this is the service I receive after paying them all that gold?! Who the fuck do they think they are? Who- I should fucking kill them all for this treachery!"

"Maybe, but that has to dealt with later. Right now there are more pressing matters. I think it would be wise to call for a retreat. To save what remains of our forces..."

"What remains... How many do we even have left?"

"Few... Far fewer than I would be comfortable with. We could maybe save twenty thousand in the best-case scenario."

"Twenty thousand, that's- By the gods..."

"Better than nothing. And it's not the battle for Alexandria yet. There is no reason to fight to our deaths in this wretched land."

"Yes, you're right. Fine, we shall retreat... Head south, regroup in some fortified and loyal town... I'll figure the rest out later. Just get whoever you can out and follow me."

The Battle of Sidon was a decisive victory for Antiochus. While the Seleucids suffered a few thousand casualties and lost most of their elephants, their opponents left the battle far worse off. By the time Scopas was out of reach of his enemies, he only had about fifteen thousand Egyptian and Greek soldiers with him, with everyone else having been killed or captured by the Seleucids or deserted the army. Scopas continued retreating south, leaving the way into Ptolemaic Levant open for Antiochus.

The Seleucid leader's first target, naturally, was the city of Sidon, which agreed to surrender immediately, with no resistance. The rulers of the city had no intention of dying for their overlords in Egypt, especially after seeing the shattered remnants of the Ptolemaic army fleeing past the city. The other Phoenician cities – including Byblos, Tyre, and Ptolemais – soon did the same, simply to side with the winning faction, as most rulers in the region did not care whether the monarch they served was based in Antioch or Alexandria.

"A great victory, my king," Zeuxis congratulated Antiochus, joining him on the palace balcony, as the Seleucids were celebrating their latest success in Ptolemais. "Just one battle, and it was enough to get all of Phoenicia to submit to us. These merchants seem to understand which way the wind is blowing."

"Thank you. You did quite well there too, Zeuxis, saving my soldiers from certain doom at the feet of the elephants," Antiochus chuckled. "Certainly one of the more interesting battles I've witnessed."

"Indeed. But many more are to come. Are you ready for them?"

"Absolutely. If this is the best the Ptolemies can throw at us, I think we will be just fine. I don't know what idiot was in charge of this massive blunder, but the leaders in Alexandria must really be lacking good military strategists."

"Best not to become overconfident though. It is still just the very start of the war… Who knows what may happen yet."

"I do. I know that this time the Ptolemaic realm will finally buckle under my forces and Egypt will finally be mine."

"Let us hope that comes to fruition. Where are you planning on taking us next?"

"Further south, of course. But not immediately, we'll stay here for a while and consolidate our gains. Ptolemais will become our military headquarters for the time being."

"I see. But may I ask – why the delay? Shouldn't we be pressing on as soon as possible? We should not give the Ptolemies any time to recover."

"Yes, that's true, but I am still waiting for Polyxenidas to secure Cyprus, I'll need his expertise and men for the invasion of Egypt. And don't think that the Ptolemies will get any rest in the Levant either. I have some allies in mind who could help keep them busy."

A couple weeks later Antiochus, with a small retinue of guards, left the city to attend a secret meeting in a designated place to the east. He had been planning it for months, and now the time for it finally came, as the king met his contact. This was Simon II, the High Priest of Israel – the highest ranking Jewish religious leader. He had expressed interest in joining the Seleucid side before, and after the Battle of Sidon, having realized how weak the Ptolemies had become, agreed to an informal meeting with Antiochus.

"Good evening, high priest," Antiochus greeted him. "I am glad we finally have a chance to meet."

"Likewise, your highness," Simon replied in Greek. "I have heard of your victories, they are impressive indeed. I am willing to hear what you have to say."

"You are the most revered Jewish figure, and your words hold a lot of influence. My armies are marching south soon, on their way to Egypt, and so the help of your Israelites would be most valuable."

"They are not my Israelites. They only bow before Yahweh."

"Right, but you are his... voice. His most loyal servant on this earth. Forgive me for not knowing how the worship of your god works, but one thing is quite clear in any event – you could undoubtedly rally the people in this land to rise up against the Ptolemies."

"I could, yes. That is possible. The question is – why would I do that though? What are we to gain from switching sides?"

"You would free yourselves from the tyranny of the Ptolemies. From being occupied by the Egyptians. Your people once fled Egypt, escaping slavery on the Nile to settle in this land, am I wrong? And now the Egyptians once again lord over you. But you have an opportunity to take revenge and free your people for good."

"The exodus from Egypt happened a millennium ago. And the Egyptians are now hardly better off than we are, considering that Egypt is ruled by Greeks. As is your realm. So I fail to see the difference and the need for us to abandon one Greek king for another."

"That is a fair point. But that's even more reason to abandon the pharaoh now. You clearly hold no loyalty to him, so why cling to his dying empire? My realm is the future of the Greek world, and my allies will be rewarded handsomely after the war is over."

"And you plan on removing the Ptolemies from the picture entirely?"

"Absolutely. Their holdouts are falling one by one, their armies are scattering, while mine are marching south with no serious obstacles in sight. The Ptolemies are also fighting Macedon in the north and local rebels in the south, and may soon be also fighting Carthage in the west. The realm's days are numbered. But your people can hasten this fall even more and be rewarded for your efforts."

"But Israel would still not be independent. It would now just be a part of your empire, I assume."

"Correct. Unfortunately, Israelites live on this crucial intersection between Africa and Asia, and so hardly any empire could allow it to remain independent. Yet that does not mean that they cannot live happy and fulfilling lives. If their religion, language, and traditions are respected, why would it matter if their region is not legally independent? This is not Carthage, we don't have elections on this side of the Mediterranean, so do the people really care whether their king is Greek or Jewish?"

"The Ptolemies could make the same argument."

"The difference is that I mean it. The Ptolemies have not really respected you, have they? For them, this region is nothing more than a buffer zone to slow down any invaders before they get to Egypt. Destined to perpetually remain a warzone. Under my rule, that would no longer be the case. Egypt and the Levant would be under one kingdom, and Israel would be just as safe as any other province, while also benefiting greatly from intercontinental trade of my expansive realm."

"That is all true. But why should we rise to help you? Why should we risk our lives fighting the Ptolemies, while we could instead just wait for your soldiers to push them out?"

"You could do that, but the war would last longer. Don't you want to help your people achieve prosperity sooner? You have been preparing for this, after all. I know that your father had refused to pay taxes to the pharaoh and almost got into a war because of that. And you have been fortifying Jerusalem and other towns – repairing walls, digging water wells, and preparing for a siege in all the other ways. That certainly does look like a man who is ready to go to war. And now is the perfect time to strike."

"That still does not answer my question."

"As I said, I am a generous man to my allies. For one, how about lowered taxes? I have many other regions to turn to for additional income. And no conscription of Jews. I enlist only Greeks into my army, while the rulers in Alexandria are now taking everyone they can find in an attempt to stop my advance. So you will never have to worry about that. Finally, an investment from my treasury – for helping you restore your temples, build new facilities, and make your towns look like proper Greek cities, which would surely attract more merchants and craftsmen here and make the region even wealthier."

"Many Jews would reject such proposals outright. Some take a very negative view of Hellenization and would prefer to keep our lands as they are and have been for centuries."

"Some, yes. But you are not one of those orthodox Jews now, are you? You are someone who can see the benefits of integrating into the Greek world. Of becoming a truly civilized land."

"I am a… proponent of Hellenization, yes. I can see how it would bring us a lot of good."

"That's all I need. And with both of us on the same side, you won't need to worry about any opposition from the conservatives. If you help me win this war, of course."

"I see. That does sound reasonable."

"And maybe, once this is over, we can return to the discussion about the state of this land. Not independence, but something that is acceptable to both sides could be arranged. I have several kingdoms in the north whose rulers have pledged their allegiance to me, but still enjoy considerable autonomy. Israel could one day become such a case as well."

"Very well. I will return to Jerusalem and tell everyone to rise up against the Ptolemies. The city will be taken, and the revolt will soon spread across the entire region. And we will await the arrival of your soldiers."

"Good. You have made the right choice, high priest. I wish you luck in your efforts."

"Thank you. If there is nothing else, I will depart now, as it is a long journey south. Yahweh be with you."

"And Zeus with you."

Chapter XXV

Euthydemus had succeeded in securing his kingdom and driving the Seleucid invaders out of Bactria. With the army commanded by Diogenes and Nicomedes shattered and its remains now scattered in India, the king had no more immediate threats to worry about. But he did not wish to simply stay in Bactria, and instead decided to take advantage of the weakened Seleucid front by striking back at the empire. After reorganizing the army and integrating the defecting Seleucid troops into it, Euthydemus once again left the capital in the care of his son Demetrius and headed west to begin his new campaign. Having received reports that Antiochus was now tied down in a war against Egypt, the Bactrian king was confident that he could push far into the Seleucid realm and greatly extend his own kingdom – or at least negotiate a very favorable treaty with Antiochus.

The king was not wrong in this assessment, at least at first, as there was no one fighting back when the army of tens of thousands of hoplites and hundreds of war elephants crossed the unofficial demarcation line. However, the army soon came upon its first major obstacle – the fortress city of Alexandria Ariana – the gateway between Iran and Bactria. This was one of the many Greek colonies founded by Alexander III in the east during his campaigns, and it now served as the easternmost stronghold of the Seleucid Empire. Naturally, Euthydemus committed to taking it and ordered his men to surround the city and begin siege preparations.

"By the order of king Euthydemus of Bactria, the first of his name, Alexandria must stand down at once and allow his highness to enter the city along with his soldiers," an envoy sent by Euthydemus proclaimed to the archon – chief magistrate of the city – Polydius, after being allowed into Alexandria to deliver the terms. "If you accept, your city will be treated with the respect given to all the cities under the king's protection. However, failure to comply will result in a total siege where no one's life in Alexandria could be guaranteed anymore. You can deliberate on the decision for however long you wish, but the longer you resist, the more your people will suffer."

"Last time I checked, Antiochus was my king, not Euthydemus," Polydius replied dryly.

"That may have been so, but not anymore. This land is now in the hands of Euthydemus – as you can clearly see if you look over the walls in any direction. It would be wise to acknowledge this new reality."

"And our army that passed through here not too long ago – where is it now?"

"We have crushed it. Completely. But many have joined our king and are now marching alongside his highness. Euthydemus is an honorable king and has no ill will towards those who submit willingly. But he is prepared to punish those who resist and threaten his realm in doing so."

"Your king is making a terrible mistake. Antiochus will return to the east soon and he will restore order here."

"I don't think even you believe that, archon. Antiochus and all his soldiers are stuck in the Levant, fighting the Egyptians. He is not coming to save you. But I won't press the issue further. You know the terms and you know the outcomes. Let us know if you change your mind, so that unnecessary bloodshed could be avoided."

The envoy left the city, and with that, the siege of Alexandria Ariana officially began. The soldiers of Euthydemus wasted no time and immediately began the construction of siege equipment, including siege towers and catapults. In the meantime, the others made sure to cut off all the supply lines to Alexandria while securing the ones leading back to Bactria, so that the army could be properly maintained and fed for however long it took. While this was not the preferred outcome for Euthydemus, it was the expected one, and so the king remained just as calm as before, carefully laying down the plans for the siege and the various ways to take the city.

The opposite was true in Alexandria Ariana, as the people immediately started panicking and the reassurances given by Polydius did not help much. The city was caught unprepared and so were the people, who had no time to flee and were now stuck in an uncertain siege. The city had some supplies and a decently sized garrison, but the prospects of outlasting their opponents still looked grim, and success still hinged on Antiochus arriving in time to relieve the city – an idea that some in Alexandria believed was as far removed from reality as the gods themselves descending from Mount Olympus to fight the Bactrians. Yet Polydius remained committed to the fight, with support from some city officials – but also opposition from just as many – holding out some hope that help would arrive and that his resistance would be vindicated.

Despite the siege, Polydius managed to get a few of his men out of the city, so they could inform Antiochus of the situation and request help. After sneaking out, they got on the fastest horses they could find and rode straight for Antioch, from where they continued to the last known location of the Seleucid king. In the meantime, the Bactrian soldiers began their siege and worked tirelessly to build the equipment necessary for its success. Before long, the first siege towers emerged, and so did catapults behind them, while more and more Bactrian soldiers flooded the area and reinforced those who had arrived first. Still, there were no casualties yet, and so Polydius argued in favor of staying the course.

A few weeks later, the archon finally received word back from the west. Antioch had indeed received the message, yet, to the dismay of Polydius, refused to send any additional soldiers and ordered the archon to make do with the resources and manpower available locally, as the king was committed to the campaign in the Levant and needed everyone in his army there. The Bactrian threat was dismissed as a more minor nuisance and unworthy of much attention compared to Egypt, with Antiochus pledging to retake it only after the war in the west was over. This made Polydius snap, as he angrily crumpled the letter with the king's answer and threw it away. The city was running out of supplies, the soldiers were demoralized, and Euthydemus was finally ready for his first major assault. Having realized that no help was coming, and that Alexandria had to look out for itself, the archon made his decision clear to the citizens the same day. He denounced Antiochus and announced the planned surrender of the city. While some were unhappy with such a state of affairs, most did not protest and were quite relieved to hear that the siege would be lifted. With Alexandria Ariana being so far away from the core of the Seleucid realm, most people in the city did not care much for their king – and far fewer were willing to die for him – and so the surrender to Euthydemus was seen as the best possible option.

The Bactrians received this news in the evening, and some began celebrating their first victory already. The next morning, the gates of the city were opened, and king Euthydemus entered it with a retinue of his most elite men. He proceeded through the main street to the acropolis of the city, where the archon resided, with some citizens welcoming and cheering for the king along the way. Euthydemus soon reached the archon and dismounted from his horse to face the city's ruler.

"Welcome to Alexandria, your highness. I, archon Polydius of Seleucia, pledge myself and this city to you, my king," Polydius kneeled before Euthydemus and bowed his head.

"Rise, Polydius. You have chosen well," Euthydemus replied. "It is good that you have taken this step before any blood has been spilled."

"Of course, my king. I should have done it sooner, but I had to convince the citizens to stand down and accept the terms first, so that the transition would proceed without issues."

"So far it has indeed been smooth. You saved me the trouble of having to forcefully take this nice city and then rebuild, repopulate, and resupply it... Would have been a shame to let the infrastructure already in place go to waste, especially in such a desolate area."

"Absolutely, my king, I completely agree. Some officials argued with me over this matter, but luckily more reasonable voices prevailed."

"I assume Antiochus is not very popular around here, is he?"

"Oh, definitely not, your highness. He spends all his time on the Mediterranean coast in the west, and treats the eastern provinces as completely unworthy of his attention, unless it's time to pay our taxes to his treasury in Antioch. We hold no loyalty to that man and are ready to help you fight him."

"As I thought. Yes, the Seleucids never cared much for the east – giving away our lands to the Indians, allowing barbarians to overrun entire provinces, and treating the region as a backwater. Well, I was not going to stand for it. I rejected the rule from Antioch and took control of the land. And now Bactria is more prosperous than ever. With your city being the latest beneficiary."

"Of course. And I thank you for this opportunity, your highness."

"I will use this city as my temporary headquarters and a launching point for a campaign deeper into Seleucid lands. I assume you have no problem with hosting us here for the time being?"

"No... absolutely not," Polydius twitched. "Would be my pleasure. Though... if it's not a secret, of course... how long will it be until your army begins its advance?"

"That depends. Could be a few weeks. Or months. Antiochus transgressed greatly by invading my realm, and he will pay. My men will march as far as they can, and then some more, so that he would be taught a proper lesson. That means I will need time to prepare and assemble a force capable of challenging him. Luckily for us, the king is busy fighting the Egyptians and does not care much for the east, as you have mentioned. We have plenty of time."

"It appears that we do, my king…"

"There is a lot of work to be done, Polydius. But that can wait until tomorrow, as we have already covered enough ground today… Now, could you point me to your main temple in the city? It would be a sacrilege to not give an offering to the gods after such a quick first victory."

Chapter XXVI

With Zimri having signed his co-suffete's laws, Hannibal was now free to do as he pleased in Byrsa Hill, with no one to stop his plans anymore. He first presented the law on the restructuring of the suffete's post – leaving only one suffete rather than two, and substantially increasing the powers granted to the man in this position – to the senate, so he could get its final required approval. Many were outraged at this, but Hannibal employed similar tactics as he had the previous time, and so secured the senate's vote with little trouble.

After the law was officially ratified, Hannibal effectively became the sole ruler of Carthage, with his powers now rivaling those of some monarchs. He had no co-suffete to hinder him, and he no longer needed the senate's approval for his actions, as the new law rendered the senate as little more than an advisory body, which could safely be ignored if one wished so. Hannibal was initially surprised by the lack of resistance in the senate in the last days of the old order still being in place, as he expected a difficult fight from his most serious opponents. Instead, the senate chamber became an almost desolate place, more of a museum exhibit and a memory of the republic's past, rather than a core government entity. Most senators appeared to have simply resigned to their fate, and abandoned the hill – sometimes even the capital itself – having given up on any more attempts to speak to Hannibal. Nonetheless, the former general was pleased with this turn of events, and continued going according to his plan.

The announcement of these changes had quite a divisive reaction in the city, as some celebrated the changes, hoping that Hannibal will now be able to set the country on a new course to greatness, while others protested the new laws and called Hannibal a dictator, a tyrant, and a wannabe king, among other things. Riots soon broke out and continued for a few days, with Hannibal's supporters and opponents now clashing openly in the streets on many occasions. The suffete deployed the army in response, in order to secure the capital during this transitional period and quell any unrest that was causing too much of a disruption to normal life. The troops arrived soon, but even their presence was not enough to stop the violence in the streets, and in some cases even intensified it. While some of his allies advised crushing the riots and dealing with the protestors ruthlessly, Hannibal decided against this idea, not wanting that much blood on his hands – especially civilian, and especially this early in his new role as the sole head of state. Thus, he left the situation as it was and hoped that it would resolve itself soon, without any need for mass killings.

Hannibal instead turned his attention to the few remaining opponents on Byrsa Hill – the judges who had refused to step down from their posts and be replaced by the new elected judges. The suffete could do little against them before, with the Court of 104 being such a revered and powerful institution, but now he had much more power and so decided that it was time to strike. One of his new laws allowed for the use of force to remove officials who were overstaying their welcome, and so Hannibal intended to put it to action, now that he was in the legal right to do so, and the populace at large was distracted by the ongoing chaos in the city.

"Good day, gentlemen," Hannibal proclaimed, as he pushed the doors open into the court chamber. "My arrival here should not be a surprise to any of you. I am sure you already have an idea of why I am here."

"Why, of course we do. To further undermine our republic and its institutions, as you have been doing for years," one judge sneered. "The only question is, what manner of mockery will you employ this time to sink this ship of state even deeper?"

"That is most ironic coming from you, a judge I do not remember getting elected. You must be one of the holdouts, I assume. One of the reasons I have come before you today. People like you are undermining our republic more than anyone! Tell me, are you not the one making a mockery of the state, refusing to move out of your seat for an elected judge and clinging to it with your life, as if defending a besieged fortress?"

"Judges were never meant to be elected! You think the proles know anything about these matters? That they know enough to elect judges, let alone become ones themselves? You have doomed our country, you fool."

"We will stand our ground. You may have neutered the senate, but we will not give away to your tyranny so easily," a second judge added.

"Be that as it may, you have no choice now. Unless you have been elected, you will have to leave and hand over your seat to those who have rightfully earned it."

"And why is that?"

"Because it's the law. And laws apply to judges too, as may be a shock to learn for some of you."

"They are your laws. Your illegitimate laws meant to only weaken and eventually destroy our country."

"Believe whatever you want, but the outcome remains the same no matter what happens. If you don't stand down voluntarily, the soldiers will make quick work of you. And I doubt they will be as patient and negotiable as I am."

"Go on then, send your soldiers in. Do your worst. See how the people like you then, after you send the goddamn army after everyone who disagrees with your madness," another judge laughed.

"Oh, I imagine they will be quite receptive to it. I have many supporters, and they would be most glad to know that I have removed such pests as yourselves, and that the country can once again function properly."

"And what are you going to do, exactly? Arrest us?"

"If it comes to that."

"For what?"

"Obstruction of justice, for one. Though I am sure I could find many more charges for some of you if I wanted. So how about you save us all some trouble, spare yourself the embarrassment, and leave now, while the consequences are still not so severe? I appreciate your stubborn defense, but the time for such games is over now. There are pressing matters that need to be addressed, and I cannot have such insolence in the government right now."

"Why, what could be more important at this point?" the first judge asked. "Do you have another war to wage? Or money to fuel into some pointless campaign started by your brothers in Iberia?"

"Easy for you to say that wars are pointless, when you have never left the comfort of the elite district of the capital. Wars have allowed Carthage to remain rich, powerful, and secure, and for you to retain all the luxuries that you enjoy."

"Keep telling yourself that, general. The last one wouldn't have started in the first place, if not for you."

"If not for me, you would all be speaking Latin right now!" Hannibal snapped. "Or, more likely, be shipped off to toil as slaves in the farms of your Roman overlords. I saved all of you shortsighted idiots! And I don't expect you to be grateful, but I won't tolerate such disruption any longer."

"Once a soldier, always a soldier, huh... Knew you shouldn't be trusted, and that you would sooner or later start treating Carthage as if it was a literal battlefield, resorting to sending soldiers to deal with all of your problems," another judge said.

"Maybe I am. But at least I am not a spineless politician like most of you here, who care for nothing but your personal short-term riches, for which you would gladly sell the country out. Maybe the republic does need a soldier to set it right and make it into a safe and stable place once again. So yes, I will use troops to remove you from here. And I will not be cowed into staying neutral while the rest of the world burns. A great war is unfolding in the east, and I have given my word to Antiochus that I will stand with him once the time comes. And I intend to fulfill this promise, just not before you are dealt with."

"Be our guest. Some of us have no intention of leaving, no matter what threats you conjure."

"Very well. You brought this upon yourselves. Here, take this," Hannibal gave a papyrus scroll with his orders and official seal to a messenger. "Bring it to the commander of the city guard."

The messenger nodded and rushed out to deliver the message.

"The soldiers will be here within an hour. You still have some time to reconsider and flee. Otherwise... I can't guarantee anything, as you will be at the mercy of the troops, and I will not be there to save you. So do as you wish, I am done arguing with you," Hannibal said as he turned around and left the chamber.

After Hannibal's orders were relayed, the commotion in the city intensified, as soldiers were now being redeployed all around and no one was really sure of what was actually happening, though many did suspect that it was part of some important change in Byrsa Hill. Some soldiers secured the harbor, while others reinforced the men already stationed on and around the walls, preventing anyone from entering or leaving the city. Many citizens were enraged at such an unexpected lockdown and protested, but they were told that it was only a temporary measure meant to prevent some suspects from fleeing, which calmed the masses down somewhat.

Finally, after all the entrances to the city had been taken care of, a unit was formed to march into Byrsa Hill and deal with the issues there. It began its march from the barracks in the west, proceeding to head to the central district of the capital. However, the soldiers were soon stopped by the rioting citizens, who were blocking their path, though this did not remain a problem for long. The soldiers were instructed to continue their march until the destination was reached without slowing down for any reason, and were permitted to use any means to clear the way there. Thus, the rioters found themselves pushed out of the way, beaten, and kicked by the troops which were naturally much better armed and trained. Due to the chaos and the lack of information, the rioter ranks included people from both the pro-Hannibal and anti-Hannibal camps, as neither side was sure whether the soldiers would be helping their cause or that of their opponents, and so tried to delay them before it became clear, though that did not have the intended effect.

As the soldiers grew more agitated, both by the protesters blocking their way and the commanders behind them ordering to advance, some unsheathed their swords and cut down the civilians in front of them in anger, resulting in the first deaths of this operation. Realizing that their own life was now very much on the line as well, most civilians scattered, going home or simply relegating the fighting to a different part of the area. The way was now clear for the troops, who soon reached Byrsa Hill and began the climb up.

"It's taking longer than I had hoped," Hannibal said as he was walking through the courtyard with Zel Baldo – his former bodyguard who had recently been promoted to Hannibal's head of security.

"Yes, it's strange," Zel replied. "Already been a few hours and they are still not here. Though they are closing in, if quite slowly."

"Do you know why that's the case? Have your men seen anything?"

"Nothing that I can confirm for certain. There were some conflicts initially, but that appears to have been resolved. Maybe because some officers refused to participate in such a mission? It is quite a controversial move, after all."

"Yes, but it needed to be done, sooner or later."

"Of course. Though the riots also didn't help. Apparently, the soldiers were slowed down by them and eventually started forcing their way through. Resulting in a few... civilian deaths. Or so I've heard."

"That's not good. I expressly forbade these soldiers from killing any civilians. This may inflame tensions even more now and the situation may spiral even further into chaos."

"To be honest, this should have been expected. Such momentous and rapid changes rarely conclude peacefully. And I'm not even saying that you made the wrong call here... but did you really need the city guard for this? Me and my boys could have taken care of this problem alone easily, no need to involve anyone else."

"I appreciate the offer, but I couldn't let you do it. I don't doubt your capabilities, but I can't just go around arresting people with my personal guards. That would set a bad precedent and might make even more people question my actions. No, we need the official soldiers for this job. Even if it seems too much, I still need to go through the proper channels."

"I understand. Though I still don't like it."

The two continued walking, with Hannibal's other guards behind them, until they reached the entrance to the complex, where they expected to meet the arriving soldiers.

"Zimri? Didn't expect to see you," Hannibal said as he noticed his former co-suffete waiting there as well. "What are you still doing here?"

"Oh, well... I needed to collect some things I had forgotten. And I heard what you were planning and so decided to stick around for a while to see it for myself. I hope you don't mind."

"Very well then, that's fine. Enjoy the show. It should be quite interesting indeed."

A few minutes later, the soldiers finally arrived and started pouring into the courtyard, with their commander at the front. Once all of them were in, they stopped, and the commander approached and faced Hannibal.

"Glad you could make it commander," Hannibal greeted him. "Are your men ready to proceed?"

"They are. It will not prove difficult," the commander Astartus Hiram replied.

"Indeed. The court chamber is just ahead and to the right, you will find it-"

"Clearly there is a misunderstanding. We are not here for the judges. We have our target right in front of us."

"Huh? Who, Zimri? He is not causing any trouble."

"No. We are here to remove you from the office."

"Remove me? On whose authority?" Hannibal scoffed.

"Mine," Hanno Nermun spoke as he stepped forward.

"Hanno? What in the name of Baal are you doing here? I thought you had ceased your nonsensical protests after the war and retired for good."

"Someone had to put things right in this wretched city. Your actions have plagued Carthage for long enough. Your disastrous reign ends today."

"This can only end badly for you. Back away now, while you can still save face. This coup of yours will fail miserably if you continue to pursue it, mark my words."

"We shall see about that. Soldiers, apprehend Hannibal. Kill anyone who tries to interfere," Hanno ordered, and his troops immediately pushed forward.

"Form up and defend Hannibal at all costs!" Zel shouted. "We need to get the hill guards here too right now!"

"They have been accounted for," Hanno smiled, as guards responsible for protecting the government complex on the hill arrived from behind Hannibal's group and were then given a simple nod by Hanno to proceed.

Hannibal's security forces were now completely surrounded and severely outnumbered. The skirmish soon turned into a slaughter, as dozens of spears pierced through the men guarding the suffete. They managed to kill a few of their opponents as well, but nowhere near enough to turn the tide of the engagement, the result of which had already been clear from the very start. Zel remained one of the last men standing defending Hannibal, desperately trying to get him to safety. Yet this attempt failed, as Zel was soon pierced through by two spears and cut down like the rest. Hannibal remained the only one from his side, and only because the soldiers were ordered to capture him alive. The suffete tried to fight, but was quickly disarmed and thrown to the ground, from where a couple soldiers picked him up and brought him to Hanno, eagerly awaiting the conclusion of the fight.

"Very good. But don't just stand around now, your work is far from done," Hanno handed a papyrus document to Astartus. "Here are all the senators, judges, and other officials on the hill who are in league with Hannibal. Dispose of them."

Astartus acknowledged the order and led most of his troops further into the complex.

"And you accuse me of destroying our republic?" Hannibal said, spitting blood on the ground. "How is this not any worse?"

"You have to be willing to fight to protect what's important. You should know that."

"The people will never accept you. No matter how many of us you execute."

"On that count you are right. They would not accept me as the ruler of Carthage. Luckily, I don't need any public approval. I have Zimri for that."

"Oh, this little worm? So he was just another pawn of yours?"

"You could say that. But you have clearly underestimated him. For instance, how you failed to notice the fact that he has been slowly replacing the guards on this hill with ones loyal to me. Such a little thing, but turned out to be so important, wouldn't you say?"

"Zimri, you fucking rat-"

"I'm sorry, Hannibal," Zimri approached the kneeling suffete in horror. "I- I did not- I had no idea it would turn to this! It wasn't supposed to be such a massacre, it's-"

"Oh, shut up. Leave us and go prepare your speech if you can't handle this scene," Hanno told him.

"So Zimri will replace me as the suffete. Is that the plan here?" Hannibal asked.

"He will. And surely, if such a weak and spineless man with a nearly spotless record did this, then it must have been justified, right? And the best part is, it is absolutely legal, all thanks to you. There only needs to be one suffete, and anyone in the government who causes trouble can be instantly deposed by the army, which has free reign here now. And you campaigned for these laws wholeheartedly. Just probably didn't expect to be on the receiving end."

"You can't use them like this! This is a perversion of the law!"

"Is it? Or are you just angry now that you are forced to reap what you have sown?"

"You still have no right to arrest me!"

"I do, actually. Everything has been well planned. I had time to think about this, and while I've had many ideas, my favorite is simply one word – treason. Now that's a word that the people love to hate. Tell them that someone is a traitor, and the accused will be chopped into pieces before he can even begin to defend himself! I worry about more important matters, of course, such as the economy, and how you are running it into the ground with all your idiotic subsidies for beggars. But that wouldn't work for the masses, of course not. So we will focus on what they want to hear."

"Traitor? You are the goddamn traitor! You are the one who cut funding to the navy and lost us the First Roman War! You are the one who campaigned against the Second Roman War for years, even after it had started! I have defended this country all my life and given it everything, while you spent decades sitting in your mansion and making sure that your profits remain as high as possible, everything else be damned!"

"Well, fuck everything else! We could have stayed safe and rich here in Africa without any need for existential wars abroad."

"You are delusional if you think we could have avoided Rome. They would have arrived here sooner or later and put this city to the torch. I made sure that they never got the opportunity to do so. Yes, the casualties were high, but I would take them any day if it meant that the Roman threat was eliminated!"

"But even Rome was not enough for you. You sold our country out to the Seleucids to fight their war in Egypt. And what would come after that? Fighting the Macedonians maybe? The Seleucid Empire itself? Mindlessly destroying everything in your path, until the country is stretched too far and implodes, like Alexander's empire did? No, this ends now. The people will hear of your insane plans, of your secret alliance with the eastern tyrant, and of your election being made possible only by foreign agents. And I have all the evidence for it."

"This is utter lunacy, and you know it! And Zimri can't even replace me, as he resigned from the post right before my eyes. Aradus would be the next suffete instead, as he was the next in terms of votes. And he would deal with your coup swiftly and mercilessly, I can assure you."

"No, because Zimri did not resign of his own volition. You coerced him into leaving. That little stunt you pulled with your men digging through the voting records? Trying to intimidate him? Whatever you tried there, it failed, and now it will only work against your legacy, while giving more legitimacy to my candidate."

"Damn you! This won't be the end of it. I still have allies. I have my brothers in Iberia, and they will have their revenge. And yes, I did work with the Seleucids – I can't imagine they will tolerate such an outrageous change. They will not take kindly to being robbed of their investment. You will be facing them too soon enough. Not to mention Macedon. Or the Italians. You have nothing, except a bunch of fat greedy yes men around you, who will turn on you as soon as they sense a weakness. You will not win."

"Still thinking like a general, I see. Only accounting for the number of warm bodies at your side. Politics is much more complicated than a battlefield. You should have stuck to the latter, instead of getting involved here. But enough. I have humored you for more than I should have. I did not want to kill you too early, so that you would have time to realize how utterly you have failed. To let the despair really set in, and to see all of your hopes for the future die. I believe these goals have been accomplished already."

Behind them, the soldiers have been dragging the captured senators and judges into the open and executing them, before throwing all the corpses into a big pile. All the officials who were known to be or even suspected of being in Hannibal's faction were executed by Hanno's orders, as he did not want any possible opposition to remain. This also included most of the newly elected judges, with the former ones receiving the promise of getting their seats back and so ensuring their support for Hanno. Some officials tried to escape, but the complex only had one way out, and it continued to be guarded by the men installed by Zimri, and so such escape attempts proved futile. The corpses of Hannibal's guards were also soon thrown into the pile, which was then set alight, while Hannibal was dragged right in front of it and forced to watch the bodies being consumed by flame.

"This could have been a great sacrifice to Moloch, though I doubt that even he would be interested in such worthless men," Hanno mused and then turned to Hannibal. "It's over, general. You have been corrupting our country for far too long, and there is only one punishment for that – death. Commander, you have the honor of finishing this."

"Won't even kill me yourself, you fucking coward?" Hannibal shouted, as Astartus approached him from behind and raised his sword.

"I'm not a soldier, and I won't pretend that I am one. But you are, and you should have stayed in your place, instead of trying to become a king."

Hanno gave the final nod of approval, and Astartus brought down his sword. In one swift stroke, Hannibal was decapitated, and his body fell to the ground. Astartus threw the body to the burning pile with the rest, and kicked the head over to his soldiers.

"Congratulations, Zimri, you are now the sole suffete of Carthage," Hanno said dryly to Zimri, who had returned after being recalled. "Just remember who is actually in control, if you don't fancy ending up in the same place as your former colleague. You will have to reassure the public that the crisis has been handled. My men will patrol the streets, but an official announcement will still go a long way if we don't want the rioters to burn the whole damn city down."

With Byrsa Hill and all the main government organs under his control, Hanno now moved to secure the rest of the city. He had already gained control of the harbor and the walls beforehand, using Hannibal's last orders as a cover to mobilize his troops, with many city guards joining them in their operation. While Hannibal did indeed have a lot of support from the military, this pertained only to the regular army and navy, not the local guards. The city guards of Carthage had their own unique culture and traditions and were far more skeptical of Hannibal. They were, on average, wealthier than a regular soldier, enjoyed stable employment, and often came from elite – including senatorial – families, as this was seen as a decent first step towards building a career in the capital. Thus, as the various senators fell into Hanno's pocket, so did their friends and family members in the city guard.

The unit was also composed entirely of native Carthaginians, rather than foreigners or mercenaries who made up the bulk of the regular campaigning armies. Hannibal was starting to question this in his last months in office, as he had secretly considered lifting such requirements and allowing non-Carthaginians to become guardsmen, in order to cut down on the capital's expenses and have more funds for public services. This information had leaked and naturally infuriated the guardsmen, who felt threatened and turned even further away from Hannibal. This was also true for Adherbal Hadash, the commander of the city guard. Hannibal's order to arrest most of the judges from the Court of 104 was the last straw, and Adherbal refused to carry out this task. While Adherbal was no friend of Hanno, the two men now had a common enemy in Hannibal, and so the commander agreed to not interfere with Hanno's coup, in exchange retaining his position after the suffete's overthrow and being guaranteed that the nature of his unit would remain unchanged by the new administration.

And so, there remained no legal opposition to Hanno's swift takeover of Carthage, as his troops flooded the remaining districts to establish control. However, that did not mean that there was no opposition at all. Many citizens continued to resist, and their riots only intensified in some areas. They demanded answers as to what was happening, but received nothing other than beatings from Hanno's soldiers. Skirmishes between the two factions continued erupting throughout the day, with the casualty toll steadily rising, but there seemed to be no quick end to the violence in sight.

Hanno ordered his men to find and kill his remaining opponents in the city, so that all the potential leaders of a rebellion would be dealt with before the situation spiraled out of control, but it proved to be a much more difficult task than anticipated. While the soldiers did manage to find some opposition figures and execute them, to Hanno's frustration many managed to evade capture. Carthage was a massive city with over three hundred thousand inhabitants, and so it was not too difficult to hide there. Aradus Reshgal, the former suffete, was among Hanno's targets, but the soldiers were too late and found his residence already vacated by the time they arrived, with no further leads as to where the wanted man could have gone.

Still, Hanno remained undeterred and proceeded with his plan, hoping that his remaining enemies would soon be found and dealt with in one way or another. He did not want to delay, as he feared that the riots might turn into a full-fledged revolution soon, and so he intended to have the new order proclaimed before too much damage was done. He assembled an armed escort, one led by Astartus, and gave it the task of protecting Zimri on his way to and from the Great Marketplace, where the announcement was supposed to be made.

"You're sending me out there? Right now? With half of Carthage being on fire?" Zimri protested.

"Yes, that's right," Hanno confirmed. "You are indeed going there to let the people know everything is under control. Hopefully that will calm those morons down for once…"

"You're insane!"

"Am I? Maybe I am, considering I could have continued to enjoy my retirement, with no worries in the world, but instead I am now here, knee deep in this shit."

"That you started…"

"That Hannibal started! I am the one who will make sure it is cleaned up. As much as it can be, before the gods take me…"

"You do realize that I might be killed on the spot as soon as I announce that Hannibal is dead, right?"

"That will not happen. I have Astartus and all my other finest men protecting you. You'll be fine."

"But you're not coming with me, are you?"

"Absolutely not, I'm not such a fucking retard to go out there and face the unhinged public. What the fuck would I even gain from that? You know how it works – I rule from the shadows, and you are the public face of the regime. So go do your fucking job, before I find a replacement. Is that clear enough?"

"Yes... Yes, I got it. I'll go, no need to threaten me anymore. But again, I'm warning you – the people will not like this. I hope you have a plan of dealing with the situation... One that does not involve committing a massacre of a scale yet unseen in our history."

"Of course I do. But that shouldn't be a concern for you. Your job is to deliver a speech to the masses. To stick to the script and not fuck it up. That's all."

"It will be done..."

"And just to make it crystal clear – don't try anything funny. If you even suggest anything slightly out of line, Astartus will cut you down where you stand. As I said, I have replacements for you. It would make my job slightly more difficult, sure, but not nearly enough for me to allow even a single treacherous word to slip out of your mouth. So don't try to be martyr, kid. It would absolutely not be worth it."

"I have stuck with you through all this, I would have quit a long time ago if I wanted. No, believe me, I realize how powerful you are, so I don't have any intention of breaking this alliance. Let's go, Astartus. Tell your men to form around me, there may be many obstacles that will need clearing along the way."

Zimri and his security team soon arrived at the Great Marketplace. They did not encounter issues along the way, though the guards did have to push some rioters out so that the way would be more passable. The market square itself was in absolute chaos, however, as the citizens continued clashing with each other and the newly arrived soldiers. Some had been pushed to the ground or even trampled to death, as the square was completely full of people who had arrived here from all over the city to await any news.

The suffete slowly got onto a podium, though he remained completely surrounded by the guards and their shields from all sides. Seeing this, the crowd started calming down and turned its attention to Zimri, while moving as close to him as possible, before being stopped by the guards. When Astartus gave a nod to confirm that it was safe enough, the suffete began his address to the people.

"Citizens of Carthage!" Zimri proclaimed, not sounding too confident. "I know it looks like dark times have come to our great city, but I assure you, everything is under control. I assume you have many questions-"

"Yeah – where the fuck is Hannibal!" a man interrupted him.

"Who are all these soldiers? Why are they here? Are we at war?" another asked.

"Why are you even here? Didn't you resign?" a third shouted.

"When will the harbor be reopened?" a merchant added from further back.

"Please, allow me to explain. You will all receive your answers soon enough," Zimri continued. "It's a complicated situation, but bear with me. While I had previously resigned, that is true, it was not my intention. See, I was forced to do so. Forced to abandon my post. By Hannibal, who is… was a traitor, and who would have become a tyrant!"

"What? That's bullshit! Hannibal was not a traitor!" a rioter shouted

"I knew it! We should never have trusted that Iberian mongrel!" one from the opposite side shouted back.

"Don't you dare speak that way about Hannibal! He is our hero!"

"Hannibal betrayed our great republic," Zimri continued, despite the crowd already starting to erupt back into chaos, "and all the institutions which are important to us. He conspired with the Seleucids, took their gold, and was in the process of subverting our country to his twisted needs and those of his… puppet masters.

He and his cronies unfairly won the election last year and already began unmaking the very foundations of Carthage. This year, I rose to the challenge and – thanks to your unwavering support – managed to dethrone Hannibal's partner in crime Aradus, to counter the former general's insanity as much as possible. However, Hannibal could not accept such a choice made by the people, and moved to depose me! He threatened me and my family, and used his fanatical followers to falsify the results of the election to get rid of me. I was forced to sign his terrible laws and step down... But I was not about to let our republic die just like that! I gathered the evidence and assembled men who are true to the ideals of Carthage. We restored order to Byrsa Hill, and now the entire capital will follow!"

"Yes! Fuck Hannibal!" a man shouted.

"Lies! Hannibal would never betray Carthage! This is an unjust coup!" another countered.

"Where is Hannibal? Why isn't he here to defend himself?" a third one asked.

"Zimri is right! What about Hannibal's men going into the voting archives? They must have changed the votes in their favor!" another rioter said.

"Listen, I know that this is all very unexpected, but we are living in uncertain times right now," Zimri stated, now sweating profusely. "I acted with haste, because who knows how much longer it would have taken for Hannibal to have proclaimed himself king? To have become a tyrant with unchecked power? Not very long, not at all. He was already in the process of dismantling the senate, and even the Court of 104 – our most sacred institution which has been here since the founding of Carthage. I took control of the situation and did what needed to be done, though it was not an easy decision to make. After finding him guilty of treason and electoral fraud, the judges agreed to remove Hannibal from office. I supported their decision and stepped in to replace the tyrant, with guards loyal to me and our traditions at my back… And, may I remind you, Hannibal himself wrote the laws that allowed soldiers on Byrsa Hill, so I only used his own methods against him. However, while we were more than willing to let Hannibal leave with dignity, he refused such an offer. Instead, he attacked us, and we had no choice but to defend ourselves. In the ensuing fight, many lost their lives… including Hannibal."

Having already been far from calm, the crowd now erupted into absolute chaos and violence. The opponents of Hannibal were cheering, and, realizing what had actually happened, joined with the soldiers in beating the pro-Hannibal rioters. Hannibal's supporters, however, became even more enraged and fought back with whatever they had, including rocks, clubs, and daggers.

"Please, everyone, there is no need for this!" Zimri pleaded. "More bloodshed will not help anyone! Hannibal has been deposed, and the old order has been restored. Life can now return to normal, as it had been before… The city will soon be reopened, the senate and the court restored to their former glory… And I will make sure this transition process goes smoothly-"

"This is for Hannibal, you cocksucker!" a rioter threw a rock at Zimri, though it only hit a guard's shield.

"But, of course, Hannibal's tyrannical laws will soon be reversed! There will once again be two suffetes, chosen at the next election. Chosen properly, with no foreign influence or voter manipulation! No more tricks that Hannibal employed to win his position!" Zimri said as he dodged a few more projectiles, including some more rocks and bottles. "You can hate me all you want, but know this – I saved you from Hannibal's tyranny, as well as his secret plans to involve us in even more foreign wars. This time as a debt payment for his Seleucid masters! Carthage will now once again be ruled by true Carthaginians, who respect our heritage and culture!"

"You said your piece, I think it's time for us to go now," Astartus grumbled, as he pushed a few more rioters who were charging at him to the ground with his shield.

"I couldn't agree more, please get me the fuck away from these people," Zimri leaned in to reply and quickly turned back to the crowd. "Please, everyone, go home now, and… celebrate this victory for our republic! Thank you, may Baal Hammon and Tanit bless you all!"

The people did not care much for Zimri's words anymore and simply continued fighting, with some still trying to get to the suffete but repeatedly failing.

"And if anyone has any information regarding the whereabouts of Aradus Reshgal, please bring it to the authorities!" Zimri said, as he was being escorted out of the area by Astartus and his men. "You will be rewarded handsomely for anything you can tell us. He is a co-conspirator of Hannibal and needs to be punished for his crimes at any cost!"

Chapter XXVII

The situation in the Ptolemaic Kingdom continued to get more calamitous every day. A large portion of the country was still occupied by the self-proclaimed pharaoh Horwennefer in the south, who could at best be only temporarily halted by the Ptolemaic forces, but not pushed back, let alone fully defeated. The kingdom was also losing its fortresses on the Aegean, where the Macedonians still had the upper hand, despite many Greek states turning against them. But the most threatening front was the eastern one, where the Seleucids were slowly but surely marching over the Levant to Egypt, with barely anyone to stop them. Antiochus had secured a major victory against the Ptolemies at the Battle of Sidon, routing the army of the Ptolemaic general Scopas and sending it fleeing south, much to the Alexandrian court's shock. What made it even worse for them was the fact that the Jews of southern Levant – now loosely allied to Antiochus – were now starting to rise up against the government in Egypt, tying down the forces of Scopas even further and paving the way for a full Seleucid occupation.

However, as some officials started to panic – Agathocles being one of them – his co-regent Sosibius remained relatively calm and continued to run the government as he had before. He promised the people that the situation was under control, and that all the threats would be soon taken care of. Far from everyone believed his message, but most had more pressing matters and so returned to their regular lives, as the enemy armies were still far from Alexandria in any direction. Sosibius also soon received an urgent message from his spies in Carthage, one detailing Hanno's coup, and he was most pleased with the outcome. Everything was going according to his plan there, and so he was ready to take the next step. For that to proceed though, he needed to consult with his co-regent and get his approval as well, and so he called Agathocles for a meeting the next morning.

"This better be important, I don't like being woken up so early," Agathocles grumbled, as he joined Sosibius in one of the inner palace courtyards with a garden, near the palace harbor.

"Oh, did I disturb your rest now? I'm sorry, that's clearly a higher priority than dealing with the existential threats posed to our kingdom. But if you don't care for it, you are free to leave your post at any time and hand over your duties to me. I am perfectly capable of ruling this country alone, if that's what you wish," Sosibius snidely remarked.

"Don't give me this pretentious bullshit. I am here, aren't I? So what is it? What are we discussing today?"

"I just got word from my spies. They have returned from Carthage with some important news."

"Good or bad news?"

"Good. The best that we could have hoped for, in fact. Hannibal is dead," Sosibius could barely contain his excitement.

"Really? Huh… Can't say it's unexpected… Though I didn't think it would happen so soon. Guess that's one less enemy for us to deal with."

"Indeed. With Hannibal out of the picture, Carthage no longer poses any threat to us. Especially as the country appears to be in flames now – perhaps quite literally."

"So how did that happen?"

"I told you before – I work efficiently, as do my spies."

"Give me a fucking break. After the failed assassination attempt before, no Egyptian would be let anywhere near Hannibal. What actually happened?"

"A man named Hanno organized a coup. He is an old and wealthy landowner, and has been an opponent of the Barcid family for decades. He harnessed the support of the anti-Hannibal sentiment from the senators, judges, and other elites, compromised the security forces, turned the city guard to his side, bought himself a private army, and then marched in and took the capital. His opponents were killed in the struggle, including Hannibal. Very nice work, I might add, the man truly is a professional. A great asset to have on our side."

"I see. I haven't heard of him before. Were we funding him?"

"Few have heard of him, as he mostly stays in the shadows. Even now Carthage does not know that he is in charge, as he has a public facing puppet to hide behind. And no, we weren't funding him. As I said, he is wealthy enough, probably the wealthiest man in all of Carthage, so it was no trouble for him to pay for all the expenses. Though my spies did provide him with some crucial information to make the process smoother. As well as assurances of our support to the new Carthaginian regime."

"Assurances? Why would he need them?"

"That was the only way to get the old man to act. Someone needed to have his back if he was to undertake such a momentous change. Otherwise, he might have just stayed in his mansion and enjoyed retirement for the rest of his days."

"It appears everything is settled. We got what we needed. What's so urgent about this situation?"

"It's not settled. Far from it. It has just begun, and we need to help Hanno so that he could secure the rest of the country."

"What do you mean?"

"This coup has its fair share of opponents, who are now organizing a resistance movement. Hannibal is dead, but his supporters still live, including his former co-suffete and ally, along with Hannibal's family in Iberia. These threats also need to be neutralized."

"Yes, but that's not our job. Let Hanno deal with the situation by himself. He got so far, I'm sure he will manage."

"Maybe, but we cannot afford to risk it. A civil war is about to begin in Carthage – if it hasn't begun yet – and we need to do everything to make sure Hanno wins and the republic stays on our side. There is simply no other way."

"Did Hanno ask for your help to clean up his mess?"

"He did. And I am going to provide it."

"What exactly?"

"Our fleet. Hundreds of capable warships to bring the rest of Carthage into line. Either by forcing Hannibal's allies to submit, or by sinking them to the bottom of the Mediterranean if they refuse. In any event, the threat will be neutralized."

"Ships? Why the fuck does Carthage need even more ships? Isn't their navy even larger than our own by this point?"

"Did you just miss the entire part about the country being in a civil war? Carthage does have a massive navy in theory, but in reality it is now divided between the various factions. Unfortunately for us, Hanno is a man of the land, and has never had much affinity for naval matters. That is to say, he has a large army at his side, but few, if any, ships. Meanwhile, the opposition still has some admirals loyal to the Barcids, and so they control the sea at the moment. But we can change that."

"And I presume you have already started planning this operation?"

"Of course. No time should be wasted. And I even selected the ships that would be going on this expedition. Take a look."

Sosibius led Agathocles through a small corridor into the area outside. The two regents emerged near the palace harbor, where dozens of ships were being inspected and outfitted for the expedition by the dock workers. Further out, in the Great Harbor of Alexandria – the main harbor of the city and the entirety of Ptolemaic holdings – hundreds more ships of various sizes were being prepared, and more still were being constructed.

"I intend to send about three hundred ships to our friend Hanno," Sosibius continued. "Most, about two hundred, will be quinqueremes, to match what the Carthaginians have, with an additional hundred or so quadriremes to add bulk to the fleet and perform lighter duties, such as scouting and maintaining blockades if necessary. There would also be twenty hexaremes as the elite heavy vanguard of the fleet, and finally a single septireme – the flagship of this fleet."

"Absolutely not. Are you out of your fucking mind?" Agathocles replied in disbelief. "This is the core of our fleet, and you want to send all these warships to fight Hanno's civil war?"

"To fight and win the war, yes. Is securing Carthage as our ally not worth sending some ships their way for a few battles? We're not even selling or giving them away – they will sail back once the job is done."

"You make it all sound so easy, but with how things have been going, I'm rather skeptical of any grand plan of yours. Just look at how disastrous the campaign in the Levant went! With the Seleucids advancing and the Jews rising against us, our army is now tatters! I'm not giving you our fleet so it could be destroyed in the same manner!"

"This is very rich coming from you. You were and still are responsible for helping the Greeks defeat Macedon, but that does not seem to be going in our favor at all either, as we are still losing city after city while Macedon remains as strong as ever. And you blaming the failures in the Levant on me is even more ridiculous. Scopas is the one at fault for losing so badly, but you were the one to hire him, so you should be blaming yourself first. I had nothing to do with that disaster, except what little damage control could be done after the fact. And I am sure the Jews wouldn't have had the gall to start a revolt against us if Scopas had won that first crucial battle. So don't you try to pin all these failures on me. I made sure we were successful in the west and prevented another front from opening. All I need now is to finish this fight, so I could redirect my attention to the east and deal with the horrible mess there. Do you still have issues with this plan?"

"I do, quite a lot of them… But I don't suppose I can convince you to drop it…"

"By all means, if you have a better plan then go ahead. I'm listening. But I'm inclined to believe that you don't have anything and are just content sitting here in Alexandria, as the kingdom crumbles all around us."

"Fine, do as you wish… I'm no strategist, so you are right, I have no alternative. Just make sure to leave enough ships to defend our own cities in the meantime."

"Of course. We don't need that many ships here – the Seleucids don't have much of a fleet, and the Macedonian one is busy fighting the Peloponnesians and the Rhodians."

"Right. And who will be in charge of this expedition? I don't suppose it will be you, right?"

"No. I'm not much of a sea man myself. And I'm not leaving the capital solely in your care, not during such crucial times. No, the fleet will be commanded by admiral Epitrophos. He is a capable strategos, one I can trust to do this job well."

"Fair enough."

"Any other questions?"

"No, I'll leave you to it. Though maybe give an offering to Poseidon in the temple, just to make sure the fleet does not sink before even reaching the damn place."

Chapter XXVIII

In Carthage, unrest showed no signs of stopping anytime soon and only seemed to intensify over the following days. While some sections of the city had been pacified, others still remained occupied by the rioters. They were mostly middle and lower class men, though their motivations were often quite different – some wanted to avenge Hannibal, other fought to preserve Carthaginian democracy, and other still joined the riots as they had heard that the new government was planning on cancelling the grain dole programs. Still, they were all united in their opposition to the coup and fought bitterly with the soldiers Hanno sent to crush them.

Among other locations in the capital, the rebels managed to take over the Great Marketplace, as well as the adjacent Great Harbor. That was when Aradus Reshgal, the primary target of Hanno's men, emerged from hiding. He rallied the opposition behind him, denouncing the coup and the new regime, and promised justice for Hannibal, as well as everyone else who had been murdered during the violent overthrow of the government. Hanno's soldiers tried to get to him, but failed, as the former suffete was too deep into rebel held territory and protected by too many supporters of his.

However, the opposition was still too disorganized and barely armed, and so it suffered massive casualties compared to the elite guards on Hanno's side, who were sweeping through the city efficiently and gaining more ground by the hour. The Great Marketplace, which had been barricaded by the rebels, still could not be breached, but some of the rebels started feeling desperate as they were being pushed back from all sides. Luckily for them, Aradus had thought of a plan and soon announced it to the public.

"Citizens of Carthage! Do not despair, as the republic has not fallen to the usurpers yet!" Aradus proclaimed, as he stood on a large flagship in the harbor, with thousands of people crowded below and ready to listen to him. "Hannibal may be dead, but his cause still lives on! We will have justice, we will avenge him, and we will reclaim Carthage! Our enemies are well armed, but we are far more numerous, and we can prevail if we stand strong! And I can tell you exactly how we will achieve that. Admiral Maharbaal Tabnit has joined our side, and I am going to sail out with him to secure the coastline and blockade the city, so that our enemies could not receive any reinforcements. We will also send word to Iberia, held by Hannibal's brothers, and join forces with them. Then, with our combined might, we will strike back and retake our city!"

The people cheered for Aradus, happy to have finally been given some hope after a long period of uncertainty.

"Those of you who have any naval experience are more than welcome to join, we need all the hands we can get," Aradus continued. "We have the rowers, but we need navigators, marines, doctors, among others. And if you have your own ship, you are also welcome to join the fleet – there is no point in letting these boats sit here doing nothing. We will find a use for any vessel. But there is a need for those who prefer staying on land as well. We need to maintain control of the harbor and the marketplace, so that we would have a clear landing area for when we return to reclaim the city. The defenses need to be maintained, and our enemies need to be kept away from here. If you care about securing a future for our republic, I urge you to help in any way that you can. I am leaving commander Milkyaton Hadad in charge of the ground operations, refer to him if you have any questions about how you can contribute. With your help, we will prevail! For Hannibal! For the republic! For Carthage!" Aradus shouted and raised his sword to the sky, as he concluded the speech.

The people, now rallied by their leader, quickly rushed to join the defense effort however they were able to. Some boarded the warships to reinforce the skeleton crews there, while others sailed out on their own vessels, taking on passengers and cargo, as instructed by admiral Maharbaal. The rebels on the ground were just as busy, distributing weapons from the armory – which had been unlocked by commander Milkyaton, a senior veteran of the Italian campaign in the Second Roman War – reinforcing the barricades, and sneaking some men out to cause more unrest in other districts of the city, so that the guards would have to redirect their attention. Even some women joined in the fight – some were the wives, sisters, daughters, and other relatives or friends of the countless officials killed in Hanno's purge, and they wanted revenge, while others were members of families associated with Aradus and other surviving rebel leaders, and so knew that there would be no peace for them under the new regime. This was quite unorthodox, but the defenders of the marketplace needed everyone they could get on their side, and so Milkyaton was willing to give weapons to anyone who could hold them.

Just a couple hours later, once the defenses were established well enough and the ships outfitted for their mission, Aradus gave the order to sail out. Hundreds of ships, from the largest Carthaginian warships to tiny fishing boats, left the harbor and sailed into the Mediterranean, where they would begin their blockade and await help from allies. It was now clear that neither side was willing to stand down, and that the issue would not be resolved as quickly as Hanno had hoped. The Carthaginian Civil War had now truly begun.

"How is it looking, admiral?" Aradus asked as he approached Maharbaal on the main deck of the flagship, several days after the fleet had sailed out.

"The blockade is working as intended," Maharbaal replied. "No reinforcements will be reaching Zimri from the Mediterranean, not before getting through us. And no one is getting through us on my watch."

"That's good. And have we established secure supply lines for our own people in the marketplace?"

"In a way. It's not a perfect solution, but it will do for now. Do not worry, your friends in the city will be fed."

"I see."

"Is there a change in plans, or are we to stay the course?"

"No, there is no need to change anything. Continue as you have, it is going well so far."

"Indeed. Still, this is a rather ragtag fleet that I'm commanding, and it would feel more secure if we had more proper ships at our side. Is there any news of reinforcements for us?"

"Well, word must have reached Iberia by now. I'm sure the Barcids are organizing a force already and may be here in as little as a week from now."

"I hope they will make it here. Their help would be invaluable. What about the other regions? Any word from them?"

"Sardinia, Corsica, and, most importantly, Sicily have taken our side. They are governed by my allies, so they are loyal to our cause. We also have cities like Hippo Regius and Hadrumetum, which are partial to us, but need more convincing to join our faction in the war. I have also sent out envoys to many other cities – Tingis, Iol, Leptis Magna – and am still awaiting some responses. However, in general most of them seem to be neutral on the matter and do not care too much for who is in charge. Their leaders are waiting for the situation in the capital to cool down and one faction to emerge victorious, so they could align themselves with it."

"That means we need to prove ourselves. Win this battle to convince the rest to join in. Take the city, and in doing so take the whole country."

"It appears so. We need to make sure we do not falter in this crucial moment."

"I assure you, my men are doing the best they can. A lot of them have little to no experience, but most are learning quickly. And like you said before, we have the numbers on our side. We can afford to have more casualties."

"Well, I would rather avoid any casualties, if it is possible. I don't like seeing my own countrymen kill each other. But... You are right, we can afford that, if it becomes necessary. I just hope we do not lose track of what we are fighting for..."

"I know how you feel. I certainly didn't expect another war to happen so soon, especially not like this. But I served under Hannibal when we were fighting the Romans – he was a great man who led us to total victory. And I'll be damned if I don't defend his honor from these bastards whose greed and lust for power has no bounds, and who can excuse murdering our hero by throwing some ridiculous charges at him. I will not stand for this."

"It means a lot to have a man such as you stand by my side. I am glad that there are still people who-"

"I am very sorry to interrupt you, sir, but there is an urgent message from one of the scout ships ahead," a sweaty marine appeared next to the two men and cut off the former suffete.

"What is it, soldier?" Maharbaal turned to him.

"We have news of multiple ships rapidly approaching our position from the east."

"What? How many?"

"Unknown. It was said that it was too many to count. Possibly... in the hundreds."

"Could it be pirates?"

"I doubt it, sir. It is said to be a large and organized fleet. Consisting primarily of heavy warships."

"Not an allied fleet, right?" Maharbaal asked grimly.

"We aren't expecting any allies from the east..." Aradus confirmed.

"And a few ships have already been lost, sir," the marine added.

Maharbaal turned to face east and climbed a bit higher to see the view more clearly.

"Baal fucking Saphon..." Maharbaal turned pale as he saw dozens of large warships appearing on the horizon in the east, with more and more emerging behind them and there seemingly being no end in sight to the recently arrived fleet.

"Why are we here exactly? What is it that you intend to show us? I think we've all seen the rebel blockade and their attempts to burn down the city already," Hyrum Baltsar asked.

The former suffete, along with some other prominent supporters of the regime, was in the courtyard of Byrsa Hill, overlooking the city and the harbor, as well as the Mediterranean to the north, where Aradus continued to maintain the blockade. At the head of the group was Hanno, who had summoned them all here, though he had not disclosed the purpose of the meeting.

"Maybe you would find the answer if you used your energy to watch and listen to what is happening, instead of asking foolish questions," Hanno retorted.

"Well, I'm not seeing or hearing anything out of the ordinary. Except for the rioters chanting below, but that is a daily occurrence now," Hyrum replied.

"And what if you look to the east?"

"I don't think- Huh... That's weird."

"What... What is that, Hanno?" Ahirom Gamon, the speaker of the senate, asked, upon noticing the ships appearing from the east.

"What is it? I'll tell you what – it's our total victory," Hanno stated proudly.

"What is the meaning of this? Are we being invaded? Who does that fleet belong to?" the city guard commander Adherbal Hadash asked as he joined them.

"No, we're not. We're being liberated. By the Egyptians, who will make quick work of the rebels and help us restore order to the city."

"Are you out of your goddamn mind? You called the Egyptians here?" Adherbal pushed through the others and was about to grab Hanno, before being stopped by his guards.

"We need their help if we are to win this war."

"And have you considered that this could drag us into yet another war? That this would allow the Egyptians to occupy the capital uncontested?"

"I have, in fact, considered such a possibility. However, I am certain that such is a most improbably outcome. The Egyptians desperately need allies, and they wouldn't dare do anything here without my approval. They can't afford to wage war against both factions in Carthage."

"And that makes it fine to just let them in here?"

"They won't stay for long, rest assured. The Egyptians are stretched thin, and these forces will have to be recalled soon for some other operation. But not before they deal with this little insurrection. But if they overstay their welcome… Well, that's why I have you here, commander. I'm sure your men would be capable of defending their city."

"This is unbelievable…"

"This is war. And we need every advantage we can get."

"So you decided to make a deal with them behind our backs?"

"Behind your backs? As if I needed approval from any of you. I had to keep it secret, so that the information would not leak and that Aradus and his crooks would be caught by surprise. Which is indeed what appears to be happening."

"You charged Hannibal with conspiring against the state with the Seleucids. How is it any different than you now conspiring with the Ptolemies?"

"It should be none of your concern, commander. But it is simple, as there is no conspiring. Hannibal was going to go to war against the Ptolemies on the side of Antiochus, that is a fact. And his supporters would most likely follow this course. Meanwhile, I have no intention of engaging in any foreign wars in the foreseeable future. This aligns with the goals of the Ptolemies, who would much rather see my regime succeed, than that of Hannibal,

Aradus, or anyone else in their camp. Thus, they sent help to us. That's all there is. We will not owe them anything, and we will remain as free as ever."

"Bullshit, I don't believe that," Hyrum scoffed.

"Believe whatever the fuck you want, it does not matter. Just see for yourself. That's why I brought you all here."

"By the gods, that is a lot of ships…" Mago Arvad said. "How long have you been planning this?"

"Long enough," Hanno smiled.

"Those are still our own people though…" Zimri muttered.

"They are traitors. They had sealed their fate when they refused to stand down and stole our ships. We have no use for them."

"But-"

"Don't you go soft now. You all knew what you were signing up for. This is the quickest way to deal with these pests, and you will soon be thanking me for saving this gods forsaken city from even more chaos," Hanno paused for a moment. "But enough about that. The show is about to begin, so please, gentlemen, enjoy the play. After all, you have the best view in the city."

"Brace for impact!" the captain of a Carthaginian ship shouted to his crew, just as an Egyptian ship smashed into its side.

While the Carthaginian opposition had expected some combat at sea, they were woefully underprepared for a whole Egyptian fleet attacking them. Maharbaal scrambled to give orders to his captains so they would get their ships into proper positions, but it was too little too late. Many of his ships were undermanned and underequipped, and the crews, in many cases consisting of civilian volunteers, started panicking immediately. While the Egyptian numerical superiority in terms of ships was not that high, their vessels were fully crewed with professional soldiers and seamen, as opposed to the ragtag group hastily assembled by the Carthaginians.

Despite these disadvantages, Maharbaal was not ready to give up yet. While some of his ships were quickly sunk or captured by the Egyptians, with others fleeing to escape the carnage, he managed to assemble the core of the fleet to combat their new opponents. The vessels with the smallest crews were evacuated, set on fire, and sent directly into the Egyptian fleet, causing some serious damage and taking down a few quinqueremes each. This greatly raised the Carthaginian morale, though it did not deter the Egyptian admiral Epitrophos from pursuing his goal.

The Egyptians continued pushing on, ramming into Carthaginian ships, firing volleys of arrows, and boarding them with dozens of marines once the targets were weakened enough. Thus, while the Egyptians were also losing ships at a rapid rate, they were compensating for their losses by seizing Carthaginian vessels and repurposing them. The Carthaginians, meanwhile, had no such opportunity, as they did not have the manpower needed to secure even the smaller Egyptian quadriremes, and so instead only focused on sinking enemy vessels and trying to hold out for as long as possible. Yet, as the hours went by and the day progressed into the evening, the situation for the Carthaginians became most dire, as the realization set in that they were losing ships at an unsustainable rate, and that there would be no help coming in time to turn the tide of the battle.

"Marines, defend yourselves! The enemy is boarding!" captain Kanmi Tabnit, the son of admiral Maharbaal Tabnit, shouted as his ship came into contact with an Egyptian one and was flooded with enemy soldiers.

The Carthaginians raised their swords and crossed them with those of their opponents – which included both ethnic Greeks and Egyptians. They managed to kill a few of the invaders, but were outnumbered and so could not retake control of their ship. Before long, most Carthaginian soldiers were all killed or thrown overboard, with only a few left standing on the very edge of the vessel.

"Captain, they have taken the ship! What are your orders?" the first mate asked, as he was fending off a few Egyptian marines.

"Just buy me some more time! Our ship is indeed lost, but I have an idea for at least avenging it," the captain said, as he shot down a few men on the opponent's ship with his bow.

The Egyptian quinquereme from which the marines had boarded Kanmi's ship had a noticeable oil spill from one of the amphoras that it was transporting, and so the captain focused on that area. After clearing the men around it, he picked up another arrow, lit it on fire from a nearby torch, and readied to shoot it at the oil spill, hoping that it would catch fire and in turn burn the enemy warship down, along with all the remaining Egyptians there.

However, just as he was about to release the arrow, a sword pierced through Kanmi's chest, as an Egyptian attacked him from the back. The arrow overshot and landed in the water, and the captain's body slumped to the ground, before being kicked overboard by the same marine who killed him. The Egyptians had now secured yet another ship for their fleet.

"It is over. I am sorry, Aradus, but I have failed," admiral Maharbaal said solemnly, as he stared into the sea with ship debris and hundreds of corpses floating there.

"You did the best anyone could have done, considering the circumstances," Aradus replied. "No one could have predicted that the Egyptians would ambush us… That Zimri would stoop so low as to allow a foreign fleet to invade our country, just so he could retain his hold on Carthage…"

"Nevertheless, the battle is still lost. There is little we can do now, as the Egyptians will take down our remaining ships momentarily."

"They will," Aradus sighed. "But this battle is just the start. This is a war, and there will be many more battles. We can still help win them."

"As much as I'd like to believe that, I don't really see how. I've lost everything now. My country, my city, my fleet... my son... There is nothing left for me here. And I will not allow myself to be captured, just so I could be paraded around the city and treated like a slave. I am ready to let the gods take me now..."

"As am I. But you are a skilled admiral, one who can help greatly in the battles that are yet to come. You are still needed."

"Me? Where would I even go?"

"West. The Barcids in Iberia still have considerable forces. And while Hasdrubal and Mago are competent generals, they will need an admiral too. Besides, someone needs to warn them that the battle is lost and that they should turn around and build up more strength, so that they would not be ambushed by the Egyptians like we were."

"Anyone could be sent to warn them."

"Yes. But it's a civil war. How would they know if it's a trustworthy source? You are someone they would recognize as being on their side and so would be more willing to listen."

"I suppose that's true..."

"And don't you want to avenge your son properly? Make sure those bastards pay for what they did? The gods are not going anywhere, you can meet them at any later point. But right now, you can do a whole lot more in the world of the living."

"Maybe. But it does not feel right, fleeing a battle just like that. What happened to the captain going down with his ship?"

"Luckily for us, you are no mere captain. You aren't bound to a single ship, are you?"

"You're right... As much as I'd like to have a glorious last stand here, pointless heroics don't win wars. I should go and rebuild our fleet. Make it a powerful force, capable of going head-to-head with the Egyptians, so that we could one day reclaim Carthage from the usurpers."

"Absolutely. This flagship is too large and noticeable, but there are several smaller ships you can take. It's getting dark, and I imagine you could escape without being seen."

"And what about you? Are you not coming?"

"No. I am just a politician, after all. A former one at that. My skills are nowhere near as valuable as yours."

"You could still do a lot of good in Iberia."

"Perhaps. But currently, I am the face of the resistance. Which means that our enemies will not rest until they find me. If we both fled, we would be pursued, and eventually captured. And then the Barcid fleet would sail right into this trap, with no one to warn them. No, I can't allow that. I must remain here, buy you enough time to escape, and let the Egyptians think that we are all still defending the city."

"You are ready to become a martyr for your cause?"

"Plenty of worse fates out there. And maybe this will make our opponents too overconfident for their own good. They would grow complicit, believe that the opposition to their new regime is crushed, even though it is just starting to grow."

"I won't stop you then. Do what you must. Just don't let our enemies take this flagship. It would be a great shame to see the crown jewel of our fleet soiled by those traitors and the degenerates helping them."

"Don't worry, admiral. No one will be taking this ship."

"Thank you."

"You should leave now though. We have little time left."

"Of course. We will remember you, Aradus. You were a great leader in our most desperate hour. And I promise, Zimri and his cronies will pay for their crimes."

"I believe you. It has been an honor, admiral."

"The honor is all mine. Now show those sibling-fuckers the wrath of Tanit."

"Admiral, we are now approaching the enemy flagship," the captain of the sole septireme and flagship of the Egyptian fleet informed his superior.

"Excellent. It will make for a fine prize for our victory," admiral Epitrophos smiled. "Our hexaremes will surround and board it from both sides. We only have to watch now."

"Yes, they are moving into position. But... It appears the ship is not stopping. In fact, it is only increasing its speed and heading straight for us!"

"No matter, it will not get through us. It will be stopped and boarded no matter what."

"Admiral, that is Aradus Reshgal commanding that ship," an envoy from Hanno, also present on the Egyptian flagship, informed the admiral in Greek.

"Is that the man we are seeking?"

"Yes."

"Even better."

"But he is wanted alive."

"Then he will be taken alive. That will not be a problem."

"It... may be, sir," the captain said. "He is still charging at us. It appears he is trying to ram our ship!"

"He can try all he wants. Ours is much sturdier and will not budge. All this little maneuver will do is stop their vessel in place."

The Carthaginian flagship then suddenly turned right and stopped, with its starboard side now facing the bows of the septireme and the two hexaremes, which were heading right at it.

"Admiral it's- We need to-" the captain shouted but was cut off.

"I can see it myself," Epitrophos replied. "He is trying to bait us into ramming. Abort the maneuver! Stop our ship right now!"

"There's no time, admiral! We need to abandon our ships!"

"Nonsense. If they want to do it this way, then fine, we will go through their puny boat. Would have preferred to secure it intact, but this will have to make do."

"No! We won't make it, their ship is being set on fi-"

Before the captain could finish, the Carthaginian flagship erupted into flames. Aradus and his most loyal supporters had stayed behind on the ship and covered it in all the flammable materials that they had, and, once the vessel was in position and the Egyptians were close enough, set it on fire. It quickly spread all over the flagship, to the horror of the crews of the ships approaching it. The two hexaremes tried going around it, but there was no time, and so they rammed into the bow and stern of the ship in full force, catching fire as well.

"No, no, no, this can't be! Fuck! Abandon ship! Abandon ship right now!" Epitrophos shouted, having finally realized the severity of the situation.

Moments later, the septireme crashed into the Carthaginian flagship, hitting it right in the center and completely destroying it. However, the Egyptian flagship was completely covered in flames in the process and started crumbling itself. While some crewmen managed to jump overboard before the impact, the ship could not be salvaged. Soon enough, the septireme turned into little more than floating debris, suffering the same fate as its equivalent on the Carthaginian side.

While the three largest Egyptian ships had been destroyed, Epitrophos managed to survive, though not without injuries and scarring from the fire. He had jumped from his flagship and was soon picked up by a nearby quinquereme, where he was treated as much as was possible. His vice admiral Tydeus took over the command of the fleet temporarily and continued the assault against the remaining Carthaginian ships. There were not many left and, after about a dozen more were sunk, the surviving captains surrendered to the Egyptians. The charred body of Aradus was also found and brought aboard to be later delivered to the

Carthaginians, despite its condition being far from what Hanno had wanted.

The battle was now finally over, with the Carthaginian rebels suffering a total defeat, though the Egyptians had plenty of casualties as well. And, by this point, admiral Maharbaal and his small escort was far away from the naval battlefield, with none of his opponents having yet realized that he had managed to escape.

Having won the naval battle, the Egyptian fleet now moved into the city of Carthage itself, with hundreds of ships flooding the Great Harbor. The rebels tried to block them, by way of nets and other obstacles, but this only slightly delayed the enemy's arrival and did not accomplish much. The rebelling Carthaginians were now completely demoralized and disorganized, having lost their leader, as well as many of their compatriots – the latter either having been taken as prisoners by the Egyptians, or sinking to the bottom of the Mediterranean. Many thus abandoned their positions and fled, hoping to avoid a similar fate, though some continued to stand their ground.

Commander Milkyaton Hadad rallied what men and women were still willing to fight and had them attack the incoming ships with whatever they had, including rocks, arrows, and fire. A few of the ships were sunk, but it was not nearly enough. There were too many vessels arriving at once and they soon spread all over the harbor. Upon docking, hundreds of soldiers disembarked at once from the ships and did not hesitate to attack the civilians who were defending the area. It was a massacre, with the well-trained soldiers of the Ptolemaic kingdom mercilessly slaughtering the terrified and poorly equipped locals, with the defensive lines being shattered almost immediately.

The Carthaginians stood little chance against the invaders and were ordered by Milkyaton to retreat to the Great Marketplace, ceding the harbor to the Egyptians. Yet even in the marketplace the situation was no better, with the Egyptians continuing to push through the defenders relentlessly and crushing anyone in their way. Milkyaton himself was killed in the fighting and the Carthaginians were left with no commander on the ground as well. What made it even worse for them was Hanno's troops finally breaking through the barricades at the same time and striking the rebels from the opposite side. Now, having been completely surrounded, the rebels accepted their fate and dropped their weapons. Those who had not managed to escape the onslaught yet rushed to surrender to Hanno's forces, preferring to be captured by fellow Carthaginians, rather than risking their fate with the Egyptians.

News of this rebel defeat spread rapidly, with some celebrating the end to the violence and chaos, and others mourning the losses and the failure to avenge Hannibal. The few men still fighting Hanno's regime across the city ceased their attacks within hours and went into hiding, realizing that there was no victory to be had against a united front of Zimri's – or, in reality, Hanno's – loyalists and the invading Ptolemaic soldiers. The revolt had been crushed. While the city itself remained mostly intact, the casualties were in the thousands, with thousands more captured either by the Egyptians or their Carthaginian allies.

"Welcome to Carthage. Your timely assistance in this matter is greatly appreciated. I assume you are the admiral responsible for this victory?" Zimri said when he arrived at the marketplace with a retinue of guards, as the soldiers were still cleaning up the scene and transporting the remaining newly captured prisoners.

"Our admiral is currently indisposed," Tydeus replied, with the Carthaginian envoy next to him serving as the translator. "I am Tydeus of Naucratis, the vice-admiral of this fleet. I will be acting on the behalf of admiral Epitrophos until he has recovered."

"I see. Send him my regards, I hope he can recover soon from the… battle injuries, I assume?"

"Yes. And you are the leader of Carthage, is that correct?"

"I am," Zimri answered, as in the Ptolemaic kingdom only the co-regents knew that Hanno was the one actually in charge of Carthage, but this information was not to be revealed to anyone else. "Zimri Germelqart, the… sole suffete of Carthage. Again, allow me to express gratitude for your support on behalf of this entire city."

"It was the pharaoh's will that we make our way here, and so we did. Nothing more, nothing less."

"Of course. I imagine you've had quite a long trip and an exhausting day, so I won't take much more of your time. I just want to establish some ground rules before we continue. First, your men should stay only in the harbor area-"

"Let me remind you that we are not your subjects. We answer only to our admiral, who answers directly to Alexandria. No Carthaginian is part of this chain of command."

"I understand that, but still… you are standing in our city. So our rules will apply to you and your men."

"Your city? Before we arrived, it was in complete chaos, overrun with rioters with which you could not deal on your own."

"We would have dealt with them eventually, but…"

"We were informed that we would have free and unimpeded access to the entirety of the city after we arrived. We have a lot of men and need the space, after all."

"I understand that, but the citizens might not react positively to seeing foreign soldiers walking freely around the place…"

"That is not our concern."

"Right… Let's put that aside for now. What about the prisoners that you currently hold?"

"We do have many that we have captured over the course of the battle."

"Yes, I know. And I would like you to return them all to us, so that we could judge them according to our laws."

"This was not mentioned to us. Why should we hand them over to you, instead of taking them as slaves to Egypt?"

"I need them here."

"Why? What use are they anymore? They have betrayed your country."

"Yes, but sending off thousands of Carthaginians to become slaves in Egypt would be a very bad look for me and would only further embolden the opposition. Which would obviously be to the detriment of both of us."

"We are not bothered by such matters in Egypt."

"Well, good for you. But we are in Carthage, and the opinion of the people matters here. If you want to make the most out of this victory, instead of wasting it, you should hand over the prisoners to us."

"I don't think so."

"What if in exchange… I allow your troops to access more of the city? Say, a quarter of it for the needs of your soldiers and sailors."

"Or we could just take it by ourselves."

"You could try. But fighting another battle would be a very poor decision on your part."

"You could not defeat these unorganized civilians on your own. You think you could defeat our forces?"

"We were not at full strength before. But we are now, we are well prepared. And the local population was previously split, but it would be united now. You think any citizen would side with your soldiers instead of fellow Carthaginians? You are here only because we allowed you to enter. So do not overstep your limits, vice-admiral."

"Same goes for you. Your republic is collapsing right in front of us. You are not exactly in a position to make any demands."

"And you are? Egypt is fighting its own rebels to the south, as well as Macedon to the north, and, of course, the Seleucid menace to the east. Oh, and I've heard there is a Jewish revolt. Let's not pretend Egypt is some bastion of stability either… Look,

Alexandria needs Carthage, and Carthage needs Alexandria, that's a fact. We have an unofficial alliance in place. An alliance of dire necessity, but an alliance nonetheless. So how about you stick to your job, which concerns only naval matters, and stop trying to sabotage what your masters in Alexandria have built? I can't imagine they would be happy if this deal fell through…"

"Fine. You shall have your prisoners. Those that survived the naval and the ground battle and were taken by us – they will be sent over to you. In exchange, we ask for access to the city – half, not just a quarter – so that we could rest, resupply, and use it as our base of operations until our mission in this region is done."

"Very well. You can move freely in the southern part of the city. Just… tell your soldiers to behave. There should not be any unnecessary incidents."

"There won't be. My men are trained professionals. You should be worrying more about what your own people are doing," Tydeus said as he turned to leave.

"If only they were as simple to control as the soldiers…"

Chapter XXIX

"My king, I have urgent news for you. May I enter?" Nicolaus asked as he approached the chamber of Antiochus in his temporary residence in Ptolemais, currently the king's southernmost conquest during his campaign against Egypt.

"By all means, general," Antiochus replies, as Nicolaus entered the room. "We were just discussing the fall of Alexandria Ariana with Zeuxis. A most unfortunate occurrence."

"Indeed. Now our eastern provinces are most vulnerable, and the Bactrians present a real threat to the realm's security," Zeuxis added.

"But we can continue this discussion later. What do you have for me, Nicolaus?"

"Well, I'm afraid it's only more bad news. And even more grim than what happened in the east…" Nicolaus sat down on the couch next to Zeuxis.

"I'm listening."

"There have been rumors about this matter in recent days, but my spies in Egypt have finally confirmed it to be true. Hannibal is dead, and Carthage has fallen."

"What? How? I need more details!"

"Of course. No one knows the full story of how everything happened, but I'll tell you what I've gathered. There has been a coup in Carthage, led by the second suffete, it seems, and it resulted in Hannibal's death. There was no public execution, so he was either killed in the initial fight or shortly after. In any event, by the end of that day the new government had taken control of the capital, though there was resistance. At first quite successful too, as the forces opposing the coup managed to take parts of the city, including the harbor and even the fleet stationed there, putting the rest of Carthage under blockade. However, these victories were short lived, and the situation turned for the worse in just a few more days. The coup organizers had allied with the Ptolemies and they... invited the Egyptian fleet to help them retake the city. The resistance was thus quickly crushed, and Carthage is now in the hands of the pro-Egyptian Carthaginians. Or Egyptians themselves. In any case – it belongs to our enemies now."

"That is... troubling, to say the least. Hearing that Hannibal has been killed this way is most disturbing. We had our disagreements, of course, but he was a great man, and could still have been a useful ally... Of course it was the fucking Ptolemies who brought their cursed ways to Carthage as well!" Antiochus snapped but quickly calmed down. "Now we won't be getting any help from them. Worse, the Egyptians now have the western Mediterranean in their grasp and Carthage as an ally, which means we will have to fight them too. Is that right?"

"Unfortunately, yes, my king. That is the current situation, by all accounts."

"I have no choice then. Zeuxis, give the order to the army and the navy to treat all Carthaginians, including their ships, as hostiles. We are at war with the republic, and we cannot afford any privileges to them."

"It will be done," Zeuxis nodded.

"Just as I thought that this was going to be a short and easy war, the gods decided to throw more obstacles in my way... Nevertheless, we shall persevere and succeed, no matter how many enemies we have to face."

"While that is a noble sentiment, my king, the enemy's naval superiority is overwhelming, and we have no answer to it. Carthage and Egypt have the largest fleets in the Mediterranean by far, and they are now working together. Even if we combine our entire fleet with that of Philip, we would still be unable to counter our opponents..."

"That may not be necessarily true, actually," Nicolaus interjected. "As I have said, a large portion of the Carthaginian fleet was taken by the resistance, and was subsequently destroyed by the Egyptians during the Battle of Carthage."

"But Carthage must have warships in other cities too, is that not so?" Antiochus asked.

"That is correct, and it may be to our advantage. Many cities still have not declared support for the new government and so their resources could be salvaged to prevent them from falling into Egyptian hands."

"I see your point, but you just told me that the resistance has been defeated. Who else would those cities turn to?"

"Well... There are the Barcids. Hannibal's family, including his brothers Hasdrubal and Mago, is in Iberia and has direct control over the peninsula. While hostilities between them and the capital have not begun yet, I can't imagine the Barcids, of all people, would simply accept this situation and bow down to whoever was responsible for killing Hannibal."

"That is true... I have met Hasdrubal personally, he has the potential to be a good leader as well. He may not reach the heights of Hannibal, but we must do with what we have. If Barcids join the fight, I will support them so that our allies could regain Carthage and kick the Egyptians out of there."

"With all due respect, my king..." Zeuxis began. "Should we really get involved in this Carthaginian civil war? We have already spent so much time and gold on Carthage, and where did that get us? Wouldn't it be better to simply cut our losses? To not escalate the conflict unless it is absolutely necessary?"

"No. I do not plan on ridding the eastern Mediterranean of the Ptolemies just so they could move west and continue to threaten us from there. They and their allies must feel the pressure from all sides, until they can no longer take it and their realm collapses. And if the Barcids are our best hope in the west – so be it, I'll help them however I can. Nicolaus, send word to Hasdrubal. Let him know that if he chooses to fight, he will have my support."

"Of course," Nicolaus replied.

"I assume not all Carthaginians are to be treated as enemies then?" Zeuxis asked.

"Correct. Only those siding with the Egyptians," Antiochus confirmed.

"And how would we know which side they are on?"

"Great question. But I am sure we will figure something out soon enough. For now, I suppose everyone will have to use their best judgement to determine whether it is an ally or an enemy."

"Very well... But what about the Bactrian attack in the east? Can we afford to fight on so many fronts at the same time?"

"We must. I expected more from Diogenes, and certainly more from the garrison at Alexandria, but the Bactrians are still too far away to be of immediate concern."

"That may be so, but we will still need to deal with them eventually."

"And we will. But not before Egypt. I am on the verge of victory here, and I'm not going to abandon the fight. I will stay here and continue the campaign until our enemies have been completely crushed. I will have my victory parade in Alexandria – the first and most important Alexandria – and then I will turn east. I will reclaim what I have lost, and I will march all the way past the Jaxartes, if that is what it takes. But while we are here, the Bactrians will be contained by natural defenses – the mountain ranges and deserts of Persia are vast, and will have to be painstakingly traversed, along with all the fortresses in the region. Time is on our side. Do you have any objections?"

"No, I agree. I stand by you, my king," Zeuxis replied.

"As do I," Nicolaus added.

"Good. You know what to do. The great plan must proceed."

Chapter XXX

"Ah, Agathocles. I assume you have already heard the news, yes?" Sosibius, sitting on the throne in the palace of Alexandria, asked Agathocles, who had just entered the throne room.

"I have. But why in the name of Horus are you sitting on that throne right now?" Agathocles replied. "This is seriously pushing the limits, even for you."

"The young Ptolemy doesn't seem terribly interested in it, so why not use the opportunity? Especially after my latest plan resulted in a decisive victory for the realm. I feel like I deserve to see what it is like, at least for a little while…"

"I really do not like the precedent you are setting. I don't care about Ptolemy, but I am a regent too. We are equals."

"Very well. I can step down to your level, if you so wish."

"You should."

"Now, let's return to more pressing matters," Sosibius said, having stood up and approached Agathocles. "As you know, Carthage is ours. Our fleet destroyed what was left of the resistance in the capital and Hanno now reigns supreme there, though now he is obviously bound to us. Everything is going according to plan."

"Does that mean that you will order the fleet to return to Alexandria?"

"Don't be ridiculous. We secured the capital, but there are still battles to come. Would be quite foolish to just abandon everything before achieving total control of western Mediterranean."

"What else is there to take?"

"Quite a lot, actually. Sicily, Sardinia, Corsica… All strongholds of the opposition. Not to mention several cities on the African coast. And, of course, Iberia. The Barcids are in control of it and they may be planning on continuing the fight against Hanno.

I doubt they will accept the new order, so have to be eliminated as well."

"Oh, so what you originally said about it being a quick operation was all horseshit. I see that now."

"I didn't say anything about how quick it would be. I just said that our ships will return home after their job is finished, and that will still happen. And, judging by our first victory, I don't think it will take very long for them to mop up what remains of our enemies in the region."

"Why am I here then? Clearly you are intent on continuing what you are doing, so why summon me here?"

"Well, I thought you should be informed. We are equals, as you have said."

"In theory, but in reality you are the one calling all the shots."

"I am always willing to hear your suggestions. But, as you never seem to have any, I am forced to make plans on my own, and only inform you of them."

"Don't act like I don't do anything around here. I make sure our treasury has gold in it to pay for all your expenses, I make sure the palace is well maintained and fully supplied, I make sure Ptolemy is safe, and I make sure the officers remain loyal."

"And you make sure to enjoy all the fine girls in the late pharaoh's harem, right?"

"That's none of your damn business."

"Maybe it isn't. I'm not judging you, but you shouldn't be judging me either, as you are using what belongs to the pharaoh for yourself too…"

"So is that the division of power now? You get the throne, and I get the whores?"

"If that's the arrangement you want…"

"Oh, fuck off…"

"Listen, I don't think there needs to be any conflict between us. You can do what you have been doing so far, and I will continue my own plans. It is working surprisingly well so far, and I don't see why this should be changed."

"In Carthage, yes, but we have all the other fronts to worry about. The south, the north, and the east. Our situation is still very precarious."

"The Greek states are keeping Macedon busy in the north, I don't think it will become our problem, not for a long time at least. In the south, meanwhile, Horwennefer appears to be losing his momentum and slowing down to a crawl, thanks to the reinforcements I deployed there from Cyrenaica. He will be dealt with in due time. The east is a problem, you are right, but nothing that couldn't be overcome. I received news that Bactria has invaded the Seleucid realm, so this may force Antiochus to split his forces. And I have a plan for defeating him for good."

"Is that so? With what forces, exactly?"

"We still have many men who are willing to fight for us. But, more importantly, we have the gold. If there is one thing that Egypt always has, it's the gold."

"To hire mercenaries?"

"Precisely. And not just one company. As many as we can afford and get to the field. No matter how many soldiers Antiochus may have, his manpower is not infinite, and the financial situation of his realm is rarely good. He will not be reaching Egypt, no matter how hard he tries."

"Right, but Scopas hasn't exactly proven himself to be the most reliable commander…"

"Never mind Scopas. I will lead our new army and face Antiochus myself. Just like in the last war with him."

"Best of luck with that."

"You will be involved as well, naturally. Both regents have to do their part to protect the realm and the pharaoh."

"Come on, I'm not a military man. Are you just looking for an excuse to send me to the battlefield to die?"

"Nothing of the sort. But you can still help by managing the mercenaries, making sure that they show up to the fight, get paid, and in general are provided for well enough so that they wouldn't abandon me when it is time to fight Antiochus. Can you do that?"

"I suppose I can. I'll start looking for companies we could get to join our side."

"Very good. We still have some time before the decisive battle, but we should not wait for too long. Antiochus is advancing quite steadily."

"I know, I know, believe me. I don't want him overrunning Egypt any more than you do. My life is on the line as well."

"Well, then I trust you to do a proper job, for both our sakes."

"I'll make sure everything is in order. Anything else you want to discuss? I have a lot of work ahead of me, so I would prefer to get going."

"No, nothing more for now. I believe we are on the right track."

"Are you going back on the throne?"

"Maybe... It is quite comfortable, you know."

Chapter XXXI

Despite Hanno's victory over his enemies in the city of Carthage, there still stood one large bastion of opposition to his control of the republic – Iberia. Most of the peninsula had been conquered by the Barcids in the previous few decades, and the process was still ongoing, as Hasdrubal continued to subjugate the various tribes in the north and make them yield to the military and economical superiority of Carthage. Thus, the region had few ties to the elites in the capital and was always the main power base for the Barcid family, even after Hannibal's death.

When news of this reached Iberia, its governors – Hasdrubal and Mago – immediately denounced the new regime and pledged to fight it. Mago organized a fleet and sent it to reinforce the rebel fleet assembled by Aradus, hoping to strike at the coup organizers before they solidified their rule, but it was too late. The rebel fleet had been destroyed by Ptolemaic forces, with the Iberian fleet being forced to turn back if they did not wish to suffer the same fate. It would have been ambushed as well, if not for admiral Maharbaal Tabnit, who had escaped the carnage and warned the Iberians about the Egyptians already landing in Carthage. The Iberian admiral Bostar Akbar took this news seriously and ordered the fleet to turn around and sail back for New Carthage, the capital of Carthaginian Iberia. Upon arrival, Maharbaal informed Mago of what had transpired in great detail and what the situation was in the capital by the time he left. This caused panic among some of his officers and advisors, with a few even urging Mago to submit to the new regime so that Iberia would be spared from the ravages of war. Yet Mago dismissed such an option and instead began preparing his realm for the eventual confrontation between the old and New Carthage.

Mago ordered more ships to be built, including some heavier warships, as the Iberian fleet was severely lacking in them.

Construction also started on defensive fortifications along the southeastern Iberian coast, including in New Carthage itself, so that a naval invasion would be even more difficult if it was attempted. Southern Iberia was quite a wealthy region and so the governor could afford all these expenses – though Iberian labor being cheaper than that of Carthaginians also helped. Mago also began a rapid assembly of a proper army that could defend the region and go on offensive campaigns, as previously he only had a small local security force at his disposal. To this end, he created a core of Carthaginian elite soldiers that recruited men from the small, but active and loyal Carthaginian settler population, and began hiring mercenaries to build up the army's strength even more. This included Turdetani, Iberian, and Celtic men from Iberia, as well as Numidians from North Africa.

New Carthage itself was a very recently founded city, established only about twenty years ago, but it had already grown into a thriving community, with dozens of thousands of inhabitants. It was also in a very defensible position, being located on a small peninsula, which was surrounded by a lagoon to the north, a narrow bay opening into the Mediterranean to the south, a bridge connecting to the Iberian mainland to the west, and an isthmus to the east. The surrounding region, including the isthmus, was also mountainous and so the city was well protected from both land and naval attacks. Still, Mago did not want to leave anything to chance and initiated a building program to further fortify his capital.

The city was now bustling with activity – ships were sailing in and out of the harbor, with dozens more being built around them, newly arrived soldiers were marching through the city, new walls were being erected, and merchants were capitalizing on the situation by selling goods from the east with an upcharge to the highest bidder in the town square, having realized that it would now be more difficult to acquire them for an average citizen, with the civil war causing a disruption in the operation of trade routes.

Mago, meanwhile, was overseeing everything from the highest level of his palace and awaiting his allies, who were due to arrive for a meeting on what was to be the next step for Iberia. Most of the others had already made their way to the city, and now Hasdrubal, returning from his latest campaign in the north, and Haspar, the son of Hannibal who had accompanied his uncle, made their way into New Carthage as well. Surrounded by an elite armed escort, the two Barcids entered the city through the east gate and were warmly welcomed by the locals, though they did not stay with them for long, as the two headed directly for the palace to meet with Mago.

"Mago! Thank the gods that you are still safe," Hasdrubal said as he entered the meeting room in the palace, where Mago was already waiting.

"Same for you, brother," Mago replied, limping with a cane to Hasdrubal and shaking his hand.

"So it is all true?"

"Unfortunately. We have lost Carthage… And we have lost Hannibal."

"I feared this day would eventually come. He had many enemies in the capital, and many of them wanted him dead even more than any Roman had…"

"Indeed. It's a most treacherous city."

"We should have been there with him! We shouldn't have left him alone, surrounded by all these schemers who care for nothing but their own gain."

"Maybe. But we had a job to do here. Which, I would like to believe, we did quite well. This gives us an opportunity to build up our forces and strike back."

"You are right. We can't bring our brother back, but we can at least honor and avenge him, as he would surely have done for us."

"We have lost the first battle in Carthage, as Zimri and his cohorts now have the Ptolemies on their side, but there will be more to come. The war is just starting."

"And you seem to be preparing for it, from what I have seen on my way here."

"I am. Soldiers, ships, forts – everything that will be needed for this conflict. What about you, what's the situation in the north?"

"Well, it's in a secure place right now. If we are going to be attacked, it will be from the south, so I am transferring my units here to give us a better fighting chance. My men have been fighting in Iberia for a long time now and have plenty of experience, so they will be a useful addition to what forces you have already gathered."

"That's good thinking. Better to keep them here, closer to the action, rather than idling in the north."

"I have left some of them there, of course, but just enough to maintain the defenses. The mountains and the sea should do the bulk of the work and buy us time if an enemy approaches from the north."

"I agree… But I think it's time I invited the others here and we started the meeting properly."

"Of course."

Mago sent his servants to get everyone else who was supposed to attend and was already in the palace. Before long, they appeared as well and entered the room, greeting Mago and Hasdrubal. Once everyone was in, the servants left and closed the doors, giving full privacy to the assembled members. Other than the two Barcid brothers, this included admirals Bostar and Maharbaal, Hasdrubal's wife Elissa, Hannibal's widow Imilce, and her and Hannibal's now fourteen-year-old son Haspar. After everyone had taken their place at the table, Mago opened the meeting.

"Welcome to New Carthage once again, everyone. I wish we could have met under less dire circumstances, but we must make do with what the gods have given us," Mago began. "As we all know by now, Hannibal – our beloved brother, husband, father, commander, friend, and the head of our republic – has been murdered in a brutal coup in Carthage a few weeks ago. From what we have learned, it was organized by Zimri, Hannibal's last co-suffete, who has now usurped power and proclaimed himself the sole ruler of Carthage. There was opposition, but it was swiftly crushed, not least because Zimri was helped by the Ptolemaic fleet, as attested by admiral Maharbaal. The capital is now under complete control of Zimri and his allies, and he is ordering all the other cities to pledge their loyalty to him, with a threat of siege if this is not done. Iberia is safe, for now, and under our complete control. Still, we don't know what Zimri or the Egyptians are planning, and our time may be running short. We need to decide how we are going to proceed."

"We need to fight back, of course!" Bostar answered. "Such treachery and sacrilege cannot be tolerated."

"I would agree, but... After what I've seen in Carthage, it's difficult to be hopeful about our chances," Maharbaal replied. "We had a massive navy on our side, only for it to be annihilated by the Egyptian fleet. Our best hope was that battle, and we lost it. How can we reasonably expect to win against not only the new Carthaginian government, but also Egypt?"

"But we have allies of our own," Haspar interjected. "We can call on their help to deal with the Ptolemies."

"Those were only allies of Hannibal. Without him, we don't really have the support from any of them."

"That's not necessarily true," Hasdrubal said. "Philip and Antiochus are both fighting the Egyptians. And so are we now. An enemy of my enemy is my friend, as the saying goes. Besides, I have recently received word from Antiochus – he appears to be willing to continue supporting our family."

"That is good to hear. We don't have many resources right now, so we need all the allies we can get," Mago nodded. "But that means we will be involved in a much larger conflict, one stretching even beyond the Mediterranean."

"We will. But what other choice, other than submitting to Carthage, do we have?"

"You are right, there is no other choice... So what would it look like? Who are our enemies and who would be on our side?"

"Well, we have Iberia, obviously, Macedon, the Seleucid realm... I don't know about Italy. The new states there may side with us, but they may just as well join our enemies. Or just stay neutral and wait to declare their allegiance to the winner. We should send envoys to inquire about the situation and try to get them to support us."

"Agreed. Hannibal was the architect of those states, in a way, so maybe the Etruscans and the Greco-Italians still hold some loyalty to him, and, in turn, to us."

"As for our enemies – there is Carthage, with however many cities they have managed to get into their camp so far, Egypt, and various Greek states that would become our enemies if we allied with Philip and Antiochus. Sparta, the Achaean League, Rhodes... Possibly some other Greek cities. And Bactria, apparently, though it is too far away to be any threat to us."

"We've faced far worse odds before. We can win, if we commit to the fight," Haspar said.

"I appreciate your enthusiasm, young man, but even with these allies, we would be lacking in ships. And, since this would be a mostly naval war, there would be no victory without a proper fleet," Maharbaal cautioned.

"I am building a fleet right now," Mago said. "It will take some time, but we have enough to make one that rivals that of our enemies."

"So it is possible for us to win?" Elissa asked.

"It is," Hasdrubal confirmed. "I can't guarantee anything though. I can't promise that all of us would survive... But victory is achievable."

"Hasn't there been too much blood spilled already?" Imilce asked. "Believe me, I want justice for my husband more than anyone, but... I fear losing what we still have."

"I would be lying if I said I didn't fear that myself. But do you honestly believe the new regime would let us live in peace, after what happened in Carthage? These are the people who organized a coup and murdered Hannibal and countless others in broad daylight, with no provocation. If we submit, they will enter Iberia unopposed and begin culling us here. I'm sorry, but I just don't see another way out for us."

"I agree," Bostar added. "They probably want the entire Barcid family and everyone associated with you eliminated. We can either fight or willingly go into the slaughter. It would be a great insult to Hannibal's memory to choose the latter option, and I would never dishonor him like that."

"I see..." Imilce sighed. "You are all right. It may very well be the only way forward for us."

"We are in agreement then. We will fight. For Hannibal, and for Carthage," Hasdrubal said.

"We will need someone to lead us though," Maharbaal noted. "Hannibal and Aradus are both dead. Who will represent our cause now?"

"Well... That's a good question," Mago said, as the eyes in the room turned towards him. "I don't think I can be this figure. I'm far from a strategic genius. And now I'm a cripple too, as everyone can clearly see. I'm not really fit to be the leader of our cause. Besides, I'm the youngest son of Hamilcar, and there is someone who is older and more experienced..."

"I do appreciate the recommendation," Hasdrubal said, as all eyes now shifted to him. "But I'm far from the perfect candidate too. I have experience in military matters, sure, but not in politics.

I tend to stay away from that. And, just like Hannibal, I have made some enemies in Carthage and other places, which may hinder our support for one reason or another. But, if it is everyone's wish for me to lead-"

"I can do it. I will lead us in avenging my father," Haspar said as he stood up.

"What? Don't be so foolish. You can't be seriously thinking about this," Imilce replied.

"Why not? I have been educated in military, political, and economic matters. I have experience in fighting battles and commanding troops, having marched against various tribes with Hasdrubal in recent times. I can negotiate and find us new allies. And I have lost the most, so it is important to me. They killed my father – I can't just stand around and wait for someone else to bring those responsible to justice! I have to lead our forces and show the world that the Barcids still stand as strong as ever!"

"You do present a convincing argument, I must admit," Bostar said after a few moments.

"It is true though. He has proved to be a very capable and intelligent young man while staying with us," Elissa added. "Wouldn't you agree, Hasdrubal?"

"Haspar has indeed shown himself to be a good strategist and a valiant soldier. And he greatly inspires the men under his command," Hasdrubal nodded. "What do you think, Mago?"

"I concur. You do take a lot from your father, Haspar," Mago agreed. "In time, you may even surpass him, if you continue on this course. We do need an inspiring figurehead if we are to succeed, and the son of Hannibal Barca himself seems to me to be a perfect candidate."

"I haven't met Haspar previously, but I don't have any objections either," Maharbaal added. "If you think he can lead us, then so do I."

"So it's only me in the opposition now, is it?" Imilce asked. "Well, as much as I would prefer for you to stay here and remain safe... I can't stop you from doing what you feel you need to do. You are becoming a man and can choose your own course in life. If this is what you wish, then so be it."

"Thank you, mother. And thank you to everyone else for supporting me," Haspar said. "I will do everything in my power to live up to my father and lead us to victory."

"I know you will," Hasdrubal said. "But we are all in this fight together, so we will all do our best to help you."

"That's right. Whatever you need," Mago added. "Now... Don't you think we should proclaim this decision to the people to let them know our position and boost their morale?"

"Yes," Haspar nodded. "I think we definitely should."

About an hour later, Haspar, with Hasdrubal, Mago, and some guards on his side, appeared in the town square to the surprise of the locals. Some had heard that an official announcement would be coming, but no one truly knew what to expect exactly. As the Barcids were clearing the way and preparing, more and more citizens arrived to see what was happening. Soon, all the local elites, military commanders, Mago's advisors, administrators, and other persons of importance – including some exiles from Carthage – had made their way to the square as well, as they had been informed to do so. After enough locals had gathered to fill the area, Haspar stepped forward and began.

"Citizens of New Carthage," Haspar proclaimed. "I am Haspar Barca, the son of Hannibal Barca. Hannibal, who secured and civilized Iberia. Who defeated the Romans and brought peace to our Republic. Who became a suffete and improved the lives of many citizens... And who was ruthlessly murdered by his opponents in Carthage. These traitors have taken the capital hostage, and much of the rest of the country in turn. Iberia now stands as the last bastion of honor and freedom from their tyranny. But these usurpers are not done yet, as they are planning to invade these lands as well and eliminate any opposition to their rule. But I will not yield to them! I will not let their coup stand! With Hasdrubal and Mago Barca at my side, I will lead our forces against the usurpers, no matter if it ends in victory or death. But for us to succeed, we will need the full support from all of you. Are you ready to stand up for what is right? Are you ready to fight to restore our republic to its proper form?"

"Yes!" some men in the crowd shouted back.

"Are you ready to defend these lands from invaders? Are you ready to fight our enemies at sea, and on land, on the beaches, in the deserts, and in the mountains?"

"Yes!" now more people from the crowd joined in.

"And are you ready to march on Carthage to reclaim it? Are you ready to avenge Hannibal and bring swift retribution to all those responsible for his death?"

"Yes!" the crowd roared back, now in full support of their new young leader.

"Then it shall be done! It will be a long and difficult war, but it will be worth it at the end. I will not let my father's death be in vain – I will continue his work and honor him in doing so. Just as he crossed into Europe and marched on Rome, I will cross into Africa and march on Carthage. All the traitors and their allies will be put to the sword, and order will be restored. Our republic will be reunified and cleansed of all that is plaguing it. And Hannibal will be avenged! For the republic!"

"For the republic!"

"And for Hannibal!"

"For Hannibal!"

Epilogue

While the port of Ostia, just southwest of what remained of Rome, was still legally a part of the Roman Republic, in reality it was under Carthaginian occupation ever since the Second Roman War had ended. The Carthaginians used it as a harbor and as a central collection point for tribute from the defeated state, and so had stationed a few thousand soldiers to guard the port, so that a beachhead would always be available for Carthage in case of a new conflict in Italy. The Romans were not pleased with this arrangement, but they could do little to change the situation.

Thus, Ostia remained in Carthaginian hands for the following years and into the start of the civil war between Hanno and the followers of Hannibal. Once news of the conflict reached the peninsula, the garrison commander of Ostia declared the port to be neutral, refusing to send forces to either side, but pledging to submit to the authority of whoever reunified the republic and restored order. For the time being, however, there was no clear winner, especially with Barcids uniting their forces in Iberia and declaring total war on their opponents in charge of the capital, so Ostia was on its own.

The garrison commander grounded the ships in the harbor and ordered the soldiers to remain in the port, while keeping all the collected tribute in the treasury. He promised to send it all to Carthage once the situation calmed down and the civil war was over, but refused to do so before then, claiming that the Mediterranean was not safe enough and that the transport ships could be seized by the various fighting factions or resurgent pirates. And so, it remained in Ostia, guarded by Carthaginian mercenaries. And while some grew concerned about events in the capital, the commander assured them that everything would be fine and the situation would return to normal before long, so they continued their regular duties as usual, for the most part unbothered by the events in the greater Mediterranean world and the war unfolding there.

"Morning, Thestor," Vindedo, a Celtic mercenary guard, greeted his colleague, as the two began their morning patrol of Ostia.

"Morning to you, Vin," the Greek mercenary replied, as he finished fixing the shield to himself.

"Reckon we will find anything interesting today?"

"I doubt it. Though it's not like we ever find anything more interesting than some unruly drunkards misbehaving."

"That's true. Maybe for the best. I'll take being bored but safe here, rather than in the chaos of Carthage. They're paying us the same either way!" Vindedo laughed.

"I heard the city was invaded by the Egyptians. Do you think that's true?"

"I don't know. I don't particularly care either. As long as the gold is flowing, I am happy. And if it stops – then I'll just find a new employer."

"There certainly is a demand for mercenaries these days, so you probably won't have trouble finding work. Especially with your skills."

"I'd like to think so too. Though I'd also like to go back north and spend some time with my family for a while. With the commander issuing this lockdown, I can't really leave the port at all, no matter how long I've served."

"Remind me, where do you live?"

"It's a small village near Populonia. Now belongs to the Etruscans, but they don't seem as bad as the Romans. My wife and three kids are there, as well as some other relatives."

"Right. I'm from Neapolis myself. Had actually signed up to join the mercenary band that was hired by Hannibal himself, but they were full by the time I arrived, so I only got in after the war had ended. Quite a shame."

"Wanted to participate in the burning of Rome yourself, eh?"

"I certainly would have enjoyed it."

"Well, don't fret about it. You are still young, so I am sure you will see plenty of battles and sieges in the future."

"Hopefully. Otherwise I should have just become a blacksmith, like my father."

"Far from the worst job there is."

"Yes, but not the most fun one."

"That's true. I'm assuming you are having plenty of fun here though?"

"Oh, definitely. Same as all the other mercs."

"I can imagine. I saw you guys making quite a mess at that tavern last night."

"We may have gotten carried away a little bit…"

"And you were with that girl, what's her name?"

"Claudia. I'm actually planning on marrying her."

"Really? Interesting choice…"

"Why? She fancies me as well, you know."

"I don't doubt it. You just don't often see us taking Roman wives. Slaves or whores for a night, sure, but most prefer to marry someone who is not a conquered enemy."

"They're missing out then. I noticed that there are few Roman men here – the population probably still hasn't recovered from the war, with so many being called to battle only to be slaughtered by Hannibal's armies… So there are a lot of single young women here, ripe for the taking. And while the Romans were enemies of Carthage, the war is over. I'm now here to make money, and my only real enemy is poverty."

"I'm not judging you, I think it's wonderful. If you want that, then go right ahead. And if anyone harasses you for it, I'll kick their fucking ass," Vindedo laughed.

"Thanks, I appreciate it. I'm now thinking about whether to- Wait, did you hear that?"

"Huh, that's strange."

"It's from behind the walls. Should we investigate it?"

"It's not our assignment. We should stick to patrolling the streets and let whoever is responsible for that area handle the situation."

"Maybe. Let's continue the patrol then... So, as I was saying-"

Thestor was interrupted again, as a guard's body dropped in front of him from the city walls. It had several arrows lodged in the chest, and, a moment later, more arrows began pouring from the outside into the city.

"Fuck, we need to get out of here!" Vindedo said as he raised his shield to protect himself from the arrows.

"Get you asses to the east gate, now!" a guard rushing past them shouted, covering himself with a shield too. "We are being attacked!"

The guards joined him and rushed to the eastern gate of the city, where hundreds of soldiers had already assembled and taken up defensive positions. Vindedo and Thestor climbed up onto the wall to see what was happening outside and were horrified by the view they were now faced with. Outside the city, thousands of Roman soldiers had assembled and were now assaulting the defenses, with more and more Romans seemingly emerging every moment from the cover of the trees and other natural features, flooding the area with their numbers. One unit also had a battering ram and, despite suffering some casualties, got it to the gate, proceeding to attempt to break in.

"Focus on the battering ram! Kill all of them, don't let them do any more damage!" the garrison commander ordered, having just arrived at the scene. "If they break through, we are fucked!"

The mercenaries managed to shoot down many Romans, but they had a severe numerical disadvantage and had some casualties of their own. The Romans meanwhile just continued replacing their lost and sending more men to help batter the gate, only further increasing the pressure on the Carthaginian defenders.

"Commander, they have broken through!" an injured soldier said as he ran up to the garrison commander.

"What? Where?" the commander screamed.

"The south gate! The south gate is breached, the Romans are entering the city right now! We can't hold them off!"

"Fuck! This was only a diversion... Men, get to the south gate right now! Everyone who is not firing a bow needs to move to the south gate immediately! We have Romans already in Ostia, they must be pushed out! Yes, you and you, and that whole group back there! All of you!" the commander roared, pointing at the still shocked mercenaries, including Vindedo and Thestor, who now promptly got back down and ran south as ordered.

"I've never been in a battle before," Thestor said nervously as he was running to the fight. "I knew it would happen, just... Didn't expect it so soon..."

"It's your lucky day," Vindedo replied. "Just don't hesitate to use that spear, as the Romans sure won't. Come on now, we need to hurry!"

The battle did not last long. It was over before the end of the day, and the port of Ostia was now in full Roman control once again. All the Carthaginians and forces aligned with them had either fled by sea or had been killed, with just as many dying in the mass executions following the fall of Ostia as in the battle itself. The surprise factor, the overwhelming numbers, and the support of the vast majority of the population paved the way for a quick victory for the Romans, though they did suffer over a thousand casualties. The Romans also captured some ships and their crews, though most had sailed away before then, taking the surviving mercenaries and refugees with them.

The ones who stayed behind in Ostia were not so lucky, however. After the garrison commander was killed and it was clear that the battle was lost, the mercenaries surrendered to the Romans, hoping to receive lenient terms for not resisting too much. Yet, to their horror, they soon realized that the Romans were not intending on leaving anyone from the opposing side alive. After the mercenaries were disarmed, the remaining two thousand soldiers were executed by the enraged Romans. Many were tied up and drowned in the nearby sea, while others were crucified along the road between Rome and Ostia. Thestor and Vindedo were among such victims, and their hanging corpses were passed by even more soldiers entering the city to secure it. The most notable among them, riding on a horse and surrounded by the praetorian guard, was Publius Cornelius Scipio, the general of the Roman army and son of the general of the same name who had died in the Second Roman War while fighting the Carthaginians in Iberia.

The younger Publius was missing in action near the end of the war and was presumed dead, but he turned up in Spoletium – the new Roman capital – after the treaty had been signed, and vowed to continue the fight. He received the full support of the remaining leadership and began raising a new army in secret. Before long, his forces surpassed the ten-thousand-man limit that the Carthaginians had set for the defeated state, but it went unnoticed as the soldiers dispersed throughout Italy. But, once news of Hannibal's death reached Scipio, he assembled his army and set out for the liberation of the Roman Republic and revenge on Carthage. With the Carthaginians having established only a limited presence on the peninsula and now suffering a domestic civil war, the fate of Italy became uncertain, and so the general took his chance. Already marching through the most pro-Roman areas, he received the support of the local population and increased his ranks even further, while the Carthaginians still had no idea what was coming for them. And now, having secured his first major victory, Publius Cornelius Scipio triumphantly rode into the city that he had taken.

Greeted by the enthusiastic cheers of the locals, who had wasted no time in ransacking the now former Carthaginian garrison along with the Roman soldiers, the general made his way through the town until he reached the treasury. There, the Carthaginian garrison commander had stored the gold that was to be used as payment for the men under his command, as well as all the tribute received from the Roman Republic. All this wealth now came into the Roman possession, with Scipio ceremoniously opening it and ordering his most trusted soldiers to transport it further inland for safekeeping.

Next, the general made his way to the forum of Ostia, where he was prepared to announce his victory and plans for the future. Excited to learn what was to come for their republic, the citizens eagerly followed their newfound leader and gathered in the forum, filling it to the brim with civilians and soldiers alike. Scipio was soon also joined by two more officials of high importance – the consuls Titus Quinctius Crispinus and Lucius Veturius Philo, who had both been recently elected to lead the republic for the year. In the late evening, once the preparations were complete, they took the stage, illuminated by the torches held by soldiers, and began their proclamation to the gathered audience.

"Citizens of Ostia, Spoletium, Ancona, and all the other towns in the Roman Republic!" Philo began. "For years we have been humiliated and forced to suffer under the terms imposed by the decadent Carthaginians. Striped of our lands, of our army, and of our resources. Forced to bow down to the spoiled African merchants and pay them tribute, while our own cities continued to burn. It was a great tragedy and a terrible time for us all. But we can once again rejoice, as this dark period has finally come to an end! The Carthaginians have turned on each other and are involved in a civil war, one which will surely mean the end of their unholy empire and reign of terror on the Mediterranean. This is a time of opportunity, the moment for us to rise up once again and show that the Roman spirit cannot be crushed! And there is no man who is a better example of this, no man who honors the gods more with his accomplishments, than our great general. A veteran of the Second

Punic War and the man who will lead us to complete victory in the third one. General Publius Cornelius Scipio!"

The general made his way between the consuls and stepped forward, facing the massive crowd that cheered for and applauded him.

"Publius Cornelius Scipio rebuilt our army, personally trained it, and marched it on Ostia, despite there being no guarantees of an easy battle," Philo continued. "Yet he took those odds, and succeeded more than any of us could have imagined. He took the city in a single day and put the Carthaginians and their filthy mercenaries on a cross, where they belong, so that everyone could plainly see what fate awaits one if he chooses to challenge Roman might. Ostia is liberated, but this is just the beginning. We have a lot to reclaim, and it will be a difficult road ahead, but it will be done. Etruria, Capua, Magna Graecia, Sicily, Sardinia, Corsica, Illyria, and even Iberia! All shall be taken back by the Roman Republic! Our glory will once again be restored, and our gods will be honored by such accomplishments!"

"We believe that Publius Cornelius Scipio is the man who will lead us to such victories," Crispinus, the second consul, continued. "But it is a war, and so our usual democratic procedures may be too slow to cope with the events unfolding around us. For this reason, we, the elected consuls of Rome, have agreed to nominate the general to be the dictator for the duration of the war, which would grant him the full authority to resolve this conflict in any way he sees fit. Do you, Publius Cornelius Scipio, accept this position?"

"I accept this honor," Scipio confirmed. "I would never shy away from duties bestowed upon me, and so I am ready to command our republic in pursuit of total victory."

"Very good. Citizens, gaze upon Publius Cornelius Scipio, the dictator of the Roman Republic!"

"Thank you for putting your trust in me. I will do everything in my power to honor Jupiter and Mars and restore Rome to its prime," Scipio proclaimed, as the crowd once again began cheering for the general and chanting his name. "I am not one for long speeches, as I prefer actions to words. Thus, I only have one thing to say – Carthage will be destroyed!"

End Notes

Thank you for reading this novel to the end. I hope you enjoyed the first entry in my new alternate history series where Rome is not as successful as it was in our world, and the Mediterranean is up for grabs by a variety of other players. Though, of course, even Rome should not be totally written off yet, as you have seen in the epilogue. And if the ending situation intrigued you enough – fear not, for the sequel is coming just a year after this book is first published, so you will not have to wait too long to continue reading the story. Currently I am planning for at least two more books – a full trilogy – but there could be far more than that, depending on how far I want to go into the timeline. In any event, the novels will be released yearly, and there will be a proper conclusion to the series, I can promise you that much. Unlike some authors, I won't make you wait for fourteen years (so far) to read the next installment in the series…

In the meantime though, you may also want to check out The Bronze Horus, my other alternate history series. It is written in quite a similar style, so if you enjoyed this read, chances are that you will find those books to your taste as well – though I would like to believe that my writing has improved over the years, and that I've learned a thing or two since the days of The Rise of Kemet, so that Heirs of the Mediterranean could be an even better offering. Granted, the two have slightly different tones, with The Bronze Horus being lighter and having more room for humor, memes, and overt references to our current world, while also being a more utopian and idealistic alternate universe. With Heirs of the Mediterranean, meanwhile, I tried to build a more realistic world with no one receiving any plot armor. I hope I managed to set such a tone well with this book, as it is the necessary groundwork for all the others that will follow.

I must admit though, I am a fan of Carthage, and it is among my favorite ancient civilizations (only surpassed by Egypt, as The Bronze Horus may have not so subtly indicated), so I may have a bias towards it. Still, I think we can all agree that the Second Punic War was quite a close contest, and that Carthage definitely did have some chances of winning it – certainly more than Germany in either World War, or the Confederates in the American Civil War, or the Soviets in the Cold War, and most alternate history works are about one of these scenarios, so I'd say Carthage defeating Rome is far from the most unrealistic outcome. And after that – well, as you have seen, it is not all fun and games just yet either, as the republic has plenty of challenges left to tackle. I had ideas about making Carthage much more powerful in my earliest drafts years ago, but I am glad that I dropped this idea to instead create a more divided Mediterranean, and in turn a more volatile and interesting setting.

I would also like to point out that most of the characters and many events were actually real in our world. For The Bronze Horus, I had to invent many things, since there is relatively little information about the Late Bronze Age, but the Hellenistic period is far more explored and so I had much more to work with. I encourage you to read about this on your own, since it is quite a fascinating and well documented era. For example, Hannibal did actually become a suffete, even after losing the war, and enacted some of the reforms mentioned in the novel. Many other Carthaginian characters also existed and so I tried to adhere to their historical personas. This includes Hasdrubal, Mago, Haspar, Imilce, and Hanno Nermun (called Hanno II the Great by historians), though I had to invent the last name for Hanno, to distinguish him from plenty of his namesakes. I also tried to keep the Carthaginian political system as accurate as possible, though I had to infer some things (such as how the voting would go exactly), due to there simply being no historical data about such matters. Same goes for the eastern Mediterranean and beyond –

history already has plenty of notable characters from that era, so I had a lot of good material and didn't need to invent many new people. For instance, all the Seleucid commanders, as well as the Egyptian conspirators are taken from the historical record. Ptolemies specifically were living through quite an eventful period, so I left their story almost the same as it had happened in our world, with only some details changed to account for Hannibal's victory in the west.

All this is to say that I didn't just randomly create these events and characters, I did my research and tried to make a world that would closely resemble our own at that point in time, with the only real changes being due to the single divergence point (Carthage winning against Rome), rather than being completely unrelated. That isn't to say that the latter method for creating alternate histories is not valid – there are plenty of interesting timelines that can be made only when using several unrelated changes in conjunction – but I just prefer the former, taking one key change, while keeping everything else the same, and seeing how much it can affect the world.

I believe that should be enough for now, but if you have any questions or suggestions regarding the series – my links are at the end of the book, I'm always happy to discuss my works with the readers or just people interested in the lore. Thank you once again for your time, I highly appreciate it, no matter what format you have or how you have acquired this work. If you enjoyed it, it would be great if you spread word about it, as I still only have a small following and any additional recommendation of my books helps. And if you didn't – well, I always appreciate constructive criticism, so I would also be interested in hearing what could be improved in future entries. In any event, work will shortly begin on the sequel, and I hope you will return to the series once it releases, as things are just starting to heat up in the Mediterranean…

Diagrams and Maps

Here are some additional diagrams and maps to help you understand the situation at the beginning of the novel better. Figure 1 represents the political system of Carthage, as it is quite unconventional and different from the other states from the period – most of the other realms are absolute monarchies, so their systems are much simpler and self-explanatory.

Figures 2 – 5 represent the relevant portions of the ruling family trees: Figure 2 for the Barcids (not a monarchical dynasty, but still very prominent in Carthage, so I felt it was important to include them as well), Figure 3 for the Antigonids of Macedon, Figure 4 for the Seleucids of the Seleucid Empire, and Figure 5 for the Ptolemies of Egypt. Continuous lines represent official relationships (marriages and children), while dotted lines represent more unofficial relationships (mistresses, concubines, and key allies of the family). Also, names in Italics show that the person is already deceased at the start of the novel, and the dates are shown in the Carthaginian system (the numbering scheme starting with the founding of Carthage in 814 BCE, so, for example, the start date of the novel is 603 in this calendar, which is the same as 211 BCE).

Finally, Figure 6 represents a very simplified map of the city of Carthage – the capital of the Republic of Carthage – which is also not necessarily to scale, but can give a general idea of how it looks like and where all the important sites are located.

The map covering the whole of the Mediterranean and beyond can be found right after the prologue. It shows the political situation at that exact time, just before Chapter I, with names in Italics denoting barbarian groups, and lighter colors adjacent to darker ones denoting puppet states (for example – Carthage is purple, and all the states in other shades of purple around it are its puppet states – though this does not apply to purple countries further away, such as Pontus or Byzantium). Unfortunately, for the paperback and hardcover versions only black and white images are available, but it should still be quite simple to figure out the relationships, as they are explained in the novel. If you wish to see the map in full color and resolution, be sure to check out the Facebook page or the Discord server for the series, you will find it there, along with other additional content and various updates. And for the map showing the situation at the end of the novel – I chose not to include it, since it would contain quite obvious and major spoilers, so it will be shown at the beginning of the second novel in the series. The remaining aforementioned figures can be found from the next page onwards.

Carthaginian Political System

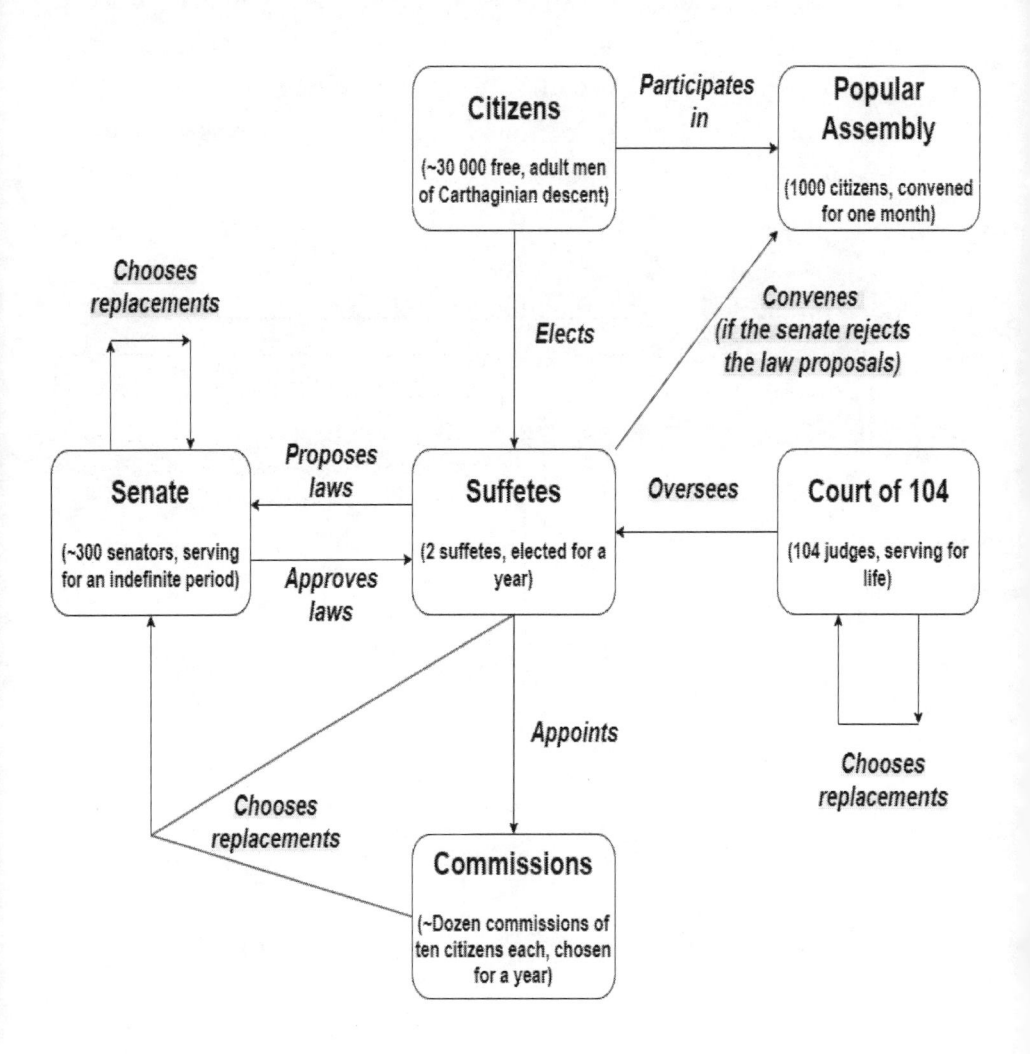

Citizens (~30 000 free, adult men of Carthaginian descent)

Participates in → **Popular Assembly** (1000 citizens, convened for one month)

Elects → **Suffetes** (2 suffetes, elected for a year)

Senate (~300 senators, serving for an indefinite period) — Chooses replacements

Suffetes Proposes laws → Senate; Senate Approves laws → Suffetes

Suffetes Convenes (if the senate rejects the law proposals) → Popular Assembly

Court of 104 (104 judges, serving for life) Oversees → Suffetes; Chooses replacements

Suffetes Appoints → **Commissions** (~Dozen commissions of ten citizens each, chosen for a year)

Commissions Chooses replacements → Senate

Figure 1

Barcid Dynasty

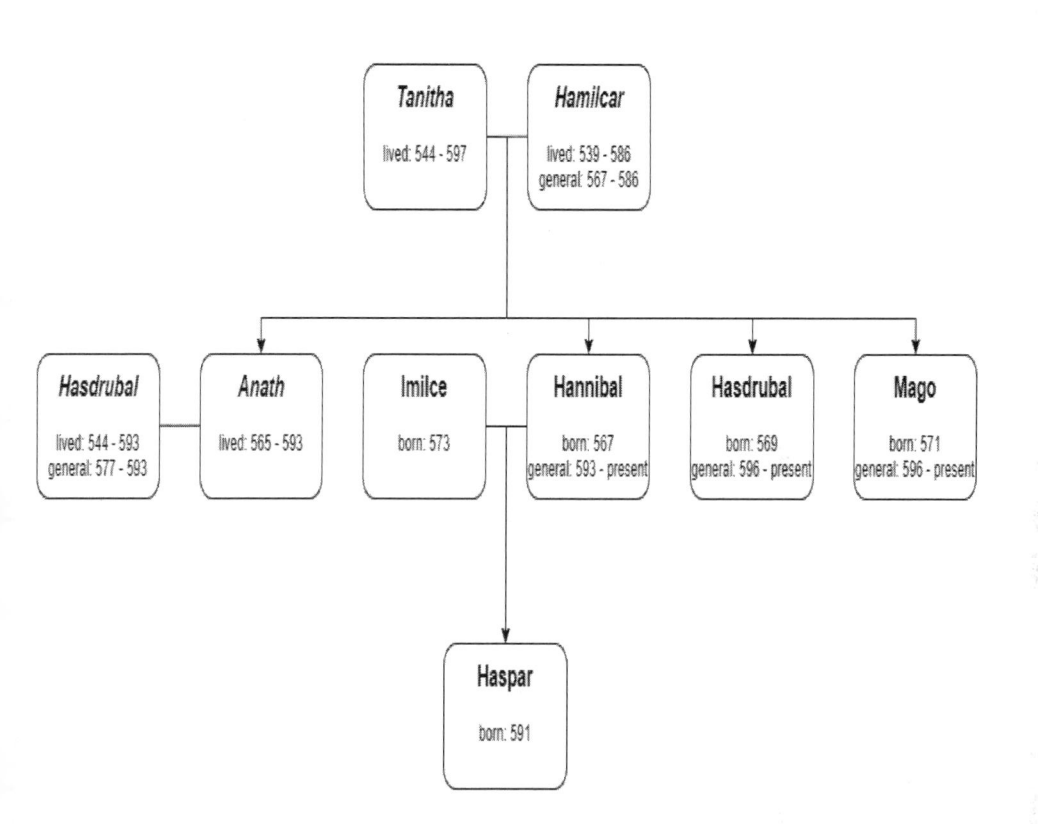

- **Tanitha** — lived: 544 - 597
- **Hamilcar** — lived: 539 - 586; general: 567 - 586

Children:
- *Hasdrubal* — lived: 544 - 593; general: 577 - 593
- *Anath* — lived: 565 - 593
- Imilce — born: 573
- **Hannibal** — born: 567; general: 593 - present
- **Hasdrubal** — born: 569; general: 596 - present
- **Mago** — born: 571; general: 596 - present

Child of Hannibal:
- Haspar — born: 591

Figure 2

Antigonid Dynasty

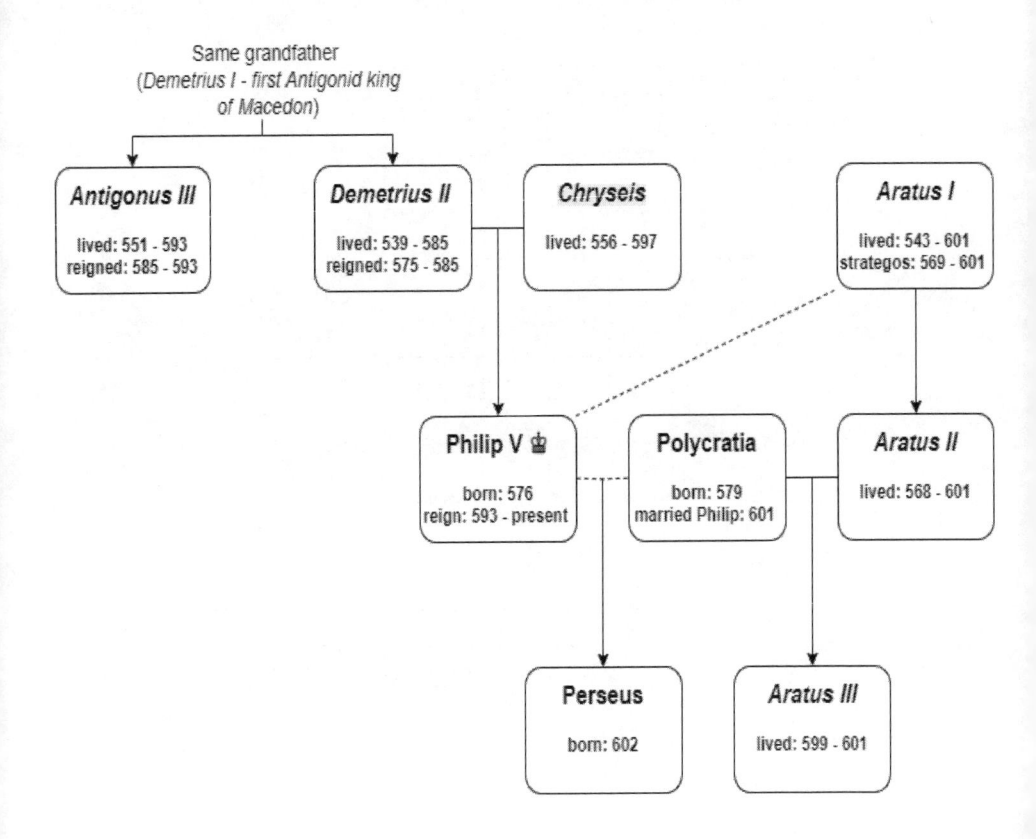

Same grandfather
(Demetrius I - first Antigonid king of Macedon)

Antigonus III
lived: 551 - 593
reigned: 585 - 593

Demetrius II
lived: 539 - 585
reigned: 575 - 585

Chryseis
lived: 556 - 597

Aratus I
lived: 543 - 601
strategos: 569 - 601

Philip V ♚
born: 576
reign: 593 - present

Polycratia
born: 579
married Philip: 601

Aratus II
lived: 568 - 601

Perseus
born: 602

Aratus III
lived: 599 - 601

Figure 3

Seleucid Dynasty

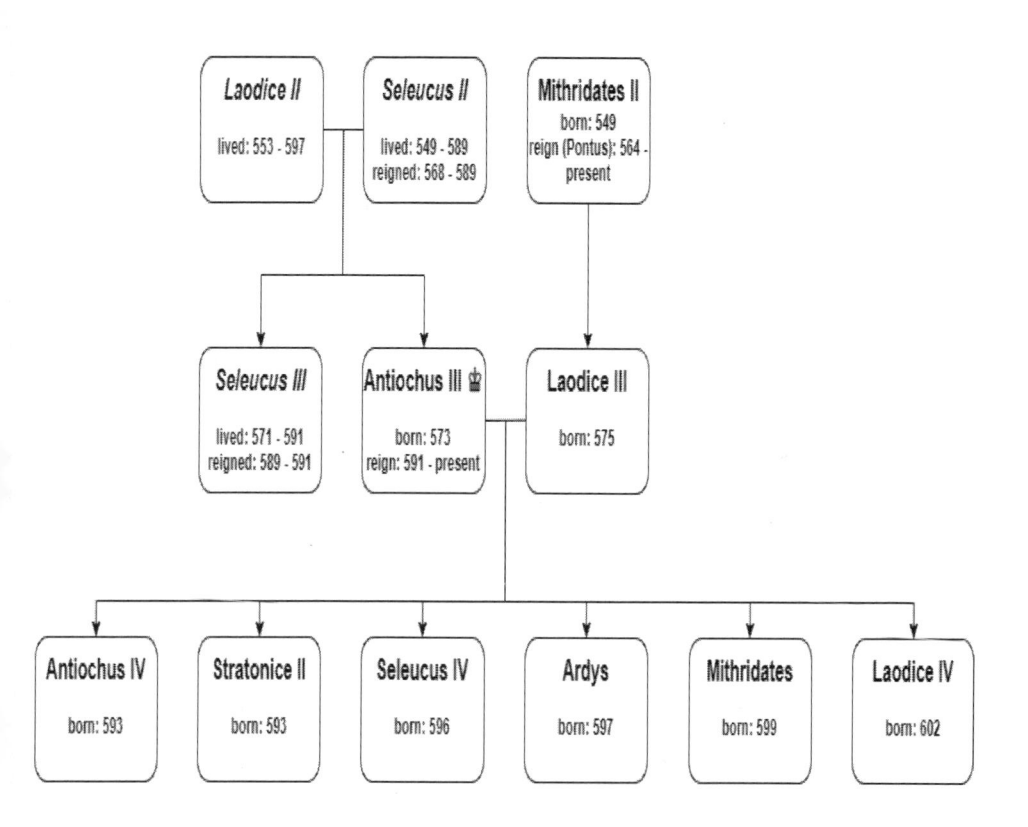

- **Laodice II** — lived: 553 - 597
- **Seleucus II** — lived: 549 - 589; reigned: 568 - 589
- **Mithridates II** — born: 549; reign (Pontus): 564 - present

Children of Seleucus II and Laodice II:
- **Seleucus III** — lived: 571 - 591; reigned: 589 - 591
- **Antiochus III** ♔ — born: 573; reign: 591 - present

Child of Mithridates II:
- **Laodice III** — born: 575

Children of Antiochus III and Laodice III:
- **Antiochus IV** — born: 593
- **Stratonice II** — born: 593
- **Seleucus IV** — born: 596
- **Ardys** — born: 597
- **Mithridates** — born: 599
- **Laodice IV** — born: 602

Figure 4

Ptolemaic Dynasty

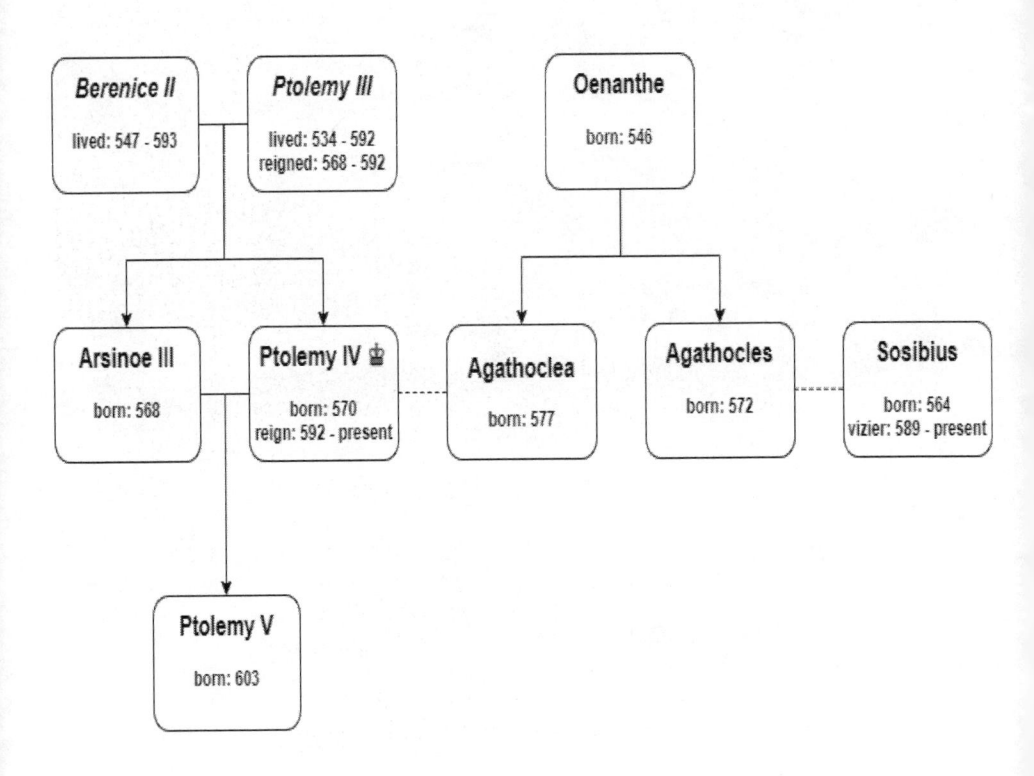

Berenice II
lived: 547 - 593

Ptolemy III
lived: 534 - 592
reigned: 568 - 592

Oenanthe
born: 546

Arsinoe III
born: 568

Ptolemy IV ♛
born: 570
reign: 592 - present

Agathoclea
born: 577

Agathocles
born: 572

Sosibius
born: 564
vizier: 589 - present

Ptolemy V
born: 603

Figure 5

Carthage City Map

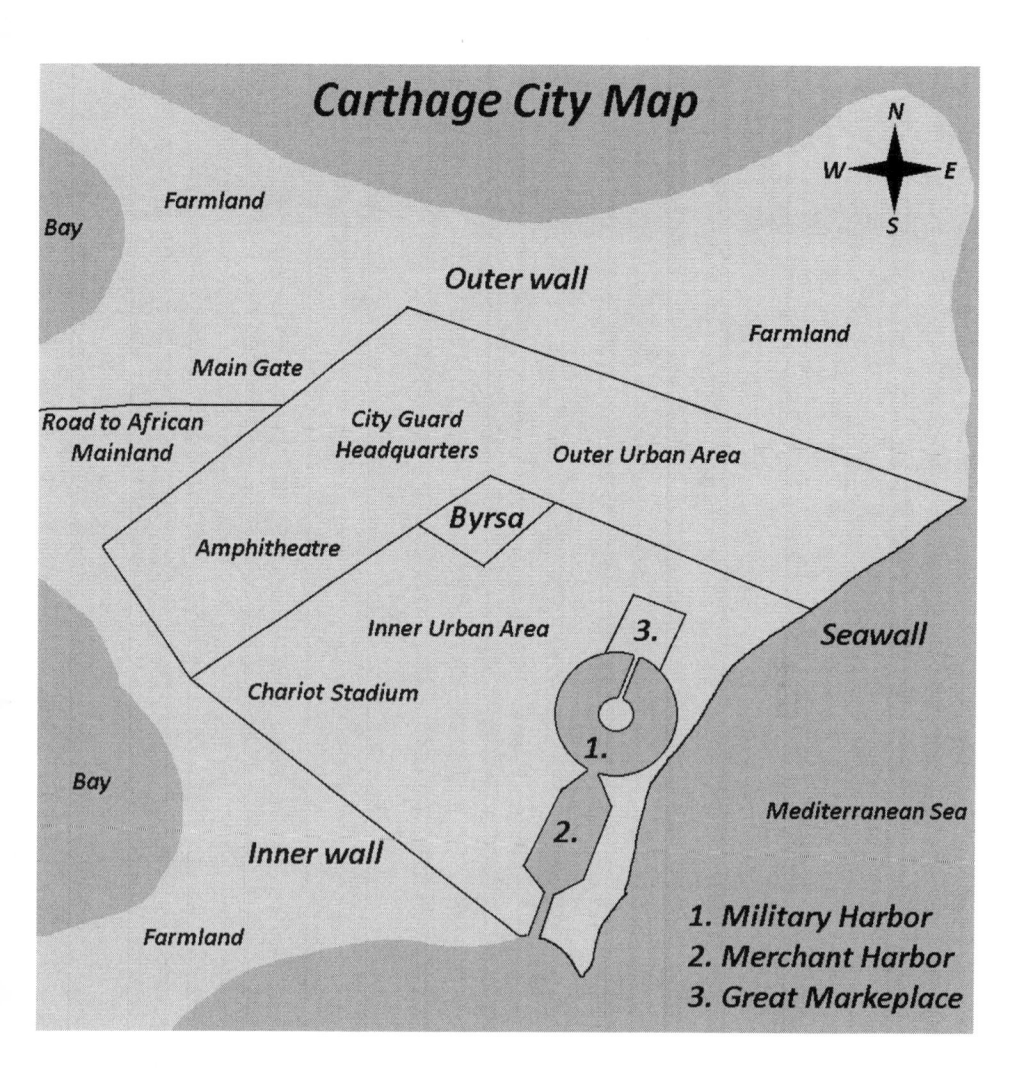

- Bay
- Farmland
- Outer wall
- Farmland
- Main Gate
- Road to African Mainland
- City Guard Headquarters
- Outer Urban Area
- Byrsa
- Amphitheatre
- Inner Urban Area
- Seawall
- Chariot Stadium
- Bay
- Mediterranean Sea
- Inner wall
- Farmland

1. Military Harbor
2. Merchant Harbor
3. Great Markeplace

Figure 6

About the Author

Julius Janeliūnas (known online as Sobekhotep IX) is the author of The Crumbling Republics, the first novel in the alternate history novel series Heirs of the Mediterranean. He is also the author of The Bronze Horus, an alternate history novel series set in a world where the Late Bronze Age collapse never happened and the Eastern Mediterranean civilizations continued to prosper, eventually reaching the industrial age. He has been an avid fan of history and alternate history from an early age, especially focusing on ancient history. Julius lives in Vilnius, Lithuania, and works as a project owner for a supply chain technology company. Yet he still has plenty of free time for writing novels and continues to release a new book every year since 2020. When not working or writing, he is most often found playing World of Warcraft or painting Warhammer miniatures.

sobekhotep.carrd.co
Discord: sobekhotep_ix
Bluesky: @sobekhotep.bsky.social

Made in the USA
Monee, IL
08 May 2025

17081835R00203